WIER&POUCE

WIER&POUCE

A Novel by
STEVE KATZ

SUN & MOON PRESS
Washington, D.C.

Copyright © Steve Katz, 1984
Part of this novel appeared previously in *Contemporary American Fiction* (Sun & Moon Press, 1983)
Cover: Katie Messborn
Publication of this book was made possible, in part, through a grant from the National Endowment for the Arts.

The New American Fiction Series: 1

Library of Congress Cataloging in Publication Data

Katz, Steve, 1935-
  Wier & Pouce.

  I. Title. II. Title: Wier and Pouce.
PS 3561.A774W5   1984   813'.54   83-40578
ISBN 0-940650-33-9
ISBN 0-940650-47-9 (pbk.)
ISBN 0-940650-35-5 (signed)

FIRST EDITION
10 9 8 7 6 5 4 3 2 1

Sun & Moon Press
4330 Hartwick Road
College Park, Maryland 20740

By Steve Katz

BUNT

Too much depended on Dusty Wier. He squared away as Nick Koros leaned back to pitch. Everything went on this bunt. Behind him the Hudson River moved, and the George Washington Bridge was there. He had the urge to look at it now. It was his bridge. No bridge could ever be that graceful. It was a gift. He wanted to look at it, not to bunt. It was his river.

"C'mon, Dusty. Let's go babes."

Swanny had got to first when Koros grazed his shoulder with a fastball. He stood on the bag, rubbing it. Dusty could see it hurt like hell. Until Nick Stamatakis' homer in the bottom of the seventh none of the Bullets had been able to hit the Condor pitcher. Nick Koros had a real fast ball, like an atomic bomb, and was blowing it by them all afternoon, and now it was the top of the eighth in the twentieth century, somewhere between World War II and the Korean conflict, and the Bullets were behind 2-1. And the next move was up to Dusty. The Condors were mean. They were never famous for their baseball, but were renowned for their rumbles. They were fighters, destroyers, a street gang with a reputation. Everyone expected a fight if they lost to the New York Bullets Social and Athletic Club, 'punks' from the Condor point of view, because these Condors owned the streets from 170th north practically to 200th, east of Broadway. There you ran onto the legendary Inwoods, a coalition of all the gangs north of

Fort Tryon Park, and though no one was sure of how
organized they really were, not even the Condors messed
with them. But the Condors owned the Bullets in a certain
way, because the Bullets weren't fighters, had no reputation on the street at all. They had new purple and gold
jackets, that made them conspicuous, but they were peaceful. They played ball, and they held dances. Until Stamatakis' home run they were resigned to losing the game,
and didn't mind, because they didn't want to fight. They
didn't enjoy it. They didn't need it. Frankly, they were
scared to death of it. But it was suddenly 2-1. They had
scored on the Condors, they had a game, and they had
some pride, and they could win. It was up to Dusty, top of
the eighth, and he could feel how bad everyone wanted
to win it now.

The Bullets were smart kids from the neighborhood.
Many of them were Jewish. They were headed for college.
When Godine scheduled the game, Eric Meyers, who
played second base and batted third, told him, "George,
no one wants to play those gorillas. It'll be a zoo. Why do
we have to play them?

"You're nuts, George. It's like playing catch with an
atom bomb. These guys . . . I'm not gonna play them."
Eric held up his hands. "Not these hands." He played the
clarinet, and his ambition was to be a surgeon. He always
carried his hands around as if they were radioactive.

"Fuck you, Meyers," said Hubby Strassburger. "You're
just a chicken. I ain't chicken of no Condors." Hubby was
the youngest kid on the Bullets, brought to the club first as
a mascot by his brother, Vernon, who quit when little
brother beat him out at shortstop. He was small and feisty

and reckless enough to enjoy a good fight. He wasn't going to college anyway. He would never finish high school.

"Why don't we vote on it?" said Eric. "This is a democracy."

"We ain't gonna vote, because I'm the manager," said Godine.

"Then I'm not gonna play," said Eric.

"You don't play this game, you don't play any game."

Eric looked to Swanson for support. He was a tall, asthmatic skeleton of an Irish kid, who smoked Luckys from the time he was eleven, and played first base because he had a long stretch, and didn't have the wind for other positions. He hit the ball, but rarely for extra bases. "I dunno," Swanny said, which was what he usually said, unless he'd drunk some beer, when he became aggressively sentimental.

"Look, Meyers, and the rest of you too." Godine stood up and folded his arms across his chest. "As long as I manage the Bullets you'll play the games that I schedule. This is a team."

"Not if we get beat up we won't be able to play," Meyers whined.

"Beat up your ass. Who's gonna get beat up?" Hubby said. He thrust his chin out at Meyers in contempt. "Beat up."

"And you'll all shut up, and if you don't like it you can quit the team, or you can vote, and decide you don't want me to manage you any more."

Eric turned around and wandered off a few steps, and stood there looking at his hands. Nobody wanted to dump Godine. Since he'd started managing the Bullets they'd enjoyed being a team a lot more. He had changed them from a bunch of straggling kids playing ball to a team with a citywide rep. They all were having more fun, and felt a lot bigger about themselves. He had got them into the Kiwanis and the American Legion leagues. He got Jake's Hardware to sponsor them for uniforms, and they travelled all over the city to play, wearing their Bullet uniforms deep into the Bronx, their spikes hung by the shoestrings around their necks. He had even got Al Bloustein to play center field for them. He covered the outfield like Dom Dimaggio, the little professor, and he could hit, and he brought to the team the spirit of a kid who lived and breathed baseball, who actually was to have a major league tryout, and played for three years in North Carolina, in the A league, and went up to the Seattle Seals for three years in the Triple A; but he was never strong enough to last in pro baseball. The Condors hated Bloustein, because he had the art of playing baseball. He had finesse. Their center fielder, Tony Galupo, a weight-lifter, a horse, a future hitter for the mob, tried to run into him and knock him down every time they exchanged positions between innings. So Godine had really brought the Bullets together, and any suggestions they get rid of him would be unpopular, and he knew it.

"Hey, you guys don't have to worry," said Nate Steiner. "My dad's coming to the game, with some of his buddies."

Nathan Steiner was their first-string pitcher, and he was free of most of the fears of the street that haunted the rest of the Bullets, because his father was a detective in the 32nd Precinct. He was a nasty kid, with a big ego, who

prodded his friends' weaknesses unmercifully. "So you
don't have to worry about your precious hands, Meyers;
but 'tits' over there is going to have to wear a bra." By
'tits' he meant Dusty, who was chubby, and self-conscious
about it, especially about the flab on his chest, ashamed
sometimes to take off his shirt and look, he thought, like
an old woman. Nate Steiner was the only person who
made him feel this way, his gut fisted up with anger. He
hated Steiner worse than the Condors; in fact, he didn't
hate the Condors at all; but Steiner, he wanted to beat him
to the ground and stomp on his neck, pull his precious
right arm out of joint, even though it was the pitching arm
of the New York Bullets. Steiner was immune, because his
father was a detective, and he had let the word out early
that any violence done on his person would subject the
perpetrator to reprisals from Gus the Ghost, his detective
dad, and from the whole long arm of the 32nd Precinct.
No one yet had tried to call Nate's bluff. Even the Condors
respected it. He didn't mind letting the rumor get around
that the exit from the game, out of the ballfield, along the
paths through the park by the river, up over the viaduct
above the drive, back to Haven Avenue, the streets—a
long walk, a lot of space for a fight to develop, for the
Condors, if they lost the game, to take it out in lumps on
the New York Bullets Social and Athletic Club—would be
protected by cops off duty guarding the route, out of
loyalty to and love for Nate Steiner, son of Detective
Lieutenant Gus Steiner, known on Amsterdam Avenue,
on St. Nicholas, on Broadway and Fort Washington, as
The Ghost.

"I'll believe it when I see it," said Meyers. It was inning

eight, and Gus the Ghost was nowhere visible.

It was hard to figure out George Godine, why he wanted to spend his time doing what he did. What did a twenty year old guy get out of spending all his time with a bunch of kids who ranged in age from 14-16? Just to coach them in baseball? Just to organize their club? Except for some part-time coolee work he did for money, he spent all his time on the Bullets. Why? Not for the girls. There was a flutter of interest among girls at school when the Bullets first showed up wearing their purple and gold satin reversible jackets and, in fact, Linda Wolfe, who lived alone with her divorced mother, wore George Zografi's jacket for almost a whole day, with his name, Zogie, stitched on the big gold B over the heart on the left side, but she gave it back; because once the membership of the Bullets was known the girls realized not much status or protection or excitement would come their way if they wore a Bullet jacket. Most Bullets had reps as 'brains', and not much swagger on the street. Zogie was the most 'mature' Bullet, as was Linda Wolfe a most mature girl. He would visit her apartment at night when her mother was on a date. He was mature because he never answered when the kids asked him what he did with Linda Wolfe in the apartment alone at night, and because he knew from junior high school that he was going to be a pharmacist, and absolutely went on to become one in Ohio or somewhere else the Bullets thought of as 'out west'.

So Godine didn't have much leverage to gain with young girls from associating with the Bullets, and he wasn't a fairy or queer either, who liked young boys. Albie Dinnerman attested to that. He wasn't a Bullet, but he befriended some of the Bullets, for reasons unknown. Dinnerman was a Jewish hoodlum, a rare type in that neighborhood. He was almost as old as Godine, but still in school because he'd been left back so many times. He wasn't stupid, but in school he was dumb, like everyone else wanted to be but didn't have the nerve. He could tell a teacher to go fuck himself, and walk out of class. He stayed in school only because his mother wanted him to graduate, and he loved his mother. He came to a couple of practices with the Bullets, and was pretty good, but quickly realized he didn't have time for baseball any more. He was supporting his mother who liked to stay in bed all the time and claim she was dying. "Nah," Dinnerman told Dusty, whom he talked to a lot, until he disappeared from the neighborhood, some said to prison, others to Florida. "He ain't queer. I've seen lots of queers. They've got only one thing to tell you in their eyes. And you look at their mouths too. They got that loose mouth that they pucker up when they see you, cause they want to suck. They all need to suck. Godine, nah." Dinnerman was an expert on queers because of the way he supported his mother. He'd go down to Times Square on the weekend and let one pick him up on the street or in a movie, and he'd get twenty bucks for it, or sometimes, he later confided in Dusty, he'd go to the guy's hotel room, and sap him, and take all his money. He showed Dusty the roll of silver dollars he had wrapped in electrician's tape, and thick felt, and carried inside a wool sock. "Knocks him out, but it don't bruise him much. Some of these guys are strong." He also carried handles from garbage can lids that he used as brass knuckles. "They cut," he said. "I

don't like 'em, but . . .'' Dusty felt a thrill when he talked
with Albie Dinnerman, of another, darker world. He was
proud when Albie asked him to come along some time,
and Dusty really wanted to go with him, at least once, to
'roll queers', but never got around to it, because it was
usually on a Saturday night, and there were dances on
Saturday night, and always the possibility that Dusty
would 'get laid'. Dusty had never 'got laid' yet. After he
did he might go with Albie Dinnerman, but first he had to
do whatever that meant, to 'get laid'. That was supposed
to change his life. You never jerk off again. And once you
'get laid' you are forever 'laid'.

Godine remained a mystery. The answer was probably
simple. He probably enjoyed bossing some kids around,
no ulterior motives. He still lived at home with his family,
and had his rent paid. He had very little ambition. He
collected dues from the team members, that went to fees
for the leagues they joined, though maybe some of it, and
some commission from the uniforms, slipped into his own
pocket; but if it was a scam, it wasn't very profitable, a
few cents an hour. He just organized, coached, and
managed the Bullets, and for that he got to boss them
around. Sometimes, to pick up a little pocket money, he'd
work, maybe with Dusty, or some other kids, as a peanut
butcher at Yankee Stadium, throwing peanuts and fielding
the quarters. That was very great to do. And he tried to
teach the kids their baseball skills, one of which was to
bunt. There was the drag bunt, which Bloustein, and
sometimes Eric Meyers, could beat out for a hit; and there
was the sacrifice bunt, which everyone on the team had to
learn, even their catcher, Nick Stamatakis, who everyone

said was like Ernie Lombardi, catcher for the New York Giants, and the slowest base runner ever to play major league baseball. A center fielder, with a good arm, could throw him out at first base on what for anyone else would be a clean single over second base. Like Lombardi, Stamatakis could belt the ball. When he got his considerable weight behind it the horsehide sailed. He was the only Bullet ever to hit it over the chain-link fence that separated their diamond from the Pennsylvania Railroad track that stretched up Manhattan along the river. He was also the only Bullet fearless enough, aside from Hubby who was too small to make a good target, to put on the catcher's equipment and squat behind the batter. Birdie Bloomklauber, a perpetual benchwarmer, would do it sometimes, just so he could play, but he was stone scared of it. He was the best mathematician on the team, and a future physicist, but when the pitch was thrown he'd close his eyes, and turn around when the batter swung, and often get hit in the back of the head.

"When you drag a bunt, or you might say 'push it' if you're right-handed," Godine explained, "you hit the ball behind your weight, because you step out with your left foot and you're on your way to first base just before you contact the ball. You show them, Bloustein." Rickie Borowski, second-string pitcher, who had more control, but less stuff than Steiner, pitched a slow one to Bloustein, who was a switch hitter, and he kissed a perfect drag bunt down the third base line, and was half way to first base, it seemed, before the ball even touched the ground.

Dusty thought he could do that, if he could bat left-handed. He was pudgy, but he was quick. Though he

loved baseball, and lived to see the flags flying on Yankee
Stadium, and his heart was full of Joe Dimaggio, and Yogi
Berra, and 'old reliable' Tommy Henrich, whose number
15 he wore himself, and he loved the myths of poor
American boys becoming aristocrats through the sport of
baseball, and though he knew he was strong enough to hit
the ball hard, he always felt this conflict when he got up to
bat, because there was someone out there on a mound
only sixty feet away, throwing a hard object in his
direction. That was the reality of it, as his gut understood
it, and his problem was to conquer first his instinct to
protect himself by getting out of the way. Putting his foot
in the bucket, was what it was called, from whatever his
stance: wide, narrow, close to the plate, forward in the
batter's box, bat on his shoulder, bat in the air. He always
felt more ready to duck than to swing, and because of this
conflict between the 'reality' of the situation and the
nature of the game, he didn't hit too well. His swing was
straight-armed and stiff from the shoulders. The few times
he'd really connected it had sounded great, and felt so
solid in his hands. It was a real American feeling he knew
he was missing, taking care of business in all the space of a
ball park. He thought about it a lot, what it was he
couldn't face. It was the 'fear itself' that he feared, more
than the baseball. He felt better when he heard what the
great pitcher Bobbie Feller said about Jackie Robinson
when he first came up into the major leagues. "Robinson
will never make it," Feller had said. "He's too tight at the
top." That stuck with Dusty. 'Too tight.' He tried to loosen
up in batting practice 'at the top.' Even the greatest had
faults and had to correct them. He started to think about

his elbows relaxed, his shoulders relaxed, and swinging
with a snap of the wrists and a follow through. He had
started to connect in batting practice that day as he never
had before, and move the ball. He had some confidence, to
watch the ball onto the bat. That was the best defense.
That was why he wanted to swing away with Swanny on
first. He would slow down Koros' fast ball just by staring
at it. "Too tight at the top," he commented to himself as
he watched Koros strike out Meyers, and thought he was
going to stand in there and connect, drop his shoulders,
loose elbows, get his hips into it, wrists snap, base hit. But
Dusty stepped into the batter's box, and looked down to
third, and there was the bunt sign. Godine lifted his hat,
cocked the brim, hooked his thumbs in his belt. Bunt. It
figured. Dusty had already struck out twice. Godine
didn't know that he intended to hit this time. It was the
only call. Move Swanny to second. Bloustein followed
Dusty in the crazy way Godine had shuffled the batting
order. If anyone could bring Swanny in from second,
Bloustein could. Sacrifice bunt. Tie the game. Dusty felt
weak, as if he was going to fill his pants.

"With the sacrifice bunt your weight is behind the ball."
That scared Dusty. "Right-handed batter moves the right
foot so his body is square to the pitcher." You face it, your
whole body, totally square to the direction from which
that hard ball is thrown. You put your full face in front of
it. Why should anyone do it? And in front of Nick Koros,
who was the fastest pitcher he had ever faced, and he was
wild, had already hit Swanny, and it was late in the game
and the ball was dirty and hard to see, and his fastball had
this hop. "The left hand grips the bat down around the

handle, the right hand slides up to the label, and you step in front of the batter's box because there's more of a chance to hit the ball fair. You hold the bat loosely." Hell, he could swing away. He could hit the ball. What did this absolutely mean in his life? Why should he put his face in front of the pitch?

"Balk. It's a balk." Hubby was jumping up and down and screaming in the first base coaching box, because Koros had stepped off the rubber after going into his wind-up. Dusty lowered his bat and stepped out of the batter's box. "That was a balk. The guy balked." Hubby was turning in circles, looking for support. The Condors glowered at him. The umpire, Vinny Falconieri, was a Condor. He turned his back on Hubby. The players on the Condor bench all stood up, cracking their knuckles, looking fierce. Tony Galupo started in from center field. He moved like a big truck on a narrow street.

"Hey, Hubby, shut up. Shut your mouth," Meyers shouted at him from the bench.

"Falconieri," Hubby shouted, but Vinny paid no attention to him. Dusty knew Vinny Falconieri. Vinny the Ginny probably didn't even know what a balk was. He didn't like baseball, didn't play the game. He was a tough guy, but he was honest. Dusty and he had a distant friendship, that began when they met once in the library, where he caught Vinny checking out a book about the life of Albert Einstein. "You can't be stupid all your life," Vinny had said, and they talked for a long time in the back of the library. Dusty was amazed. Vinny played the piano, classical. The Bullets had all the Condors stereotyped as thugs, greasers, junior racketeers, gang-fighters, and there

Dusty was in the library talking from his heart to Vinny
Falconieri, who had a rep as one of the roughest on the
street, and he went to Catholic school, and yet both of
them knew, it was absolutely felt between them in brand
new blood pumping through their veins after they talked
philosophy for hours, that if it weren't for their separate
loyalties to the Bullets and the Condors they would be best
friends; in fact, in a way, they were. Vinny ignored
Hubby.

"What is this? A balk? What fuckin' kind of baseball?"
Hubby was calming down. He took a last look at Godine,
and got no response. Godine was a fanatic in his own way,
but he wasn't going to argue this balk. He was super-
stitious too. When his team got a hit, or just a man on base,
he stopped moving, except for his hands to give a signal,
but never his legs. At a Kiwanis game once, when
someone else was coaching third base, he bent over to
pick up his hat just as Bloustein got a double, and he
stayed bent over that way till the rally was over, while
they batted twice around the batting order, and scored
eleven runs. He couldn't straighten up after that, and the
next day had to go to a chiropractor. He was fanatical, but
not stupid. He knew, as did most of the rest of the team,
that with the Condors anything was an excuse for a fight,
and if they tried to press a technicality at this point, the
eighth inning, 2-1 the score, a balk, try to explain it, then
there would definitely be a slaughter right then, and they
would never finish the game.

It had been peaceful so far; ominous and sullen and
dangerous, but peaceful, just like the cold war, which was
the politics of the time, the Eisenhower years, the

McCarthy era, negotiated through the game of baseball, maintained with a precarious edge by kids who lived in a neighborhood that yielded to the bigger government some years later a certain Henry Kissinger, who was neither a Bullet nor a Condor, was too old at the time, probably finishing his Ph.D. in the Ivy League.

This game was territorial, it had that significance, and that made every move important. The Bullets were playing for their right to use this field. After the Condors had intimidated them out of the park on 175th St., and had pushed them out of the schoolyard, they had come down here and found this field by the river, and they had practiced here unmolested through the rest of the summer, when at the end Godine had started coaching them. The Condors would have pushed the Bullets off this field too, out of sheer meanness, but they didn't find out till the start of this summer, and lucky for the Bullets Godine had managed to negotiate a ball game, to delay an immediate show of power by the Condors, and some instantly busted heads among the Bullets. The Condors were ruthless and greedy when it came to territory. Only Hubby on the Bullets was ready to die for that, so the whole team was relieved when he finally gave up about the balk. Tony Galupo turned and moved back to center field.

Everyone thought the Bullets would be losing by more than one run in the eighth, especially after the Condors scored two runs on errors in the first; but power on the streets didn't necessarily mean power on the ballfield. You had to hit the ball. You had to score the runs. Even big Galupo looked like a fish strung out on a hook, batting

against Steiner. Only Koros' pitching kept the Condors in
the baseball game, and he was a ringer, had become a
Condor, who knows because of what intimidation, only
just before the game. Baseball was not a Condor specialty,
and the Bullets realized they could win, and they wanted
to. Why not? Win or lose the Condors could jump them
after the game. Dusty felt in his spine and in a faintness in
his wrists all the desire of his whole ball club. And good
old Stamatakis had blasted one onto the railroad tracks,
and Swanny was on first shaking his fists at Dusty. Oh
how he wanted to swing away, to prove it to his team, to
himself. Aside from poor Birdie, he was the lowest, his
only mean consolation that he could play better than the
spastic mathematician. He needed this redemption:
shoulders loose, elbows free, wrists snap, base hit.

Dusty looked down the third base line to Godine. He
was staring into right field. He hadn't moved his legs.
"C'mon Dusty. You can do it babes," from Bloustein on
deck. Dusty could hear him boning his bat, not to make
the wood harder, he explained, but to attract horsehide to
wood, like flesh to bone. Everyone felt it, even the
Condors. If Swanson got to second, Bloustein would drive
him home, and that would change their world. Godine
didn't move. "I'm going to hit that mother," Dusty told
himself. Then, the sign. Godine shifted his hat, hooked his
thumbs in his belt.

"Front of the batter's box, weight forward on the balls of
your feet. See the ball hitting the meat of the bat. Put it
there with your eyes." It depended on Dusty. Koros
wound up. Swanny was on first, rubbing where his arm
was hit. The ball would come right in Dusty's face. Did he

have a choice? Condors glowered at him with evil eyes. He had to face it all, square away, and bunt. He couldn't tell where his knees were going when he heard the first pitch explode like a grenade in the catcher's mitt, and he didn't open his eyes till he heard Falconieri call, "Strike one!"

"That Koros," he remembered Zogie saying. "He's got a fastball that rises, and about as much control as a kid with a busted kite string." Nick Koros grinned from the mound, more of a sneer to tell Dusty he had him in his hip pocket. There was the sign again. He stepped out of the batter's box and looked around. You could have feelings and still swing away, but you had to be cool to bunt. All the Bullets were silent. They wanted to win real bad. O for a wild pitch that would get Swanny to second, and then he could swing away. He didn't want his friendships to be riding on this bunt. Koros, a small guy, looked big as a bull on the mound. Dusty stepped back in to face it. Koros wound up. Open, Dusty told himself, keep the eyes open. As Koros' arm swung down, Dusty squared away again. He saw the ball leave Koros' hand. Watch it onto the bat, he ordered himself. See it on the meat of the bat. The bat stunned his hand, and vibrated, and there was a bomb of light in his head, and for a moment, nothing.

"Go, Dusty. Come on. Run." Hubby's voice, and the voices from the Bullets' bench. Dusty ran like a blind man in the direction he knew first base to be. "Safe," shouted Hubby, and Dusty stood on the bag with a hand over his right eye. What happened? He slowly opened his tear-drenched left eye. Swanny was on third. Koros had fielded what looked like a perfect bunt, and he threw the ball into center field trying to get Swanny who had stumbled on the way to second. Now he was catching his wind on third, and Dusty was on first, and Bloustein was up. Dusty had laid down a perfect bunt with his eye. The ball had glanced off the bat, bashed his eye, and rolled neatly to the right side of the infield, stopping between the pitcher's mound and first base line. No one seemed to know it but himself. The body of the batter is foul territory. He should have called a second strike on himself. "Attaway Dusty babes. Attaway, babes." He should be at bat again, swinging away, but he knew that with one eye shut there was no way he could find a pitch. He'd take it, then. The Condors deserved it. He'd take the bunt. He'd take the eye. Him and it.

Tony Galupo had picked up the ball in short center field, and he walked it in, faking a throw, squeezing the horsehide sphere as if he would crush it. "Gaw ahead. Try to score, you faggot. Break for home," he shouted at Swanson. "I'll sink this fuckin' ball between your ears." Everyone was up from the Bullets' bench and screaming, "Great bunt." Hubby was beating him on the butt and giggling. He turned to look at Hubby, and pulled his hand away from his right eye.

"Holy shit," said Hubby, stepping back. "You're gonna have some shiner, man. When did that happen?"

Bloustein was up. The bunt and error had taken something out of Koros. Bloustein jumped on the first pitch for a triple, and Dusty carried his swollen eye, that weighed a ton by the time he rounded second, past home plate with the run that put them ahead. He stood by the bench and held a sweatshirt over his eye while his teammates celebrated around him, and he tried to look

casual, as if he was walking out of Macy's without paying
for the sneakers he had slipped under his coat. Steiner
walked the first man in the top of the ninth, but struck out
the next two, including Galupo, and the last man hit a high
fly to right center field, a shot that Dusty, in right field,
didn't even see; but Bloustein, ranging wide from center,
pulled it in without trouble for the third out.

Not a sound from the players. A tugboat hooted on the
river, towing a line of barges out to sea. The Bullets
tiptoed in from the playing field, as if someone was
sleeping whom they didn't want to wake up. The Condors
watched them sullenly. The world could have ended right
there. But the finish of the game, and the way they had
lost, dampened the meanest energies of the Condors. They
gathered their stuff together silently, and quickly, and
prepared to leave, like a giant army surrendered to a
nation of runts.

Godine laid an arm on Dusty's shoulder. "I couldn't
believe that bunt, Dusty, when I saw it roll out there. I
guess I really coached you good. Thanks, kid." Dusty
lowered the sweatshirt from his eye and looked at Godine.
"Jesus, Dusty." He put his hand up as if to touch the eye
swollen shut. "Looks like a horsefly bit you. When did
that happen?"

"I don't know," Dusty said. "It suddenly happened."
His throat dried up when he lied, so he could hardly say
'happened'.

"Okay, where's your famous father, Steiner?" Meyers
asked.

"Don't worry," Steiner said.

"You don't worry. You said he'd be here. You don't

have to worry. They won't touch you.''

"They're here," Steiner said, waving his arms at the trees as if to indicate there were cops hiding behind them.

"Well, we better all leave together," said Meyers, looking over at the Condors that seemed to him to be milling around like a tornado about to hit. "There's safety in numbers." He looked at Dusty. "That was a great bunt. That was a Richie Ashburn bunt. Hey, look at your eye. What happened to your eye? Look at Dusty's eye." The whole team gathered around him, and stared at his eye, and made him feel like a frog in a bio lab. "That's gonna be a beauty," someone said. The Condors shuffled past them as they left. "Punks," mumbled Tony Galupo.

"Hey, let's not let them get too far ahead," Meyers whispered. "We don't want to get ambushed."

"We won't get ambushed," Hubby said.

"Just keep close enough so we can see them," Meyers said. "So where's your father, Steiner? In the woods?"

"Yeah. He's in the woods with your mother."

Dusty hung back as all the Bullets left together behind the Condors. He didn't want to talk about the game, and his bunt, and his eye. He wasn't ashamed of it, but didn't want to hear about it. In a sense the ill-acquired bunt wasn't his, it was theirs, a gift to the team. They had won more than a game, and this had been more than an infield hit. But the bunt was important only to the extent that he was a Bullet, and that wasn't everything. Now he had his eye, and it was swollen shut, and he had himself. He walked slowly and watched the old men fishing off the tar-smeared boulders by the river. He could hear them talking to each other in Italian. Up ahead on the asphalt path he could see Vinny the Ginny sitting on a bench, waiting for him. He stood up when Dusty got close.

"Hey, you put a big Kosher steak on that eye when you get home," Vinny said. "Porterhouse." He fell in step with Dusty on the path. Dusty knew as soon as he looked at Vinny that he'd seen it. He'd been the umpire, behind the plate.

"You could have called that ball foul, Vinny. You saw it."

"I never liked baseball that much anyway. I only like football a lot. You know me, I like to get in there and beat on people."

"You saw it, didn't you?" Dusty pointed at the swollen eye.

"What are you, stupid?

"You saw it, and you didn't call it. My eye is foul territory. That could have been strike two."

Vinny shrugged his shoulders. "What do you want from me? I can't help it, Dusty. I like the underdog." Vinny pointed at the old men fishing. "You know my grandfather Renzo used to come down here to fish. Sometimes he took me. This was the only thing he ever enjoyed after they brought him here to this country. He caught eels. He didn't like the crabs, they were for the Chinese, he said. It was the only thing he really enjoyed. Not me. I was bored stiff."

"I can't believe it," Dusty said.

"Look, that was a good bunt. You gonna bother me about it, fuck you. That was an original way to lay down a bunt. That was a great way to play baseball, more like football. Besides, I don't believe in ruining a good story by telling the truth.'' They walked quietly for a while.

"It was real creative,'' Vinny finally said. "Listen, I gotta catch up with the rest of my animals up there. It's almost feeding time, and I don't want them to get too mean, and I don't want them to see me talking to the enemy.''

"We're not the enemy.''

"All punks are the enemy,'' said Vinny the Ginny. "Remember to take care of that eye. Kosher meat.'' Dusty watched him run ahead and jump on Tony Galupo's back, and watched them wrestle around. There was no fight between the Condors and the Bullets. At one point, he later heard, Galupo had picked up Nate Steiner on the viaduct and dangled him over the traffic, but his own guys quieted him down. The Bullets practiced unmolested on their field from then on, and on the streets the Condors were almost friendly.

Dusty left the path to walk along the stones near the river. The tide was coming in, pushing the smell of the ocean upriver. He watched an old Chinese man pull up a trap with three crabs in it. The man carefully removed the crabs from the wire net and dropped them in a straw basket with other crabs under wet newspaper. Dusty grinned so wide his eye was throbbing. He loved this Chinese man pulling crabs from the Hudson. And he loved the Hudson. A police siren on the bridge far above sounded like the whine of a mosquito. He loved the bridge. The Chinese man looked at him, expressionless. Dusty walked away. Who would ever understand the Chinese? He touched the tender skin around his eye. "This is good,'' he grinned. "This is real good.''

When his mother took one good look at his eye she would rush him to Emergency at the hospital. The last place he wanted to go was Emergency. He remembered the storm sewers Vinny had told him about once that wound around inside the high walls of the drive. Dusty didn't want to go to Emergency. Vinny had said that he went down the sewers sometimes, just to be alone and think. This had filled Dusty with fantasies of hidden worlds and secret passages, but he never had the courage to go down there himself. Right now the sewers sounded better than having to explain the eye to his mother, and letting her turn him into her baby again.

Just past the viaduct, at the top of the first flight of steps that led to Haven Avenue, was a manhole cover, entrance to the sewer. Dusty stared at it. This was the opening to the underworld, to the passages that wound around under the whole city. He could go anywhere in them, and come up under anyone secretly from beneath. He lifted the cover and slid it aside, and let himself down by the iron rungs cemented into the wall, then he pulled the cover back over the hole, closing the daylight over his head.

It was dry at the bottom, and dark. With one hand on the wall he worked his way towards someplace slightly brighter down the tunnel. He was Jean Valjean under the streets of Paris. He was Tom Sawyer in the cave and would feel safer only if he had some Becky to protect. Stealth was his middle name. He got to a barred window high on the thick stone wall, that allowed the sewer some dim illumination. Narrow stone steps climbed to the window to let you look out, or scramble out of the way to hang on to the bars if water started rushing through. He knew how to survive. From the window he could see the river, and hear the highway traffic, his river, and his bridge across it, and his palisade cliffs on the other side.

It was all so great. He had never been in such a place before. He climbed back down and looked up at the grey patch of sky behind the barred window. This was enough to do, to put himself in prison for his own cheat. He sat down against the wall, and the next moment he remembered it was getting darker. He must have dozed off. He climbed back to the window, and laughed out loud, and his laughter echoed down the tunnel. He was a maniac. No one had ever spent a night in a place like this, not even Vinny the Ginny, and he was going to do it. Then he saw the egg in the sky. He was going crazy. A peculiar lozenge of light crossed the sky, moving towards the bridge, subtly changing color. It brightened and darkened and got brighter again. "Say something to me," he shouted. "Tell me." He wished someone else was there to see it too, because was it really moving there, or was it inside his head? One eye was not enough to know. "Space people," he shouted. "I love you." It was going to be like this for him, he understood, one eye open, flattening out what was there, the other swollen shut from inside, rendering the 'truth' into all its dimensions, never ruining a good story.

It could be an omen, or a vision, but of what? He watched it with a mixture of skepticism and awe, one eye inward, one eye out, like a bunt. It was so delicate as it bisected the arc of the bridge, and rose out of sight. It was pure speed. Had he seen it, or not? Why make such a thing up? He watched the darkness come. He would never

forget it, any more than he could forget this night. Lights
from cars turning down the West Side Drive cast a shadow
of the barred window against the back wall. The warning
beacon started to turn on top of the Jersey tower of the
bridge. Red then white then red then white. There was a
light wind by his ears, and a whirring sound as bats,
hundreds of them, flew past his head out of the window
into the night. "Bye-bye bats," he said. He was a maniac.
Baseball was a dream in the afternoon. Night had come
and he was alone for the first time in his life.

   He climbed down and leaned against the wall and felt
his heart flapping lightly as the wings of a bat. "I love all
the people," he whispered. He picked up his baseball mitt
and brought it close to his face as if to make a meal of the
smells of leather and neatsfoot oil and sweat. "I love you
Jimmy Piersall baseball mitt." He shouted loud as he
could, his words echoing down the corridors. "I love all
you people who wonder where I am tonight. I love you,
my mother." He laughed. He was a maniac here. He
screamed it out. "I love you, police, trying to figure out
where I went. I love a telephone. I love Nate Steiner the
suck and his father The Ghost. I love the Condors. I love
Vinny. I love Nick Koros who threw the baseball that
smashed into my eye. I love baseball. I love you swollen
eye that wins the ball game in the afternoon. I love you
bridge and I love you flying saucers." He lay down in
darkness, his mitt under his head. "I love the bunt," he
said. "I love George Godine and the mystery of George
Godine. I love the stupid Bullets and the stupid purple and
gold satin reversibles." He snapped the jacket around
himself, and the darkness folded down on him. "Ha," he

shouted, and closed his eyes to watch the terrifying thoughts nudge his mind. Dungeon thoughts. Trapped forever. No morning forever. Ha. He was a maniac. He jumped up.

"I love you, rats," he shouted, because rats were sniffing around his shoes. Of course there were. The sewers were a rat's house. "Welcome to you, rats." Not even Vinny had ever spent a night with the rats in a sewer. He could hear them chewing on his mitt. Dusty climbed to the window and looked out at the night, one eye swollen shut and throbbing, the other wet with tears, and he had the thought for the first time in his life that when morning came (would it come?), that would be the first day of the rest of his life. He had heard something like that somewhere in a song, but he couldn't remember which song.

COLLEGE DAYS

---

1. Freshman Year:

W ad   I mpatient   E ating   R affle   &   P anoramic
O bverse   U glification C acodyl E mbower

"Wad up those girly mags and toss them in the lake, and toss your girls in too," E. Pouce tells the other abject freshmen on his corridor, horny scavengers without dignity, who could be led into war for a piece of tail, or a bite of meat. Impatient to the extreme, his father would empty the scalding contents of the soup tureen onto the bare feet of Delia, one of their maids, if the dinner was even slightly delayed. Eating well is a privilege you inherit, or earn with difficulty, and rabble can't even know what the experience means when they get the opportunity to taste a truffled paté. "Raffle these nonentities," he'd hear his Grandpa Pouce shout frequently, though he never really understood it till he began to develop in his own spheres of influence. & E. Pouce taunts Dusty Wier every day with his modus operandi, fiendish though still hypothetical. Panoramic devastation is a fantasy Pouce savors. Obverse madman, Dusty calls him, finding something more essential in the E. Pouce phenomenon than mere perversity. Uglification is a small aspect of the evolution of his whole design. Cacodyl, and other foul-smelling poisons flow from the tunics of

Pouce's schemes, and Dusty ponders meanwhile his own purpose on earth. Embowered in his heart is a love for everything life illuminates, but what stuff is the E. Pouce heart, and what steers it, beating, through his vision of ultimate darkness?

I dyllic	E clectically	R ailroading	&	P alm
O ceanic	U mpteen	C aricaturist		E ndpaper
W arranty				

Idyllic scenes cover the drapes and bedspreads of E. Pouce's rooms in the dormitory. Eclectically decorated they exude a sense, albeit illusionary, of good nature. Railroading motifs, the whole history of locomotives and rolling stock, run in a lively frieze from window to door. & once a girl enters this room she is persistently wooed by scents and sounds. Palm trees rustle in her ears. Oceanic fragrances mingle with gulls' cries to give her the seashore illusion. Umpteen females are deflowered just by the atmosphere in there. Caricaturist and feminist Elizabeth Zinberg, who in a fit of self-hatred ends up in a disastrous marriage with Pouce, returns to the room again and again, fascinated by something there she can't yet define. Endpapers of his books hold her sketches, sometimes morbid, sometimes gay, always mysterious, that she doodles while waiting for him to wake up, or to return from class. Warranty this relationship with my words, he tells her, but there is no guarantee.

E cuadorian	R ationality	&	P atent	O nion	U lulant
C aste	E rratic	W eather	I llative		

Ecuadorian folk musicians stroll the dormitory halls playing panpipes and guitars, trying to keep winter spirits up. Rationality demands firmer evidence to support what Dusty is beginning to know in E. Pouce as so terrifying he needs to blame some of it on paranoia; not that he is paranoid, but he finds it too unnerving to attribute the whole scope of this evil to one E. Pouce. & Elizabeth Zinberg keeps him posted as she digs up more E. Pouce info, all of it amusing to her, still not ready to find him sinister. Patent designs for instruments of torture, a mill that processes human bodies into paper fit for printing bureaucratic forms, poisonous wastes to pour in the ear of the planet, Elizabeth shows him these as if they are tricks she has found in his room and has copied in triplicate. "Onion, my Onionhead," she calls him. Ululant, piercing sounds issue from his room in the early morning, but when they open the door no demons, just E. Pouce asleep alone in his bed. Caste can't be the only excuse, though Pouce's wealth and privilege make it easy for him to presume to interfere on a massive scale in the lives of everyone else. Erratic as is Dusty's thinking at school on most political issues, he identifies E. Pouce with certainty as a most serious threat, one of the few who owns the world in conflict with the rest who don't. Weather quiets their life through most of the spring, giving Dusty the time to reflect in a warm room. Illative, and therefore not totally reliable, Dusty has to presume, are his conclusions about E. Pouce's schemes.

2. Sophomore Year:

R ectification   &   P epper   O rgan   U nderexposure
C hapultepec   E ra   W etback   I mplement
E ighth-note

"Rectification my right rectum," Dusty tells Elizabeth Zinberg. & he pushes her back into the easy chair, where she starts to sneeze. Pepper spilled from the shelf above his hot plate drifts on the air currents. "Organ selection is only one of his ideas, ahhhh-chooo," and she explains how E. Pouce would take the best organs from the poor to rectify deficiencies in the systems of the privileged few. Underexposure to just plain folks could be his problem, and Dusty is willing to search for an answer. Chapultepec Park, a few days just sitting in it, watching poor people, could ignite the spark of his humanity. Era one of his life has been indulgence in total privilege. 'Wetback in reverse' will be the next. Implement this plan immediately, Dusty resolves. Eighth-notes played incessantly outside his door by Ecuadorian panpipers will begin to put Pouce in a trance.

& P harmacy O ysterman U nconscious C hippewa
E xecution W ent I mpassive E nable R elevant

& this is how the plan unfolds. Pharmacy Phil puts out the pills to keep Pouce docile after panpiper hypnosis while Dusty and Elizabeth carry him unconscious to his car and they head for Mexico to execute a prank that lasts through spring break and beyond. Oysterman Acapulco

Eddie shucks the big ones into the bathtub, where they lay
the drowsy E. Pouce down in the heat of the day.
Unconscious till evening, as the sun goes down he gets up,
covered with cool, lubricous mollusc meat. "Chippewa
spoken here, only Ojibway," E. snaps as he sees the
Indian faces watching expressionless as his white body
rises in the middle of Chapultepec Park from a bathtub
full of oysters. Execution of this prank demands that
Dusty and Elizabeth keep out of sight, so E. Pouce can feel
what it means to be alone among plain folks, vulnerable,
subject to ridicule. "Went well," Dusty tells Elizabeth,
whose sympathy for E. in his dilemma threatens to ruin
the results. Impassive and sophisticated Mexico City
residents soon ignore the stupid sight of E. Pouce climbing
from the tub and shaking off the indignities, though the
condors that drop from nowhere out of the polluted air, to
dip up the oysters, attract a lot of attention. Enable E.
Pouce to become human, Dusty prays to the gods of shock
therapy. "Relevant to whom is this silliness, to those
birds?" exasperated Elizabeth asks Dusty finally, and she
grabs a bath towel and rushes forward to pat E. Pouce dry.

P lane   O ctober   U ndisposed   C oin   E xtrovert
W hip   I mpertinent   E mpiricist   R equire   &

Plane geometry of emotions put Elizabeth Zinberg in the
arms of E. Pouce for the duration of the trip. October
weddings, they decide, are best, because her moon lies in
Sagittarius where he has his rising sign. Undisposed to this
turn their scheme has taken, unhappy that no progress has
been made on the E. Pouce case, Dusty leaves, rides a

train alone through the jungle to the Yucatan. Coin makes
power, and the passion for coin corrupts, Dusty reflects in
his depression, but something even more complicated is
working in the case of E. Pouce. Extrovert Mayans,
hustling hammocks in Merida markets, joke Dusty out of
his funk, and guide him through the ruins for a few coins.
Whip or snake, or snake that functions as a whip, held in
the claw of a batlike god, this image fascinates Dusty at
Uxmal, and moves him to near extrasensory experiences.
Impertinent to claim it changed his life, but he does feel
different about the world on his return to school.
Empiricist still to the core, nevertheless Dusty relaxes
subtly into acceptance of a mystic order in the ancient
ruins, and the modern ones as well. Require the dream in
yourself as reality, and the whole new realms of being
unfold their petals. & he begins to feel at school a new
openness in his spirit, and he meets Olivia Pink, a
mysterious girl, destined to become his wife, the mother
of his children, and she provides the preoccupation that
mediates his obsession with E. Pouce.

3. Junior Year:

O badiah   U nionize   C ogitation   E verything
W hite-perch   I ncorporate   E nthymeme   R evel   &
P lacer-mining

Obadiah preached to those who imagined they dwelled
safely in the clefts of high places that even they would be
brought down, as would E. Pouce eventually, Dusty
thinks. Unionize the spirits of all the people below him, to

give him what he deserves. Cogitation in college,
however, he knows is not action. Everything in his own
life, he fears, is almost too copacetic with Olivia Pink as a
partner. "White-perch I caught myself in the lake, just for
you," she blows a kiss as she sets the lemon and
dill-scented dish in front of him. "Incorporate what you
learn at school into your daily life, otherwise your
education is useless," he explains. "Enthymeme, a word I
learned, or me and you which makes love the implied
conclusion, and that's a gloss on our relationship I took
from my rhetoric class, and this is delicious," and he
kisses her with a mouth half-full of boiled potato. "Revel,
on the other hand, in stupidity, as the other kids do around
here, and you end up with someone else in control of your
life." & Olivia Pink believes in him, and in herself, and
their mutual intensity is a buttress against the ubiquitous
know-nothing party people encouraged by E. Pouce to
waste their own minds. Placer-mining of their feelings in
adversity could save these people some day, perhaps wash
them down to the few grains left of their finest feelings.

U nlock   C onduct   E ulogy   W hoopee   I nfectious
E ntrap   R ift   &   P oem   O bservatory

"Unlock the secrets of this box and change all our
lives," she whispers, raising an imaginary container in her
hand. "Conduct your conversations outside of lab," says
Miss Pumice, the graduate assistant. "Eulogy or elegy,
which is it?" asks Vinny Falconieri, worried about a
literature exam coming up for him next hour.
"Whoopee," shouts someone who has finished.
"Infectious but not fatal," she says in Dusty's ear,

speaking of love. "Entrap someone with rhetoric like that and you'll get yours later," Dusty replies in a hushed voice. "Rift butter, that's what I call it, and that's all I'm after," says Darryl Krek, lifting a retort by its spout, and getting a worried glance from Miss Pumice who finds him attractive and a little dangerous. & so the college days go on with a sense of their own priorities. Poem, if you can write one here, is as important as Job later will become. Observatory love is also significant, and they make use of the facility even on cloudy nights.

4. Senior Year:

C onsanguinity   E spalier   W ilt   I nnate   E quation
R obber-baron   &   P redilection   O ffbeat   U xoricide

Consanguinity doesn't guarantee friendship, Dusty realizes, as he watches the rift between himself and his brother widen. Espalier education, that's how his brother got his degree, went on to graduate school, trained to conform, to lie flat as he climbed the academic trellis, not the kind of development Dusty aspired to. Wilt not, and be not wasted, Dusty thinks, but his brother is training his own mind to bend to a pattern, virtually to wilt itself. "Innate ability, talent, courage to just go ahead with it should count for more in our economy, in our arts, and that's why there's so much confusion, incompetence, waste in our marketplace," Dusty spoke out in his Theory of Capitalism class. Equations with a factor of freedom, and discipline as a result, figure in Dusty's sense of what is necessary, of his own destiny, but self-initiated, self-imposed discipline, not his brother's dull surrender to a system. Robber-baron offspring E. Pouce chuckles in his corner of the lecture hall at this futility because he knows he owns this popular Professor Swank. & Dusty, with Olivia Pink on his arm, confronts E. Pouce with Elizabeth Zinberg on his arm after class. "Predilections, predilections of the rabble don't make for talent," E. Pouce taunts. Offbeat, gentle Olivia Pink pulls off her brassiere and snaps the elastic at E. Pouce's rear as he walks away. Uxoricide is possible, something Elizabeth Zinberg will have to be careful of with E. Pouce, Olivia tells her in confidence, but never with her Dusty Wier.

E mission   W inter   I ris   E thos   R upee   &   P roject
O ne   U se   C rimp

Emission rather than graduation is what Dusty feels this process to be by the end of his senior year. Winter melancholy turns the university into a gross, sluggish internal combustion machine, standing in place, students as fuel, graduation the exhaust. "Iris of my soul," Olivia calls him. "Ethos starvation, this homogeneous environment of a university is something I'll gladly leave behind," Dusty explains to Olivia. "Rupee and ruble of my heart," he says into her eyes. & as their College Days draw to a close they draw closer to each other, finding in their love the security lost after leaving alma mater. "Project our relationship into a lifetime together, and splendid," he tells her. "One person, you and me, one future," she sighs. "Use each other while you can," says E. Pouce, passing them in cap and gown. "Crimp yourselves together with marriage."

5. Graduation:

W inter inmate entraps rationality & poem one unlocks
cogitation era

I ris eating relevance & predilection observatory
uglification coins everything whoopee

E mpiricists revel & patent onion ; umpteen
caricaturists embower whip implement

R upee & pepper, Obadiah ululant, caste emission went
infectious eclectically

& panoramic October uxoricide crimps eulogy weather
impatient Ecuadorian requires

P alm oysterman use Chapultepec espalier, wetbacks
impassive enable robber-baron &

O bverse undisposed Chippewa extrovert wads illative
equation rift & projects

U nionize conduct, erratic white-perch, impertinent
eighth-note rectification & pharmacy organs

C acodyl execution warranties idyllic ethos railroading
& placer-mining offbeat exposure

E ndpaper wilt incorporates enthymeme raffle & plane
oceanic unconscious consanguinity

"Damn," Dusty sheds his cap and gown. "Free at last."

"Did you understand that speech?" Olivia wore only a swimsuit under hers.

"Just a few of the words, but I didn't get how it went together. I was nodding off. I couldn't listen."

Olivia hugs him close. "Now we can finish that van off, and then we're gone."

"Travel. Go to Europe. Leave this school stuff behind. Run your own life. Move to Tangiers. See the underbellies..." he whispers in her ear.

"And we can have our babies," she whispers in his ear.

Dusty doesn't hear that. He watches E. Pouce pull away in a silver limousine.

BABEBIES

"She was a whore? Well, so what?"
"Furba," said the carriage driver, who was taking Dusty across Lecce to look at one of the Signora Foti's apartments to rent. The driver tapped his skull to indicate how smart he thought the woman was. "That one deserves respect. So she was a whore? My mother was a whore behind my father's back. During the war everyone had to survive, even Il Duce. At first he was a good man, but then even he became a whore for that Hitler. So what could that poor girl do? She was young. Everyone needs to eat. She sold what she had. At least she was smart. She saved her money, not like some of the other women who squandered it like water. Furba, this Signora Foti, this Padrona of Via Casoti 24." He flicked the reins and his little horse moved. These horse-drawn carriages were the cheapest taxis in Lecce, usually used only by poor people, but a great luxury for Dusty, a special treat; and more appropriate, he felt, to ride around on the paving stones of Lecce's ancient streets to this light Boccherini of hooves.

After the American troops had left the Salento the Padrona left the profession and invested some of the money she had saved on a statue of Mary Magdalen. The figure of Magdalen was dressed in pink kneeling at the feet of Christ in a blue toga. It rested on a pedestal in the patio of her apartment in the complex she was building on Via Casoti. Her neighbors, the Leccese bourgeosie, respected her reluctantly, but kept their distance because they knew she had financed her apartments with money gathered from services rendered to the American Colonel and visiting staff officers. The Leccese didn't rent from her, because they didn't consider her apartments respectable. She kept them rented, however, full of 'foreigners', Milanese assigned to manage franchises in Lecce, or strangers like Dusty who came from abroad and didn't know or care about her past. She had concentrated her resources on raising her own two children, and had fleshed out in prosperity all the curves that had made her desirable on the postwar marketplace. She was a powerhouse, willfull, strong. She stood in front of her apartments when her neighbors walked by, her arms folded across her breast, and the usually animated Leccese conversation reduced itself to hushed whispers as they passed her by.

"Another American," she said. "Che cazzo." She grabbed Dusty's cheek between her thumb and forefinger. "And so young. And married?"

"Yes."

"Children?"

"Two boys, and my wife is pregnant." The Italian word, 'incinta', sounded to Dusty like an imprisonment, whereas 'pregnant' sounded like a mental condition. When a woman gets 'incinta' you sympathize with the man, whereas if she's pregnant you worry about the woman.

"What a pity. So young." she said, and led him up the stairs. "My own son lived in this apartment, but now he's gone away for a while, and I don't know for how long. I didn't want to rent it, but since you're a stranger, and an American, where will you live? I like the Americans. I will rent it to you." The place was spacious: a big master bedroom, and a small room for the kids adjoining, a sunny dining-room, a big living-room with a balcony over the street. The Padrona was particularly proud of the closet built into the small bedroom, because you rarely find such conveniences built into Italian apartments. Their furniture always includes an elegant wardrobe for hanging clothes. "If my son comes back, you will have to leave."

The couple from Torino that lived downstairs explained that the son was in prison for counterfeiting ten thousand lira notes to pass off on tourists during the Rome Olympics. All southern Italians, these northerners explained, are thieves, barbarians, Africans, and Dusty would have to be very careful. They hated living down here, in the Mezzogiorno, but what could they do? The 'company' had transferred him, and they had to make the best of it. They had no friends, spoke to no one and, as if this was some kind of imprisonment, they left their apartment only to buy groceries.

Dusty discovered a trap-door in the floor of the built-in closet, that led to a tiny, cell-like room below, accessible by a clumsy ladder, the ceiling so low he had to bend over, inconvenient for storage, good to hide a counterfeiting operation. Dusty could see them, rolling out the phony bills, bent over like peasants.

"You have to call the electrician," said the Padrona, when he showed her there were no sockets or light-fixtures, just a jumble of bare wires. When a tenant moves, she told him, he takes all that for his next house.

"Okay, that," said Dusty. "Now tell me this." He led
the Padrona into the bathroom. "Is there a seat for this
toilet?" The Padrona shrugged. Dusty tapped the bare
ceramic pedestal. "A seat. A top. A cover."

"Non capisco, Meestehr Doosty. Don't understand."

Dusty tried to mime a toilet seat, but the Padrona had
decided she couldn't get it, and she didn't, no matter how
graphic his gestures.

"You have to speak to Aldo. My son-in-law. Aldo speaks
English."

"It's a toilet seat. Nothing. Not complicated." That
Olivia would arrive pregnant, two little boys, unfamiliar
language, peculiar food, strange customs, filled Dusty
with a sense of responsibility again for being a father and a
husband. Silly as it was, he wanted to protect Olivia seven
months pregnant from the alienation of sitting down on a
cold toilet pedestal. It was one of those petty obsessive
worries.

"In a couple of days Aldo will feel better, and you can
come and ask him. I don't understand. Io veramente non
capisco."

Aldo was the husband of Gioia, the counterfeiter's
sister, and with their little daughter, Angelica, they lived
in another of her mother's apartments. The family was
filled out and served by two small women, Rana, and her
daughter, Nulla. They worked eighteen hours a day for
ten thousand lire a month, room and board, their rooms
windowless cells, and their food whatever scraps
remained after the family appetites were sated.

Bringing in each piece of furniture was a day's work. In
this part of the world you bargained even for aspirins at

the pharmacy. The Italians loved to enrich the human interaction with haggling, but after a week of trying to deal with the language and the prices Dusty was totally docile, and agreed to pay anything, just to get out of the marketplace.

Dusty stepped onto his balcony that overlooked the Padrona's patio. This was early fall. A warm wind herded some pale pink clouds across the sky, and brushed his face with sea-scented Adriatic feathers. A thin reek of ammonia occasionally drifted up from where Rana was on her hands and knees scrubbing the patio stones around the statue. The Padrona, huge in her flowered housecoat, stood by the Mary Magdalen with her arms folded across her chest, directing Rana to the places she wanted scrubbed. Rana saw Dusty and paused to smile at him and wave, bringing down a torrent of abuse on her head, which she knew how to ignore.

"She's lazy," said the Padrona, looking up at Dusty. "And she's stupid. If you don't watch her every minute nothing gets done. She ruins everything. A little crazy."

Dusty's most generous reflection on this 'slave' relationship was that the two of them were one person, Signora Foti the soft one, storing up the fat and exercising only her brain, as if her function was to hold a reserve of flesh to carry them through the next war; and Rana was all the muscle, all the extension of the will of the Padrona into function within the household. They were hardly ever separate, did virtually nothing without each other.

The Padrona stepped closer to the balcony. "Meestehr Doosty, you doing fine? You've got some furniture now? I hope you didn't pay too much. A pity Aldo is still in bed.

He could help you to buy. He speaks English."

"I've got almost everything."

"When your signora comes, it will be so nice for her here. So listen, Meestehr Doosty. Aldo feels a little better, and tonight, for a little while, he can talk to you about your question. Is that good?"

Dusty had almost forgot about the toilet seat. "It's alright, Signora. It's not necessary. I'm glad Aldo is feeling better, but I don't need to ask him anything."

"Don't worry. Aldo speaks English very well. Tonight I will come to your door, and I will take you to Aldo, and you can talk." In the realm of her household and holdings the Padrona was unopposable. She had absolute authority. Dusty could not refuse. She walked up behind her servant and slapped her across the ear. Rana reacted like a scolded dog; as if she deserved whatever abuse she quickly crawled to another corner and started to scrub.

That evening she came to his door in a pink chenille bathrobe. She had flamed her mouth with a glistening lipstick that seemed to float in front of her face independent of her olive skin. "Meestehr Doosty, come with me." She put a hand in the small of his back. "You look so strong this evening, I don't know how to say it. Very cowboy, very masculine." She urged him across the hall to her daughter's apartment.

Nulla, daughter of Rana, pulled open the door as they approached. She stared hard at Dusty as if she believed nothing but a miracle could have made such a strange being appear in her world. She ran to open the bedroom door, her coarse grey smock rising above her callused knees as she lifted her arms. The Padrona pushed Dusty into the bedroom. Dusty took a last look at Nulla's wide, innocent face, as if looking for someone else who acknowledged even slightly how strange all this was.

Gioia wiped her husband's brow with a damp rag as Dusty approached. Aldo's eyes were barely open. He lay under a featherbed, his head propped on the bolster. Gioia fluffed up another pillow to slip under his head. The dark headboard was carved with dour-faced angels, making an arch of admonitory scowls around Aldo's pale, drawn face.

"How do you do? My name is called Aldo. Who is your name?" The strain of his debut in English threw Aldo into a fit of coughing, and his wife poked a dish under his chin to catch the saliva.

"See how good he speaks the English," the Padrona whispered in Dusty's ear. "Bravo, Aldo. Veramente bravissimo, come parla Inglese. Gioia. Bravo." Nulla grinned from the doorway, her mother standing nervously behind her, nervous that the Padrona would turn and rap them for not being at work.

"My name is Dusty. Mi chiamo Dusty."

"Parla Inglese. Speeka Eengleesh. Non parlo molto bene, ma capisco abbastanza. I understand good the Eengleesh. I am very happy to meet of you, Meestehr Doosty. Very much happy. Why do you want at me? Or do you say, *for* me? You must correct me, so I speak Eenglish better." Aldo started to cough again, and was ministered to immediately by his wife. Dusty turned back to the servants at the door. The sight of them relaxed him, they looked so amazed at everything. A glance from the Padrona sent them scurrying back into the apartment, however, and she shut the door. Dusty was trapped.

"Ees good, zee Eenglish, very important, for to make zee money," Aldo wheezed. "Verrrry necessario." Aldo's was the face of a man incarcerated and tortured, gaunt, covered with stubble, red-rimmed eyes, a man with all privileges denied. His skin was translucent, ghostly, and his voice dwindled into incomprehensibility as he tried to hold back his coughing fits.

"I'm sorry to disturb you," Dusty said.

"No. No disturb. Please..." Another coughing fit. "My pleasure. Eet ees nuthfft..." He fell back on his pillow with the exertion of trying to pronounce the 'th' sound.

Dusty started sweating in the stuffy room, all the windows closed, curtains drawn. He had hoped to slip through this conversation easily, explaining it was just a misundersanding; but it looked now like Aldo was ready to die over his toilet seat.

"So tell heem what you want from eet pliz? What can I help you?"

Dusty decided it would be too complicated to explain the misunderstanding, that he would have to go straight ahead. "I wanted to buy a toilet seat." How embarrassing. How ridiculous it sounded. "I asked the Padrona if there was a toilet seat."

"What ees eet? Towlit sit?" Aldo looked at the Padrona and back at Dusty.

"To cover the toilet. A seat."

"Towlet?" Aldo shrugged. "Ma che é, 'sit'?"

The women shrugged. Dusty felt he was in the midst of an international misunderstanding of minor proportions. He tried to mime a toilet for Aldo, and the seat that covered it. Nulla had pulled the door open again, and she started to giggle. "Via," the Padrona snapped at them. "Stupide."

"Ah," said Aldo, his head rising, then sinking back into the pillow. "But you have the towlet. Is towlet appartamento. Do not worry, Meestehr Doosty, my friend."

"But a seat," Dusty pursued. "On top of the commode." It was the first time Dusty ever remembered having said 'commode'.

"You have commode. There is commode." He looked at his mother-in-law in disbelief.

"Okay," Dusty said. "It's not important."

"No. Ees eemportant. Tell me. Tell Aldo." The sick man was excited, his eyes tearing, red speckles like abrasions flushing his cheeks. Dusty didn't want one of his first acts as an American in the Salento to cause the death of a native in a misunderstanding over a toilet seat. He tried to mime it one more time, sculpting the pedestal in the air with his hands, forming the seat that would cover it as an embrace. Aldo rose higher on his bolster, as if his life depended on this. The veins swelled in his temples. Gioia rushed to his side.

"Aldo. Aldo. Per piacere, signor Doosty," Gioia exclaimed.

"Ahhhhh," Aldo finally exclaimed, as if in his terminal delirium he'd had a vision of eternity, and he slowly collapsed, as if over a spear that had been thrust into his chest. "Sediola. Coperta. Capisco, finalmente, grazia a Dio." He doubled over, and Gioia rushed forward to lean him back on his pillows. "But why, signor Doosty?" he asked, feebly. He could barely make the words. "Towlit sit? Che bisogno? Why you need eet?"

"I don't," Dusty said. He felt foolish.

Aldo's breath had become very shallow, and his eyes rolled up into the top of his skull, and he faded away from the conversation. Gioia covered his face with a wet washcloth.

Dusty stared at the man in horror. He showed few signs of life. "He's right," Dusty apologized. "Aldo ha ragione. Non ho bisogno. I don't need the towlet sit." He pronounced the word as Aldo had. Aldo's nose twitched.

"A little tired, but resting now," said Gioia.

"I'm sorry," Dusty said.

They turned off the light. "Eh," the Padrona shrugged. "É così."

As they left the room Dusty felt the Padrona's hand in the small of his back, not pushing him, a friendly hand. She slid her other hand up his arm and steered him into the salotto, this strange mausoleum of a room common to the homes of the aspiring middle class in southern Italy, used only for very special company, and then just very briefly. The marble floor of this one was scrupulously polished, an enormous, marble-topped sideboard against one wall, an ornate, gilt-framed mirror hanging above it, reflecting the big chandelier of plastic beads that hung from the ceiling like an udder. She led Dusty to a candy-striped love seat, burgundy and grey satin protected with clear heavy vinyl.

"E allora, Signor Doosty. Now what do you like? Some Vecchia Romagna, brandy? Or some Grappa? No. Grappa is too strong. Maybe a little digestivo, some Cynar, or some Cinzano, cin-cin.'' She spoke slowly, her voice deep, trailing innuendo, as it must have done once for officers of the American military. She held onto Dusty, pressing her flesh lightly against him. She must have been invincible, he thought, when her younger body formed itself around these wiles.

''Sit down,'' she said. ''Rest a minute.'' She pushed him gently into the love seat. The plastic crackled as he slid back on it.

''So. A little glass? What will you take?''

''Si. Yes.''

''Bene. What?''

''Some Cynar?''

''Good.'' The Padrona smiled. ''It's made from artichokes. Good for the stomach. And good for the man.'' She winked at him, and pumped her fist up and down in a vulgar gesture, then slid out of the room on the big, terry-cloth slippers women wore in the house to keep the floors polished as they moved.

Nulla leaned against the doorframe, staring at Dusty again, something unself-conscious yet melancholy in her look. How had they given her that name, he wondered as he smiled at her, a word that means 'nothing' in Italian? In a novel it would seem too obvious a signal. She had tied a soiled red rag around her forehead, that made her look like a samurai. She didn't return his smile, but kept staring as if she couldn't recognize his species, or as if he had just stepped into her life off a UFO. The Padrona gruffly shooed her back towards the washroom to work when she arrived with the drinks. She handed him the little glass of Cynar, and sat down with him. ''Your wife,'' she said, leaning towards him. The chenille robe slipped to reveal her stretched and wrinkled cleavage. "She is very beautiful, yes?" Some fresh cologne was vaporizing between her breasts, and Dusty felt himself enmeshed as this woman, almost three times his age, three times as big as she had been herself at twenty-three, bellied out the ancient nets of perfume and flesh. "And you don't want her to put her little culo down on a cold commode."

"It's not important," Dusty said. He sipped the Cynar, that did taste like artichoke, bitter and sweet.

"You are a very good husband. A strong young man."

"Thank you."

"Why don't you buy this at Upim?"

"I know."

"They have a fixed price. You don't have to bargain. The people here have a certain mentality. Like Africans. They bargain. They try to take advantage, to get a little more. Upim is better for you. More like America. Fixed price."

"Presso Fisso."

"Bravo. How you've learned to speak Italian." The Padrona stroked his cheek. "And tell me. Our Aldo. How well does he speak English?"

"Signora," said Dusty politely. "He speaks well."

The Padrona's eyes held an ageless, complicated, seductive darkness he didn't dare gaze in for long. "Signor Doosty. Our Aldo, he is an honest man. An educated man. A good man. But he has no job. And how will he pay for all this?" She looked around the room. Dusty was beginning to understand what this business was. "If a man speaks English, he can get a good job. Make a lot of money. Please tell me, how well does Aldo speak the English?''

"Signora, honestly, I don't mean an insult, but Aldo could speak very well if he studied a little more. If he took a few lessons.''

The Padrona straightened her back and looked at him coolly. "Study, eh?'' Dusty nodded. She stared at him in silence, and then she sighed, "Bene,'' she said, pulling back, as if she had got what she wanted and now could switch off certain channels. "Have you finished your drink?'' Dusty put down his glass, still half-full, and she immediately picked it up. He felt foolish, as if some game had been played, and he hadn't learned the rules, and he'd been exploited, and had lost. He didn't even know where that feeling had come from. The Padrona left the room, and sent in Nulla to show him out.

It was late when he got back to his apartment, but he couldn't go to sleep. He stepped onto a balcony and breathed. This unfamiliar air. Too much. The streetlamps were out so the stars were big in the limpid humidity, like luminous eyes swimming below the continental shelf. Too strange. He went back inside and sat in one of the crude cane chairs he had bought cheap, and he stared at the wall and reviewed in his mind how he had got into the movie he was living now called southern Italy, and how he had ever left what he remembered as the hallucination everyone called America.

After the Padrona's daughter's elaborate rooms his apartment seemed empty, despite all the furniture he had struggled to buy. He preferred the vacancy. The bare walls suited him. Nothing he could hang on them would make this place feel like his own. That was okay. The

beige plaster surface was wide and soothing. What
madness had moved him to leave his family in Nevada
and make a pilgrimage to this strange place? The walls of
this apartment were the color of the side of Buckskin
Mountain, where he had last worked, outside of Paradise
Valley, south of McDermott, for a prospector con-man
chipping at a hopeless vein of cinnabar. They carried ore
out from the face in buckets, to have samples to show his
investors in Montana. Mining to sell stock. Why had he
left them, Olivia pregnant with two boys, one morning in
Winnemucca? With a light pack he had walked to the east
end of town and stuck out his thumb. And why had Olivia
come by in their VW van at 1:00 P.M. to find him still
there, and she with his lunch, and the bewildered face of
his two-year-old son riding shotgun in his car seat? He
could still see his worried face. Why had he insisted, when
she came by at 5:30 again to tell him dinner would be
ready at six, on standing out there for just a little longer?
He could have got in the van with her and gone home. And
why had that Buick Special stopped, just as he was ready
to give up, go home, change his plans, go to Mexico
instead? This guy had stopped, a salesman of office
equipment, headed for Salt Lake, and that's how Dusty
had got started on his pilgrimage to Florence, where on a
wall of the Brancacci Chapel of the Santa Maria del
Carmine was a fresco by Masaccio of the tribute money
that had obsessed him reproduced in his book of Italian
painting. Whatever it cost, he had to see it for real. That's
what he told himself. Maybe it was a weak excuse to bolt
from his responsibilities. Their sense, these Italian
painters, of the proportions of men in a landscape. He

wanted to be close to that. How they made men appear to stand firm on the earth. The mystery of the space around the figures. The distances between them. How had this vague, peculiar drive finally put him in contact with the Padrona, this ex-whore, this entrepreneur, her weird menage?

In New York he waited tables at a Longchamps restaurant till he had enough money for third class passage on the last voyage of the Saturnia, an old Italian liner steaming to Gibraltar, Barcelona, Patras, Palermo, and finally Venice, where he got off, and gazed for a while at Piazza San Marco, but had to get to his Masaccio, so he got on the road again outside of Venice in the rain and caught a ride finally on a truck going in. He took a room at the Pensione Bartolini and headed immediately for the Carmine, where he stared at his fresco for three days in darkness before he realized that a fifty-lire coin would turn on the lights. What for? What had he got out of that to sacrifice the stability of his family? He'd destroyed his eyes for a week, and had learned to say Vitamin A, Weetahmeena Ah, in a pharmacy on the corner of Lungarno Guicciardini and the Santa Croce bridge. And why had he answered the ad in the Rome Daily American for an English-language teacher to work 'somewhere in southern Italy'? And no reply. And he was ready to leave Firenze, deal his way back to Nevada, when his wash got caught in the rain, and in the extra day it took to dry his clothes a letter arrived from Bari offering him the job. And why in the hell had he taken it, to come down here and be with this Padrona et al.? It paid on the Italian economy not even enough to be sure his family could survive. And why had he wired them that very day to pack up and spend the last of their savings on a ticket to Rome? And now they were on their way. Pregnant wife. Two small boys. Aiiieee. He had almost forgot the Masaccio fresco. Christ and the apostles grouped on the right, their haloes sloping, confronting with utter calm the arresting officers, the mountainous landscape bare, a few stricken trees, a bit of architecture on the right, and kneeling at the stream to the left a solitary man, St. Peter, pulling gold coins from the mouth of the fish. Himself, Dusty, kneeling alone at the stream.

That night a warm rain fell in his dream. He walked through dense foliage, his clothes soaked and steaming. Through this jungle he suddenly came on an immense structure, a pyramid, like some he'd visited in the Mayan ruins. It was so smothered in foliage he couldn't make out if it was of stone or what. Where it was visible through the leaves it had the glint of brushed steel. He reached in through the foliage to touch it and felt something yield to his hand. The substance of the pyramid was resilient, alive. His fingers suddenly penetrated and his arm was pulled in by a powerful suction the same time as a putrid gust of wind, as if from the bottom of a swamp, crossed his face. He distinctly heard the name, 'Pouce', as the rest of him followed his arm into the substance of the pyramid. He oozed through the wall as if it was made of warm sponges, and pulled free in a large chamber, the kind of room that people who claim to have been taken into flying saucers describe. He stepped slowly around in the subdued light, afraid to touch any of the growing panels. Underfoot felt in substance no more than a cloud, yet it supported him. Above his head, suspended like a chandelier, was a cage in the form of a pyramid, holding a luminous yellow eye that slowly rotated to survey everything. On the other side of the large room was a broad control panel. Through a window in front of it, spread-eagled and strapped to an illuminated table, was his friend from college, Elizabeth Zinberg. It was a shock to see her, but she didn't seem at the same time to really be there, but to contain within the form of her presence an enormous void through which clouds of interstellar dust circulated in a cosmic wind, and galaxies, and whole universes expanded and disappeared within her form.

"Elizabeth," said Dusty. "I still have a pair of your sunglasses."

The man seated at the control panel, pushing buttons and levers with a sure touch of his hands and feet, turned to face Dusty. This was a shock. This was E. Pouce, his problematic friend from College Days.

"Dusty, welcome," he said in a voice that was not reassuring. "Welcome aboard the S. S. Pestilence."

Dusty noticed that Pouce was barefoot. "Should I take off my shoes?" he asked.

"Just be careful," said Pouce, and he pointed at the cage suspended from the center point of the ceiling. The eye had become a mouth, from which a yellow tongue slowly extended all the way to the floor. As soon as it touched there was this sudden feeling of acceleration.

"Where are we going?" Dusty asked.

"We're just going to finish up," said Pouce.

"Finish what?"

Pouce picked up a mandolin and strummed some

melancholy chords, singing, ''I learned to be a carpenter, I
learned to be an engineer, I learned from a nurse in Africa,
to drop the dumbkeitschaft of fear.''

Dusty began to have trouble breathing, the acceleration
was so rapid and intense. He had to sit down. He was
trembling. The air seemed to be parceled out in bunches
so he had to time his breaths to catch them as they crossed
his face.

''You got troubles, buddy?'' asked E. Pouce.

''Where are we going?''

''Going is nowhere.'' E. Pouce touched the controls so
Elizabeth rotated, and her body, or her bodiless figure
brightened till it lit the room so harshly he could see
nothing. ''No place nobody has been.''

Dusty lay on his back and closed his eyes against the
brightness. ''Exterminate the whatever.'' He heard E.
Pouce's voice, and just before he woke up he heard E.
Pouce speak again, a voice that erased all images from his
dream. ''Everything here is hunky dory.''

*   *   *

''Happy,'' sang Avrum, Dusty's oldest son, on the train
south from Rome. ''Happy. Now we're happy.'' Olivia
stared out the window with her hands folded over her big
belly. Nick, still in diapers, not yet able to speak much,
watched from under his mother's arm for a few minutes
as the bare, mountainous landscape slipped by, and then
he fell asleep. Avrum too fell asleep soon after that,
muttering 'happy' to himself as his eyes closed.

''This is going to be really good for us,'' Dusty said to

Olivia. "To learn a foreign language, to cope in a strange place, strange people, unfamiliar customs."

"Yeah," said Olivia, sleepily.

"I mean, strange. Wait till you meet this old whore we're renting from, and her slaves, and her son-in-law. I won't describe it. You'll meet them. But it's going to be good for the kids to learn Italian, and they'll probably learn Leccese too. And they'll get to know a life that isn't sterile supermarkets and white bread and plastic, and it's been good for me so far, even though a little weird, and you'll be able to have the baby with a midwife, and you'll learn Italian." Olivia had travelled a long way, seven months pregnant with two little kids. As they talked she smiled at him, but she was tuned out, her eyelids heavy. "And these towns, look at them," Dusty pointed out the window. "How they built them for defense on the tops of hills. In one of these towns, between Lecce and Taranto, they don't even speak Italian. They speak Albanian..."

Olivia was asleep. Dusty smiled at them asleep across from him in the compartment. Unimportant what words he'd said. A warm pulse throbbed in his breast, tears brimming under his eyes. Here was his wife and kids. He'd resisted in every way admitting to himself that he was bound in a marriage. He'd denied it, too young to be shackled with it; but it was his reality now and he was suddenly in love with it, with this sleeping warm cuddle of a family, and he would make it good, what the hell, as much good life as he could squeeze into this predicament.

As a gift on the arrival of his 'signora' the Padrona gave them a half hour of the service of Rana. "She will do your wash, Meestehr Doosty. But you have to watch her carefully.'' The little servant attacked their clothes, standing on a stool at the tub. She ground away at them on the saw-toothed washboard peculiar to that region. She was very thorough, worked fast, and all their American fabrics, woven to be tossed lightly in washing machines, shredded and dissolved in her red hands.

''Ask her to stop,'' Olivia said.

''She's a gift. It would be impolite.''

''There go your t-shirts.''

Dusty lifted one of his t-shirts out of the tub, full of holes. He held it up in front of Rana. ''Bad. Male. Male,'' he said. She agreed, shaking her head enthusiastically, and went on washing.

The Padrona returned in exactly a half hour. ''Look at her,'' she said, amused at Rana pumping up and down over the washboard, a big dull grin on her face, as if there was nothing she'd rather be doing. ''She is very stupid, signora.'' The Padrona put an arm around Olivia and felt her belly. ''But she's strong, and I gave her to you as a gift, as a welcome, and you pay nothing.'' She stroked Olivia's belly. ''How big you are. I think it's a girl. Only a girl comes to a point like that.'' ''She says your belly comes to a point,'' Dusty translated. ''So it's a girl.''

''That's good,'' said the Padrona. ''Two males, and now you'll have a female. How many months?''

''Seven,'' said Dusty.

''I'll find a midwife for you,'' she said. ''Don't you worry about it. Leave it to me. I will do everything.'' She kissed Olivia on the forehead. ''Okay, stupid,'' she said to Rana. ''Andiamo via. Enough for free. If you stay any longer they have to pay.'' She dragged her servant away by the arm.

"She seems like a nice person," Olivia said.

"That's a whore's job, to seem nice."

"Dusty, that's not nice. That's mean. She gave us her maid's time. That was nice of her."

"How would you like to be that maid?"

"Yeah. That's weird. Anyway she does say she'll find us a midwife. That's nice of her. That makes it easy for us."

"We'll see what it costs."

"God, Dusty. You have to trust someone."

"I trust her. I just intend to watch her around my wallet. She's not the kind of person who does someone a favor without getting something back for it."

Olivia pulled a t-shirt out of the washtub and held it up by the shoulders, big holes ground through the chest and back. "So this is life in Italy. A life full of holes."

"She just made room for me to expand into all the pasta I'm going to eat," Dusty said.

*   *   *

Food was the absolute focus. What they were going to eat, how it would be prepared. Everyone talked about it constantly. Olivia and Dusty held long discussions across the table about what to buy for dinner. It was the most direct entrance to the culture. Dusty biked to the market every day, a limitless pleasure in there among the mountains of oranges, the fresh figs, the tubs of ricotta not more than seven hours old, the delicious, small, three-pitted fruit called nespoli, the artichokes, finnochio, fresh fish, fresh fave beans, exquisite tomatoes, peaches

with a perfume to drown in, brown bread bent into thigh
shapes, bread baked with salted olives, or with herbs, all
called into the air at the covered market by merchants
with voices like jungle birds. Every day Dusty moved
from stall to stall through the subaqueous light in a daze of
bargaining, and would emerge after an hour with an
armload of stuff, each item packed into a cone of
newspaper. "Professore," his students asked him. "And
what do the Americans eat tonight? The hamburger? The
patate frite?"

When he got home with the groceries, Nulla usually met
him at the bottom of the stairs and offered to carry the
groceries up to his apartment, for which he would give her
a few grapes, or some peanuts, luxuries she rarely got to
taste in the house of her mistress. This day she looked
worried. "La signora piange. La signora." She kept
pointing at her eyes to illustrate tears.

"I can't cope with this," said Olivia, sitting at the dining
room table.

Dusty put down the groceries and went around back of
her and rubbed her shoulders.

"I can't even talk to her. How can I talk to her? I don't
know what she's saying. The kids'll go nuts. I will too.
Every time I send them outside to play she brings them
back up. And she scares them. I don't understand what
she wants. They go bonkers in here all day, and they drive
me bananas too. It's not dangerous for them out there,
except for her."

"I'll talk to her," said Dusty, stroking Olivia's face. He
hated a confrontation, particularly with the Padrona. "We

should go for a walk, then I'll talk to her when we come back.''

"What's in that?'' she wrinkled her forehead, and pointed at one of the packages that seemed to move slightly.

"Snails. They were real cheap. Fifty lire a whole kilo.''

"What for? What do we do with snails?''

"Cook them.''

"Are they still alive?'' She lifted one of the corners of the paper cone.

"Yeah. That's how they stay fresh.''

Olivia gave Dusty her 'you're such a wise guy' look. "I've never cooked a snail before.''

Nikolai bounced into the room in his yellow jump-suit, clutching his blanket. He grabbed Dusty's knee. "Hey, Nick. You want to go for a walk.''

"Going,'' Nick shouted. Learning to speak, Nick found the present participle the most efficient way to communicate. Going. Eating. Sleeping. Hitting.

"What should I put them in?'' Olivia touched one of the snails with her fingertip.

"Put them in the pot till we get back.''

Nick ran into the other room shouting, "Going. Going.'' to round up his brother, who with his head down peddled his red tricycle at top speed around the corner and into Dusty's legs.

"If I go nuts,'' said Olivia. "If these guys can't go out and play by themselves...'' Olivia stood up, and hugged Dusty, her big belly like a melon against his. "Forget it.'' She was a little more cheerful. She unfolded the

newspaper full of snails and shook them into the pot. She
was from the American West, and had a birthright of
'wide open spaces', raised on a Nevada mountainside,
miles of unpopulated sagebrush vista to expand into.
Anywhere in Europe would be too confined for her spirit,
for her sense of how much space her children needed.

On their return Dusty went directly to the Padrona's
apartment.

"I'm so sorry, Signor Doosty," said the Padrona. "I
disturbed the Signora. But I have fear for your children, to
be alone outside, no one to watch them. Shame on you.
There are bad people here, Signor Doosty. Dishonest
people, who will grab the little ones and run away with
them. Then they hide them, and they ask for money.
American money. When I go on the bus," she confided,
showing him the diamond rings on her fat hands. "I turn
the diamonds around. They will cut off your finger in the
bus if they see them."

"Signora, excuse me, but our children need to play
outside, by themselves."

"Why?" The Padrona shrugged. "What are they, like
the children of Naples, or Taranto, without shoes? Our
Angelica does not play outside."

"American children play outside."

"America. America. Porco dio. Here someone always
should watch the children. Who keeps their clothes clean?
You buy them new clothes?"

Dusty had noticed that her granddaughter never went
into the street unless she was dressed like a tiny adult, and
her mother hovered over her constantly, brushing her

skirts straight, fixing her hair. There was no getting down and scuffing your knees, no luxuriating in the mud, for the deprived kids of the Italian middle class who unlike the urchins of Naples and Taranto had no freedom, but were used in public as mannequins, to exhibit the prosperity and propriety of their middle-class parents.

"Dirt never hurts them, Signora."

The Padrona wrinkled her face in disgust.

"It's just a different philosophy, Signora. It's the way we raise our children in America."

"Ah, America." The Padrona put her arm around his shoulder. "Always America. Meestehr Doosty, now you are living in Italy. Soon you will have an Italian child, a Leccese child, with a Leccese godmother." She pulled Dusty around and squeezed him against her breast, a move she could use on him with complete confidence, that Dusty didn't know how to resist. "This evening," she said, "I will bring the midwife to your house. She is the best midwife. She delivered our Angelica, you understand. She delivers good babies. The best in the Salento. She will come to look at the Signora tonight." She let Dusty loose.

"Thank you," Dusty said, and they parted, and he felt once again there was a contest going on, and he didn't understand the rules. The term 'Italian Godmother' stuck in his mind. Whatever the game, the Padrona had won another round.

"O damn. Goddamit," Dusty heard Olivia shout as he walked into the apartment.

"Yelling," Nick waddled out of the dining room, up to

his father. Avrum came around the corner, his tricycle on two wheels. "It's dad. C'mon Dad. Hurry up. Something happened."

Dusty crunched something underfoot as he rushed into the dining room. Olivia was standing precariously on a chair, stretching to pick something off the wall. Her big belly kept her from reaching it.

"Dusty, this was your idea."

"Easy, Livvy. Please come down. Get off that chair before you fall."

He helped her down. "You were going to get fish. That's what you said. At least fish is dead. These guys aren't even housebroken."

"The midwife is going to come look you over this evening."

"I hope she approves of your pets."

The snails had pushed the cover off the pot while they were out, and now were fanned out all over the room.

"The snails are running all around, dad." Avrum was delighted.

"Going," said Nick, significantly.

"We weren't even gone that long. They're goddam fast. Who said snails were slow?" He picked one off a table leg and watched it first suck in its shiny, knobbed antennae, then retract its head, and slide its foot back into its shell, pulling closed its little trap door.

"How will I cook them?" Olivia asked. "I'm beginning to like them. It'll be disrespectful."

"Just be nice to them. Tell them it's their punishment for all this mischief," Dusty said, as he picked a few off the balcony doorsill.

"Are we going to kill them, dad?" Avrum asked, looking worried. "Will we make them dead?"

"Son, you have to kill anything you eat, first." Dusty felt he sounded like some form of Daniel Boone when he talked this fatherly to his kids. "Even a carrot you pull from the ground and it dies, and then you bring it back to life in your belly."

"Just like mommy," Avrum grinned.

"Killing," Nick sang out.

* * *

"Maschio. È maschio," said the midwife, her hand on Olivia's belly. "It's a boy. I'm sure." "I thought a girl, signorina," said the Padrona. "It's so quiet. It comes to a point."

"No. Definitely a boy." The midwife stood very straight, in a black dress, trimmed with lace, a sheer maroon scarf tied around her neck, a dark woman, with pale golden eyes that gleamed with confidence.

"You are very healthy, very good, darling," she told Olivia. "I'll come back in another month. Then we'll begin."

"I think I like her," Olivia whispered to Dusty. "She seems real competent."

"She should eat a lot of finocchio," the midwife said. "You know the finocchio? You boil it. A little salt. Pepper. Some basilico if you like. Some olive oil. Eat it every day."

The Padrona hefted her bosoms. "Good for the milk."

"Of course," said the midwife.

"You have the kitchen to cook it in." The Padrona

turned on the light and looked into the kitchen. "What is this?" A grey froth was boiling out of the pot on the hot-plate. The Padrona grimaced. "Signora, what?"

"Oh, Dusty. O my God. The snails exploded," Olivia covered her mouth and started to laugh.

"Che?" The Padrona looked at Dusty.

"Conchiglie, signora."

"Conchiglie? You eat the conchiglie?"

Olivia reached in through the froth and turned off the hot-plate.

"Signora," said the midwife. "Before you cook the snails, you feed them. Feed them sawdust or polenta for two or three days, to clean out their systems. They eat for a while, then you eat them."

"You eat the snails in America?" The Padrona was incredulous.

"You boil them," the midwife went on. "Then you take them out of their shells, saute them in a little butter and garlic, a little lemon. A lot of work, but delicious. First you feed them."

"Those were our first snails," Dusty said.

"It was his idea. I wanted fish," said Olivia.

"Now they're dead," said Avrum.

"Look how beautiful these little boys," said the Padrona. She patted Olivia's cheek. "What treasures. Now you will make the third one. Poor signora. So young."

*   *   *

"Meestehr Doosty. My good friend." Aldo stepped out of his apartment as Dusty headed down the stairs to work. His head stuck out of a towel wrapped around his neck, tucked into a burgundy smoking jacket. His complexion was grey as phlegm. His legs barely held him up as he gripped the bannister, descending a few steps, looking like the victim of a TKO. "Just one moment, my friend." Dusty grabbed his arm. He could see Gioia watching from the half-open door of their apartment, the Padrona behind her. Aldo pulled a trinket from his pocket, a miniature urn big as the top joint of his thumb, and held it out to Dusty.

"Thees ees of you, my friend. You must take eet back."

Dusty had bought several of these little pots to give to his sons, and when poor Nulla admired them he had given her one. Her delight had been far out of proportion to the value of the gift, which cost less than a penny in the marketplace.

"I gave that to Nulla," Dusty said. "It's nothing. It's okay."

"Eet ees not okay, Meestehr Doosty, I must beg you. Do not give to Nulla. No geefts. I must tell you."

"Why?"

"Eet ees very bad. Eet poots her jealous. It makes her stop to work."

The Padrona stepped out of the door in front of her daughter, and stood at the head of the stairwell. She had sent Aldo first as reconnaissance, and now was ready to lower her heavy artillery.

"Signora," Dusty appealed to her. "That was only five lire."

"Five lire. Five franchi. Five dollar. No difference. Never give her. The disgraziata. She gets ideas. And now she runs away."

"She ran away?"

"Yes. She escaped. The disgraziata. Gone. You give her something, and then she gets ideas."

"Maybe she gets ideas, Signora, but it's not because of my trinket that she runs away."

"Ah, my son, Signor Doosty," the Padrona sweetened her voice. "You are an American, so you don't understand these simple people. She is not meant for gifts."

"Simple people...not meant for gifts..." It seemed so outrageous Dusty could hardly speak. "Fuck off, lady. Goddamit." He clenched his fists. "It's goddam slavery," he said in English, turned and ran the rest of the way down the stairs.

In the hallway below Rana was sweeping, and as Dusty passed she followed him out of sight of the Padrona, and grabbed his sleeve.

"Nulla," she said. "Via." She spoke mostly Leccese, little Italian, so she communicated with him mostly in gestures. "Fuori Citta." So Nulla was outside the city. "Uomo. Giovani. Signorino. Forte." With a young man. Rana seemed proud of it. "Fare bebe." To make a baby.

"Fare bebe?" Dusty asked.

"Si. Si." Rana grinned, and curved her arms to rock a baby in an imaginary cradle. "Bebe. Si, bebe."

"Angelica. Figlia Gioia e Aldo." The little girl. "Cresce grande." Grows big. "Ha bisogno." Needs. "Una donna servizio." A servant. "Come me. Come Nulla." Like her and Nulla. Rana stood up to her full four and a half feet, and thrust out her chest like someone proud of her profession. She held out her hands to describe a belly swollen with pregnancy. "Mia figlia." My daughter, grinning and proud.

The impact didn't hit Dusty at first, but while he looked at the faces of his students around the table struggling to retain a few English phrases he suddenly said to himself, "Omigod. They let her loose so she can breed." His students were staring at him when he recovered from that, as if he had suddenly gone catatonic in front of them.

"Big excitement in the compound," said Olivia when he got home. "Nulla disappeared. She ran away."

"You bet. They tried to blame it on me, on that little trinket pot I gave her. They took it away from her." He set the pot on the table. Olivia picked it up.

"She loved this little thing. God. I don't blame her for running away. I have nightmares about being stuck here forever."

"She didn't run away."

"They don't even seem really worried about her though. They were in good humor. It's the first time I think I ever heard them laughing. What do you mean she didn't run away?"

"In America you can run away and disappear. There's no place to hide here. They sent her away. To breed."

"Breed?"

"Yeah. They put her out to mate, with a young guy. Rana told me. She's real proud of it. They let her run off with a young guy, and they hope she comes back pregnant. Then they'll have a servant for their little Angelica, if it's a girl. I don't know what they do if it's a boy. Slaughter it for veal.''

"It's so weird here, Dusty. I want to go home.''

"Every place is weird, Livvy. This place is time-warp weird. It's the middle ages here.''

*   *   *

The Padrona knocked on the door and Dusty opened. She had a grip on Avrum's forearm, and in her other hand his red tricycle. Her eyes were narrowed to slits, her lips drawn tight. ''Signor Doosty,'' she said, her patience stretched thin as her voice. ''Look at his clothes. This is impossible. Look how dirty he is.'' In the corner behind the Padrona stood Nulla, her head hung low. She was back, totally humiliated, like an abused draft animal. They had shaved off all her hair, and had hobbled her around the ankles with a coarse rope. She stood staring at the ground, standing there as if she wanted Dusty to look at her.

"She's hurting me, dad.'' said Avrum. Dusty unfolded the Padrona's grip from Avrum's arm and he ran into the apartment.

The Padrona turned on Nulla and snapped at her. ''Why did you follow me? What are you doing here, you disgrace.'' She slapped Nulla across the ear. ''Back to work. Go inside. You miserable.'' She lifted her arm to hit the wretch again, but Dusty grabbed her arm. Nulla went inside. The Padrona let her arm fall and turned back to Dusty. ''They are stupid, like animals. They make it difficult for us.''

"Real difficult,'' said Dusty, the sarcasm in his voice lost in the translation. He took Avrum's tricycle away from her.

"We can't have this, signor Doosty. Your Abramo is such a beautiful boy. I would not let my godson get so dirty. Why do you do it in my house?"

Dusty turned to step back into his apartment without answering, but the Padrona grabbed his arm and pulled him back towards herself. "Don't run away. I like you, signor Doosty. You make me think you don't like me." She slipped closer to him, was almost whispering in his ear. "Don't you like to live in my house?"

"Signora..." Dusty hesitated. What could he do? He was too dependent on this woman's help when the baby came. "Of course. Yes, I do."

"What do you think when you go to a house and there are dirty children, dressed in rags, playing alone out front?"

"If they are healthy and happy, signora, I think it's good."

"Meestehr Doosty, I love these children like my own grandchild, but it is not good. The whole neighborhood talks about your children. How dirty these American children are."

"Signora..." Dusty sighed. She drew him closer. Something. It was crazy. What was it? Something he despised in himself made him powerless to resist. A passivity, a weird, druggy lassitude assaulted him when she was being most persuasive, caught between a cream-puff and a soft place.

"So I like you, and this is a nice house. A good place to live for you, and you should keep your children in the house, where they are safe. Where nobody will hurt them.''

''Are you threatening my children, signora?''

''Ah, signor Doosty. You think I am so terrible. Like my own grandchild. Like little Angelica I love your babies. But the people here, I know them. They are not honest people. I speak for the good of your children.''

Give it up, Dusty thought. No use. He changed the subject. ''I see Nulla is back, Signora.''

''Yes. The disgraziata.''

''So do you think it worked? Is she pregnant? A little girl, we hope?''

The questions startled the Padrona, and she looked at Dusty as if to figure out if she'd understood him, then she grinned, and a mischievous sparkle came to her eye, and she embraced Dusty, and whispered in his ear, so close he could feel the warm moisture of her breath. He felt innocent, and young, but she said, ''You are a wicked boy. A wicked wicked boy.''

She held him there for several eternities before she turned him loose.

*   *   *

On the evening she went into labor, despite the pain, Olivia put the boys to bed herself. ''I didn't want them to think anything was wrong,'' she said, as Dusty helped her into bed. The midwife was making preparations in the kitchen. Dusty went into the kids' room. They lay there with their eyes wide open.

''Did I ever tell you guys,'' Dusty said, ''about the night

Shaughnessy O'Diddley Dewdrop went to bed and when he woke up in the morning he suddenly had a little brother.''

''What was his name, Dad?'' Avrum asked. Nick held his blanket close to his cheek and sucked his thumb.

''Well, Shaughnessy called him Toodles O'Diddley Dewdrop.''

''I won't call my little brother Toodles.''

''Toodles,'' said Nick.

''It could come out to be a little sister.''

They heard Olivia moan in the other room.

''Does it hurt mom, Dad?'' Avrum asked.

''It's not like getting hurt, buddy. It hurts, but it's like happy pain, because she knows there's a baby at the end of it.''

''It better be a brother,'' said Avrum.

''Hurting,'' said Nick.

''I can play with a brother. I can let him ride my trike.''

Dusty kissed them both and went into the other room. Olivia moaned deeply. The Padrona and her daughter folded sheets and stacked clean rags at the foot of the bed. The midwife entered swirling a blue flame in a porcelain bowl. Her face seemed to float ghostly in the flame across the room. Olivia came out of the pain of a contraction and smiled at Dusty. ''Listen to Nick,'' she said. ''Baby. Baby. Baby.'' Nick sang as he was falling asleep.

This was different from the way his two other boys were born, Olivia secreted away from him in a hospital, in the hands of a male doctor, treating the birth as if it were the recovery from some kind of sickness. That all had happened somewhere in the groin of a hospital, where

under the auspices of men, babies were issued, those men
called doctors practicing more or less honestly the sleight
of hand called medicine with as much arrogance as they
cared to assume, with the airs of omnipotence for which
their education had licensed them. But this room was
different, an ancient woman's mystery here, for which he
could be, at best, merely a satellite.

The midwife wrapped their washboard in a clean towel
and slipped it under Olivia's back. "They put me on your
side of the bed," she said to Dusty. "Do you think that
means something?" She took Dusty's hand and never let
go of it. The Padrona and her daughter bellied a clean
sheet in the air and layed it across Olivia up to her neck,
then folded it back up her thighs, and lifted and spread her
legs, bending them at the knees.

"Tell your signora she has to push," the midwife said.
Dusty's function was as translator.

"What did she say?" Olivia asked.

"She told me I had to tell you to push."

"I've done this before, remember?" Olivia winked at
him.

"Not me," said Dusty. He squeezed her hand and
smiled, but no response, because the pain had come, and
she closed her eyes to accept it into her breathing. Her
whole body shuddered as she tried to push and her small
hand crushed Dusty's with a strength he never imagined
she could have.

"Tell her push. Tell her push," the midwife said.

"Push. Push." Dusty translated. Olivia's fingers sank
into the meat of Dusty's palm as if she would transfer
some of the pain to him. He wanted to pull his hand out of

the clamp of her grip, but he also wanted to accept the pain, as she had to, and how did she stand it? The Padrona and Gioia each had one of Olivia's legs, and the midwife gently massaged her belly. "Push harder," said the Padrona. "No. Not now. Don't push now," said the midwife. "She's going to die," said Gioia. As the contraction diminished so did the pressure on Dusty's hand. Olivia hummed from behind her clenched teeth, "My Darling Clementine", a song about a miner's daughter, and she was one, of course. The midwife covered her legs again, and continued to massage her through the sheet. Olivia kept a light, firm grip on Dusty's aching hand. The Italian women couldn't interpret Olivia's Anglo-Saxon grit and restraint. They brought their children into the world with wide-open screaming and imprecations to God. They took her quiet humming as a bad sign. "She'll die. She's going to die," the Padrona's daughter kept saying. "She's too weak." Then the bag of waters burst, and the midwife shouted, "Push. Spingere. Spingere," and Olivia pushed, gouging Dusty's palm, singing just a little louder, "But alas, but alas, but alas, she was no swimmer," as the top of the head appeared.

"I'm afraid for your signora," the Padrona whispered to Dusty. "She's too quiet. Too weak. She is going to die."

"I won't translate that," Dusty whispered back.

And Olivia went on pushing, powerfully, but quietly, and the midwife worked efficiently, and the Padrona and daughter saw death approaching, and Olivia pushed, and gouged at Dusty's hand drawing all the strength from his body, until it seemed all her pelvis had opened up free from its joints, and she was turning herself inside out and

with one immense contraction she drew from somewhere
out of the magma of the earth she thrust the head of their
third son into the world, and the rest of him slipped out
like an oily channel swimmer, and Olivia lightened up on
Dusty's numbed hand, and sighed and farted, it seemed,
forever, and the midwife set the little body bawling on the
bed beside the mother, umbilical cord still attached, and
started to clean Olivia up.

"They should take care of him, not me," she whispered.

Not until they finished attending to Olivia, and moved
her to her own side of the bed, did they clean and swaddle
the baby, wrapping him like a little mummy. The
strangest moment for Dusty, the most beautiful came
when all the other women were gone, and he looked on
the bed, and there was his wife, exhausted, still awake,
smiling, and the brand new son swaddled, sleeping beside
her.

"What's his name?" Olivia asked softly.

"I'll tell you in the morning," Dusty said, and full of
weird tremblings lay back the blankets and slipped under
to lie down beside them, a privilege no other man he knew
had ever enjoyed, and Olivia slept, and he lay there all
night awake thinking how full of divinity and love and
mystery was all this creation, and he felt his left hand still
throbbing deeply with the pain from Olivia's grip, as close
to the pain of childbirth as he would ever come.

He slept towards morning, and woke up after Olivia,
who had propped herself up with some pillows, and was
holding her new son to her breast, despite being warned
against feeding him her first milk.

'Rafael' was in his mind as soon as he woke up. "His

name is Rafael," said Dusty. "What do you think?"

"Hi Rafael," said Olivia, pulling him smiling off her nipple.

* * *

Donald Troyer, Church of Christ missionary from southern Illinois, fat, self-righteous, dressed in a bright green double-knit of U.S. manufacture, arrived unexpectedly just before the circumcision. He had been living in Lecce for almost ten years, envoyed by his church to convert the Catholics to Christianity. He had turned the money pleaded and squeezed out of his supporting congregations at home into a luxurious life for himself, his Jenny-Lou and their four kids—an American car, a big apartment with all the appliances, the luxury of cheap servants afforded by southern Italian poverty. "I tell you," he said, walking uninvited right past Dusty. "We had a midwife when Jenny-Lou was pregnant with Wendy-Joe, and she was big as a house; and as you know the doctor comes just if there's an emergency, and I sat by the phone every minute, because you just can't predict." Troyer sat down in the living room. "And where's the little one blessed of God?"

"If you mean Rafael, he's asleep."

"You know Jenny-Lou was so weak after the delivery I had to clean her out by myself. I got in there with a washcloth every night. It was a mess in there."

Avrum rode in on his tricycle, circled the room, and rode out again, Nick running after him, dragging his yellow blanket. "Bless them," said Troyer, then he leaned back and sighed. "You know I always say that I haven't got much, but every foot of it belongs to Jenny-Lou.''

Whenever Troyer said something gross it made Dusty feel a little sick. He said stuff always out of context, unexpectedly, and a habit of speech that in some other man of the cloth could be interpreted as charming earthiness came through in Troyer as petty decadence just under the surface, the real coarseness of his soul. The Italians loved to pronounce his name, even those few who, for whatever material reward, he claimed to have converted. ''Padre Troia,'' they liked to say, because the word meant 'sow' in Italian. ''Troia,'' old whore in Roman slang.

''With kids it's no picnic living here,'' Troyer went on. Olivia stopped in the doorway and looked at them. ''Especially if you come here from America and are used to using oral medication. Everything is suppositories here. Aspirin. Vitamins...'' Olivia came up behind Dusty and whispered in his ear. ''What's he doing here?''

''You bend them over the bed just like they're going to pray. It's not easy with kids. You have to spread their little cheeks...''

''What's he doing here?'' Olivia insisted, loud enough for Troyer to hear.

''I don't know,'' Dusty whispered back.

''And sometimes, I tell you brother, it's tough. A tough fit, even with the child-size suppository, that little hole is so shut down tight.''

''Ask him.''

''I will.''

''But they need their vitamins. Everyone does. The little ones especially. Of course, it's a lot easier with

Jennie-Lou. She's opened up down there, a real tunnel."

"Damn it, ask him. The doctors will be here any minute." She stepped between Dusty and Troyer. "Mr. Troyer, please..." She hesitated, nervous in anticipation of the doctor.

"Okay, Reverend Donald," Dusty took up the slack. "To what aspect of God's grace do we owe this visit?"

"Dr. Errante must have told you."

"What?"

"Well, he spoke to me about the circumcision, and mentioned there was no Rabbi in Lecce, so I offered to be present in my capacity as a man of God."

"I hope God knows about it," Dusty said. "Look, Troyer. This ain't no religious ceremony. I just want the good doctor to snip a little so when the boys grow up and stand together at the urinals they don't see any difference. No one's got anything extra."

"Well the doctor thought it would be a good idea."

Olivia went to the door for the doctor's ring. Dr. Errante and his assistant were learning English from Dusty, and offered to do the circumcision as a present. He had never done one before, but had seen it twice, once at medical school in Chicago, and once at a briss for a Jewish family he knew in Milan. That latter was why he had brought a bottle of wine, spumante, in honor of the ancient Jewish ritual.

They used the kitchen table, and what in an American hospital took just a few seconds dragged on and on for Dusty who was holding little Rafael's feet. Troyer was bent over the little body, watching with vulgar curiosity. "I had mine circumcised," he said. "Though nothing says it has to be, but it is probably more sanitary. Who knows what kind of gunk can collect under there? And a foot or two more or less doesn't make any difference."

"Padre, please get away. Get back." Dr. Errante pointed at Troyer with his scalpel.

Olivia looked in briefly. She didn't want to be there for the cutting. "You okay, Dusty?"

"Sure," Dusty swallowed hard.

"God. You're white as a ghost."

"I'm just fine," Dusty said, and that was all he remembered saying as the doctor touched the scalpel to the stretched foreskin.

He revived in the living room, a cold towel across his brow, and the first thing he heard was Rafael sobbing in the bedroom as he fell asleep. Olivia held his hand, kneeling by his side, and behind her was the vacant face of Troyer. The good doctors were still there, lifting their glasses of wine as Dusty sat up.

"Auguri," said Dr. Errante. "He's a very healthy boy." The doctors stood up. "Now we have to get back to the hospital. We were staying only till you revived."

"How long was I out?"

"A few minutes."

"How embarrassing. My mother wanted me to be a doctor too."

"Well, it's your own son, so it's different," the doctor said.

"Please stay and finish your wine."

"We can't drink the wine. Too many operations this afternoon."

"No more circumcisions."

"No, signor. Not in Italy."

The doctors left. Dusty returned to Olivia.

"I was telling your wife," Troyer said. "That I can use ordinary tap water. It will serve just as well."

"How's Rafael?" Dusty asked Olivia.

"I'm sure it really hurt him a lot," Olivia said. "I'm glad we only do that once. He's almost asleep now."

"Of course I could run home and get some of the water we brought from Illinois, if you're worried about it. Just a little jiggerful of that stuff can work in a whole sink of water."

"What's he talking about?"

"He wants to baptize Rafael."

"Go home, Troyer."

"As I told your wife, and I feel obliged to say it to you, the soul of that child does not belong to you. It belongs to God, and every child needs to be baptized.

"I'm Jewish, Troyer."

"Every child should be baptized, whatever the beliefs of the parents. Now I don't want to stick my nose in your business, but for the sake of the little one blessed of God I am willing to go home and get my water. Your Mrs. isn't a Jew, is she?"

"Troyer," said Olivia. "My mother is a Quaker, Christian Science, Hindu, and my father was a Catholic. I didn't follow this fool with two kids in tow and seven months pregnant all the way from Nevada nine thousand miles to Italy to have my baby dipped in water by some Church of Christ...some Church of Christ..."

"Don't say it," Dusty said.

"...hypocrite."

Troyer looked up at the ceiling. "It will be on your own conscience."

"What is this fetish you've got, Mr.?" Dusty said. "You like to dip little babies in water. They ought to lock you up."

Troyer seemed to be looking through the layers of ceiling into the face of God itself. "If you don't take advantage of my offer, and I make it without asking for a contribution to my church, although God knows we need the money, your little one can face possible eternal damnation."

"Can we get him a few years off for good behavior?" Dusty grabbed Troyer's arm and moved him towards the door. "I think Jennie-Lou needs you. I hear her calling. You'd better leave. We need to be alone."

Troyer's double-chins were quivering by the time he reached the door. His face was bright red. "I wouldn't say anything but for the sake of the little one blessed of God. If the child needs me, I am always available."

"I'm sure, Troyer. Thanks." Dusty pushed him out the door. "Let me ask you one thing." Troyer turned back, and almost smiled. "Can you baptize with suppositories?"

Dusty closed the door and the place was quiet. They walked into the bedroom and looked at Rafael asleep now, Avrum and Nick playing quietly on the balcony.

"That was close," said Dusty, drawing Olivia against himself. "I guess that's America. Troia America."

"Hey, Dusty," said Olivia, putting her cheek on his shoulder. "We had better be on our toes. We are surrounded by heathens."

* * *

"Meestehr Doosty," said the Padrona. "I say this to you once. I explain it, and then I step out of the discussion. This is not my business." They sat down at the kitchen table, the Padrona, Dusty, Olivia, and the midwife. "I don't know what the custom is in America, but in this country the custom is to pay the midwife four times. Once you pay when the baby is born. Then when the cord falls off you pay again. Then when you register the baby in the City Hall, and the last time is when the baby is one year old."

"Do you believe this," Dusty said to Olivia. "Now we have to bargain for Rafael."

"That's the way we do it," said the Padrona.

"Signora Foti. We already paid 20,000 lire for the baby. A friend of mine in Tuscany, he lives near Siena, paid only 8,000 lire for the midwife, for everything."

"That you have to discuss with the Signorina." She pointed her chin at the midwife, who sat with her back straight, her head held on her shoulders like a precious cup of pride. "Now I have nothing more to do with it." She brushed her hands together, washing them clean of the issue.

The Padrona whispered to the midwife who had taken the baby from Olivia to examine him. She looked at Dusty. "Eight thousand is for a baby of the second class, Signor."

"Second class?"

"Of course." She held Rafael out in front of herself, facing Dusty. "This is a baby of the first class. You must pay more."

"How do you tell the difference, Signorina?"

The midwife gave Dusty a disdainful look, as if she had never faced such ignorance before. She placed the baby on a blanket on the table in front of Olivia. "Look at your baby," the midwife said.

"The Signora doesn't speak Italian," said the Padrona.

"It's okay," said the midwife. "A mother understands."

"I speak a little now," said Olivia.

The midwife placed her hands on Olivia's shoulders. "Signora, does this look to you like a baby of the second class?"

Olivia looked at Dusty, who shrugged.

"Well," she asked again. "Is your Rafael a second class baby?"

Olivia rolled her eyes up to the ceiling, as if in thought, then looked at Dusty with her most impish grin. "Sure," she said to the midwife. "Why not. Do we get a discount?"

"O, Signora," said the midwife haughtily, and she turned her back on the baby and walked away to stand next to the Padrona. "I do not deliver babies of the second class." The midwife left, and they never saw her again. Before she stepped out the door with the midwife the Padrona turned and said in a sympathetic voice, "You know the signorina is very disappointed in you, Signor Doosty. But it's none of my business."

After she escorted the midwife to the street the Padrona came back smiling, radiating all her charm. "Ah, Signor Doosty." She put a hand on his shoulder. He knew by now that any time she touched him some obscure con was coming down. "It is so very hard for you in a foreign country. You don't understand all the customs. Now I must tell you that you have to take the baby to the City Hall.''

''Why?''

''Of course, you don't understand.'' She patted his cheek. ''Here, in the City of Lecce, you take every baby to Piazza San Oronzo, where we have the City Hall. Every baby has to do it. You register the name of the baby there, and the name of the godmother. Then you get the certificate.''

''What will they do if I don't do it?''

''You must do it, Signor Doosty.''

''What will they do? Put the baby back?''

''Signor Doosty, before three months every baby is registered.'' She took Dusty's face in her hands. ''Then little Rafael will be a citizen of Lecce. Don't worry. I can go with you. I can help.''

Dusty had never seen her this way, slightly out of control, a little too enthusiastic.

''Little Rafael will need a godmother.''

''No,'' said Dusty. ''It's not necessary.''

''Of course. Of course. You don't understand. The godmother must sign the certificate. Otherwise the baby is not legitimate. Every baby must have a godmother.''

She really wanted this honor, Dusty realized. Why? ''We don't have anyone to be a godmother.''

''But I will do it for you, Meestehr Doosty. I will do it.'' She was like a little kid of the third grade, jumping up with the answer. ''I will go with you. I will sign the certificate.''

''No. No.'' said Dusty, enjoying an opportunity to tease her a little. He turned to Olivia, and spoke in English.

"What do you think, Livvy? You think we want an old whore for Rafael's godmother?"

"Don't be such a prick, Dusty."

He turned back to the Padrona. "It's too much trouble for you Signora. It's not necessary."

"Yes, it is necessary. And no trouble for me, Meestehr Doosty. I am a good woman. We can go together. We go Wednesday, eh?" She pinched his cheek. "You are a good boy."

For the excursion the Padrona put on a black dress printed with fat pink gardenias, covered her mouth with an ellipse of glistening red lipstick, and wore her shiny red high-heeled spikes that she hadn't worn since she was a working girl. Rana and Nulla, her hands folded over her growing belly, grinning in the doorway, watched them go. Dusty suggested a taxi, but the Padrona insisted that a walk would be good for them, and she led them on a roundabout route through the aisles of the covered market, and the back streets near it, down to Piazza San Oronzo, around it, past all the cafes opening up, to the City Hall. The Padrona carried the baby, and Dusty carried Nick, and Avrum ran to keep up with the parade led by the Padrona strutting as she remembered how to strut, the image of Signorina Foti moving lithely somewhere within the grosser body of the Padrona. "This is my godchild," she told the tripe butcher. "This is the American family that lives in my house, like my own family."

"I am the godmother of this American child," she said to a little woman standing by a mountain of tangerines.

The market people pretended indifference as Signora

Foti approached, but watched with extreme interest after the parade had passed.

"Look," Dusty heard a man who sold toothbrushes and key-rings off a table next to the market shout to a companion. "Look how the whore has made herself a great lady."

As they moved into the piazza and passed some of the finer gentlefolk of Lecce the Padrona's manner became even more haughty. "Please," she said to some people who stared at her from a table at a cafe, and she held Rafael out to them at arm's length. "My godchild. American godchild."

"I want my baby back," said Olivia.

"Wait," Dusty said.

They entered the City Hall, where the bureaucrats hibernated permanently, and the Padrona shouted in a voice so resonant it opened some eyes behind the brass and marble wickets, "Signori. Here is Rafael. Here is my godchild." One bureaucrat actually rustled some papers. "We have come to arrange his certificates."

The Padrona took care of everything. From what Dusty heard they didn't need a godmother, the baby didn't have to be present, just one parent had to be there to make the certificates. Dusty signed, and so did Olivia, and then the Padrona. She stood back from the counter, stretched to her full height, and proclaimed in the full resonance of her voice, as if she were making a summation in a court of law, "I am the Signora Foti, owner and proprietor of Via Casoti 24, and I am the godmother of this American baby, of Rafael, this little American boy."

"I want my baby back," said Olivia.

"It's okay, Livvy. Let her get hers. What do we lose? For Rafael's godmother we get a Leccese whore. That's a bonus, an expatriate plus."

The Padrona was ecstatic as they left the City Hall. Her face glowed golden in the late afternoon light. This was a part of her redemption, how she was finishing off World War II in herself. She paraded in front of Dusty and family again, past the Leccese bourgeoisie, sipping aperitivos at cafes on Piazza San Oronzo, as the swallows began to swing across the pale blue sky. They crossed the mosaic of the wolf in the center, and walked by the partially excavated Roman Amphitheater, and the Padrona whispered explanations of everything in Leccese in Rafael's ear like a tour guide.

She walked back to her home, her statue of Mary Magdalen, her household of slaves, her enfeebled son-in-law, cruising at an altitude she had longed to reach since World War II, when she had sold off some of herself to survive in that world in this town, and though she'd never get back anything lost, she could by being godmother to this American child put an extra notch in the weapon she needed to wage the war that had been going on in her life since the Americans had left. The little game they had been playing was over for Dusty. She had scored all the points she needed, and he knew he might score this or that in this strange place, but he'd never let himself, or be allowed to win enough to live inside this world. He was trapped in the skin of his own, in the America, where he had never yet found a place to put himself down.

REPERTOIRE : SUPER CONQUERANT

Dear Reader: I never expected, nor did I ever desire to say 'dear reader' again, but here I must beg your indulgence just one more time, so I can shed some light on, though I can never adequately explain, the passages that follow. Whatever qualities each of you attributes to them as you read I think you will find your reactions share one aspect in common. One down thing in common. That it be the way it be because of the blues. Cause of the blues. 'Cause who can tell the story right when you have got the blues? And who can listen, who can hear, when the blues has got you down? The story of Dusty and his family broke up. The story of Dusty losing the woman he loved so bad. The story of losing. The history of loss. That's the blues. The blues in our time, that no one needs to learn about it skins us each so close. It aggravates in the heart like you're allergic to the dream. Men driving women crazy and gone; women destroying men on their way. However you want to talk about it, baby, it don't come out told right. It comes out wrong; because fellas and girls, let me tell you this, some sweetest things is begun with a kiss; but when it's over, she's away and gone, it feels like your heart's shaved down to the bone. Sliced in to the bone. It's the blues in the bone. Down bone blues. And the blues don't talk. And you just don't ride in her Chevrolet no more. The blues don't talk, they cry out, they wail. So, dear reader, you see, I gave it up, trying to tell you the story myself, and I

left what could be told of it to the alphabet, which I have
known impersonally by heart since I was six or seven or
so; and when I had the mixed fortune to be alone in
France, where loving has long been a popular myth, the
world capital of love, and it came to me to write these
passages, I bought this notebook called Repertoire : Super
Conquerant, and set myself travelling from town to town,
from A thru Z, and in each town I allowed the cipher itself
to dictate what could be told and how. If anything of the
place itself, or its people, is suggested by the content or
mood of the text, it was not by intention, and I apologize to
the people. It's not their fault. It's just a situation. I hope
this telling be anonymous as the breeze of alphabets; and I
thank you, dear reader, for allowing me this last 'dear
reader'. And before I pull my voice away from you now I
want to pay my respects to W.A.G.—Webster, Abish, and
Gangemi, all masters of the alphabet, and innovators of
alphabetical fiction, down whose swath I humbly rake up
the rakings. Now I recede, deep as is possible in such an
account as this book be, back into that anonymity that
neither embarrasses nor persuades.

                                             The Author

Arles 2/25

At An Acute Angle the Alleys or narrow streets Arrive. A
smile Appears, Appeals. An Angel At An Angle
Apparently. All Americans Appreciate Amour. Is it lost
Alice, or Antonia Afresh with an Alibi? Dusty Approaches.
Angel Aura Awkwardly evacuates Aisle, Alas. The
Algebra of Allure. Dusty takes three steps towards the

Alps. Three steps towards the Arno. Three steps into Africa.

Nine steps Away Altogether

-Anywhere is better, says Alan, his Amis.

-Anywhere's An Attitude, Dusty Argues, As is Anyone, or Anything.

-Astute, Alan Agrees. -Au revoir.

Amour is a French word, and l'Amour is an Affliction, Acronym for lost Also miserable over unfulfilled relationship. Dusty Arrives in Anguish. Does Amour Always = Anguish? Angoisse is a French Adult Ambition Acceding ennui.

-Are All Adults Alone After Amour, Dusty Asks. After long marriage, After Another long Amour's Amiss, Aieee! Alone Appears As Absolute Alternative. - All women Are Alike. All men Also, Dusty Apostrophizes.

-All Are Abnormal.

Béziers 3/4

-Breaking up, Dusty Breathes - is so hard to do, But why does it make a Boy so Boring to his Bivouac of Buddies? Babbling and Bawling, Boring himself about Bitches and how they Betray you.

-Bachelors Beware, he Bellows - Beautiful Bait Binds then Busts.

-It seems Bleak, Beverly, his Buddy, Beckons.

-It's a Blitz. A Bummer.

-Don't Beef. Button my Blouse. I'm Buxom and Bad. Dusty is Baffled. Ball Beverly? Blimey! You're Being Boorish, he Berates her.

-Don't Bother then. But a Balmy day with a Beautiful Body on a Beach in the Barbados or Bermuda could still Be Bliss. Dusty Blinks and looks into the Blue.

-Or take the Bahamas, says Beverly - I can Baptize my Bikini.

-You'll Burn and Blister in that.

-Better my Brave Baby Buddha. Buoy yourself up. Bundle with Bev.

-Best Behave, Dusty Bickers. I Be Burned out. Bury my Brain in Booze and Beer then Bed down.

-Boo, said Beverly Brunette Bouncing Between the Blankets Dusty Belched and turned his Back - Too Blasted.

-Breaking up, Dusty Blabbers in the morning, Beverly Bellying Beside him. - Is the Blues.

Carcassonne 2/28

Clever Cunts Connive Causing Catastrophe.

Cooler Cucumbers Consider Connections Carefully.

Too Cruel. Dusty Cares too much. Cries. Clings. Complains to his mirror. Cramps his Corpse into a Corner of the Cot.

In the Cul-de-sac Closing this Century Couples Cannot Continue Coupling. Crazy. Confusing Children Continuously.

Come to Carcassonne, mon Coeur.

Centuries Collapse into this Crack.

-I am Cool and Clear. I am still Conscious, Dusty Cants over the Chaos. - Let me Chant in a Cloister, Commune with Celibates in a Chalet or Chambre, or a Change to Chaps for a Change. Chuckle with a Chum. Conviviality

and Comradeship. Cuddle with a Clam or Coyote. No Coy
Crucifixions, Charming Castrations. Cupid Crushes when
Caresses Curdle. Chop it off. Cut me loose, Dusty Cackles.
-Let 'em use use Carrots or Cukes or Cauliflower (Cough).
A Cosh or a Candle for Chrissake.
Collapse of Cold Carnal Capacity.

Digne 4/17

-Daniel was Damaged, as was David and Dirk, Drew
Drawled. The Dames are Deep these Days, Dusty.
-Dawn it Drizzled and now Deigns to Drip all Day on my
Dungarees.
-Don't be Downhearted.
-I'm Downright Depressed.
-Discuss it with Dolores. She's a Dyke, a Decidedly
Different Dilemma, a Deviate but Discrete.
-D-D-Dog Diarrhea.
-Dusty Don't Despair, Dolores Discoursed. - Dawn Distills
the Dew and Daily Dinner is Delicious. Don't Droop,
Darling. Dawdle Delirious Dimpled Dutch Damsels in
Denmark. I Don't Dice my Diction. Disasters with
Dispassionate Daughters are like Dandruff. Discomb,
Dislodge, Drive on.
-Don't Dally, Dolores. Dose me with Dope or Drink. My
Domicile Disintegrates. My Dipstick Disconnects.
Dusty Departs. Drives his Diesel to a Discotheque and
Drinks and Drinks and Drinks.
-It's Dark and I'm Damp, he says to the Doorman, a
Drudge from Detroit. - I'll Detonate Damned Dynamite
and Destroy the Diocese.

-We'll Do a Duet, the Doorman Drooled

*E*nserune (l'oppidum de) 3/4

Empty nights. Energy Ebbs. Endure Encroaching
Existence. Eddies of Ego. Erections Elapsed. No Ewe to
Exhort, Embrace. Embalmed. Evacuate. Expose your
heart and Everyone Evacuates.
Eleanor is Elegant in the Elevator. Everybody Estimates
Eleanor's age as Eleven, plus or minus Eighteen years. An
Empress in the Elevator, but Dusty not Enamored. Too
Edgy. Not at Ease yet with an Eleanor, an Esther, an Eve.

*F*rontignan 1/29

Family. Fuck it up like a Foul Fiend. Dusty Festers.
-Face it, Dusty Fastens on Fred. - I get Furious with
Formers. It's a Feminist Feud. Flakey Foxes up a Flagpole.
-Forget it. It's Fiction, Fred Faints.

Gignac 4/12

-Giggling Girls make me Growl, Dusty Grumps. - Why
Goose their Glands with my Gherkin?
-Get away. Go to Greece, Gloria Gropes. - or to Greenland
to Gripe. Gag a Guerrilla with a Grenade in Guinea. Gaff
a Grubby German Gynecologist and Get Going. It's no
Good to Grieve.
-Grrr! Grrrahh! Dusty Growled.
-Grrrrow up, Gerry added.
-Generous Gents with Gilded Grizzle Grappling Groins.

Gergh, Dusty Gagged.

-Gloom Goes. Gertrude Gestured at the Giraffe Grazing the Gladioli. A Gorilla Gargles Glue and Gags. - Glee Gleams on the Gloomy Globe.

-Get Giddy with a Girl and Guffaw, Gerry Gulps. Gather the Gossamer Glamor of Guileless Gorgeous Gurgling Gals. Don't Grovel in your Grief.

-Aren't you a Gemini? Gertrude Guesses.

-I'm Giblets. Dusty Gripes.

*Hé*rault (vallée de l') 3/12

-Honey it Hurts. My Heart is Heavy. Can't Handle it, never to Hold you again. It's Holy Hell. Help me, baby. I feel so Horrible. A few blond Hairs Hanging from a Hairbrush make Him Hanker for Her. Her Hair. Helas. Her Hair. He holds it in His Hand, could Hang Himself with it.

-Hush now, He Hears, Hallucinating Her voice. -Here I am. How could the Habit of Having Her Hello Hold Him, make Him Hysterical, Humiliate Him? He Hurries Home and Hastily dials Her House, Half a world away, Holding His Hand over the speaking Half, just to Hear Her say Hi, Hello, wHo is it? He Hangs up.

Henry Howls at his Hang-ups. - I'll Heckle you till your Heart is Healthy again, Dusty.

-So Hollow.

Henry is a Hack writer but Has a Heart of Gold -Read Herzog for How it Honestly Happens, then Hunker down and Hold your own, says Henry.

-I Had Her to Hold for two and a Half Heavenly years. It's

Hard, Henry.

-Hell with Heartaches, and Hip Hip Hooray for Houston Street, for Houston, Texas, for Hollywood. That's where the girls Hang out. Hip Hip Hooray. Say it.

-Hip Hip Hooray, Dusty says Haltingly.

-Hip Hip Hooray from your Heart.

-Hip Hip Hippopotamus, Dusty's Heart still in Hiding.

*I*sere (pont de l') 4/8

-Ice. Impaled In her Igloo of Indifference. Isolated. Ignored. Insults Instigate Injury, Implant Ire. I'm not Invalid. I won't be an Invalid, Dusty Intones.

-Immigrate to India, Ira Insinuates Irrationality - Insight Into Intelligence, an Inkling from Ikons Isn't Irrelevant.

-I'm Insomniac, Impotent, Irreconcilable. It's Insane.

-It Isn't Irredeemable, Irene, Ira's Intended, Interjects.

-Inside It's an Inferno. I'm Infected with Ill-feeling.

-I've an Idea, Ira Inserts. - An Idyll In Iceland.

-Inky Innards. An Infantry of Infants In Incest. Inhumanly Inlaid with Iniquity. Impressario Idiots Immersed in Iodine. Intercede O Israel or Iraq. I.

*J*onquiers St. Vincent 4/15

-Joy aint Just Jollies, Jack. Jump on the inner Joy if you ain't Jaded, Judy said.

-Just don't Jerk your Joint on my Jeans, said Jeanette. - You give me the Jewish Jitters.

-The Job Job in the Jordan Jailhouse was no Jubilee, Dusty; and that's you auJour'd'hui. So Jam your Jacknife in the

Jukebox, Jake, you're Jinxing the Joint; you're like a Jumbo Jap on a Judo Jag.

-Don't Jest with me Judy, said Dusty Joyless. - My life is a Jumble, my heart a Jelly Jungle. I'm off on a Journey in a Jiffy, a Jugoslavia Jag, a Jog to Jamaica to Jettison my Jewels.

-Jeez, Jessica Joined in. - June and July are Juicier than January to Justify a Jaunt.

-All Joes are Jerks and Jellyfish, Jennifer does not joke.

Kerveoc'h (auberge de) 5/25

Kith and Kin, Dusty Knows, are Kollapsing.

-A Kiss on the Kipper under the Kilt could be Kinky in the Kiosk, Kathy says. Kathy carries a Khaki Knapsack full of Knockers.

-Who today Knits Knowledge and Kindness, Dusty asks.

-Kneel, says Kevin. -Tell me who filled the Kettle-drum with Ketchup. It's not Kosher.

-We are the Kittens of the Kibbutz, say Kathy and Klaus. To Knit Knowledge and Kindness. Kith and Kin, Dusty Knows, are Kollapsing.

Laroque 3/12

-Latin Ladies are Lollapaloozas, but Lousy Lovers. Their Lust is Lame. Dusty Listens to Lenny Letting Loose.

-Lenny, Dusty says. -Labia is Labia. It's Luscious Local or from Leningrad, or even Latin. I'm too Lazy. I've Learned my Lesson. Once it was Lavender and Lovely. Now it's Lemons, Leeches and Lizards. I need to Loaf as a Loner.

-Latin Ladies Lead Lurid Lives, Leonard Lingers on the Litany. -But they Lose that Leavening, that Lightness. They become Lumpy.

-I'm Licked, I'm Lapsed, says Dusty.

-Lapse into Lap, Lucinda Laughs.

Lecce 4/1

-Love was Ludicrous and now I'm a Loner too, says Larry. Dusty Listens.

-But Lust, Laura asks. -Does Lust Lessen? Do you Learn to Leave it?

Dusty Listens.

-Lust Lingers Like Lint on the Lapel or Lice in the Linens. Dusty Listens.

-Then it Lurks Like a Lynx in the Lairs of Luxembourg. Dusty Listens.

-You Lug it around Like Luggage, Like some Loot. Dusty Listens.

-It Looms in the Literature. It Lunges at the Listless. Dusty Listens.

-Its Lewd Lullabies Lambaste the Lazy and Lechery Lassoes the Liberals.

Dusty Listens.

-Loving is the Logarithm of Loss. Llamas Lift Loggerheads of Loins with Lusty Lullabies.

Dusty Listens.

-Are you a Lesbian? asks Lou.

-Leave me Lie. You've a Lisp on your Lips yourself Lady-Lover.

Dusty Listened and Left and Lamented aLone in the Lobby, aLas.

Montpellier 5/20

Modern Morals Make Marriage Messy. Marrieds Muddled in a Morass of Mistakes, Molasses of Misconduct.

-Don't Meddle in My Misery, Mother, Dusty Moans.

-I'm not your Mother, Morton Mumbles.

-It's Monstrous, Made of Mondays, Mosquitoes, Mole-Mittens. What's Marriage? Mucus in a Monsoon of Moths.

Outside their Motel a Mandarin Motivates a Mountain towards a Morsel.

Mr. M. Mates with Madam X at Midday.

Ms. T in Mufti is Melancholy.

Dusty Meditates in a Monastery on a Mexican Mat.

Meanwhile Manhood Mocks Maternity, Masturbates with Marbles.

-Murder, Marianne T. Mentions Mildly.

-Murder, Murder, Murder, Mimics Dusty.

Midnight now. Our Midget is not Meek. She Minces under the Minarets in Mauve Masks of Midnight Mass, a Mini-Minion in a Miniskirt.

Under a Mongol Moon the Mulatto Mounts the Mustang, and Mushes the Mule to the Mouflette.

-Miso, Miaos Millicent the Manx.

-Make no More of these Mysteries, Dusty Manages to say to Morton.

Molly Marauds the Menagerie. Myrtle's Mop on the Moon.

Nimes 3/7

Nervous about New Relationships as Never before Dusty thinks Never. Never again.

Nancy Notices him, thinks though he seems Nasty, underNeath he's Nice. She Nods at him, thinks they'll Never meet. Neighbors, Nothing more.

News is Nuts, Dusty off his Noggin. Never see her agaiN. Nesting in his New Nook in New York. Nobody calls. Nobody comes. No Next woman please.

Nancy that Night dreams about Dusty. -Nip my Nectar, it's Nourishing, she says. -It's Necessary.

-Necessities are a Nuisance, Dusty Needles her dream. -Nobody Needs them.

-You're boring without Novocaine, Dusty, says Norman, his dentist.

-I Need it to Numb my heart, Norman. Nick me with the Needle, as my friend and dentist.

Nancy is a Nurse and knows Norman. She's Nosy about her New Neighbor and Nudges Norman for an intro. Norman Never Notices, Not professional. That Night Nancy kNocks on Dusty's door. No answer.

Nobody, Dusty thinks, Nodding till his Nose Nips the Newspaper. I want to see Nobody.

Nice 3/27

-Not a Normal November, says Dusty's Niece, Nelly.

-It gives me Nosebleeds, makes me Nervous and Nauseous, Dusty Notes.

-Get Nude uncle Dusty, you're Not a Nun.

-I'm Not New-age enough.

-Nothing a Night of Neutral Nimble Nooky won't Negate, Nourishment Notwithstanding.

-No, guess Not, Dusty Nonplussed by his Niece.

*O*range 3/11

-O! Oy! Oh! Ohhh! Oyvey! Ooooo!

-O you Oaf. The Orgy's Over, Otillia tells him Off.

-Orangutangs, Osprey, Ocelots, Owls, the Ostrich, even Ordinary Oxen are more Open to love.

-I'm Open to Opium, Oink. Ointment Oozes from his Orifice.

-You're not the Only One.

-The Only One is Odile, Dusty responds.

-And what makes her so Out of the Ordinary?

-Ouch! Oliver and Odile. Ouch!

-What is it?

-The Ozone. It finally hit me.

-What Of it?

-I've drawn this circle, and now I'm in it.

-So that makes me an Outsider, says O.

-Obviously. I guess sO.

*P*aris 2/9

-Passion would be more appropriate, Dusty tries to calm himself down. -in Paris, Pompeii, Portugal, Prague, Port-au-Prince; but to have it unrequited after she unmercifully leaves you is not Pleasant; it's Painful. It's a Pilgrimage through Purgatory.

Paris 3/20

Pixie Pairs with Panda Produces Peculiar People. Pleasant Publicity Pisses Punks. Phallic Protuberance Prospers in Pygmy Pajamas, but Power Plunge Postpones Performance.

-Poke me, you Pig, says Patrice. -Penetrate my Pinafore. Dusty Peeks at her Pants and Pouts.

-Pivot Piccolo and Produce your Prong.

A Puny Philosopher Ponders his Problem. -Physique is a Phantom that Prances to Procreate Proteins. The Physical is a Prison. Dusty Pulls a Pistol from under his Pullover and Presses it to his Pelvis. -Pow, right in the Penis. He Pumps the Piece. A water Pistol. A Pot-shot, or more Precisely, Potty shot.

Paris 6/3

-I don't Pooh-Pooh the Pederast in the Penthouse, or the Placid Prostitute, or a Platoon of Pinups on a Picnic. I'm just Puzzled Presently. Prefer Privacy. Peace of mind. Pouce of mind. Poison mind.

Quarante 3/4

He's Quiet, Quick to Quit a Quarrel. He would Query a Queen, but feels Queasy about it. Is life better Queer? He can't Quash his Qualms. How to Quit this Quagmire? He Quivers in the Quaint restaurant by the Quai in the Quinine Quarter and orders a Quantity of Quail Quavering in Quince. He prays for a Quake to Quack his Quandary.

Roma 4/5

-Relax, Rest, be Reasonable, Ralph Reasons. -Out of the Rubble Rises ...

-Relatives, Dusty inteRRupts.

-WRong, Ralph Responds. -Ribald Relationships.

-Ruining Reunions with Rancor.

*S*ete 1/29

-Sex is Simple, Sandy Says.
-Scratch Sex and Survival is Simple, Says Dusty.
-Sexless life is Stupid, Susan Simpers.
-Sex Succumbs to Sadness inevitably, Sidney Screams.
-Soon Sorrow Seizes Someone Sexy, yes, Slater Syllogizes.
-Sans Sex Says Satyananda Souls Surpass Samsara, Sally Swears.
-Several Sexes Survive Simultaneously, Stuart Says Sweating.
-Stop Stupid Stuttering Sex-talk. Savor the Sunset, Someone Screeches.

*T*oulouse 2/28

-Tough Titty, Tiger, Tom Talks to Dusty. -These Tragic Tussles are Too Typical Today. Too Trite to Titillate.
-It's a Toboggan To the Tomb, Tom. It's Tizzy Time for Toddlers. Timid Tots Torn to Tatters, Dusty Tells.
-Tomorrow Together and Thursday The Tantrum, The Terminal Ticket To Trauma. Tom Tells Dusty To Transcend The Thorns of Treachery. Tricky Torque, Dusty Thinks. Trudge To the Tolerable.

*U*zés 4/8

Unctuous Undertakers Undulating in Undies make Dusty Uneasy. He's Unsure, Unnerved, Unwed, but Undaunted.

Wants to be Unstuck. Undertakes to Unscrew, Undo Unique Uneasiness. Cannot Undo Unkindnesses but can Unfasten, Unspin, Uproot Unreasonableness and as an Uninhibited Ump Unmasked Usurp Unfairness and Undertake a U-turn.

Verona 3/28

Veronica was a Virgo, Vivacious and Vigorous, with a Versatile Vocabulary and a Velvet Voice. Dusty Vowed Vegetarian Vengeance, to Vitalize her Vagina with Violets and Vitamins, then Vitiate her Vivacity with a Vase of Vinegar, with Vapors of Veal, and Vaccinations of Vermouth.

Their Venue was the Venetian Verandah. She lifted her Veil.

-I'm not a Virgin now, though a Virgo Verges on repeated Virginities.

-That's Valid, said Dusty. -But I wish I could Vault the Vatican and Vanish. Veronica, with you I feel Velocity. I feel Vast. I've been a Victim. You make me Viable. It's been Vicious, this Vogue of Vivisection between man and woman. The Virile and the Voluptuous both Vilified. It's a Volcano in Voile. Vulgar, Venal. Dusty reVealed all. -If I could Vault the Vatican into the Void.

-Give me some Vodka, said Veronica. Take me to Vienna in your Volkswagen. Virtue is a Vulture's Virus. Get a Vasectomy and I'll be your Valentine. Your Vertigo is not in Vain my Vassal. Is this the Viper or the Virgin, Dusty Vondered.

Wence 3/26

alence 4/8

Wacky Women Wonky Woo, Whoops
Wager a Wart in Williamsport
Dusty Watches, Whistles and Waits
Wedlock with a Witch in a Water-closet?
Wild Wives Wake the Wizard of the Womb
Wearing Wellingtons Wheezing Wee-Wee
Why Woo Wonders Dusty
Weak Weasels Wedge into the Weeds
Withdraw in Wisdom With Wine
Warily Watch the Waning Wanglers
Whack-off With a Warm Whip
Worship Warheads in Wartime
Waltz With a Wallflower Walrus
Watch the Wasps Waylay the Weasel
Dusty Weeps Without a Woman
Wistful Wolves Writhe in Woolens
Without a Wife in the Wings
O Wreck of a Wriggler Wrought
Welcome the Wolves and Whales
Whisper to the Walnut, Work the Weeping Willow
Without Wedlock you're a Winner

X en Provence 4/16

("X should be very difficult to find," said Marc
Chenettier.
("I'll use aiX en Provence," I explained.

("Of course. What an idea. But you know how we pronounce the letter X? We say 'eeks'. You're going against your rules."

("Rules become pertinent only when you X them.")

X es of interseXion.

X es of affeXion in her letters.

-An Xess of Xtasy Xpressed by your X Xibits anXiety Xposed in her Xema.

-Now it's your X with the X wife of my X lover's X mistress.

-Xtraordinary!

-His fear of Xpulsion is Xenophobic in the Xtreme.

-It's not Xalted to be Xcluded, Xavier.

Love is a tune Xerted on a Xylophone : teXt teXt. X. X.

Yssingeaux 4/26

-Yvette, Yesterday You Yelled like a Yente at the Young Yodelers and today You Yawn. Y?

-I Yearn for some Yanks, Yvette Yelped from a Yoga pose. Dusty was philosophical. -Youth Yields its Yeast. Yonder in Yugoslavia the Yogurt Yellows. First I'll urinate in the Yard, and then on the Yacht, Yvette. You know what, on the Yacht.

-Yes, Yes. I say Yes.

Zone ... .../...

Zero

Zip

Zilch

THE DEATH OF BOBBY KENNEDY

On the huge patio a small band was warming up. Dusty Wier heard the musicians and thought it was good. He was at the party that had been going on forever. He watched Abby below haggling with a kid who had pulled in a gorgeous bluefish. Music and roast fish—great. The kid turned his back on her, took a few steps away, then turned around, came back and took her money. She lifted it by the gills and held it away from her body, and stepped around the tarballs as she slid it up the bank towards Dusty through the spiky grass. The exploded fish-gut left a trail of slime on the rose-thorns. There was a breeze in the pines. There was a hint of plutonium in the air.

"How much did that kid take for that fish?" Dusty shouted.

"Fifty-three bucks," she shouted back.

"Swindled," he said. "Do you carry that much money in your bikini?"

"Wouldn't you like to know." She laid the fish at his feet. "Maybe I charged it."

"It's big enough to be human," said Dusty. "You should give it back."

"I thought we were hungry."

Dusty squatted and poked at the fish. "Fifty-three bucks."

"I spent my own money; besides, you're not my husband."

That's true, Dusty thought. All he knew was her name:
Abby.

"And even if you were my husband," she said, then
paused and reflected on it. "But that won't happen again.
I'll never get married again. I'm perfectly happy single,
thank you."

"I don't think anyone should eat a fish that costs as
much as a person."

"You'll eat anything if you're hungry enough," Abby
said. "An hour ago when we met one of the first things
you told me was that you liked fish, and now you've got
one." She looked down at the boy on the beach who had
sold it to her. "I spent all my money to get us one." Down
there he finished counting his money, shoved it into a
pouch that hung around his neck, and ran off into the
dunes. Dead fish still rose here and there on the calm
water. They glowed red in the descending sun like distant
neon.

*   *   *

From the French windows that let onto the balcony of
the second floor of the mansion he had leased just for this
experience E. Pouce grinned down at the scene. It was a
good beginning, he thought. The mist nest he had stretched
across the flyways of the little birds bellied in the wind.
He had also dynamited the waters of the bay, so his guests
could have fish. Some had their fish, and some climbed
the stepladders to pick nightingales or larks off the nets.
The guests could roast them on the spits he had provided
if there were some wood to burn; but he had had the

grounds cleaned of dead wood, so that left no fuel. They'd eat their dinners raw. E. Pouce was pleased. Raw fish. Raw little birds. Raw people once he was through. He would love to do Baltimore next, once he had practiced here. Or he might be ready for New York. New York, a city of nose-pickers. The band was about ready below him, and the whole crowd seemed poised to dance. The bass player looked to the sky to check out the weather. It wasn't what he would call a beautiful evening, but he couldn't call it bad weather either.

*   *   *

Abby ran off to wash her hands in the brook while Dusty arranged some rocks to make a small barbeque pit. He wove some fresh willow twigs into a grill to lay over the fire. This was enjoyable. It reminded him of being at his own place, in Cape Breton, by the sea, where life was basic. There you reached into the ocean and got a lobster. A bunch of kids had volunteered to get wood for his fire, but they couldn't find any, so they ran around near his fish making a lot of noise. When she got back from the brook Abby watched them and grimaced. She hated little kids, especially noisy ones. She didn't like to be reminded that people kept having children, because she had figured out that she didn't want any. They were like a threat. The mother and father sat at a distance, looking shy and helpless from having coped too much already.

"I'm sure glad you got a big fish, now," Dusty said.

"I hope you're kidding," Abby replied. "We can't feed all those kids. The way kids waste food. We can't feed the whole world.''

''For fifty-three bucks we should be able to feed one family.''

Abby grabbed one of the older children by the arm. ''We don't need any more wood, so stop running around our fish and go back to your mother and father.''

''There is no wood,'' the child said.

''Go to your parents,'' Abby insisted.

''My daddy said we could play with your fish and my daddy said we could stay over here,'' said a sassy little girl who came up and looked Abby in the eye. She was the kind of kid that looked like it often bit grownups.

''Well I guess I'll just have to go over and talk to your daddy, you little brat.'' Abby turned to the parents.

''Take it easy on the kids, Abby,'' Dusty said.

''Yeah,'' said a couple of the kids.

''Don't patronize me,'' Abby shook a finger at Dusty. ''And my name is Abigail, and I'm not your wife.''

''Jesus,'' Dusty mumbled as he watched Abigail walk over to the parents, followed by the little kids. He sat down by the fish and put his hand on it as if it were the shoulder of a friend.

Abigail was angry, but didn't mean to take it out on Dusty. She couldn't help herself. She was irrational about kids, because she had been raised to believe she was destined to have a big family. She had been one of seven kids herself, and it was a difficult decision for her to give up the idea of children. When she saw a couple so oblivious, so rampant in its breeding, she just got pissed. What a world to force a horde of children to grow up in. Her decision had been an act of conscience, and her anger was justifiable, she thought.

The parents wore orange cotton pajama-suits, loose fitting, and sandals that laced up their calves. The bracelets on the woman's wrists rang like wind-chimes. They both had long blond hair, and looked like they came from a tribe of southern California surfers.

"Look," said Abby. "Your kids are just pests. They're bugging us. I don't mean to sound too harsh..."

The blond man stood up and grabbed the heavy pewter ankh that was beating against his chest. "Hi," he said. "My name is Penis." Abby was stopped in mid-sentence by the grin that flew onto her mouth at the name. "And this is Vagina, my old lady."

"Are all those kids yours?" Abby asked her. She looked too young, like a pretty girl on a record jacket.

"We're real sorry about the noise," Vagina spoke very softly. Two kids were hugging her thighs. "Six are ours. Two just showed up."

"I don't mean to be snoopy, but are you some kind of Catholics, or what? I mean I don't mean to offend. I was a Catholic, I mean my parents were."

"I've had four abortions," said Vagina, wistfully.

"I'm an abortion," said the sassy little girl as she jumped on her mother's back.

"Shut up. You are not," said another kid.

"Look," said Abby. "We've only got one fish, and all these kids; I mean, do you have a fish?"

"That's very nice of you to ask," said Penis. "We don't eat fish. We'll eat some seaweed." Penis grabbed a fistful of grass from the lawn and chewed on it. All the kids imitated him, pulling up roots and all, muddying their mouths. The lawn let out a low growl, resenting the disturbance. "You know you've got to keep kids busy these days. Otherwise tragedies happen. Situations you can do without. I don't want my kids to drown in a ditch, or take a drug. That's my theory of kids."

"We don't eat fish," Vagina said.

"Okay," said Abby, a grin still stuck on her face. "We do have a big fish. It's as big as a small person."

"Oh," said Penis. "We don't eat people, and we don't condone cannibalism, not even on Donner pass, or in the Andes. Not even when it's socially sanctioned, part of the culture, like Idi Amin. But big fish is good. After you eat it come back and shoot the breeze, and bring your friend. This is a weird party for us but the people are nice though. But I know how evenings can get sad. My evenings used to get very sad in California, so I used to swim a lot, swim till morning. So you eat your fish and come over and we'll pass the time."

"And thanks a lot," said Vagina.

Abby returned to Dusty. "The guy's name is Penis and she's named Vagina. They don't eat fish anyway. They eat seaweed. They're kind of new-age people."

"It's no use anyway, Abigail. There's no wood to burn here. We can't cook the fish, and it's too dark now to go look for some at the beach."

"I wonder if they got their names from Rajneesh, or some other guru. Why can't the guy's name be Vagina? That would be better, a guy named Vagina and a girl named Penis, or Cock. Why not Cock? I don't think their parents would give them names like that."

Dusty leaned over and stared into the fish's eye. "You

can eat raw fish. Or I could take a chance on some wood on the beach in the dark. Do you remember where any wood was when you were on the beach?''

''Why do you think anyone would want to call themselves by those names?'' Abby sat down next to Dusty.

''It's really dark down there, but I should go anyway.''

''I guess they are pretty words. Penis. Vagina.''

A breeze full of dope noise from the patio cooled them. Abby felt her anger dissipate, and she rubbed Dusty's brow that was furrowed with indecision. He grinned, and blinked stupidly. A thick paste of mellow rock music oozed onto their laps. ''I'm real hungry,'' Abby said.

The lawn seemed to undulate beneath them. ''We'll figure it out,'' said Dusty, and he laid an arm across her shoulder, and laid his other hand on the fish.

* * *

Elizabeth came up stealthily behind E. Pouce at the window. She didn't want to give him the length of a whole room across which to build up his verbal onslaught. People hated E. Pouce, though they didn't mind coming up to his parties. The rope burn, like a pink viper on his neck, as evidence of the hate. Elizabeth's abhorrence was intensified by her having married him once, and complicated by her divorce still pending.

''Hello, Betsy. Don't think I don't know you're there,'' he said, without turning around. ''You're about as subtle as an oil-tanker.'' E. turned. He had no lips, or nose, or eyebrows. It still shattered her peace of mind to look at his talking skull. He had been widely recognized as handsome when she married him, a man whose regular features inspired trust, and duped young innocents like herself. Now he had just one ear left.

"At least not one of your oil tankers," Elizabeth said. "Not any more."

"Good, Betsy. Very good. You're coming into your own."

He never told her what had happened to it. Two years after their wedding he returned from one of his frequent South American business trips sans face. He was a different person for her from then on. The illusion of good qualities had been stripped away to expose the absolute morbidity of spirit that dwelled beneath. He leaned toward her and she stepped back. He used to say, "Kiss my teeth," when he put his face in front of her, a cynical lustfulness in his voice that parodied all joy. He knew it was her habit as a dutiful wife to obey and kiss it, and he relished taking advantage of it, though he took no pleasure from it without lips. At first she got a weird thrill from the feel of his dry teeth and slimy gums, but at a certain point she couldn't do it any more. She developed a defensive vindictiveness, and said things like, "Pucker up first," and turned away from E. .

"Ssssssooo," he hissed. "Did you come up here for the view? Or did you bring me my tea? A new religious experience? Communicated through a revolutionary system of massage, very ancient?"

"Stop."

"Just what are you into now, my little Betsy? That new dress? Very provocative. The erotic violet. My favorite color."

She shouldn't have worn the dress. She knew it. Gauzy and see-through. "I'm not 'your little Betsy'."

"But what's mine is yours, darling."

"The lawyers will figure that one out, E. dear."

"Zu-zu-zu," he moved his faceless head close to hers. Something sinister was going on, nothing new for E. Pouce. She wanted to get out of there as soon as possible.

"Your mother is in the hospital. That's what I came to tell you."

He grabbed her arm and pulled her to the window. "Look. Look how many thousands have come." He fluttered his fingers in an arc across the view of patio and lawn. "Sixteen languages spoken. Twenty-seven races present, and the old people and the young people. They all came. Ambassadors. Waitresses."

"And all of them hate you."

"Yes, and look how they have nothing better to do. They say, 'Someone we hate is throwing a party. Good. Let's go.' It's a phenomenon, Betsy. It's like having Moscow in your heart."

"She's resting well. I promised her I'd tell you."

"Yes. Little bunches of thousands of people. Did you notice the lawn when you came? It's a new hybrid my people have developed. Very complicated. It's carnivorous. They manufactured it with sheer molecular botany. A hybrid of sundew and flytrap and pitcher plants and buffalo grass and artemisia and other stuff and does it like to eat. See those little kids playing all the way over there? Watch them. You might even be here at feeding time, Betsy. You keep this lawn fed and it keeps itself mowed. Fuel conservative. That's the advantage of this grass.''

Elizabeth couldn't see the grass, but she could see the people dancing under the patio lights, and off in a corner some were meditating, and others were doing Tai Chi.

''How long has this party been going on, E.?''

''Forever, darling. At least since the death of Bobby Kennedy. But I don't think of it as a party. It's an experiment. However, now that you're here it's a party. You look so delicious.''

''I'm going to leave now.''

''I still don't get it. Why did you come in the first place?''

''Your mother...''

''Yes. My mother. But in that dress? You could have worn jeans to deliver the message. Or sent a friend. Or telephoned. But to come as the seductive Betsy in your most tempting transparent violet.''

''Goodby,'' she said, and turned to the door, but he placed a hand lightly on her shoulder, and turned her back too easily towards the counter of the bar.

''You can't leave without a taste of my new Mongolian Whiskey.''

''I should be leaving,'' she said. She knew her weakness, but didn't know how to correct it. She was never able to tell E. Pouce what she really thought of him. She couldn't make the decisive move. And she had worn that dress, that made her feel erotic and perverse. Was his decadence, not even decadence, but unmitigated evil, really still attractive to her? She took the glass of smoky liquor that he handed her.

''You can never resist playing Beauty and the Beast with me, can you Betsy?''

"I never do that," she said.

"Even though I'm repugnant to you. Even though I make you want to vomit, you like to get me aroused."

"Not true." She took a sip.

"I return to the issue of that dress. You wore it because you knew I couldn't resist you in it." He reached out as if to touch her body, but then withdrew his hands. She felt her skin tingle.

"I'm not like that, E., and you know it. You were married to me long enough to know that I don't play games." She looked around, felt a little silly. She sipped some more. "Only racquetball with Jennifer, and she's better than I am."

"Just for amusement's sake let's say hypothetically that you're playing this game." He moved closer to her. "They say that sometimes divorce makes a relationship more erotic."

She felt the exhalations from his nares in soft bursts against her cheek. She didn't like this at all. She regretted her curiosity about this new whiskey. "I'm not attracted. Not even hypothetically." She backed away from him, and her arms felt suddenly heavy. A froth of drowsiness started to fill her head. "And I don't really know why I came here." She sat down in a wooden armchair he had slipped behind her. Her glass shattered on the floor. "Did you drug this whiskey, E.?"

"Mongolian Whiskey is a drug, sweet."

Her eyes wanted to close, but she kept them open. It looked to her that E. had exposed himself, and was swinging his peculiar penis in front of her.

"E.?"

"What, my pet?"

"I feel very strange. My head is leaving my body."

"You'll feel much better, Betsycups, once I get you tied to this chair." What she had seen as a penis was actually a rope he was winding around her body. He yanked it tight around her legs, so her mind flew open and she saw what he was doing.

"E. Don't be a maniac. Stop. Please." He was winding the rope around her entire body. "You've got no brains in your head."

"Thank you, Elizabeth."

"All you've ever had were those diabolical horror films screening between your ears."

"Betsy you have to relax, and enjoy your visit. You don't think I expected to be doing this? Not in a million years. This is totally improvised." He paused and scratched his chin. "But even so I want to give it an edge. A special something." He cinched the rope around the back of the chair, and stepped back in front of her.

"Undo this, E. It isn't funny."

He placed a hand over her mouth. "Shh. Don't be silly. How do you undo? If there's an itch anywhere, I'll try to scratch it for you, but nothing more." He stepped back and looked at her as if she were a design he was creating. "Ah," he said, and raised a finger. "Now I've got something." He disappeared into the pantry at the other end of the room. Elizabeth closed her eyes. She would have screamed but knew she wouldn't be heard above the music. In the first place she should have known better than to come. The telephone ringing somewhere in the house made her want to cry. She had let herself in for this.

She opened her eyes to see E. standing there with a kitchen knife and some linen napkins in his hand. The knife was an old Sabatier.

"This is going to be grand. You'll feel so much better about it, Betsy."

"Wait, E. Please stop. Don't do anything more fiend..." She stopped talking when she saw him put the knife to his final ear and exclaim 'sharp' as he cut it off. He held the ear like a baby bird in the palm of his hand and looked at it a moment. "So there it is," he said. When he looked up at Elizabeth his eyes were peculiarly baffled and tender. The blood oozed down his neck and she felt sickening compassion battling the rage in her heart.

"It's always been in my mind to do the right thing with this piece," he said, as he approached her chair. A premonition made her shake her head violently from side to side, till he grabbed her hair, then squeezed her nose shut. When her mouth flew open for a breath he slipped the ear in like a wafer, and followed it instantly with a linen napkin. "So great," he said, looking up through the ceiling. "Thank you." He tied another napkin around her mouth. She choked at first, but then propped the ear against her palate with her tongue. "And for you too this is great, Betsy." He looked in her eyes lit with apprehension like ambulance lights. He moved a table onto the balcony over the party, and as if she weighed nothing he lifted Elizabeth in her chair onto the table, propping the front legs on the balcony railing. He tilted the chair in such a way that any movement to escape would cause the prisoner to topple from the balcony and impale herself on the spiked gate below.

"Betsy, you know you were wrong about the brains,"
he said. "I have two of them. A little one in the skull, and
one at the base of the spine. And don't worry about my
mother. I'll go to see her in a day or so, and I'll tell her you
gave me the message." He walked away, but before he
went out the door he turned to look again. "Now there's
the edge that makes life sweeter."

As soon as Elizabeth heard E. Pouce close the door she
started to have thoughts.

*   *   *

Dusty slept with his face on the grass and Abby no
longer had an appetite. His lips were nearly kissing the
mouth of the fish. On the patio a new band had started to
play country swing, and she would have liked to cross the
lawn to dance with everyone, but meeting new people still
gave her goosebumps. She just didn't have the gumption
to go there herself. She had been an anorexic teenager and
in her late twenties still felt occasionally the same deep
shyness that had partially caused that condition. It made
her feel enormous and unattractive to think of breaking
through alone across the lawn onto the patio flagstones
where people were dancing. How many people were
there? She felt the weight of all these strangers inside
herself. And Dusty Wier, fallen asleep on her like a baby,
his body softened into the grass as if pressed there by the
weight of the atmosphere. And she didn't even know him
yet, and in a way didn't care. She had picked him up to be
with for the time being. That was a pattern in herself. She
had got married that way, when she was a junior at Cor-

nell, had just got a grip on her condition, was eating regularly and putting on some weight, and was suddenly freaked by the attention of men; so she grabbed one for herself, a fraternity boy, a business major moderate weekend drinker occasional pot-smoker, who taught her to play bridge, and took her to Watkins Glen for the Grand Prix. She clung to him in a self-annihilating way that most women can do only once, serving his needs, erasing herself on the pages of his ambition. She kept house, cooked, sewed, worked to raise the money to put him through Harvard Business School, until one winter evening after he told her he wanted her to stay pregnant and have his baby she found herself walking aimlessly in a blizzard around Harvard Square and realized she had reduced herself to an appendage of an arrogant, boring man. She cured that condition as she had her anorexia, by leaving it behind. She hitched to the coast, joined a theatre group, tried all the drugs, made love with male and female endlessly. That gave her a lot of self-confidence, but finding herself suddenly in a situation like this, at a party where she knew none of the people, where she didn't even remember how she'd got there, she was thrown back to the old pattern, condition one, where she needed someone, and Dusty would do, if only he'd wake up, to help steer her course for the time being.

She bent over and touched Dusty's shoulder, trying to get him to stir, and what she saw was truly strange. A steady line of small caterpillars moved from the fish mouth into Dusty's mouth, iridescent ones, like a line of blue sparks moving. When she was buying the fish she had the feeling that all this was happening not in her life, but in a novel, like *The Old Man And The Sea*, or when she saw the big house it was like *The Great Gatsby*. The whole experience had a literary flavor for her, because like a character in a novel she hadn't chosen to be in this situation. But what she saw here was more strange, not like some American fiction, rather like a dream. She touched the fish, thinking she would move it if she could, but her hand sank in, as if the creature had turned to foam; a fifty-three dollar fish evaporating like a soap-bubble. It wasn't funny. The scene was getting stranger each moment, and she knew no one would have an explanation. She went back to the family sitting quietly now on some stones.

"Where's your old man?" Penis asked.

"He's not my old man. I just met him here. I don't have an old man, thank you." The kids played cat's cradle with a piece of string, passing it from one to the next. "You know, but I wish you'd look at Dusty for a moment. He seems to be swallowing some worms."

"Worms are nothing," said Penis, standing up. "Once I saw a man swallow a whole raccoon. It was a small one, and the guy had this huge mouth. He just opened up and dropped it in."

"This is different," Abby said.

"The raccoon thought so too. Found it real inconvenient. Tore the boy apart inside and might've got out if he hadn't suffocated."

"I tell you," said Abby, as they crossed back to look at Dusty. "I really don't know how I got here. Maybe I just blacked out on the train. I was on my way to Easthampton. Some people from my company - I'm an actress -

rented a house for the summer, and I dozed off and..."

"Don't worry about it. We don't have an invitation either."

They looked down on Dusty and the fish. His eyes were open now, crossed on the caterpillars entering his mouth.

"See. This is unreal," said Abby.

"At least it's not a tragedy," Penis said. "That guy Frank, he was a crane operator, drunk all the time till he met his last raccoon. Frank died. Dusty's okay. Besides, those are caterpillars, not worms. And caterpillars are no raccoon."

"But what I mean is," Abby explained carefully, "that fish becomes those caterpillars and those caterpillars move into Dusty's mouth and now they're in there." Dusty raised his arm as if in agreement. A fragile webbing in the shape of a fish was all that remained. It popped and disappeared as soon as she reached for it.

"See. A whole fish gone. Isn't it weird? That fish cost fifty-three bucks."

"There goes inflation for you," said Penis. "What's a buck worth to the average man?" Penis looked back at his family. "You see, we don't eat fish at all, and let me tell you something, even a live little squirrel can be a tiger once he gets down in your gut. That's one good reason we're vegetarians." Penis suddenly reached out and cupped Abby's breast. "I'll tell you, Abby. I like you, but I've got to go now. Vagina isn't philosophical at all. She gets real jealous. So when you're ready to shoot the breeze come on over and we'll shoot it."

Penis left. Her breast was still warm where he had covered it. She squatted down to look at Dusty. His eyes were shining, his face, radiant. "You okay?" she asked. He turned his face towards her. The inside of his mouth was white where the caterpillars had begun immediately to spin their cocoons. He seemed alright. "I'll be over there with Penis and Vagina, in case you need something," she said. Dusty lifted his arm to acknowledge that.

He could hardly taste them or feel them in his mouth, but knew he had to be careful moving his tongue. They had moved in for a reason, though he didn't know yet what it was. Something happened whenever he and E. Pouce were thrown together, some turn of events, perhaps already turning, for which he became responsible. E. Pouce was dangerous. He'd always heard him called E., never by name, and as far as Dusty was concerned E. stood for Enemy. So he nurtured this metamorphosis in his mouth. It had originated in the sacrament of a fish, and he knew that in the stories of Atlantic tribes like the Micmac and the Arawak fish meant clairvoyance. Something would soon come clear. He stood up. Through the lavender haze the dancers on the patio looked like they moved behind the wall of an aquarium. He waved to catch Abby's eye, and indicated he was crossing to the house.

He understood the lawn was dangerous, especially in the evening when it was accustomed to taking its food. He knew the reasons for a lawn like this. It took little care, kept its green late into the fall, rarely needed reseeding. Voracity was its only drawback, compensated for by its vigor and beauty. It had the astonishing ability to coordinate its efforts in feeding, as if the whole sward was one creature. This was a great triumph for Dusty's botanist friends who had been employed in this research. Imagine a poor drunk who wandered onto it at feeding time, tripped by a sudden rising of the surface in one corner, and a quick sweep of the grass blades under his feet. He falls to the grass, thinking it's his own fault for drinking too much, and he lies on his back babbling about the splendid stars and the dignity of the universe. Suddenly he is inundated by digestive juice this lawn can mass at any point on its surface, and before his dissolution he has splendid visions, due to psychotropic principles present in the juice, all his synapses firing, and the absorption of flesh and bone happens so swiftly that within a few minutes all that remains of the former tippler is a shadow on the grass. Failing a drunk the lawn takes a diet of lean red meat. Dusty wasn't afraid for himself, because he had an understanding with the lawn, but he hoped those parents kept their children close by their side.

* * *

The angle at which E. had placed Elizabeth Zinberg-Pouce made it possible for her to see almost everything though people 'having a good time' at a party didn't interest her much. She never got pleasure out of it herself, to dance, get drunk, stoned, hustle someone. Now she was in her own situation, not 'at the party', and she had been raised to make the best of any situation, a 'stiff upper lip' inculcated by her father, an expatriate South African photographer, intrepid mountaineer, member of Alpine rescue teams, who enjoyed survival trips, and big game hunts with his camera. "Danger," he liked to muse, sucking on his big briar. "So you get into dangerous situations, and suddenly you're right up on the void. Where do you go? What should your reaction be? I say, relax. Neutralize your fear. Tell yourself a story. It's just a signal, that's what fear is. A trouble light. Acknowledge it. There's the fear, you say; but don't dwell on it." Elizabeth looked down at the spikes on the gate below, and she relaxed. This calm was like her patrimony. "Don't dwell on possible consequences." He'd put his lighter to his pipe then roll to the window and look out at the snow-covered Vermont mountains. "You should have the attitude of 'no outcome', just the situation as it is. That's where I slipped up, Elizabeth. If you have your mind fixed on the harm that can possibly come from some situation then that harm will come, because whether you know it or not you have attached your will to it. You make it happen. The mind is sneaky. Sometimes your own worst enemy." He rolled back her way and reached out for her to hug him. "But if you can relax and empty your mind you leave all possibilities open and remain conscious. You see when this happened to me," he slapped his crippled legs. "I was too distracted. I shouldn't have gone on that climb. Your mother gave me too much to think about, and I ran off to escape. I hoped the danger would erase my preoccupations, and that's a dangerous way to go. You should never let yourself do that. You should know yourself first."

Maybe the numbness in her legs made her think of her father. Maybe that she was in what he would call 'a situation' made her remember him, dead now seven years. As a little girl she held him a mythical person, an archangel of kindness, heroism, power, out of her dream of the perfect man. She remembered when he took her with him once on an assignment to an island off the Alaskan peninsula, so long ago, before she'd even started her period.

They rode a small steamer from Anchorage that delivered mail and staples to island settlements inaccessible by air. This was June, the month with mildest weather and the least fog. Though it was sunny and bright she wore a heavy jacket because she enjoyed to be cold and snuggle against her father's chest. He held her with one arm and rested his Leica on her head as he shot pictures of the tiny harbor. How pretty, and how scary to live there, she thought, in the pastel pink, blue and yellow prefab houses on top of cliffs, naked in northern light. Fishermen hauled crates of salmon out of a shed to load onto the steamer. The dock was slippery with fish-slime, and the salmon were bigger than she was. She walked between barrels of salted cod and mackerel. She remembered thinking there could be bodies in the barrels.

They stayed with a Danish fisherman and family. His wife was an Eskimo, with a great circle of a face, a habit of speaking very softly, her eyes lit with good humor. The big Dane was loud and crazy and funny. He liked to snatch Elizabeth off the ground and shove his thick, rough fingers between her legs, and laugh with a deep preoccupied ho ho ho, like Santa Claus. Her father pretended not to notice this, preoccupied with his project, and although she never blamed her father, this was the first time she ever felt that confusion of anger and pleasure in the perception that there is some conspiracy among men to humiliate women. When Toolooluk, the Dane's wife, thought he had gone too far she would reprimand him in her quiet voice that had all the authority of silence, and he would move his enormous body to a chair in a corner and sit there like a scolded puppy chewing on some dried salmon. They had two little daughters, and a son about her own age, whom she would remember forever. His name was Svenchuk. He was a dwarf with a huge head. At first he sat across the room from her and stared, very shy, and if she happened to look at him he would stand on his head and kick his feet in the air. She hadn't yet taken an interest in boys, though six months would change her radically; but by the end of her stay she developed a unique love for Svenchuk, deepened in conspiracy; and he lost his shyness and would sit at her feet in the evenings crooning the soft atonal lullabies he remembered from his mother.

In the winter the whole family slept in one room with the stove, but in the summer the kids slept out on the porch, where Elizabeth was given a cot, and the parents slept in the bedroom, their only months of privacy, and her father in the kitchen-living-dining room. Elizabeth looked down from the balcony at the chic, the luxury, the excess of this party: booze, cocaine, hashish, designer clothes, leisure for come-ons, propositions, rejections, and she felt privileged to have this experience to remember: their first simple meal of fresh salmon and turnips, the first time she had ever eaten a turnip.

On the first night there she woke up at 2:00 A.M., thinking it was morning because it was still light, and she got out of bed and walked around the house where she could see the sun flattened on the horizon, and the long

rust-colored shadow of her father who stood on a rock
with his hands on his hips the way he did, contemplating
the light of what she then remembered he had told her
would be the midnight sun. He was there without his
camera, because he liked to experience light before he
used it. "You can feel it," he told her once. "Light has
texture. You experience that when you go to a new place
where light is different." The air felt cool and warm at
once and she wondered if that was light she was feeling,
and she wondered what her father was thinking, her
orange father in the glow of it, if he was thinking about her
mother, who had left him a few months before to live in
southeast Colorado with a commune of women, a terrible
hurt in Elizabeth's life, their break-up, that made her
father forget how to laugh for a long time.

He had come to photograph grizzlies, and huge brown
bears. "The biggest bear in the world," he told her.
"You're the biggest bear in the world, daddy," she
replied. "In fact, it's the biggest mammal in North
America." She already knew it, but he explained anyway
that a mammal was any animal species where the mamma
produces milk to nurse its young. From just that moment
she began to feel her breasts ache and tingle as they started
to grow. She was a mammal. That feeling made her wonder how men ever learned that they were ones too. And
it was almost as soon as they left the island that she started
to have her period.

Tied to a chair with these memories. Precarious over the
crowd that mingled below and couldn't see her in the
shadows. A new rock band was setting up some speakers,
huge ones, and detonating amplifiers, a sound heavy

enough to vibrate her off her perch. It was like a Fellini
movie down there, but she was performing in an old serial
melodrama, The Perils of Pauline. She couldn't laugh. It
would shake her down. She had to put her mind back in
the bears.

Her father took Elizabeth on short excursions while he
shot tests of deer and eagle and raven and mink. He
wasn't ready to see the bear yet, though any short hike up
the Little Blue Sack River would put them close to some.
The bottoms of streams ran silver and black with salmon
crowding inland to spawn. Eagles sometimes dropped to
snatch one away, and ravens waited by the shallows to
peck out the eyes of exhausted salmon. One of her father's
most famous pictures was of a raven with the eye of a
salmon looking out of its beak.

The hikes weren't easy. There were a few trappers'
trails, but her father usually wanted to go cross country, or
up some little stream bed, and they often had to crawl or
climb over windfalls of hemlock and spruce piled ten feet.
The foliage was thick and lush, the forest deep with moss
underfoot, parasitic mosses hanging from the trees, hills of
huge, thick-stemmed ferns, and dense thickets of sallal. It
was not as she'd imagined the north country, but rather
the tropics to be. Then they would come to a clearing
opening to the west and the snow-covered peaks of the
Blue Sack mountains.

They built a fire and her father was about to cook the
trout he had caught for lunch. Elizabeth stared at a huge
heap of bear excrement, shaped almost like human turds,
but colored a mysterious violet by the berries they were
eating. This color she still remembered, luminous as gen-

tians. Her father suddenly grabbed her arm. "Don't move." She was about to ask why when his hand clamped over her mouth. It smelled like tobacco. He turned her face towards the bear, the first one they had seen. He had waded into the small stream from the other bank to snatch a salmon. He rose on his hind quarters to sniff the air, and as he rose looked like he could keep rising forever, bigger than the trees or the mountains, big enough to pull the sky down from the heavens. "Don't move." Her father's hot breath in her ear. He looked in their direction for a while, waved his head back and forth to get a good sample of their scent, then dropped down and disappeared into the thickets.

"Not like polar bear my father sometimes hunt," said Toolooluk. "Sometimes hunt my father. White bear no fear of people. Like to eat them up." Her husband grabbed Elizabeth and nibbled on her belly through the sweater. "That's right. Like that," said Toolooluk. "But brown bear we live with now they eat the salmon, they go up on the hill and eat the berries. Don't mess with people." She pulled Elizabeth away from her husband, who was holding her in a bear hug. "But these bears are cranky people. Don't surprise them. Don't bother mama with her cubs." She unbuttoned her husband's shirt and pulled it down to show his scarred shoulder. "Peter was drunk," she said.

The fisherman laughed and moved his shoulder back and forth. "Not drunk. Ho ho ho. A big mama bear dragged me by the arm. I didn't know she was there. I didn't see her little ones. She was mean." Elizabeth had never seen anything like the maimed shoulder, wrinkled like a brain. "But I was smart. I make loud noise, like I put my voice over there, and mama loosen up, and I go in the river under some roots and lie dead there till she go away."

Elizabeth stared at the shoulder till he covered it. "Smart bears," Toolooluk said. "Show them cameras, and they know what you want to do. Tell them who you are. They like people from cities. They like to smell the aluminum."

"Smell the aluminum?" her father asked, but Toolooluk didn't say any more. She smiled and drew her hand across her mouth like a curtain.

Her father took her along for the next few days as he observed the bears through binoculars. They saw the cubs playing on the hillsides, raking berries into their mouths. They watched them stand in the streams fishing, like big Russians in overcoats. With one quick slap of the paw they could flick a huge salmon into the air. "Some nice teddy-bears, Betsy-boo," her father would say, as if she was six years old.

Once he started to shoot pictures he abandoned her, and moved into a world that admitted no one else. She watched him leave at 2:00 A.M. in the spooky light of the midnight sun, with his cameras, a big tripod, and a backpack full of accessories. No one went with him, because he wanted nothing to interfere with the privacy of his communication with his subject. It was the first week of August and the fog had begun to come in bad, making it dangerous because easy to surprise a bear. When she waited for him to return at evening she was bothered by the image of the Dane's mangled shoulder. Maybe he won't get back, she thought. She'd sit on a rock outside the house and listen for the cowbell he tied to his pack to tell the bears he was coming.

She watched him leave for the first few days, swallowed instantly by the fog, and could barely keep herself from going along, if only to protect him, though what could she do? It was more than that. She wanted to watch him. His concentration was awesome when he took pictures. There was an aura around him of someone leading a sacred ritual. "It's me, this island, and the bears, Betsy-boo. I'm the privileged student." His cameras were like votive masks in a dance her father did between light and substance. This was her inheritance, a dance she needed to learn, or at least to keep witnessing, so she started to follow him. How could she resist, even though she knew how horrible it would be if he caught her, because his feeling was absolute, that she could not be admitted to the world of his mysteries, that it was not even his to share with anyone; and she understood even at that age that one of the unspoken conditions of his love for her was that she never even ask him to share it. He had his privilege for which he would take his risks, and she was assuming her risks in order to claim what she felt was her own privilege as his daughter, that of watching him at his secret work.

It was easy to follow the sound of the cowbell as it rose out of the fog in the mornings. She hid in the brush on the hillsides to watch her father work around the huge, solitary kodiaks feeding on berries with their cubs, or when the fog burned off she followed him to the stream bed to watch him shoot them fishing. It seemed riskiest for him there. He waded out in the streams with them, circling slowly with his Leica in one hand, sometimes not looking through the finder, but shooting from the hip. He liked to get close. At most he'd use a 120mm lens, so as not to flatten the image too much. "The long lens," he told her once, "erases that sense of intrusion and risk you feel in a real photograph, the interaction that's implied. It puts too much optics and technology between the hand and the print. It's the difference between being a spy and having a commitment to the image. In a real print you feel that commitment."

He moved among the bears as if immune. They noticed him, but it was as if they understood something about him, that he shared their aloofness, and their gentleness, which so few humans have ever observed. She watched him without tiring, stayed absolutely still, transfixed by the slowness and grace of her father's movement. Her quiet was absolute, and she was sure of it, but one day it was tested when she heard some movement behind herself. She suddenly felt chilled. Her own death appeared in her young mind like a grey shadow. She would rather die than have her father find her there. An icy sweat broke out on her body. A creature was moving behind her. She threw her hand over her mouth to keep a gasp from flying out. Something like a bear cub was moving there, but too stealthy for a cub. She suddenly felt her body to look like Peter's shoulder. "Dive under the roots," she said to herself. Warm pee turned cold as it ran down her legs. She was ready to be silent forever, and said to herself, "God, God, God," wishing that just once she had learned a prayer. It crawled closer to her through the brush. She would not cry out. It came into the open just behind her and raised onto its hind legs, and she turned, and her courage gave way to relief, and then to trembling exhaustion, when the apparition came into focus as Svenchuk, the dwarf, who took a step toward her with a finger on his lips. He settled down beside her, and she leaned against him, and they both watched her father till he was done.

That soon became a liaison in mischief and adventure. They sneaked after her father together from then on, and between them they cooked up the miserable trick she played on him, an interlude that it embarrassed her even to remember, an experience as precarious as being tied to a chair and perched on the edge of a balcony.

*   *   *

Dusty got to the patio just as the rock band was testing its speakers. They were going to be loud, they were going to blow this party into the stratosphere. "Dusty. Dusty Wier. Hey." A woman called his name, and came at him across the dance floor. He recognized the voice. She was backlighted weirdly by the lavender spots, her shiny pants suit glowing at the edges, as she rushed his way, pausing only to point her Nikon and shoot. What was her name? Jan, or Fran? He knew it was someone he'd once spent several nights with, intimate nights. He could remember the noise of her sighing. It wasn't Nana. He could remember everything else, even meeting her at dinner in a Thai restaurant. She was the friend of the sister of his girlfriend at the time, and they all were eating at the place

on Bayard Street, near the courthouse. He remembered
the meal: skewered beef in hot peanut sauce, mussel soup,
broad noodles and ground pork, sea bass with shrimp and
vegetables, and one more thing. He couldn't remember it.
What was her name? Sam? No. He knew a woman named
Sam. It wasn't this one. His girlfriend, Julie, and her sister,
Anne, both were sick at the restaurant, had got their
periods at the same time, and Anne's boyfriend, Andy,
offered to take them home in a cab. He remembered her
words: "Don't spoil your dinner, Dusty, just for me. I'll go
home. You stay here with ... and finish your dinner (It
didn't work. He still couldn't cough up her name. Pam?
Tam? And she was still coming at him with her camera.) ...
just phone me later." That left him in the restaurant with
this woman, a good-looking lady, high-strung, smart,
titillated, he could see, by the potentially naughty
situation. She stared at him over a dish of Yum Squid, that
was the name of the other dish, but still not her name; and
he knew this was going to be something nice, some sweet
cheat, a sexual digression neither of them would be able to
resist. Her leg found his under the table, completing the
circle of energy that had begun in their eyes.

They went to her apartment, the ground floor of a
brownstone in the East 50's. He called Julie from there
and spoke soothing words while... (Sue? Lou? It still
wouldn't come.) ... paraded in front of him, shedding her
clothes. She touched down on his lap just as he was putting a loud goodby kiss for Julie into the receiver, which
this woman picked off his lips before he'd even set the
phone in its cradle. The walls of her apartment, he
remembered, were covered with masks from all over the

world. Her boyfriend helped her collect them. He was a photographer who travelled everywhere documenting tribes that were disappearing, and animals near extinction. He sent her masks from Africa, Polynesia, from everywhere. Dusty remembered one particularly she said he had sent from Puno on Lake Titicaca. Rafael (good lord he remembered the boyfriend's name, but not hers - Leslie? Wesley? Chesley? - and she was coming at him, shooting pictures, shouting his name, her outline glowing weirdly lavender, her dark hair like a liquid helmet) had gone there to do his story on the floating islands and the Uros. This mask was made of masks. There must have been forty-three different faces attached to the central one, which was a buddha-like grinning presence, from which caricatures of all human emotions were dangling, some of them so specific that he could tell, for instance, that one was of a man grieving over the death of his nephew, his sister's son.

She, whatever her name was, handed him a plastic mask, the face of a young Chinese woman with red lipstick, while she put on the translucent mask of an older man, and became a distinguished gentleman with pencil-thin moustache, crow's-feet, and small, firm breasts.

"Makes it a little kinkier with these." She rubbed the lips of her mask against the lips of his. "And it's good for Rafael, just in case he looks in the window. He's strange. I hate him to do that but that's why I keep the curtain open, so he can see."

"If you hate it then let's close the curtains," Dusty remembered saying. "I'd like the curtains closed."

"I wish I could, but I can't. This is the way we work out

our relationship. He loves to look in.''

''That's totally nuts.''

''And that's another reason it's good for you to wear that mask too. Sometimes he takes pictures.''

''Through the window?''

''Well I'm certainly not going to let him into the bedroom. I'm not into it that much. I mean he threatens to kill me if he catches me with someone else, to kill both of us. Can you believe how unfair that is? He always goes to bed with someone else, usually a young boy. He shows me pictures.''

Dusty removed his mask. ''Forget it. I think I'll leave.''

''Don't. Don't leave. Don't believe everything I say. Sometimes I tell a story just to make it interesting, a little kinkier for the both of us.'' She put his mask back on. ''But I tell you he is jealous, and that's crazy, because I mean I do love him, even though we never even have sex. He only does it with boys any more. How can he be jealous?''

''Kinky, huh?'' Dusty reached for the lightswitch.

''You have to leave it on,'' she said. ''I like it with all the light.'' She started to unfasten his belt. ''Besides, I want him to have enough light for his pictures. The image is dark enough.'' She brushed a nipple across his mouth, a barnacle stuck to a jelly fish.

He looked to the window and though he could see no one there a thrill of fear radiated through his flesh. She took his penis like a handle and led him to the bed.

A thought occurred to him. ''Does he carry a gun?''

''I think he does. He says he does, but I don't think he knows how to shoot it.'' He felt his jaw tighten up, as she pulled his pants over his ankles. She tapped on his erection.

"I hope you're going to put that inside me," she said.

Just as he started to do that he saw a shadow at the window.

"Dusty Wier, finally," the woman said as she got up next to him. He still didn't remember her name. "You don't know me but I know a lot about you. One of my reasons for coming here was just to meet you. They said you'd be here, and I've been very curious. I've read your work."

He opened his mouth to say something, and two crimson moths slipped from between his lips and fluttered heavily up into the light.

"I love it," she said, and she surrounded Dusty with her Nikon. "It's wonderful the way you live your work. My friends all talk about you, and now I meet you."

Dusty tried to say something again, but three more moths flew out, which she caught in a sequence from his lips to the light. She touched his shoulder. "I hope you don't mind I take all these pictures, but I feel comfortable with you. My name is Leonora, by the way."

"Lucinda," Dusty remembered. "Her name was Lucinda, not Leonora." Dusty lifted the woman's hand, lowered his lips to it, and left a crimson, iridescent moth drying its wings on her knuckles.

* * *

A new band. The test of the lead guitar bolted up Elizabeth's spine and rocked her chair slightly. Relax, she told herself. Mind in the bears, she thought. In the bears.

"Bears are big people with great overcoats, and dangerous mittens," Toolooluk told her father after Svenchuk brought back the news that Elizabeth had been snatched by a bear. "Each one like to be alone. No friends. Not like human people. Bears like first people in their overcoats. Human people want those overcoats, and bears do not want human people in their berries or fish. Bear people are first people, alone people."

"Where did this happen?" her father asked Svenchuk, impatient with Toolooluk's talk.

"On the mountain. On the Tens Peak," Svenchuk said. "Lady bear pick Elizabeth up in her mouth and carry her away like a big salmon."

"Sometimes mama loses her cubs," Toolooluk said. "Sometimes papa bear eats them, and mama bear will find the human baby, carry it away. Story says that happened here once."

"But she's not a baby," her father protested.

"This bear was gentle with her," Svenchuk reassured him. "She came right by me, passed as close as you to me. Elizabeth she smiled, she said, 'Goodby. Goodby, Svenchuk,' and they went fast up the side of the mountain."

"This happen, Zinberg. Before once, that everyone remembers the story, from long ago when my people first come to this island. A big brown one takes a two-year old Eskimo child, and this one keeps it two more years before they find it alone picking berries on the mountain in the summer, mama bear gone to mate again. The child is a little bear, think like bear, move like bear. It make bear noises. This is a small bear in the mountains. Learns to stand and walk all the time again, and speak with human tongue. Everyone love this child then. Respect it for being the bear, and come to it to ask about bear people, but that year the white man come here and bring bad influenza, and many die, bear-boy-person too; but even now every year someone from his family carve bear from walrus tusk and bury it at his grave up there above White Eagle Cove."

"Then this did happen?"

"Yes."

"It's crazy. It's impossible. Elizabeth is gone."

"We were picking the huckleberries," said Svenchuk. "She was over there. I watched her. A big mama bear stood up, picked her up, went away up the mountain."

Svenchuk was lying, of course. Even today Elizabeth feels a pang of conscience at the deception. At the time she knew she did it just to force her father's attention to herself. Watching him had become too much, and she was jealous of his cameras, of the bears, of the light and the wilderness and all the business. She wanted more of him, so despite the discomfort she stayed away in the cold and fog in a little cave by the sea where Svenchuk had led her, and walked along the beach when it was foggy and she couldn't be spotted, and watched the seals play from her perch when it was clear. Every evening Svenchuk came and cooked some fish, and told her what was going on. She loved it then, this pinnacle of naughtiness, but hated herself a little for it forever after that.

No way, her father thought, that he was going to wait two years for a bear to decide to wean his daughter. He should never have brought her in the first place, but it was too late to think about that. Now he had to find her. Svenchuk took him to the mountain where he said he last had seen her, and when the fog cleared pointed in the direction the bear had carried her. The fog was tremendous. Her father always loved it, to shoot in it, the way it cleared from or filled in the spaces, so he carried his Leica as he went; but this fog was a hell of a disadvantage for finding anyone, and dangerous. He enlisted the help of a Coast Guard air-sea rescue helicopter, but it soon had to give up because of no visibility. It was like looking for a needle in a haystack, when you couldn't see the haystack. Peter, who knew the island like the inside of his mouth, led them on a search from den to den. Everyone had to make noise, beat on pots, carry bells, so they wouldn't surprise the huge bears in the fog. Once Elizabeth realized how many lives her prank had put in danger the thought of her prank made her sick. For the first time in his life her father carried a gun as well as a camera, and though he got some of his most mysterious pictures then, he knew the gun violated the understanding he had established with the bears, an understanding that had made Peter say, ''I never saw such a thing before, a man and the bears. Not Eskimo. Not Indian. Not White Man.'' But that was over. He could never establish that equilibrium again. The assignment was finished.

After ten days of around-the-clock search his daughter began to seem imaginary, as did his own sense of grief. They moved through the grey mists over an hallucinatory landscape of killing: three big bears, one deer shot in the fog by Peter with his 45 Magnum. He hated this killing of animals. Though his heart was ripped with loss he didn't believe in this stupid, futile search, that only killed the bears from whom he had learned so much about nobility. He would never find her, and he even blamed it on her, the loss of his magic among the bears, and he despised his own paternity, that had become just a distraction that broke the spell.

Svenchuk brought her fish, and turnips, and potatoes to roast in the coals, and sometimes they'd throw some oysters on the fire that he'd picked up in the shallows of the estuary near the settlement. They sat and ate on the edge of the cliff and watched the seals, and the fog bunching up at the headlands. They leaned on each other in the warmth of their conspiracy. Svenchuk pulled out a cigarette, broke it in half, handed half to Elizabeth. She had never smoked before. She placed a hand on Svenchuk's big head. "Smoking stunts your growth."

Svenchuk smiled warmly, innocently. "Svenchuk was born with no growth."

Elizabeth started puffing on the cigarettes with him. They tasted evil. The first smoke on her tongue flashed like lightning through her system, but it felt necessary too, as it got dark, the hot smoke in her mouth giving a sense of warmth, enriching their companionship, the both of them puffing. That acrid taste in her saliva, she thought, must be the way a person tastes to herself all the time after she gets older. She liked the whiteness of the smoke out of her mouth, blown into the fog, moving, as she felt she was for the first time out of her childhood, and into womanhood. And this now was a feeling of agelessness and wildness and the void dissolved into forms and corralled by the conspiracy of herself and her friend, Svenchuk, the dwarf.

"You are the nicest person I ever knew," she told him.

"Yes," he said enigmatically, "and half of it still left behind." His mouth grinned, but from his eyes she knew she could understand all that he meant by that. "Now you should go back to your father," he said, a deep bank of melancholy lowering on his dark eyes.

Elizabeth was sitting by the stove when her father came back from his hunt for her. She expected a great rush of love, an embrace as soon as he saw her, but she didn't get it. He seemed relieved, but kept his distance. For him it was an anticlimax. "Betsy. Betsy, where have you been?" was all he asked, and he didn't pursue it. He didn't even kiss her. A new feeling rose in her along with her shame and confusion, and this was anger at, rather than admiration for, his manly restraint. When she followed him around spouting the wonderful tale she had invented about her time with the bears he hardly listened, his occasional glance at her full of skepticism. For him an enormous chore had come to an end and they could finally leave; which they did the next day, a rough crossing back to Anchorage, Svenchuk on the dock giving her the longest, most sincere kiss she had ever tasted.

She never found out if her father believed about the bears, or knew she had been playing a prank. He ignored her, seemed to forget the whole thing. At first she felt a lot of remorse about what she had done, along with anger at him; but once she saw the pictures he had taken while searching for her, some of his best work from that period, she didn't feel so bad, because even at that age she understood enough about his art to know she had provided the distraction that got him out of himself and allowed him to do more than he knew. When they got to Anchorage she menstruated for the first time, and her mother told her on the phone that her heart would never be the same, and that from then on she would have the rhythm of the moon.

The band erupted into heavy metal like a chorus of 45 Magnums and her chair jumped an inch, and settled back. No way she was going to drop onto the spikes for E. Pouce. The story of the bears had so far passed the time for her, and it was a good one, and she had enjoyed spinning it out for herself, though it wasn't true. She had never seen a bear, no less an Alaskan Brown, except in a zoo. And her father was no photographer; he never got beyond the Instamatic. He was no angel, but a son of a bitch, unscrupulous as far as she could remember. He owned a chain of seedy restaurants where he had poisoned a lot of people. They called him Ptomaine Harry Zinberg. But that wasn't true either, just another story she could spin out if she had the time. If she had the time to write all this down she would ask for the reader's indulgence: "Dear reader you must forgive me for putting you on so crudely, but I told the story for my own survival, to keep my mind free of this predicament, and now, goodby." But not goodby. She had no time for asides, no time to write the story down, because her chair was rocking to the heavy beat, and now to keep from falling she had to listen, get her body into it, and then she could hold on because she didn't want to give E. Pouce the satisfaction of his fiendishness. He would have to learn that she could endure, that her womanhood was powerful, that she had the rhythm of the moon, that she knew the way to survival at that still point inside the beat.

*   *   *

Dusty Wier hated this music. It hurt through half his
bones. He couldn't call this 'noise', a person could hear
noise, but you didn't hear this, this bypassed the eardrums
to spring the sutures of the skull. It paralyzes the sphinc-
ters, crosses the chambers of the heart, throws blood into
the eyes. It turns back the peristalsis of the gut, cauterizes
the asshole, and the turds shoved out the mouth are
passed as song. The filthy air is magnetized by this so
pollutants accumulate on the bodies of the people like a
layer of slime. Drought descends where heavy metal
plays. This moves tidal waves, raises locusts from their
sleep, to drown the cities of the shore, to devour the corn
again to its roots, and this lifts from the sewage a great
serpent of sludge that goes in the night to dig at the sex of
the dancers, so sores erupt in their sweetest parts and
green maggots attack. When from above the broad angels
hear this they fold their clouds around their harps and
leave us to the buzzards that drop into this human sump
and dip dark beaks in blood. Fangs are bared in the night,
night fills with knives the intercourse of lovers, and with
this lovemaking a commerce of bombs is born. This is the
cries of the close and the dead without hope, that keeps
the gopis ever from dancing again.

He covered his ears, but his body shook with this. He
looked helplessly up through the lavender haze to the
heavens, so distant, unreassuring. And he cursed aloud
this music that reduced rock-and-roll to its demons. Then
the lightning flashed, and he heard thunder, as if he was
being answered from up there, and a parting of the haze,

and as clearly as he had ever seen anything in the sky he saw leaning on their magenta clouds a gauntlet of pudgy angels, like the wise babes of Murillo, or the mischievous kids of Tiepolo, all grimacing in sympathy, their fat little hands over their ears. He followed the lines of the little spirits from the center of the sky funneling towards the ground where the haze closed in again, and their line ended, pointing like a finger at a balcony on the second story of the house, where he saw a seated figure swaying slightly in the shadows on the balcony in front of the French doors. He moved closer to see it better, Leonora still trailing behind him in a wake of snapshots and talk. Dusty moved close enough to see it was someone dangerously perched on a chair above a gate of iron spears. It was a woman tied to the chair, and the dreadful music made her sway. He recognized Elizabeth, Betsy, a woman he had always admired. E. Pouce had married her, and he always feared that would come to disaster. This was his work. He had tied her up and put her in that position. Dusty opened his mouth to call out Betsy's name, but no sound came forth; instead the moths flew up in a crimson swarm, like bats leaving a cave.

* * *

Mellow and boring, that was Penis and Vagina, right on the image Abby always held of blond California people, brains mostly evaporated in too much sun. She often got stuck in ruts like this, particularly at parties, because her shyness always kept her from making the next move. Soporific conversation for the whole evening while across the room, or on the other side of the lawn in this case, the interesting stuff was going on. The kids seemed tired. They played quietly at the edge of the grass. The couple was telling Abby more about themselves than she wanted to know.

"My husband," said Vagina. "Used to bring other women home all the time, my first husband I mean, and they sat there and got high and ignored me, and I'd go to bed, and we had this king-size bed and they'd crawl in even while I was there, and Edward would ball her right in the bed, with me in the bed. It really made me feel unwanted. That's why I'll never get married again."

"When she met me," Penis said, "she didn't even know who I was."

"And there was this picture of him on the front page of the Santa Barbara paper that said "Who Is This Slick Swimmer?" And what I saw above his head in the picture was just the word 'penis' shining there in all the colors of the rainbow. It was like a UFO experience for me. I mean, 'penis'. What do you want, Cirky?" The oldest girl was staring at Abby.

"Nothing," she said.

Penis whispered to Abby, "When she came to meet me and I heard her say she saw 'penis' above my head I thought this was a crazy woman, but then I looked at her and saw 'vagina' above her head and I thought that was far out."

"Why don't you go back with the other kids?" Vagina told the girl.

"I want to tell her a story," she pointed at Abby.

"Don't point, Cirky, and it's not nice to tell stories."

"So that's how we got together and we've been together ever since," said Penis. "And that's how we got our names too."

"You know the funny thing about our names," said Vagina, "is that I never even used to say words like that. And I don't want my kids to use them either."

"That's admirable," said Abby. Penis stared at her as if he wanted her to say more. "That's a very romantic story," was what she thought of.

"I want to tell her about when I went down to the worms," said the little girl.

"It's her imagination," Vagina shook her head. "It's cuckoo."

"But I did go to the worms and they took me down to where they live and showed me what it was like under the ground. And how they keep warm, and how they eat, and how they watch the little worm TV, and read good little worm books. And they showed me their bedrooms. They have little worm turkeys on Thanksgiving, but I don't think they call it Thanksgiving."

"Now stop. Do you think grownups want to hear that stuff?"

"But it's true, Mommy. You know it. They were nice to me. But they brought me back because they didn't have anything good for me to eat."

"Cirky!"

Abby stood up. "I'll go look for Dusty, I guess." And a great relief to have said it.

"Well when you find him," Penis said, "bring him back and we'll shoot the breeze."

Abby stepped off across the lawn, happy to be on her

way to the rest of the party. The lawn was ready to feed, and it looked Abby over with some interest, if the scrutiny of a lawn can be called 'interest'. Abby had plump breasts for the size of her frame, and some small meat on her buttocks, but the lawn was quite discriminating in its own behalf, and it knew, if you could call it 'knowing', that it had energy to feed only once, and such a bony woman would not be as much to its benefit as the horde of plump children that sauntered out to play near its edge. Such was the reasoning of the lawn, so Abby's crossing was without incident. And she arrived at the rock-and-roll, where she wanted to be, in the heavy metal she loved, that lunged right into her bones, and threw her to dancing as soon as she hit the patio stones. She loved this sound that drowns your whole being, that in its motion takes you into the essence of motion, that connects all the rhythms of your body to its beat and moves you to another time, not your own, but no one else's either, a time shared by everyone beneath the flood, tuned to the grace of music, a communal pulse that moves everyone and all the spheres. She danced by herself, tossing back her great mane of black hair, and she danced with everyone, and the choirs of heaven gonged in her flesh, and slow hordes of grace moved from left to right, and rose and fell, and ordered themselves in dancing contingents displayed like the configurations of the stars that shine through the skull of heaven, that holds the constellations in their lines.

She saw Dusty near the house. He was looking up as if to talk to someone on the balcony. It bothered her that he could stand still in this music. She liked to watch men move, and learned more by seeing them dance one time than by listening to them rap for weeks. When she got closer to him, she stopped dancing, and watched the moths fly up through the spotlights from his mouth. "Dusty," she said. "My God." The whole cloud of them settled on the figure seated on the balcony, that looked like a Cardinal in an iridescent crimson robe, about to address the gathering. Dusty closed his mouth as he breathed the name, "Elizabeth", and this miraculous coordination of moths flew up with all their little claws gripping Elizabeth. They picked her off the balcony and gently fluttered her down next to Dusty, then they rose again and disappeared in a spray of blue sparks.

Now she understood the damn novel into which her life had been diverted; one of those trippy South American books, written from a position of privilege and political apathy, oblivious to the oppression that surrounded them, these reactionary authors in their academic ivory towers. Aieeee! Imperialism! She couldn't stand it, these disenfranchised fantasies that oppress the people with indifference. She was involved in an art, in a theater, that was going to restore conscience and political consciousness. She loved Brecht, and learned from the early Odets, and would revive Karel Kapek; but couldn't tolerate Marquez, or Donoso, or Borges, or Beckett. The world of her art was populated by real people, made for real people, even those asleep, whose conscience she was driving to forge here and now.

Dusty untied Elizabeth, and she slumped forward in the chair, sighing, her eyes shut. He squatted and looked into her face, more sensitive, he noticed, now with some age on it, than when he first realized years ago at school that he liked her. He kissed her lips till the pink returned. She opened her eyes and smiled.

"I'm glad I got here in time, Betsy. I knew there was some reason I was put in this party."

Elizabeth's mouth opened and she pushed out with her tongue a full yellow rose that fell from her lips into Dusty's cupped hands. He stared at it astonished. It was the yellow forged in the mind of a mountain, in the forge of the sun.

"I spit on all this baloney," Abby said.

"Dusty, you know how I hate all that Prince Charming nonsense," Elizabeth said. She embraced Dusty. "But just this once I want to hold you as if you are He."

"I spit on Prince Charming."

"That's okay," said Dusty. "We'll live happily ever after, but just for a minute."

"I include myself," said Abby. "I spit on this whole bourgeois sexist fantasy, and all of you I spit."

Dusty and Elizabeth stood up, still holding their embrace. When they separated he turned to Abby. "I want you to meet my friend, Betsy. Elizabeth Zinberg-Pouce."

"I spit on Zinberg-Pouce." Abby hacked up a clam, curled her tongue, and sent the glob flying their way.

"Terrific," said Leonora, because she got there at the decisive moment, to snap a picture of Abby as the sea-green arabesque of phlegm left her tongue and arched across the yellow rose in Dusty's extended hand.

*   *   *

E. Pouce never panicked. He had absolute faith in the logic and order of experience. Everything worked itself out to his design. So his pilot quit and stole the small chopper. He'd fly the big one himself. Now that he understood it he knew that was the way it was supposed to happen. What was his pilot's name? Harry Fuller. He made a mental note never to hire anyone named Harry again. "Don't expect relief in this world from doing it all yourself. The bastards don't let you rest." That's what Grandpa Pouce always said as he squeezed little E.'s shoulder so hard it brought tears to his eyes. "And if I were you, when I grow up I'd go out and kill the whole brazen lot of 'em. Big mistake that I didn't do it myself when I had a chance, put 'em out of their misery." That was advice E. Pouce remembered as he grew up, and followed with increasing intensity. He took more pride in Grandpa Pouce than in all his other relatives. He liked to meditate on the old guy, even more than on his great aunt Iola who loved to poison anyone who went to dinner at her house, family or not, by feeding them blowfish liver paste, delicious and deadly. Grandpa Pouce was more profound, more universal, like the difference between a mortar shell and several megatons. "I was a pilot," he'd say. "Hate the goddam pilots. Hate the ground crews too. Killed six of 'em once, just cut 'em off the runway. That's how I lost the hearing in my left ear." E.'s mother called her father-in-law's outbursts Grandpa Pouce's shitfits, and for good reason. When they lived in Chicago, in his waning years, he'd crap in his pants while he was having one. He loved to try to embarrass the family, especially when they were entertaining guests at a fancy dinner.

Sarah, their Irish maid, who had raised E. from a sprout, often tying him to his bed at night to keep him out of trouble, set the ceramic tureen of clear turtle soup on the table, and his father began to ladle it into the shallow bowls. The guests watched, with their hands in their laps, as the steamy essence dropped like an emerald cord into gold-rimmed porcelain bowls. E. always knew when Grandpa's shitfits were coming; it was like a baby pushing to load a diaper. First came the smell of the quiet farts, that made the guests a little edgy because they feared it was the aroma of the soup, then Grandpa turned bright red as he squeezed the shout out, as loud as his voice would go, raising the guests half out of their seats: "Worked in the damned mines. Damned molybdenum in damned Leadville, Colorado. Hated the filthy miners. Killed three of 'em on a hoist. Hated the bosses too. That's why I've got this steel plate in my head." They looked nervous, but were reassured by the steady green stream of soup into the bowls, that didn't even waver at the outburst. Everyone ignored the old man, except E. who sat next to him and helped spoon the food through his trembling lips. It was still a mystery to E. how Grandpa had become a capitalist in the course of doing everything else in the world. "I worked in the woods. Hated the damned loggers. Killed seven of 'em with a choker chain. That's how I lost my right hand. Hate the damned doctor who sewed it back on too." He'd been a fisherman, he'd taught civics in high school. "Killed twenty-six students. That's when I lost the sight in this right eye." He'd been a telegrapher, a shipfitter, a railroad brakeman. He'd run a trucking company. Maybe that was where he began to amass his fortune. But to E., when he knew him, he seemed too mean to make money. He must have been more friendly once, seemed friendly anyway to the world; but before he died he hated everyone without prejudice, including his own family. But to make money he must have been ingratiating and hypocritical at one time, charming enough to manipulate a few people, different from this personality distilled from his essence in his later years, which E. admired without reservation, that condensation of misanthropic pique and absolute grievance. "Worked on the docks. Hate the damned unions. Hate the stevedores. Hate the shippers too. Killed seventeen out there. That's how I crippled my right leg."

E. looked after Grandpa Pouce once the stroke paralyzed him. He couldn't move his mouth to eat then, and couldn't speak anymore, so there was no way for him to articulate his shitfits. E. spent a lot of time in his grandpa's room just looking at him in his armchair, motionless, but still filling the air around himself with emanations, his eyes still alive as an entrance to an old mine, his body like a heap of radioactive waste. He saw the fit coming in his grandpa's eyes like a loaded ore car at the tunnel mouth, and he'd try to time it just right, and speak for him. "Worked in a steelmill. Hate the goddam steelworkers. Killed a dozen of 'em. That's how I got the scars on my belly." Eric imitated him. Grandpa Pouce hated this presumption, E. could tell, though the old man stared just as blankly out of his paralysis, but throughout the room E. could feel Grandpa's greyest vibes intensify, and a chill would fill the air, and just a fleck of saliva would foam out at a corner of the old guy's mouth.

In Grandpa's last summer E. liked to roll him along the
lakeshore, or take him to Lincoln Park, or Buckingham
fountain, and he'd leave him sometimes by a beautiful
woman sunbathing on the grass, just to torture him,
because he knew how much Grandpa hated women,
bragged about killing two of his wives, liked to provide
financial aid for rapists at their trials. One buxom young
woman in particular enjoyed to have Grandpa parked at
her spot. She did her stretching exercises in full view of
him, and maybe her motive was charitable, to give a dying
old man a treat, by displaying in her bikini for him some
nicely rounded Iowa meat. She didn't know Grandpa
Pouce. E. came back one day to fetch him while she was
doing a headstand, and saw Grandpa Pouce bearing down
on her in his wheelchair, top speed. Who knows how he
got the chair moving, sheer force of his malicious will,
probably, and before E. could reach her he had smashed
into her tender body, and they kept going, the astonished
girl in Grandpa's paralyzed lap, till they were stopped by a
wire-mesh trash can, into which she dropped, bruised and
bewildered, but not badly hurt. E. helped her back to her
blanket and apologized, though he'd enjoyed watching it,
but she was too confused to talk, and he wheeled Grandpa
away, and felt in the handles of the chair the vibrations of
his hidden laughter.

The last event that impressed him was just before the
end of the old guy's life. He wheeled him along the
lakeshore near the Field Museum and they stopped by a
fountain for a drink. Nearby was an unattended baby
carriage with a black and white dog tied to it. "Give me
that kid over there." It was unmistakably his Grandpa's

voice. That was the first thing he'd heard him say in two years. E. stepped around to look in his face. ''That kid over there, give it to me,'' Grandpa Pouce talking, his voice peremptory and youthful. E. looked around. The parents might have been those people drinking beer and talking to someone in the parking lot. What the hell, E. thought, indulge the old bastard at the end of his life. The dog didn't make a sound when he lifted the kid out of the carriage. Grandpa always said he hated the little titsuckers, and this one was gurgling, its diaper loaded. He placed it in Grandpa Pouce's lap, and watched. For a moment E. thought Grandpa was getting sentimental in his senility, because he looked like he was kissing the kid, but the baby's eyes flew open, his arms shot up, and a shocked expression flew onto his face. When Grandpa lowered the brat Eric saw that this was still the same old Grandpa Pouce because the old man spit out the kid's little ear. He bit it off. His mouth was working again and he put it to use. E. grabbed the kid away just as Grandpa was going for its nose, and as it started to scream he dropped it back in the carriage, and the little dog jumped in with it and howled as the parents came running, the father tossing a can of Stroh's high into the air. When Eric turned back he saw the father strangling the little dog, the mother bent over her baby on the ground. Grandpa Pouce was something else, rotten till the day he died.

Now shoop. Shoop. Shoop. Shoopshoopshoop. The rotors of the big chopper shooped, and he loved it. He touched each of the three napalm cannisters leaning near the door, then strapped himself in. Three was all he could get, but it would be a good taste, enough to cover the patio,

the house, and some of the strays. A good tribute to
Grandpa Pouce on the seventh anniversary of his death.
He would learn something, and so would his guests, about
what happens in the world. He pulled back on the stick
and lifted off. Loved the rising of it, the suddenly airborne
sensation, like Christmas morning. Opening the presents.
Tiny lights blinked on the enormous tree, and it was still
dark outside, and he always got lots of presents, and he
always deserved it, because he was a good worker, and a
dutiful son.

First out over the bay, where two of his tankers were
idling. From high up he saw the glow of the gathering
around the estate he was about to sacrifice on this
occasion, and in the bay the glitter of his ships. All of it
would be glowing better soon. The noise of the rock band
rasped evenly, like someone filing the blade of an ax. That
was a pretty sound, and the sound would get even prettier.
And pretty flames. And pretty screams. And the tide was
right, two-foot waves running at the shore. That beach
would cover with oil in no time, a wash of burning diesel
going home. He circled the two ships several times. He'd
already lost his chopper pilot, and wanted to make sure he
didn't have to move the ships himself, but he was paying
the crew too much for them to desert, and paying them in
gold. This was dangerous, but men loved gold. Fun. They
moved about on the decks, waiting for his signal. He lit the
flare and let it fall, and hovered there a moment while the
big diesels revved up. One of the ships swung around so
graceful, the invisible arabesques of its wake married the
small waves in moire with the moon. It set a position to
ram its explosive bow into the oil-filled midships of the

other tanker. O for a film crew. Why didn't he have one at
this event. Why did film crews set up on other locations
where they had to make movies? What good were movies
anymore when the special effects were happening
everywhere else. Right here inside his coat. That's what
he'd do when he finally had his way, he'd let them play
the movies out on all the sets at all the locations, just let
them do it there, and he'd turn the cameras around to the
three hundred and sixty directions and make them suck
light. "Good boys," he shouted to the ships below. "Just
what the doctor ordered." He buzzed the tugs waiting at a
safe distance to pick up the men, then set off at a lope for
the onshore festivities.

* * *

Reginald loped down the beach. Like this he could go
forever, that's why they called him Long-toes. He ran till
his ankles flowed, ran till his ears sailed in the darkness,
he ran through the backs of his eyes, ran away from the
noise, ran to the shores, ran with the pouch of money
swung from his neck, two hundred and sixty bucks from
hustling fish. Hang around white folks by the water and
you get to hustle fish. He could have cooked it for them if
he'd stuck around, and doubled his money: that's what
Ptomaine Harry would have told him to do. Get the
money. Ptomaine Harry knew how to hustle the white
folks, was more or less white himself, though more greasy
and gray than real White white. He'd been like a father to
Reginald, that studious old grubby Italian man, who sold
sandwiches off a cart by Stuyvesant High School, near the

projects where Reginald lived. He took care of Reginald, like his mother couldn't and no one else in the world wanted to. After he rented a storefront across the street from the school Reginald went to work for him in the early mornings and after school. He was just seven years old. His mother let him sleep in the store, because she was pregnant, and had four others at home. At least Reginald was off her mind. The warmth of Ptomaine Harry's ample heart embraced Reginald like a son. "Had a daughter once," he said, "but she don't come to see me no more, and I don't want to see her no more. I don't even remember what she looks like. " He helped Harry prepare the sandwiches at night, and ran some deliveries after school in the neighborhood. "I like you, little Caffe Latte, you make some noise in my life, it's good," said Harry, "and you a serious boy, no bum." He was called Ptomaine because there was a rumor he had to leave Flushing High with his cart when kids started to come up poisoned from his sandwiches. This was years back, in the early fifties, but it wasn't true any more, probably wasn't even true then. Harry was clean, and he made good sandwiches, real Italian cheese wet down with good olive oil. When an occasional fingerprint turned up on the bread it was always Reginald's, and Harry would point at the bread and say, "Hey sporchetto, you wipe you little black ass with that finger?" They'd wipe it off if they could, and sell it anyway, and Reginald would keep his hands clean for a few nights after that.

He slept on some flattened cardboard cartons in back of the counter, under a moth-eaten wool blanket, with his head on a lumpy pillow he had found on the street. When it got really cold the old man crumpled the *New York Times*, or the *Christian Science Monitor*, and stuffed it in a burlap sack for him to sleep under like a featherbed. "Makes good insulation," Harry said. "As long as you don't read it. It freezes the heart to read a newspaper these days, but it keeps a little boy warm in bed." After Reginald was asleep at night Harry usually went home to Flushing where he kept an apartment, but sometimes he'd stay late in the store and read. He'd light a kerosene lamp because he said the Italian language didn't look good under electric. Reginald lay under the counter breathing the incense of salami and oregano and listened while the old man said this Italian poetry aloud. It sounded like another kind of music, very important and sweet. It made Reginald vow, as he looked out at the shadows flying in the lamplight, that he would go to Italy some day himself, where people must be nice to each other, because they spoke this nice language. "Hey, boy, you asleep?" Harry would say. "Listen to this." Behind his voice the trucks crushed garbage, taxi drivers complained about tips, men and women went at each other in their apartments. "Ascoltate, Otellino."

"'O voi, che siete in piccioletta barca,' that means, hey you guys over there in that little boat. Ascolta. Ascolta. 'Desiderosi d'ascoltar, seguiti / retro al mio legno che cantando varca,' very important, my little one, to have a song, whatever the song, wherever you go." Reginald would doze off. "'...Che forse, / perdendo me, rimarreste smarriti.' Oh you know how I want to see Italy again, and I never will. My beautiful Capri. Some day you go to Capri for me. You like the Dante? Me, without my Dante, I

would be nothing. I would be an empty man, senza
cuore..."

Reginald slept deeply to the smooth Italian words, and
in the morning Harry was gone, the kerosene lamp blown
out; or he was asleep, cheek on the table, some roaches
scurrying near his mouth.

Reginald was almost fifteen now, Harry dead some
seven years. He guessed about the death when he woke up
one cold morning. It was a smell, like big empty rooms.
No breathing. The kerosene lamp still burned, and
roaches ran around in the old man's open mouth. Reginald
closed the old man's eyes, as he'd seen them do it on TV.
Dead men didn't scare him. He'd seen them before, shot
down on 14th Street, and once when he was real little his
mama's boyfriend died in his blood on their big chair.
Reginald shooed the roaches out of Harry's mouth and
tried to press it closed, but the jaws were locked, so he
plugged it up with a heel of Italian bread, then covered the
head with a dishtowel. Reginald stayed out of school all
that day, and made the sandwiches and opened the store,
and he even sold a few prosciutto and provolone heroes to
some of the kids, before a teacher came in on an early free
period, Miss Makaroff, a regular customer, a
thirty-year-old spinster, with Kleenex sticking out of her
bra. She always ate a green olive and ricotta sandwich,
and ordered one that morning before she noticed that
Ptomaine Harry wasn't breathing. She lifted the towel
from his face, pulled the bread out of his mouth, and
jumped back gasping when some roaches scattered out to
hide under the edge of the table.

Reginald kept the Dante, Cavalcanti, Petrarca, and he

still had them, and he intended some day, when his hustles didn't take up all his time, to learn to read them. "You a lucky boy," Harry had told him, "light enough to look Italian, like latte macchiato, and that's more easy than black in this crazy country. Because if you're a white kid and you hustle the white people they think it's cute and darling and free enterprise, a baby Rockefeller; but if you're a black boy and you hustle them maybe even they love you at first, but soon they slip up and finish you off, easy as that. I've seen it. I've seen a lot of things here in America."

A lot of things, Reginald thought, that he wanted to be, but no way he wanted to be dead. That's what was so crazy about some of the kids he lived with at The Settlement. They took death drugs. They did death crimes. The difference between a hustle and a crime was that a hustle you could fold it up and run, a hustle could disappear back into the mind, but you add a piece of chain to a hustle, and you've got a heavy crime about to happen, because you lower that chain on a shopkeeper, or on some dude you're jacking up in a doorway, and maybe you'll have to squeeze the trigger, just squeeze it, and that trip was one way. Dead was dead. Dead was equal rights.

A small helicopter hovered like a mosquito above him. Cops? How could they bust him for selling the fish? Maybe they thought he had blown up the water. Shit. As he watched it, the helicopter suddenly turned bright orange, and it wobbled in the air, and a roar hit him like all the subways at once. He saw the flames back there on the water, and felt a rush of heat against his skin. Jesus. He'd never seen an H-bomb go off in his life yet, and didn't ever want to get to see one; but that fireball he was looking at back there now was one big hot motherfucker, and he'd seen pictures of that mushroom cloud before. O, shit. He didn't want to be dead. He sank to his knees and clutched the canvas pouch of money hanging from his neck. He wished he remembered how to pray. Flames shooting up by that big house. Folks out of their skulls over there. Grown up people, destroying themselves.

"Hey, kid." A voice behind him.

Reginald turned to see a big bearded dude coming at him from the helicopter. "What?" His face was bright orange. The whole place was lit like an inferno.

"Listen, kid, what time you got?"

Reginald lifted his arms to show he didn't carry a watch.

"I thought maybe you were a kid with a watch," the bearded man said. "I would've bought it from you. Maybe I would've traded for my helicopter." His face was ugly white under his beard. Grey mice crawled under his eyes. He had put too much alcohol, too many drugs through his system too often. "What do you think of that? If you had a watch I would have traded you my helicopter. Pretty good, huh? A watch for a helicopter."

"You can't tell time with a helicopter."

The guy didn't laugh. He looked around like a dummy. "Get in the helicopter. I'll take you."

"I ain't getting in that thing with you."

"That's my chopper. You could have had it for a watch, but you didn't have one, right; so get in, I want to have a chat with you. I need your support. This is an election year."

"I'm too young to vote, and you're too stupid to be a politician."

The bearded one grinned. "That's what you think." Reginald saw the sickening suck-pucker of his lips. He'd seen that one before. "So get in and sit down."

"What are you, the helicopter fairy? Why do you want to take me with you?"

"Look, the place is burning. My name is Anthony. I'm a hemophiliac."

"Okay, Anthony. What's a hemophiliac?"

"Your blood don't clot. I'm a bleeder. Now get in. We're wasting gas."

"That's rough on you," said Reginald. "Your blood don't clot, you bleed a lot." Reginald knew what this guy was, a hemophiliac faggot. The helicopter sat there like a dragonfly on a twig. Except in the movies he'd never flown in one of them before.

"So that's why I need you," said Anthony. "In case I start to bleed. Someone's got to help plug up the blood."

"Why don't you use a Tampax?" Reginald said.

"Come on," said Anthony.

Reginald looked back at the flames. The faster he got away from there, the better. "You'll take me where I'm going? To the settlement?"

"Of course," said Anthony.

Why not, thought Reginald. He was still alive, and all this shit was burning. Do it, was one of his philosophies. He climbed into the seat, and the dude climbed in next to him and helped him strap down. Then he pulled back on the stick and they went up. It was great, Adidas with wings, the flying sneakers. Down there was burning, a thousand tongues flicked off the water. Where was the Coast Guard? The land was burning too. Where were the fire departments?

"So you're a bleeder, Tony?" Reginald said, as they banked sharply and kept rising.

"My name's not Tony. It's Harry Fuller."

"Why'd you tell me your name was Anthony?"

"I brought you up here to tell you about Jesus."

"I've heard about it. Why'd you give me the wrong name?"

"I'm carrying you closer, little brother, closer to the Lord, so when you meet Him, you take Him in your heart."

Reginald stared at him. A gust of wind shook the chopper. This was dangerous now. "Look, you could have saved me down below, and saved gas too." It was a big risk, a mean religious queer in a helicopter. Reginald picked up a beat off the rotor and tapped his foot for consolation.

The dude stared at him, his lips a fat pucker.

"Do you know what it's like," said Harry, "to be a fat man in a thin man's world?"

"Look, I'm not prejudice. A fat man's cool. Fat Harry, Fat Anthony, as long as you can fly this thing." They had gone up so high it looked to Reginald they were closer to the moon than they were to the earth. "I was a chicken once, but they never let me fly before."

The dude grabbed Reginald's hand to his mouth and sucked on the fingers. "Hey, it's the flavor of the week. I hope you liked it." He pulled his hand back. Harry grabbed the other one and rubbed his beard in it. "I want to tell you about the Buddha." He held Reginald's forearm like it was a jammed lever. "You know, you can fly like this and you don't even need a helicopter."

"I need a helicopter," said Reginald.

Harry threw his head back and laughed like a fiend. He started to bring the chopper down in the direction of the fires.

"Hey. That's where I came from. You told me you'd take me where I was going."

Harry looked at Reginald and laughed some more. "We're picking up the trash. Rich trash down there."

"No," said Reginald. Someone should have warned him about the white faggots in their helicopters.

"Cut some gold fingers. Cut some diamond ears." Harry grinned.

"You crazier than I thought, white man. You are a deep white creep." He paused and looked around. "But I guess this is your bird." He closed his eyes and hummed 'Great Speckled Bird'. Of the Bible.

When he opened his eyes Harry was staring at him through some mean, puffed-up, biker-faggot eyelids. "Why didn't you tell me that?" he said.

"What?"

"I don't fly with no nigger-boy, boy. Why didn't you tell me first?" His knuckles were white where he squeezed the controls.

"Hey. Do your mama got the King-Kong clap? You a fat hemophiliac Buddha faggot Jesus-freak motherfucker."

"I just don't fly with them," said Harry, sitting straight up in his seat.

"You can suck on my nigger, white man. You don't fly with me? Okay. Take this chopper and put me down over there where it's burning. That smells like the ghetto over there."

Harry said no more. He unsnapped his harness and turned away from Reginald. "Wait," said Reginald. The dude looked like he was leaving. "Teach me how to fly this thing first." Reginald glanced at the control panel. There were numbers showing on those instruments that he'd never seen before. The sucker was crazy. He swung his legs out the door. "Hey, let me shine your shoes first, before you go. You'll bleed to death down there." Harry slipped his ass off the edge, hooked the heels of his boots on the strut, and held onto the top of the bubble with one hand.

"You just lost my vote, man," Reginald said, as Harry zipped open his fly, and pissed into the flaming waves below.

* * *

At the far edge of the lawn that had just consumed their children Penis and Vagina lay in each other's arms. Her head was turned away from the cluster of shadows left on the ground where the little ones had been playing, but Penis stared directly at the spot and thought how he had failed as a parent. He should have played catch with them more, should have read them more Dr. Seuss, they definitely should have been more closely supervised. Now a tragedy, and right before their eyes. It had happened so fast they couldn't move to rescue them. "Look, Cirky, quick, look..." was the last thing they heard little Rhombus shout. So happy, he'd sounded. Then Circle stood up and spread her arms. Her face was shining, ecstatic, as she dropped to her knees, then to her belly, and she rolled over and started to dissolve. "How pretty. O I love it so much. How pretty the air is. So full... O Mama..." and that was all. Vagina's instinct was to rush to them as soon as she saw them globbing into the lawn, but it was already too late, and Penis held her back. They melted like some slugs her brother used to cover with salt on the basement steps. "What's happening to them?" She still felt pulled their way, but Penis held her cuffs.

"We can't lose you too," he said. "Don't go over there. It's too late for them."

"Why can't we do anything?" She sat down and felt numb, and guilty as she remembered how much more violent her reaction could be to tragedies on the tube. There was nothing else they could do. They had watched the fires explode on the party across the lawn, and had seen their children disappear. It had been a lot to take in, and now it was time to go home and turn on TV. The music kept coming over the cries and troubles out there, and the message was as usual that the beat went on, that rock and roll would never die.

"You know what I keep thinking?" he said. "Maybe I seem callous, but I keep thinking that we always said we shouldn't have had children so young, and suddenly we don't have them now. It's like it was erased, like the mistake was on paper."

Vagina started to sob, so fast she hyperventilated. Penis laid her down, and kept his hands on her body till she was calm. "At least," he whispered in her ear, "they seemed to be happy. It wasn't a hideous death. How many people enjoy to die?" He could even think it was fortunate that the children went this way, if they had to die. They were gone, and buried in one gesture. It was ecological, and was it too cold for him to acknowledge that it was also economical?

"Are they really dead?" Vagina lifted her head, breathing regularly now.

"That's a good question," said Penis, "because they became grass. How can we say 'die'? All flesh is grass."

Vagina sat up. Penis was correct. Where their children had been looked like an erasure on the lawn. "How strange. I feel so distant, so...nothing." She gazed across at the fires exploding into the trees. This party seemed to keep going through all the tragedies. "It's so far out. It's as if we never had them. Maybe tomorrow it'll catch up with me. Suddenly we never had them. God." She covered her face. "I was so much older before this happened, and I'm feeling so much younger now."

Penis kissed her hands, and she pulled them down from her face. "We've never known each other without children before," she said. "What can we do?"

Penis pulled her back to the ground. "We do it. That's all," he said. "We do it."

"I guess you're right," she said. "Okay." She lifted her hips as he slipped her jeans down. A blanket of pain-muffling music settled on them. His implement was hard when she touched it. He established his position above her. Heat punched at them from the burning party. Penis inserted his device in the well-oiled socket, and he and Vagina coordinated a motion that separated them into their own dreams, away from the dream of things, moving towards the universal dream, in a dance that led them beyond functions and gross signals in this world.

*   *   *

Elizabeth and Dusty in the frame. Abby in the background. She hit the shutter release. Picture. She advanced the film. Difficult for Leonora to shoot behind the foliage of smoke and fire that separated the four of them from the chaos at the party. When the napalm fell, a smell like grease in the nose, they took shelter under the overhang of a stone tool shed. Lucky that none of the burning mess had slopped onto them. Pain like a weather report out there, others trying to party while it burned. Dusty found a hose coiled on a hook and they sprayed each other to keep the heat down. The steam fogged her lens, but focus wasn't critical. Abby was in the frame. Dusty sprayed Elizabeth. She tapped the shutter release. Picture. Spray drenched the lens. She advanced the film.

"E. had cruel parents," Elizabeth said. "You can't blame it all on himself."

"He never would have become your husband if you'd listened to me at school." They were nose to nose in the fireglow. "And you can't blame parents for cruelty of this magnitude."

"This is about Vietnam Karma coming down on us now, that's what it is," Abby said. "Who paid for Cambodia? The Khmer people are just the latest genocide. What are we doing about it? And can we turn our backs on Soweto? Does fascism in Argentina have no effect on us?" She grabbed the hose and sprayed it on herself. Leonora snapped in a dry 28mm.

"E. went on a camping trip once with his father. He was only eight years old," Elizabeth said. "His father tied his wrists to his ankles and hung him from a tripod above their campfire. He said that if he survived he'd live forever. E. survived.''

Dusty pressed her sweating palm against his lips. ''Even when we were at school I loved you. I could love you now.''

Abby turned the hose on them. Steam rose from their shoes. ''Can you spare a little love for the displaced Palestinians? For the Kurds? Armenians still live somehow in southwest Russia. When have you thought about hunger in Micronesia?''

''You remember me at school, Dusty. Then I loved anyone who wore a black leather jacket, jack boots, had a big bike. A beard made me wet automatically.''

''True. I was in tweeds and dungarees. I couldn't even get in the door. I was Mr. Peachfuzz Moustache. But that doesn't make a difference any more.''

''On that same camping trip his father, and he always seemed like a decent man, a little stuffy and humorless, but basically decent, put little E. in a net bag...''

''I never know if you're making it up or what. E. never told me about this.''

''And the Macedonians?'' Abby waved the hose above her head. ''Where are they today?''

''Then he attached a rope to the bag and swung it out over a cliff. If he was going to live forever, his father told him, he'd better get used to this.''

''So them we ignore, right? Just because they live somewhere in Bulgaria, right? Would you call Bulgaria an okay place?'' Abby sat down.

''Now listen to this. His father covered his whole little

body with molasses. That was probably the worst thing he did. He left him there with ants crawling all over him, to find his own way home. His father told him he needed to experience the bears and the bees."

A long moan suddenly emptied the air from their alcove, and a putrid smell rolled in like sewage in the mouth. They held their throats and backed against the wall. A wind full of charred flesh blew across them and another moan from a diseased planet jellied their spines. Leonora courageously lifted her camera and snapped a flash in the direction of the noise; then she hid the camera under her sweater and mumbled her mantra. A huge slug of black sludge moved towards them. It swelled and diminished in the flicker of light, dark, atavoid, suffering.

Abby pointed the hose at the creature like the muzzle of a gun. Elizabeth pressed into Dusty. "Just hold me," she said. Abby closed her eyes and played the full spray on the apparition. It lifted its forward end and made a sound that was almost human. From beneath the thing a pink hand reached out, a human hand clutching a human wallet, and it made some sounds, nearly human words. This was a human being, clothes and flesh so charred it seemed covered with fur.

"Excuse me. Excuse the introoj...jun," as if suddenly realizing it was in company it was embarrassed. "If I interrupted something, I'm very sorry. Veruh sorroooh..." The front end collapsed again.

Dusty knelt beside it, Elizabeth gripping his ankle. He saw a human face, charred like a piece of wood, eyes burnt shut. "So this," Dusty said solemnly to himself, "is the glooming of the human condition." "Forgive me," the man said. He laid the wallet in front of Dusty. "And ask them to forgive me. Tell them I loved them despite..." The human expired. Dusty opened the wallet and found a snapshot within of a family posing in Yellowstone Park next to some bears. There was a wife, a husband, and 2.3 children.

*   *   *

An exodus of possums, heading for the bay, their pups on their backs, crossed the patio, sifting themselves through the fallen bodies, risking the feet of those still dancing. They peeped as fire singed their hair, and scorched their white hides. Occasionally a dancing foot sent one squealing into the air, its pups hanging from its back. Bank swallows and martins swooped at the possums to grab the fleas that escaped their flaming bodies, and sometimes birds carried into the flames, where they exploded.

*   *   *

Pouce had missed the bandstand, as was agreed in their contract, so the band kept playing. The bass player watched the burning tide advance and retreat to the beat. It was intolerable. They were disgusting. He loved it. This was excruciating. Those who hadn't succumbed yet still danced. Even those felled by the flames kept beat with a foot, or a finger, or a nostril if it wasn't burned. After all, this was the party they had all been waiting for. A young woman whose friend had succumbed stripped off his still smoldering jacket and danced with that. This was the party they all had known was going on somewhere, that they always came for. Seven long-haired young men greased their hair with burning jelly and whirled. This was the party they never wanted to leave.

*   *   *

As soon as he put the chopper down Harry Fuller forgot about Reginald, and grabbed a burlap sack from behind the seat, and headed for where the bodies were thickest. He stopped on the way to pull a wristwatch off some moaning, burnt-up dude. Reginald thought he looked like the black hole of Santa Claus, with his beard and greasy sack. Reginald didn't want any of that dead man's shit. Even if it was rubies. Even a winning lottery ticket. Okay maybe he'd take a winning lottery ticket if he found one, but he didn't want any of that other dead man's watches, dead man's rings, dead man's snakeskin boots. The world was full of dead man's shit, and this white music was dead man's music for the dead, who kept on dancing instead. And if they were hurting, nobody said. These folks felt no pain, white folks, black folks maybe too. Who could tell? Faces covered with soot. Bloodshot eyes shining out. The band paused and he caught all the other noises, napalm still sizzling, cries of pain under the squeals of pleasure. A possum rubbed against his leg. "Hey, possum, how you be?" Not good. He picked it up, the little thing half cooked alive. It pretended to be dead in his hand. He put it back down and looked around. He should leave again, he thought. This disco, this dancehall, had a dress code: burnt clothing, blister skin. He passed a large fountain, some party people face down in it, napalm floating around them like burning jellyfish. On the ground at the rim of the fountain a woman lay moaning, curled in a ball. He bent over to touch her but another woman grabbed his arm and turned him around.

"C'mon, honey boy." He couldn't tell how old she was under her damage. Her polyester slacks were smoking on her legs. "This could be the last dance of the evening; but maybe not, honey boy." Her hair was smoking too.

"Don't that hurt you, lady? You burnin' there."

She tried to pull him close. "Come danser, bajar, ballare, tanzen, tanzen."

"Hey," he said. "If a man don't want to, just let him lie." He pushed her back just in time, as her clothes flamed up and she went spinning off like a rocket, with an ecstatic or anguished scream that fell into the music.

He watched Harry Fuller fill his sack across the patio, as he chopped off swollen ring-fingers with his hunting knife, and ears with their jewels cooked in. A man fell into Reginald's chest, "Ohh." A small, thin man with two days' beard, red rings around his eyes. A dab of the burning grease slopped from the man's sleeve onto Reginald's cheek.

"Damn," Reginald hollered. That shit burned. He brushed it with his hand, and it kept burning on his palm, like it would sear a hole clear through it. These were some high people, some stoned people, not to feel it. He plunged his hand into the fountain, but that stuff still burned under water. It burned till it was used up. He kneeled by the woman still curled at the fountain's rim. She was quiet now. She hadn't been damaged at all. He felt the blister swelling on his cheek. He'd be alright. He rolled her over.

"Take your damned paws off me." She didn't open her eyes.

She was just a girl, no older than he was. She didn't belong at this party any more than he did. And he was ready to split right now. He slipped his arms under the girl's body to pick her up.

"Go maul up somebody else," she said, and opened her eyes and saw Reginald. "O. Not you." His was the nicest face, she thought, that she had ever seen.

"Shhh," he said. "Come on. We can go away now."

"I can't leave my mother here," she said.

"Your mama is too busy dancing, and she'll stay here anyway, but no reason for you to stay." He went to help her up, but she straightened out and stood up herself. "I can walk," she said. She looked across the havoc. "Mama told me she went to a party, but look at it. Grownups are so weird."

"Shhh." He covered her lips. "We've got some place to go, lady." He put his arm around her as they started to leave. She kept looking back over her shoulder at the diminishing fires. "O my God," she kept saying. Reginald took the lead. This time he would get back to the settlement. No faggot helicopter pilots would ever turn them around.

*   *   *

No refuge and no refugees. A bomb on the house should have dropped. E. was the perfectionist. It always fit in the big design. He carried five thousand rounds here, but he wouldn't strafe. Bullets were little messengers, hot little tongues. They made one on one, not his game. All the moon was full and he would strafe the moon. This was no power trip. Noisy big whirly-bird. Could hear only the edges of music. And "God Bless America." What did Anton Webern sing when Himmler listened in? And what did those citizens sing below? Stand up when you do God Bless America, boy. That's an Irving Berlin tune, and he was Jew. Something in it all, something in it below that he envied. The wolf and discord. The irrational amok delightful. His own life too straight too harmonious. Always in the big design. Orderly, integrated like pomegranate, perfect cobblestone fragments in place, white membrane to hold in sets. White life in control. If something to drop on him from above okay. Or something else would be better. Or put it up to chance. Any dance anything on a planet of skunks. Another life of more essential orbits. Could anyone more vigorous be more alluring to the gods? Who were watching. Half-amused half-Chinese. The other half grabbed him by the bones and shook to see what rattled loose, and nothing. Nothing loose, like Grandpa Pouce. Chopper full of black smoke. He rises out of it and opens the vents. Below this isn't big enough, this isn't enough of what he wants to do because he has appetites. He takes big bites, a mouth to garage the world. Pretty oil slick flames bright orange a fringe of blue here and there across the back of a breaker in the moonlight. He goes for altitude and a look at the whole thing. The range of smokes and flames enough some heaps of dying enough some lamps still lit enough a beach of refugees enough shadows of dancers intrepid enough the flaming seas the flames enough, and in the distance headlights and taillights remembered on could be the planet of his dreams almost enough. He could call it art, if this weren't deeds, a fanciful ephemeral beauty putting time on a shuttle. The audience stands up, stretches a little, gets to the aisle, hands in pockets, gets to the streets again where the first words are, ''What now? Well, what now?'' Yes what now? Bigger chunks. Bigger death. E. Pouce, the biggest. This limit of the world where the light of all destruction illuminates what? Emergency exit. He flies a wide circle for the last time around the image below, of his creation, and tilts the chopper towards the big city. There he'll set it down on the wharf, and his driver will take him to his flat. A small bitch there, an acquaintance of his pooch, is having her fourth puppy. He breaks his orbit and vectors towards the city. Disrupt, he complains. More disorder. He breaks the construct and flies away.

* * *

Dusty got out first, followed by Leonora, by Elizabeth, and then Abby. Abby went in the other direction. She knew she could walk away from it, because she'd never volunteered for this experience, and she had no ambition to pursue a friendship with anyone in this work of black humor. Black humor, that's all this was, outmoded, and that's how she interpreted it. None of this demon-charged existence belonged to her needs. It was a fantasy, an imposition. Another puff of smoke and she'd be gone,

back with her friends, back at the rehearsals of their new
piece, terrific, she had the lead, about the life of Isabelle
Eberhart. Back to the ha ha reality of her life, this novel
behind her forever, like the music of this bass player, the
last musician on stage, still looking at the stars, still
playing his line, who would probably keep on playing
after they pulled the plug from his amp, but disappeared
from her, deleted like her memory of this.

She felt a light touch on her shoulder and turned to look
into the potent blue eyes of a young man whose face had
been badly scorched. How many times had she seen this
same gesture, his hand paralyzed with burns, held out to
her, stooped shoulders, body turned away slightly, ready
for rejection and retreat, that smell on the bowery of urine
and vomit, a barrier to the exchange, and at the same time
a ploy to hasten the transaction; except this was the smell
of burnt flesh, and these were living eyes, not the
depthless murkiness of the bums where she lived, that she
had to move off the stoop of her loft building every day in
order to get in or out. He couldn't speak. His lips had been
seared into a kind of pucker, the tongue moving slightly
behind it like a yellowed infant in an incubator. He tried
to express his need with a slight movement of the neck.
Abby was touched. She couldn't resist that he had picked
her out. Pity attached itself like a light pink sound. After
all, he might be quite sensitive and nice to be with had she
met him in some other dream, or a novel of more gentle
fates. That's how she was forced to explain this finally, as
a dream or fiction mutually conceived by its participants.
Conceiving it that way she at least had some flexibility,
some control over her part and didn't have to be revolted

or terrified by all these mutilations and characters untraumatized, as if they'd lost the mechanism to acknowledge the damage. In fact she recognized something about this one. He probably was someone she had seen before, someone from her own neighborhood, the young painter who lived around the corner, and he was here just as she was, an artist out of his element. He wanted a cigarette; that was clear from the way he held out his hand and raised it to his lips. His hands would have to heal before he could ever paint again. Now she remembered. She had seen some of his work in a group show at a co-op on Mercer Street, and it was very good, a gentle painting, abstract, somewhat geometrical, but that nonetheless seemed to display the power of his social commitment. The patio lights flashed and expired and the bass player, his power cut, sank to his knees and breathed fitfully as if his oxygen had been snatched. Abby tried to hand the young man a cigarette, but he couldn't hold it. He let out some small moans to indicate how much he wanted it. She was on the right track. The last time she saw him was in Fanelli's. She sat at another table and listened to his heated conversation with another painter. She loved to eavesdrop, and adored this conversation, about making art for fashion or making it out of need, out of your guts and spirit, and she knew which one he favored. She remembered his turning to her once, the same shocking blue eyes. What good fortune for her to meet him here. She could help him. She led him to the rim of the fountain and they sat down. She lit a cigarette and put it to his mouth, but he couldn't close his lips on it to draw the smoke. A few sycamore leaves, their pale blue

undersides up, floated in the pool behind them. She filled
her cheeks with smoke, and moved her lips against his,
lightly brushing his, and blew the smoke as far as she
could into his lungs. He pressed her shoulder with his
forearm to reassure her that she had done it exactly right,
and she felt a nice thrill that placed her more or less in the
evening, and grateful to be there, and she watched the
smoke he exhaled rise towards the stars that seemed,
those of them not obscured by constellations of black
smoke, quite convincing in her eyes.

*   *   *

The lawn inched over the patio towards the party
leftovers, leaving a wake of digestive froth. Dusty and
Elizabeth went to the front of the house, then turned to the
left and moved quickly through the rubble to the edge of
the dark woods that bordered the unhappy estate to the
South. They peered for a while into the inky atmosphere
then looked at each other, took a last deep breath for
courage, and stepped into it.

*   *   *

Leonora followed them at a distance to the edge of the
woods and stopped when she saw them go in. She'd gone
far enough to meet Dusty Wier. She'd have to save it for
another time, when she could dance with him. She was far
from a verbal person, especially in first attempts at
communication. Dancing made it easier. All that ice
seemed to break automatically. It was like her camera that

made it easier for her to circulate in crowds of people. If someone stopped her to talk it was usually about her equipment, and that was okay. She saw them disappear almost immediately into the darkness. No way she would take that plunge. Maybe some other time, Dusty Wier, on some other terms, at a new place to dance. She turned back. This party was over, as suddenly as it had begun for her; gone in a way she couldn't have anticipated. Not a sign of it. It was like she'd been at a movie, some Fellini that sputters out at the end. She was glad she had it on film, had taken so many pictures, and could hardly wait to get into her darkroom to develop what she had.

She pulled her flashlight from her purse and played it over the dark remains. Vines had captured the old estate again, loosening the shingles, penetrating broken windows. The crumbling fountains were covered with moss. The lawn was defeated by weeds. Half the front porch had collapsed years ago, and on the other half a middenheap of baby-food jars and beer cans from the squatters who had to be driven off a few years back. The wrought-iron lampposts that once filled these elegant gardens and patios with gorgeous lavender light were darkened forever, bent or fallen. Extinguished was the splendor of this estate from the golden age of American millionaires. That epoch would never return, she thought, not to the shores of this republic.

She walked back to her Toyota. Sometimes it wouldn't start, especially when it was damp by the sea. She cranked it over a few times. No response. She hated the cars. She cranked it again. Nothing. Maybe she wouldn't be able to get out of there. Trapped there. What a dismal place, what an atmosphere of ghosts and corruption. She slammed the door hard several times. Sometimes that worked. She didn't know why. It did. The motor kicked, sputtered, and went. She'd never understand it. Machines would always be a little bit of magic in her life.

*   *   *

Dusty and Elizabeth moved through the woods in silence in a direction they thought might get them to some expressway. Actually they weren't sure, but there was the trace of a line that had been cut a long time ago through that forest, and the trees left there to decay. They glowed now slightly along the way, a pale blue-green light. The two followed that subtle light of decay through the woods, bright as a torch once their eyes accommodated. They followed wherever it led, out of the woods was what they hoped.

THE MESSAGES

The enormous pockets of the New York Public Library were filled with the unemployed. And the unemployable. And degree candidates, their heads asleep in the caves of scholarly journals. And silver-haired gentlemen with thin moustaches, Wall Street actuaries retired from the world of numbers into the world of images. And Manhattan's health widows levelling their eyeglasses at the next page of Scheherazade. Dusty was out of work, and this library was his occasional escape from the city. He enjoyed entering it from the street, into one of the big rooms, to look down the rows of heavy blond tables, like a plowed like a plowed field at sunrise, at each workspace a green lampshade, a cone of white light, a disarray of texts and notebooks, and people diminished by the massive tables, and stacks of books, and high ceilings, and the voluminous silence that magnified the tap of a cane along the floor.

He handed in his requests and sat on the bench with the others waiting for their numbers to flash on the callboard. The year 2000 was coming. In a few months his unemployment insurance ran out. Would he have some work by then? 2000, a triple goose-egg year. Three zips, like smoke-rings off the lips of his boss who regretted, but. Would there be benefits to apply for in the year 2000? How much would a glass of water cost? Will the mutant bacteria find nourishment in New York City? Will these people receive their degrees? Will there be clones? Will they have anything to eat? He could work in a motel, will motels be extinct? Who will confront the tyrannies lurking in computers? Will there be any metal left? Will the name Andy Warhol ring a bell? 2000. Like a locomotive. Like a family of swans. You hold on the neck of the '2' and ride.

His number 129 flashed and he took his book into the North Reading Room, where there were fewer people. The library was one place on the island of Manhattan where you had enough space to enjoy the idea of America in yourself, and didn't feel the Calcutta or Port-au-Prince that the streets were becoming. A few people here and there in the North Room, their reference books fanned out on the table, homesteading in their notebooks with felt-tip pens. He opened his book and read, "But wait a bit. There is more to America's past than appears upon the surface...permanent colonies of Celts, Basques, Libyans, and even Egyptians." He looked up from his book when he heard a cane tapping on the floor. An old woman entered the room, one of the shopping-bag ladies without her shopping-bags, stockings bunched around her ankles, tatters of old drapes flowing from her shoulders. She pompously tossed the frayed ends of her rags over her shoulders as the librarians watched her following the tap of her cane around the room. She stopped at each place to see what the people were reading.

"Don't worry about her. She's crazy. Every day she's here." The swarthy, balding man on Dusty's right, reading books in Italian, leaned over to say that. "Because so am I, so I see her."

Dusty heard the cane stop, and the woman cackling quietly behind him. She leaned over his shoulder and picked up his book. She smelled of rosewater. "America, B.C., America, B.C., by Barry Fell, who never got up." She put the book back down and placed an index card on top of it, and tapped her way out of the room. A message was printed on the card in raised letters: *I'm Mrs. Bread in The Age of Aquarius. Can't make me without yeast.* Dusty folded the card and put it in his pocket.

"What does it say, that card?" the bald man asked. Dusty pulled it out to give it to him, but he held up his hand. "Don't give it to me. I know what it says. She's probably got a son on Wall Street and a big apartment on Central Park West. I come here every day and I'm tired." Dusty put the card back in his pocket.

"But let me tell you, you see me reading in Italian, and so what. I try to keep up with my Italian. I used to live in Italy. I mean I'm American, my family's been here from Italy for three generations, but I went to live in Italy for a while, just to check it out, because I didn't have a father, you know, just my mother, and she didn't know where my father was, she didn't even know who he was. She played around a lot before she got sick, but she was a good woman." He pulled a silver cigarette case from his inside jacket pocket, placed it in front of Dusty, and opened it up. The case held a faded picture of a woman, and was full of fine ashes. "Don't blow on it. That's my mother. I never knew what to do with the ashes, so I carry her around with me. The rest of her I've got sealed in a box that I check in the cloakroom when I come here." He closed the case and took it back. "That's why I wanted to talk to you, because I saw you reading that America, B.C., and I thought maybe that was before Columbus, so I thought I'd say something."

The man leaned back in his chair. Dusty flipped his book open again to some Phoenician symbols found carved in stone in Vermont. Realm of the Mother Goddess, was the caption under the pictures. How amazing, Dusty thought, that they were here, and the Celts and the Libyans, and all of them, and they still are. He turned the page. The man leaned towards him again. Dusty knew that he'd either have to move, or forget reading and let the guy talk. What the hell, Dusty thought, he wasn't committed to the reading. He just woke up in the morning and came to the library. He closed his book.

"I tell you it's Italy where I learned I was American. That's where I became aware of it for sure. I lived there in Lecce, that's in the south, in the heel of the boot. You know where that is?"

"I worked on a ship, and we stopped in Taranto once."

"That's like in the instep. Lecce is close, about ninety kilometers away, but it's a whole world of difference, a different language, different people. I got a job there. I taught English in that town, in an American language school."

"Leche means milk, doesn't it?

"In Spanish, yeah, but in the dialect there it means wolf. There's a big mosaic of a wolf in the pavement of Piazza San Oronzo there, and there's part of a Roman amphitheater excavated right in the middle of that piazza. When I first got there you know I hung out with the students. They were the rich kids. This was '61, and they had their little Fiat millicentos, and we'd run the nine kilometers to the sea at San Cataldo. Beautiful blue sea.

On a clear day you could see across the Adriatic, the mountains of Albania."

"Albania," Dusty repeated. "Amazing."

"Yeah," said the man, sliding his chair closer. "On the road between Lecce and Taranto there's a town where they speak Albanian. It was settled by Albanians. You know what this world is like. Everyone is everywhere." The man stopped talking as a librarian rolled a cartful of books past them up the aisle. Dusty watched the old woman tap her way out of the reading room. Why did she have to tap her cane, if she wasn't blind?

"Yeah, I hung out with my students at first," the man went on. "But then I realized something," he tapped his chest with his fingertips. "That I wasn't one of them. I don't just mean I was American, though I was learning what that meant; but these were rich people. They owned the tobacco plantations. They were the professional people. Some of them talked about their 'contadini', their 'peasants', as if they were lower than animals. They understood to feed the animals, but they complained that these 'disgraziati', they called them, wanted to eat meat every day, wanted shoes. And they were mad because the poor people were deserting their land to earn money in Germany or Belgium or Switzerland. Then I began to feel this American blood in my veins. I mean whatever you say about America, and I'm out of work right now, a poor guy has still got a chance to make it in this country; but there, forget it. See I realized that the peasants these people were talking about were my people, who came to this country to escape fat vultures like themselves, and these rich guys I was hanging out with would never go to America except as a tourist, and my people had to leave Italy, which is a beautiful country, because of jokers like them.

"So I started to ride my bicycle, and take a trip on my own every weekend. Oh was it beautiful. The light was beautiful there, and the colors that would come up in the sky. My skin would touch the air and I'd get all jammed up with sensations. You have to experience what it's like to see an olive tree. I mean the whole volume of it standing in that light, and a thousand years old. You've got to see it for yourself. I mean I felt closer to those olive trees, they made me feel more like being an Italian, and I had more to say to a tree than I did to all the elegant rich guys that I hung around with before. That's why I could never understand in my heart how people, American people could support the Shah, or some of those creeps in South America. But maybe I'm a little nuts.

"There's a town there called Calimera, which means good morning in Greek, and they speak like ancient Greek there. I mean they speak Italian, but that's their dialect, Greek. There's a tiny monument there, a stele given them by the city of Athens, that's inscribed in Greek, *You Are Not A Stranger Here In Calimera*. And you hear the people there calling the sea 'thallosos', and calling a man 'anthropos'. I got a thrill out of that. I mean how far back can you go just by hearing some words? I'd bike to the sea from there, a town called San Foca, with a little church and a priest in a brown cassock, who sat out front in the sun, and two women always scrubbing, and a lot of little kids running around calling him pappa. In the piazza there the fishermen sold 'ricci', sea urchins, and these rich padrones would drive down in their Mercedes, and sit there on a painted chair holding a napkin, their leather coats open, their hats tipped back, while the fishermen cracked the urchins open and with a little spoon would scrape out the orange eggs and lay them on the rich guy's tongue.''

The man paused and looked at Dusty. Dusty lifted the front cover of his book, and let it drop. ''You want to listen to this story some more?''

''Sure,'' Dusty said.

''I should be able to make a buck telling about Italy. They do that. They go around giving lectures on places, and they make money. You know I could kick myself for never taking any pictures while I was there. I could show slides, tell a story, make a buck. I mean Italy is beautiful, and if you live in this city you want to hear about someplace that's beautiful, and you'd pay a couple of bucks to hear about it, wouldn't you? That's what I think.'' The man reached over and touched Dusty's arm. ''You don't have to pay me nothing, though. I'll tell you the rest of the story; I mean, you talk about beauty. You go from San Foca south along the coast, and there are all these watchtowers from the twelfth century built within sight of one another to warn the people about raids from the Saracens, and there are some Mussolini pill-boxes built there too, that the fishermen use as crappers now. I biked that road to get to Torre dell'Orso, my favorite beach. About halfway there are these ruins of Metapica, an ancient city, never been excavated. Just sitting there. So it was time for me to rest, and I went over to sit next to this guy sitting on the sea-wall. He was half asleep, and I saw this little homemade bomb in his hand. The air was real humid. I pulled out my cigarettes and gave him one, but it was so wet we couldn't keep it lit. 'Scirocco,' he said. The wind was full of fine sand they say gets picked up off the Sahara and carried across. 'When the fish come, boom,' he said, making the shape of an explosion with his arms. I asked him if it wasn't illegal to fish with explosives, and he got this big grin on his face because he understood then that I was a foreigner. If you're poor in Italy it's no disgrace, like it is here. You try to make a buck. 'During the war I was in Africa,' he said. 'Then I was in Greece. I was a prisoner there.' He never asked me where I was from, and I never saw him throw that bomb. The water rode up in a funnel of smoke and spume, and I stood up and he still sat there, till the fish began to rise, and glitter on the surface like coins. 'Mo, vediamo,' he said, and disappeared down a stairway carved into the rock. That was one guy I met. A lot of them had real nostalgia about the war. That was the way they had spent their youth, you see, so they reminisced about it. They ate pretty good too, as British prisoners, or American prisoners, don't kid yourself.

"But talk about a beautiful beach with nobody on it, this Torre dell'Orso is the place. It's formed like a shallow bowl with the bluest water and the cliffs on either end shaped like bears. That's why they call it Orso, that means bear. It's the most beautiful place in the world. A pine woods grows right out of the dunes. Even in the summer it's hardly ever crowded. In the fall and spring, nobody, maybe this old man I talked to once who sits there when it's warm under a black umbrella. That water was like diving into satin bedsheets. It was like floating on a kiss. I felt so good it was like I'd just been born when I came out of there. But that old guy under the umbrella told me to be careful. I think he was a little nuts. He told me about giants under the water."

"About what?" Dusty asked.

"He talked about under all the oceans, these big giants, and that they would rise up. He really believed in them, so that was why he stayed there whenever he could and watched the water. He probably thought it was a relative. He always brought his lunch."

"What was this guy's name?" Dusty asked.

"Domenico Modugno. I don't know what his name was. What difference does it make? Just a goofy old guy, probably dead by now. If he's not, you go there, you see him."

"I want to tell you I saw one of those giants," Dusty said, leaning towards the man. "It was under the water."

"That's okay with me. That's good you saw one. Not everyone sees one. I never saw one."

Dusty turned to the picture of the Cerne giant in his book, an enormous figure carved by the ancients in the chalk bedrock of Dorset, in the south of England.

"That guy's got a dick if I ever saw one," the man said. "Thirty-five feet long, that's what it says. This old guy never mentioned anything about dicks. Just he was waiting for this giant to come up."

"That's not so strange," Dusty said, stretching as he looked around the room.

"Hey, look, I'll lay off if you want to read. I understand when some people don't care about Italy." He looked as if he'd been scolded and beaten back. He withdrew into his seat.

"No. No. Keep telling it," Dusty said.

"I mean it's such a beautiful place. People like to hear about beautiful places. And I've been there." The man slipped his hand inside one of the books, and slowly looked up to the ceiling, as if searching in the high shadows for the cause of the sadness that had come down on him. "I mean you got to know who you are, or else who are you? You know what I mean? That's why I went to Italy, to find out. I mean..."

"Okay. Go ahead," Dusty said. "Tell me about it."

"So then," he sighed. "There were these kids standing by my bicycle. I mean they were teenagers, and in my neighborhood you see a bunch of teenagers and you stay away. They're mean. They burn bums with gasoline. But this wasn't my neighborhood. I mean this was big Italy, not Little Italy, and there's a difference in the people. So I went over to them. They were just some curious kids, because they'd never seen a bike like mine before.

"'Deutsch?' one of them asked when I got there.

"'No,' I said, and I didn't want to tell them I was American because to those poor people that always meant money, especially to the kids, and it always got stupid after they knew you were American. So I explained about the bike, and how I bought it in Holland, and how it worked with the gears and axle casing, and they thought I was Dutch, but I told them I wasn't Dutch. They went through Greek and Danish and Portugese, and even Chinese for a joke. Then one of them asked me what was my name. I said 'Salvatore.'" He stopped for a moment. "My name is Salvatore, by the way. What's your name?"

Dusty hesitated, because he couldn't figure how to put

his name into this story. "Okay. My name is Dusty." He held out his hand.

Salvatore took Dusty's hand in both his. "Dusty. Very pleased. What kind of name is Dusty? That's not a New York name, that's an American name. That's a John Wayne name from the West. You know how you say that in Italian? You say, 'polveroso'. It would sound real funny. Like my name means 'savior' in English. Mr. Polveroso meet Mr. Savior. You see what I mean? Like a joke. So those kids, they said, 'You're not Italian?' and I said, 'No.' 'Then what are you?' they asked, and I didn't answer. 'Was your father Italian?' they asked. 'I don't have a father,' I said.

"'What do you mean you don't have a father? Everyone has a father.'

"'I don't have a father.'

"They started getting real close to me and I was kind of jumpy because I didn't know what was going on, so I said, 'Va bene, va bene, Americano sono. I'm an American.' Just to end it right there. They got real quiet, and I was a little spooked, so I threw my leg over my bike to show them I was ready to leave. 'Un Americano bastardo,' one of them whispered, and he rubbed his thumb against his fingers in the gesture that means money. American means money to them. I started rolling my bike, and they pressed up against me. 'Eh joe, gotta cigarette?' one of them said. I started to pedal away and they ran along with me. 'Eh Joe, choongum. Eh Joe, pretty leelseester.' They'd heard maybe stories about the wartime from their parents. I got out of there, because you see what I mean about telling them you're American. Their parents told them about

American soldiers.

"I was better off with the landscape than getting up close to the people, but I could understand that the people were part of the landscape too. Poverty people, poverty landscape. The salento, that's what they call the heel of the boot, is like a limestone shelf, mostly rock, with soil deposited like in pools here and there that the people work, slave over, and olive trees hanging on for a thousand years. From just north of San Foca I take a shortcut inland to the highway to Lecce. This is a dirt road, and as soon as I hit it my tire goes flat, so I had to walk. This was a high, flat, rocky place with a little soil here and there, and the old men with little donkeys and wooden plows, and women in black bending over this pale green young autumn growth, and girls bent over in plaid smocks and red kerchiefs, and the old women in black, beating clumps of sod with short-handled spades. All the young men had gone north to make the money, and I kept thinking as I walked my bike along, that this ruin of a place, with people of the ruins, was my place, my olive trees growing contorted around the stone walls, like the bent bodies of the people working, and that blue was mine of the sky, of the stones, of the olives, and the clarity of the air around the blue fig trees. And these people were singing these strange songs, monotone, like Arabs singing, slowly, slowly, almost no melody, poor songs, my songs, impoverished as the soil. I could stay there forever was what I felt as I walked along. I had always been there, was what I felt. You see what I mean, Dusty, how you get to know who you are, and sometimes it's so strange."

Dusty looked around the room. The sound of Salvatore's

voice rode out to fill all the enormous space of the library, but no one seemed bothered by it.

"You're lookin' around, Dusty. Listen. The story'll be over in a minute, just a little more I want to tell you now, although I gotta say there's a lot more stories I can tell. But let me finish this one. Okay. By the time I got to the main road to Lecce the sun was going down. I sat for a minute under this big fig tree. I was tired. The 'tramontagne', which is a wind from the north, began blowing down with the evening, and it was chilly. Not many cars passed at this time of night because everyone in town was dressed up, walking on the streets, and talking about what's for dinner. Then I saw these headlights coming from San Cataldo, and I got up and crossed the road because maybe I could get a ride. This car was coming real slow like the driver expected the road to disappear. It was a big Ford station wagon, and a woman was driving, and her husband next to her, and some kids in the back. When they spotted me they sped up. I shouted, 'Hey, I'm an American. Hey. God bless America,' as they whizzed by. They knew I was there, but they didn't even look at me. There was a sticker on their rear bumper that said, *We Are An Air Force Family*. I was tired, and for some reason that pissed me off, that they'd gone by so fast, and the Air Force family stuff. I shouted, 'Porca Miseria; putana Americana,' which are curses in the Italian language.

"So I picked up my bicycle and started walking. Soon I got to where the road slopes slightly downward and you begin to see Lecce, the campanile and old buildings. Behind me was this vermilion sunset haze, and the stones of Lecce in front of me glowing orange. I felt like I was in the Bible, Dusty, going to Jerusalem, or Bethlehem, or Gomorrah. Then this cart, they call them 'traini', one of these painted carts with big wooden spoked wheels, pulled out of a field next to me, and the driver stopped his little horse, told me to throw my bike on top of the pile of artichokes in back, and to climb up front with him. We started off. The night was on top of us. He pointed his whip at Sirius spraying its colors out of the north, and Lecce looked so beautiful in front of us, all blue and yellow lights and red neon, glittering like a sequinned leg.

"I told him about my whole trip, and that I'd walked more than eight kilometers, and he sympathized. I really liked this guy, a quiet guy, one of the poor people who have no flesh on their faces, big hollows scooped out of their cheeks and necks where the hunger settles in.

"'It wouldn't have taken long if I didn't get a flat,' I said. 'I ride my bicycle all over.'

"'When I was young I rode a bicycle; but I'm older now, and my little horse has four legs. But it wasn't long ago that I'd take my bicycle from Merine to Gallipoli to see Giovannino, my friend. But he's dead now, a long time.'

"He whispered little phrases to his horse for a while, and teased him with the whip. The horse was a brown, hollow-flanked veteran who was happy to trot along, though not too fast. I was glad the Air Force family had passed me by. I really liked this old guy, Dusty. I didn't know why, but I liked him.

"'You speak Italian well,' he told me. 'But now you have to learn Leccese. It's a beautiful language.' You see it's not like here, Dusty, where there are accents, but you understand American wherever you go; but ten miles away in southern Italy and there can be another language.

'''Why should I learn Leccese?' I asked.

'''Why?' he repeated. 'Because it's easy. Because you know Italian already. Because you live in Lecce. Leccese is very beautiful. It's not like Barese.'

'''Barese is ugly,' I agreed.

'''You've heard it. Barese is very ugly. Leccese is the best language. You come to Merine, to my house, and I'll teach you Leccese. You just ask for Odiseo. Everyone knows me there.'

''I promised to go see him, although you know I never did, and in my heart I feel bad about it, Dusty. He told me this story that he said was a song, but he didn't remember the song. There were two dogs, one from Lecce, and one from Bari, who meet on a road. The dog from Bari has a luscious piece of meat in his mouth, and the Leccese dog is very hungry. So the Leccese dog approaches the Barese dog and asks him where he's from. The Barese dog is not very smart, but he's proud of his city, and he answers, 'Sono da Baaaaaaaaari,' pronouncing the broad, extended 'a' of the Barese accent, and that makes him open his mouth very wide, so the piece of meat drops to the ground. The Leccese dog quickly snatches up the meat and holds it in his mouth tightly. The Barese dog is a little embarrassed but confident that he can get the meat back using the same trick. 'Where are you from?' he asks the Leccese dog. 'Sono di Lecce,' says the Leccese dog, in the clipped, clench-toothed Leccese accent, the meat still held in his mouth, and he trots away with the meat. So you see how good the Leccese is. Smart language, he tells me.

''I asked him if he was always from Lecce. 'Of course I

am always from Lecce,' he said.

'''And is your father from Lecce?'

'''My father?' He laughed and laughed.

'''Yes. Your father could come from somewhere else.'

''He put his arm around my shoulder, still laughing. 'Figlio mio,' he said. 'My father was the wind, or a plow in the furrows of the earth of Otranto, or a fig tree in winter with no leaves. That was my father. Who knows who my father was?'

''I looked at him while what he was saying sank in. And suddenly, Dusty, this thrill came over me. 'So then you're a bastard,' I shouted. 'You are a bastard.'

''Dusty, I was never so happy to call someone a bastard. 'Si, figlio mio, pur troppo,' he said, and shrugged his shoulders. 'Who knows where he's born, or where he'll die?'

'''But so am I a bastard,' I shouted, and I stood up in the little cart and waved my arms. And I sat down and threw an arm over his shoulder, and he threw one over mine, and he began to sing a song in Leccese, translating a difficult word or two for me into Italian. This was a song about Maria, who takes a basket of clothes out to wash, and bends her broad back over the tub; and the song was about her breasts that slip out of her blouse, and they are as big as the moon, and they are magnificent.''

Salvatore stopped talking. He opened one of his books and riffled the pages. Dusty blinked and looked around again. His mind as if it had been dilated to adjust to the story, had to readjust to the library.

''That's the story,'' said Salvatore. He closed his books and stacked them. ''So you're probably wondering why a guy like me, I graduated from N.Y.U., is out of work. Well I'll tell you. I had a job, Dusty, and I got laid off."

"I got laid off too," said Dusty.

"That's what I figured. That's why you're reading." Salvatore closed his books. "I still say a guy ought to be able to make some bucks in this city telling stories about Italy. You just need the right connections. It's a crime what goes on today." Salvatore stood up. "It's been a pleasure talking to you, Dusty. I never talked to anyone named Dusty before. And that was a story just for you. Now I gotta go get my mother and take her home. You know she worked her whole life and put me through college, and I graduated from N.Y.U., and I graduated with honors, and now I can't even find a job, and that's a crime, Dusty. That's a crime against my mother's ashes."

Salvatore left. Dusty sat staring at the cover of *America, B.C.* He had chosen to read that book for some reason that was muddled in his mind at this point. It was to get the information, to center himself in his idleness, and rebuild his resources. He couldn't open the book again that morning. It was almost noon. The numbers from his two other books were still lit on the callboard. Okay, he said to himself, back to the street for the time being, back to America A.D., and a sandwich in the crowd.

He bought a felafel at a tiny counter on 42nd Street, facing the library. This America A.D. was Arabs on the street, and African women in dashikis, and Chasids in black, and saffron-robed monks from Sri Lanka, and black kids prowling in sneakers, and bag-ladies at the waste-bins, and a cripple with a flute and a hatful of coins, and Puerto Rican messengers on skateboards, and glutinous packs of Japanese tourists, a moving frieze projected onto 42nd Street as if it were a screen for the spontaneous cinematics of this whole planet called The Earth.

Dusty threw his napkin into the trash and pulled out the index card the old woman had given him. He looked at the message again and was about to throw it away when he saw the bibliographical entry typed on the other side: Dent, P.P.; BATS OF THE AMERICAS, Baltimore, 1884; 3 Vols. illust. 301 Plates. Bats, he thought, and he looked up and down the street at people off for lunch or going back to work. For him it was either a stroll up Fifth Avenue to the Museum of Modern Art, or it was bats. He looked at the reference again. P.P. Dent. Illustrated. And why not bats? It gave him a sense of employment on a December afternoon.

The Dent volumes were tucked away in the rare print room at the end of a hallway on the library's fifth floor. Dusty had to be fingerprinted, give several references, and explain that he was writing a book about bats, before they led him to the locked gate. The librarian sat on a high stool at the other side of the room at a shelf-like desk. He was a sloppy gentleman in his mid-forties though his threadbare tweed suit, several sizes too small now, but probably a good fit before he put on weight, showed that he once had cared more about his appearance. A single incandescent light shined on the crossword puzzle held to the table with a fold of his belly-flesh. His pencil he held poised above the puzzle like a dart that when he turned seemed ready to be launched at Dusty.

"You want in," he said, as he unlocked the gate. "I

smell felafel. If I knew you could have brought me a sandwich." He grabbed Dusty's hands and scrutinized them. The librarian's pudgy fingers were scrubbed pink and carefully manicured. "Only pencils in here, you know. Not even ball-points allowed in here." He held up Dusty's hands. "Now take those into the washroom and scrub them up there. Give me your book request first. Dry them good too."

When Dusty came out he found the books laid out on a piece of green felt. He sat down and opened them. They were large format, with almost no text. The pictures were carefully done and minutely elaborated etchings of bats of every habitat and species known at the time to P.P. Dent, who was the John James Audubon of the bat world. These winged mammals are held repugnant, even sinister, in the bestiaries of the West, though for the Chinese they bring good luck, and the Maya worshipped them, called one of their eighteen months, Zotz, or bat, and one of their gods, Cama-Zotz, is depicted as a bat who holds a sacrificial knife in one hand, and in the other a severed head. The work of P.P. Dent, because of superstition and prejudice, has been kept, like its subject, in the shadows.

Dusty noticed that aside from the librarian the only other person in the room was a man of ascetic appearance poised over a book of pictures at the second table. Like a praying mantis he was utterly still, only his mouth parts moving, as if he were actually taking the pictures in.

"Where'd you buy your felafel?" The librarian came up behind Dusty to examine his pencils.

"Across the street on 42nd."

"They make better on 6th Avenue. They give more

there." He leaned over Dusty's back. "So you like the bats?"

"This book is interesting. It's beautiful." Dusty leaned back.

"So you think they taste good?"

Dusty looked at the librarian. "What?"

"The bats. You know they eat the bats in some places." He was grinning. Lines of saliva gleamed from the corners of his mouth like stretch marks.

"I've never had the opportunity to taste one."

"Well, who knows what you'll eat?" The librarian turned away and talked to himself as he shuffled back to his stool. "They eat rats already in this city. In a few years everyone's gonna be hungry. What are they gonna eat then?" He settled onto his stool and turned back to Dusty. "Lizards. Snakes. Sparrows. Roaches. Bats. Bats. Bats."

Dusty was relieved when the librarian settled back into his puzzle. The pictures were beautiful to look at, and it was interesting to imagine P.P. Dent descending into the caves with carbide lamps and candles to sketch the creatures where they slept, shadows of stalactites waving like the flags of hell. What a commitment to the darkness. He showed each species as it flew, as it slept, as it fed, and recorded such minutely observed details as the suck-pads on the foot of the tropical South American disc-winged bat, and the death's head pattern on the body of the black and white bat of the Southwest. Victorian mores didn't restrain him from showing the bats giving birth, nursing their young, even fornicating as they hung upside down. Dent sometimes luxuriated in sentimentality, one plate of a large, female red bat clutching its offspring to its breast in a crack in the bark of a large hickory. Its teeth are bared in protective defiance as a huge horned owl swoops down, wings spread wide, claws about to snatch.

One picture in particular captured Dusty's interest. This was of some fruit bats native to Haiti, flying around a mango tree and landing on the fruit. It is late afternoon in this detailed etching. In the background a garden party is in progress at a typical French Colonial manor. Barefoot black servants in colonial dress carry trays of food to the wealthy white people sitting under the gaslamps. What first interested him was that he knew the Haitian revolution spanned the turn of the eighteenth century, and by 1884 Haiti had been for a long time an independent black republic, free of slavery and colonialism, though not of internal tyranny. So for P.P. Dent, who lived in New Orleans, and was from a Mississippi family of impoverished aristocracy, this was a bit of ante-bellum nostalgia, to spice up his design, which was otherwise impeccably accurate. A man leaned over the balcony on the second floor of the manor, talking to a young woman holding a suitcase on the patio below. French doors opened behind the man into a large room. Although the print was black and white the walls of the room had a blue glow that drew the eye to the interior.

P.P. Dent was a master, in a way. The etching was done with great ingenuity, in uncanny detail. Dusty kept coming back to it, not to look at the bats so much as to examine the background tableau that took up just a small portion of the whole design. He kept looking into the glowing room behind the French doors. To see it better he needed a magnifying glass. He looked around the room.

The librarian was snoozing on his puzzle. The other man hadn't moved in his seat, as if his bones were riveted in place under his grey suit. Dusty approached him on the chance he'd have one. He was examining some nineteenth century fantastic drawings, projecting cities into the twentieth century. His eyes scanned the pictures from left to right, top to bottom, as if he were reading a text. When Dusty asked him for a magnifying glass he pointed, without looking up, to one side of the librarian, where there was a compact edition of the *Oxford English Dictionary*, with a magnifying glass in the little drawer on top of the slipcase. Dusty sneaked around the sleeping librarian and took the magnifier.

He could see through the lens that the glow on the walls was not produced just by a stippling effect, as he had thought; but each of the dots was a minute etching of a tiny bat, and the blue was the blue of their eyes. Their eyes had to have been tipped in after the etching was complete, with the care of a master miniaturist, who used a single delicate hair dipped in some microscopically atomized cerulean pigment. He'd heard a story once from a friend of his brother about some tiny bats like these. They cover the wall of a room, he remembered. Deep in the shadows of this room he made out the dim outline of a body, a head with no features, no hair, no ears, like a skull. He knew who it was. And the man on the balcony looked like himself, with his beard and stocky frame, and at the table a man who looked like his brother's friend, Fletcher, who had told him the story of the bats; and the host, at the head of the table, was tall and lanky like the other man in this library room. He put the magnifier down and leaned back in his chair. His own breath made him dizzy. He closed his eyes to try to stop the sense of disorientation that rose from the base of his spine.

"You can't trust the equipment." Dusty opened his eyes and looked at the man from the other table now standing behind him. "It's all defective. Eyes. Ears. It's all used stuff. Borrowed equipment." His arms swung back and forth as he spoke as if he were pumping out the words. "Do you know what you see?" He pointed his fingers at his eyes. "Do you trust your eyes?"

"You'd do me a favor," said Dusty, "if you'd take a look at this picture for me." He handed the man the magnifier. "Tell me what you see."

"You can't trust them," he said, examining the magnifier as if it were a flower; then he bent over the picture and looked at it through the lens.

"What do you see?"

"Edges."

"I mean what's there? Who do you see?"

The man looked up at Dusty. "You have to be careful. Shadings. The color blue. You don't verify too much at once. Not with this equipment."

The guy was a fanatic, Dusty thought. A little crazy. "Look again. Does anyone there look like me?"

"You," said the man, scrutinizing Dusty. "Another face." He looked back at the picture. "Aha. There you are." He pointed at the figure on the balcony.

"And that looks like you," said Dusty, pointing to the figure at the head of the table.

"Of course. The host. I'm sick of it, frankly. But who knows what I look like? To look is through eyes, and that's a fog with the best allotment here. You can't trust the stuff."

"But we see the same thing in this picture. We see ourselves."

"Coincidence. Everything is coincidence. I don't know if I have to explain it to you or not." He leaned over Dusty with his body at an impossible forty-five degree angle, as if he were welded together at the hips. "We live on a grid of experience throughout which coincidence is maximized at the interstices. Everything happens all the time, and that we achieve these apparent congruencies of perception is the result mostly of conditioning, patterning, programs. Similar programs. Just nearly the same. Just enough so you can follow me. Do you follow me?"

Dusty had been a science fiction buff when he was twelve, and remembered following threads of speculation such as this. "You are a metaphysician," he said.

"Not at all. Not at all."

"How did we get into this picture?"

"All of us are somewhat human, my good man, and time is a rolling cylinder that slowly enfolds us. Partly people, and part of it is in pictures."

"I'm not sure I get that, but I don't think I agree with it."

"Proves my point," said the man, straightening up. "A slightly different program. I want to ask you one question, and you are not obliged to answer." The librarian woke up, flapping his lips. "Are you very sure," the man asked, "that you live on the planet Earth? I mean do you know that this is the planet Earth?"

"Of course I know it," Dusty said.

"Are you quite sure? Absolutely?" His voice resonated down his whole body and filled the room.

The librarian turned to them, with his arms folded over his belly. He glared at the two men through bloodshot eyes, and walked over to them. "You have finished with the books, and are through with that magnifier, please hold your conversations outside the room so as not to disturb the other readers." He yawned.

"There are no other readers," Dusty said.

"I read more books in an hour than you can browse in a week," the librarian replied. "And when you come back bring me a felafel sandwich. From 6th Avenue. Lots of sauce. I have an appetite."

That picture was a coincidence of some magnitude, that he would have to return to for sure. Dusty and the tall man descended the stairs together. The man talked, looking down on Dusty as if he were dropping words on his head. "So you're one who believes that this is the Earth. You'd even say that you know that this is Earth."

"We say Earth. That's just the name we give to this planet," Dusty said. "We give names. That's what makes us human."

"Don't depend on that. Don't depend on being human either. This is not even the planet you might think we have named. This is not that place, and you are not that human, and I'm sure I can show it to you. This is not even the quotes Earth."

New York was full of kooks, Dusty thought. You step into one of their closets and it's your own fault if you're subject to their harangues, or worse. He expected the man to go on expanding his theory, but he fell into a peculiar

grinning silence. They reached the balcony above the
main lobby and looked down on the people staring into
the showcases. The man was still silent. Dusty followed
him down the wide, shallow steps curving to the lobby.
He looked up at the man a moment, who was scanning the
space at his eye level.

"I didn't catch your name," Dusty said to break the
silence, and to perhaps start to take his leave. "My name
is Dusty." He offered a handshake, and noticed his palm
was sweating.

The man took Dusty's hand by the thumb, lifted it to his
face and scrutinized it. "John," he said. "I'm John Doe."

The name made Dusty feel uncomfortable. It could have
been phony, in which case Dusty was sorry he'd said his
real name. Or it could actually be his name. "So you're the
John Doe," Dusty said uneasily, wishing he hadn't. "I've
always wanted to meet you."

"It's too late," said John Doe. He wiped Dusty's hand on
his jacket and let it go.

They stepped out onto the library plaza, above the gaze
of stone lions north and south. It was unseasonably warm,
the air full of smoke, and all the crowds were out. Every
horn was honking. Tourists gazed from their buses.
Jackhammers crackled above wailing compressors at the
edge of the broken pavement. The intersection of 42nd
and 5th was jammed up. A young woman with a purple
streak in her hair climbed into a trash barrel and jumped
up and down while some tourists took snapshots and
her boyfriend shouted, "Maureen, you jerk." Some
'Moonies' on the corner chalked out their cosmology on
a blackboard while the police watched. A haunt of bag-

pipes wound through the noise like a thread of smoke.

"There," said John Doe from the top of the steps. "This is some proof of it."

"What proof?"

"Dusty, my gentle fellow, this is not the planet Earth, believe me." He swept his arm in an arc across the panorama. "How can you call this the planet Earth?"

A cop prodded two drunks asleep, embraced at the base of one of the lions. A line of 'Guardian Angels', in red berets, counting cadence, marched cockily past the police on the corner, and down the steps of the subway. Some brakes screeched and a man flew up over the hood of a taxi and fell to the street. The driver jumped from his cab and shouted at the man lying on the pavement, "Cross at the corners, asshole. Get off your cloud." The man got up, holding his hip, and collapsed again as he lunged towards the cab driver. Cops moved his way like blue pellets through the crowd.

"They told you this was the Earth from the beginning, and you believed it. This stuff is not the Earth, Dusty."

"Who told me? I don't remember anyone telling me."

"It's the ones who programmed all this fake conscious-ness out here. All this confusion and mess. The actual Earth people. The ones who live on the real Earth, and use this as the dump."

A wailing ambulance pushed around the traffic down the sidewalk through the crowd. The victim rose again and shouted at the police who grabbed him. "No. No. I got a meeting. Five minutes I got it." He tried to jump through the crowd, but the cops restrained him. Attendants rolled a stretcher out of the ambulance and they tied the man

down. "No," he screamed. They slid him into the
ambulance. Dusty and John Doe started down the steps.

"Maybe the Age of Aquarius is coming, Dusty, but not
on this Dump. See, you never thought about it before, but
the real Earth is beautiful, full of intricate trees that speak
to you in the night. Happy humans. Tidy winds. Water
chuckling in clear rivers. What have we got here we could
claim to be Earth? Look it over, Dusty. Have you ever
proved to yourself that this stuff was the Earth? No. You
were told once, and that was that. You went to the
planetarium, looked at the orrery there, someone pointed
at the third planet from the sun, and said that was it. How
could you doubt it? I don't blame you, but I suggest that
some night if you're in a place where you can see them
you look up at the stars. Spend some time looking, then
you'll know something is wrong. You'll realize you're not
in the right place. Not a chance."

The crowd around the accident was dispersing. Dusty
noticed a man crumpled up in the street, moaning. "If you
look at the stars, if you're lucky enough to be some place
where you can see them, and you look at them long
enough, you'll notice that it feels a little precarious."

There was blood around him and he was twisted as if his
hip and collarbone were broken. They had taken the
wrong one to the hospital. Dusty approached a cop. "Hey,
they made a mistake." He pointed out the guy still on the
pavement. "That's the one who was hit."

John Doe followed him. "You look at the stars and feel
like you're going to fall off." He was oblivious to what had
happened on the street. "And it's not really comfortable
underfoot, and you'll feel like you've got somewhere to

go, but no way to get there. Maybe you fall down. Some vague intuition tells you you should be somewhere else. Another place, another orbit. A peaceful place. The Earth is a beautiful place."

Cops prodded the victim on the street. He moaned, half conscious, like a drunk. Dusty grabbed the cop's shoulder. "Hey, don't hurt him. He's the one who was hit by the cab. The other guy was a mistake." The cop turned on Dusty, and shoved a nightstick into his ribs. "Okay, wise guy. Get away from here. Just move on."

"That's why they don't like to let you see the stars." John Doe pulled Dusty away. "They don't want you to know."

"That guy you're poking at is the one who got hurt," Dusty shouted at the cops. "He needs help." The cops ignored him.

"All of us are hurt," said John Doe. "We're all the Victims, not the People. That's why we're here, and not on the Earth. The real People on the real Earth call this the Dump, where we are, and we don't know about it. We're too stupid."

"Leave me alone. You're fucking crazy," Dusty turned on John Doe.

"That could be true," John Doe shrugged. "With the equipment we get to work with. They keep all the up-to-date new models, and we're the wrecks, and they throw all their old used-up parts into us. It's mostly gone when we get it, and then we wear it out."

"We've got to help that poor guy."

"You can't help anybody, not with the equipment we've got. If we got a fresh pair of eyes, or a fresh sniffer, then it would be a different story. Do you think we'd smell what we smell out here? If we had some elbows, like the People get on Earth, then maybe it would be a different story." Dusty watched them manhandle the accident victim into a police car with the two drunks. It rolled away, lights spinning, siren blazing a trail through the traffic.

"We get this skin, Dusty, and misery is the tattoo that comes. It's our skin. Buddha says misery is inevitable. But look at it. Buddha was a ringer, from the real Earth, and so was Jesus and Krishna and Mohammed. They were sent here to keep us off balance with messages they call spiritual. Make us think we should be satisfied in misery. The opiate of the people, Dusty. Karl Marx was as smart as a Dumpling can get. Avatars, so-called, spreading propaganda, sent here from the real Earth. Attain Nirvana, enlightenment to escape misery. I'll tell you, Dusty, no one on this whole wide Dump attains. Earthlings come here and radiate this aura so Dumplings follow them like sheep. On the real Earth, by the way, that aura is standard equipment." John Doe grinned like a kid who has just made some points on a debating team. "So tell me now, Dusty. Do you still believe this is the Earth underfoot?"

"Okay. I've got to think about it."

"Good. Think. But remember that even when you think you're using worn-out equipment." John Doe looked across the street. "There she is." Dusty saw the old shopping-bag lady who had given him the index card with the Dent reference. She was waving at John Doe, and he started across the street towards her. That he hadn't said goodby made Dusty feel a little uneasy. Did John Doe expect him to follow? He looked up and down the avenue through the thick, dusty air, and felt disoriented again, as he had when he looked away from the print earlier. The man was probably nuts, but there was a grain of truth in John Doe's rap. What better to do with the rest of this day than to follow a grain of truth?

He crossed the street to where John Doe was kissing the woman who had given Dusty the message that had led him into this experience.

The woman had been waiting for John Doe. Dusty was amazed at how much younger she was than she appeared to be in the library. When he was introduced to her Dusty mentioned that she had given him the reference card that led him finally back to meet her again through John Doe. "Amazing coincidence," was all she said. She had less trouble keeping up with John Doe's long strides down the street than Dusty did. She told him her name really was Bread, Lavinia Bread. Her first husband was an architect, had designed the famous Bread Pavilion in Caracas. She left him as soon as she met John Doe. "He's so crazy. I love him. He understands everything." She looked now like a woman in her mid-thirties, and getting younger... She shook her head and smiled when she noticed Dusty staring at her.

"Yeah. Okay. I forget how different this looks," she said. "I used to dress normal, but then I started to get real angry when some jokers on the street tried to hit on me. I got violent. Once I put the point of my umbrella through a man's cheek. He was just some poor jerk on the subway rubbing my ass with his hand on his briefcase. I followed him into the street. I hate it. They make you feel like a piece of meat on a hook. I figured best to put an end to it. I'd rather be disgusting and repugnant. No one gets hurt. I get some peace of mind if I look like a bag lady. Now I love to be out and walking the streets to see what's going on, and some jerk doesn't come up to me any more. I've even begun to enjoy looking like this."

"I think she's really ugly," John Doe put a hand on top of her head, "and that's why she loves me." They turned the corner at 52nd Street and walked towards the East River. A cold wind followed them, clearing the air.

"But I don't think she's ugly at all. I don't think you're ugly," Dusty said.

"Watch your mouth." She glared at him. "I don't have to talk to you." She spit into the street.

"It's just like I was saying, Dusty; if she were on Earth she'd have a chance to be beautiful, but on the Dump beauty has to be in the eye of the beholder, and with this equipment." He dolefully pointed at his eyes. "We're all rotten beholders."

"This is the man who knows," said Lavinia. "He knows his shit, and he knows his Shinola." She touched his shoulder. "And he's really stupid too."

"And you look like garbage, Lavinia. You look disgusting." She put her arms around him and kissed his jacket. A peculiar way to get along, thought Dusty. But not so peculiar as what was to follow.

They lived in a spacious apartment overlooking the East River. Lavinia had two little girls, six and four, both pretty. When Dusty pointed this out to John Doe he explained that pretty is possible at first, but it soon begins to fill up with junk. The apartment was full of elegant stuff: fine rugs, original Eames chairs and a Mies Van der Rohe sofa. A big Frank Stella painting arced across one wall, a glass table-top sat on some structures by Sol Lewitt, a box by Joseph Cornell on the mantel, a series of drawings of tools by Jim Dine along the walls of a hall, all high-priced contemporary art. "I know what you're looking at," said John Doe. "Once I used to believe in it, but let me tell you now that all this stuff is no good."

"And I'll tell you, John Doe, that I'm out of work, and just one of these pieces could support me for the rest of my life."

"And what good would that do you? To what end? This is all a compromise. This stuff just gilds the illusion. That we need it at all is part of the Dumpling's burden. Just to get the slightest sense of exaltation. On the real Earth no one needs artists to create the sense of order and beauty."

"And what do they do when they're out of work, and they're broke?"

"No work. No money required there." John Doe handed Dusty a snifter of fine plum brandy. "So have a seat for a minute. There they don't even need a chair to hold their equipment. Comfortable is built-in. But you sit down. I want you to meet someone. I'll be right back."

Lavinia was reading to her girls in another room. John Doe left him alone. Comfortable built-in, he thought. What an idea. He crossed the room to sit in one of the chairs, and relaxed under the umbrella of rich plum brandy. A ringing of bells came quietly from the hidden speakers. He sipped and closed his eyes. The little girls giggled with their mother somewhere deep in the enormous apartment. Then as if his ears had been plugged all sound suddenly stopped. He opened his eyes. In the silence in the opposite corner of the room in an exact duplicate chair he sat in was what appeared at first as an apparition, a man with a face nearly a skull, no nose, no ears, no lips. This was E. Pouce. He recognized him and rose in his seat, then settled back.

"What are you doing here?" The silence until the response seemed interminable, then E. Pouce opened his jaws and issued back the question as if he had squeezed all the juice from the words, a sound so coarse and sinister and slow that it made Dusty squirm. "What . . . are . . . you . . . doing . . . here . . ."

"Do you know John Doe?"

There was a grim pause. "Do . . . you . . . know . . . John . . . Doe . . ."

The words floated back into the drafts of the room like empty husks.

"It's been a long time since we had a chance to talk," said Dusty. It had always been unnerving enough to look at E. Pouce, but now it was just as painful to listen to his dessicated voice echoing back from some caves in the valleys of the dead. They both stood up when John Doe came back into the room.

"So you two have got acquainted?" said John Doe.

"We've been acquainted," said Dusty. "We went to school together."

"School . . . together . . ." E. Pouce echoed.

"But we don't have much to say to each other any more."

". . . any . . . more . . ."

"Nothing to talk to him about, Dusty. Once you meet

him, that's the lesson. Since you already know him..."

"At school he was a playboy, and a perpetrator of nasty pranks to humiliate his fraternity brothers. The revolutionaries thought he was a revolutionary and the fascists took him as a friend." Dusty mused. "But now there's something more sinister, something horrible and self-destructive, some fascination for...I'm afraid to try to say it. It's not just what's happened to his face."

"It's perfect, Dusty. The face is right on. That's what I've been rapping to you about." John Doe leaned towards Dusty, his arms swinging. "Refuse the equipment. Trash the trash. Nose in the nosebin. Eyes in the eyebag."

Dusty looked at the spectre in the other corner, and noticed that the eyes were blank. E. Pouce had given up his eyes. He felt his heart fill with trembling ghosts.

"The way he acts, that's the way you get him," John Doe went on. "For his visionary acts, that will finalize this Dump." Lavinia entered the room in pale blue silk, followed by her daughters dressed like her in miniature. Her hair that had been pulled back and covered with a sooty bandana now flowed down her shoulders in an auburn wave. "Finalize the seven seas," E. Pouce said.

"He does everything out of greed, the meanest heart. Profit."

"Not so. Does he need more profit? Just he knows that our imperfect story needs a perfect ending. To finalize the atmosphere."

"I have this horrible feeling," Dusty said.

"E. Pouce is the embodiment of everything I've been explaining to you. An end to the claptrap of species perpetuated in futility."

"That what I really need to do is kill him," Dusty shut his eyes to say this, and felt his words echoed back immediately by E. Pouce. "I . . . need . . . to . . . kill . . . him . . ." Saying this E. Pouce stepped towards them across the room. He walked directly to Dusty and faced him, as if he could see through the red-rimmed opaque white scars that were his eyes.

"This boy has a problem, this Dusty Wier. And that problem is..." E. Pouce reached out as if he would pinch Dusty's cheek, but Dusty brushed his hand away. "That he's got no sense of humor."

"Where are your lips, E. Pouce?" Dusty said.

"Drinking water finalized," said John Doe in his revery.

"I kissed them goodby, Dusty Wier." E. Pouce turned to John Doe. "This boy needs some dusting off. He needs a change of style."

"Hey, like honey..." John Doe said.

"I want the girls to say goodnight and go to bed," Lavinia interrupted.

". . . cancer drips through the lost ozone E. Pouce."

Dusty looked at Lavinia and the girls so blue and red in the madness of the room as if in them was some kind of hope. She lifted the youngest girl, and he picked up the other who pressed her warm lips to his cheek.

"So we went to school together," E. Pouce said, "and he learned and I didn't. Or maybe I learned something, and he didn't. This boy needs to go back to school."

John Doe extended his hand towards the face of the girl in Lavinia's arms and she kissed it. "That's the vision. That's the truth turned through E. Pouce. The end of the Dump." Lavinia carried the girl to E. Pouce and Dusty said "No" and closed his eyes when the little one leaned with her lips puckered towards the fleshless face. The girl in his arms squirmed and jumped to the floor. Her mother picked her up and she too kissed E. Pouce.

"Sorry to hear you're out of work, Dusty Wier." Dusty stepped back as E. Pouce approached him again. "It won't be hard to find you a job for the time being."

"You girls go to bed. I'll be in in a moment." The daughters skipped out of the room and Dusty watched them disappear, darkening down a hallway, and then watched the hallway after they were gone.

"A little job," said E. Pouce.

"I don't need a job."

"For a school chum, no problem." E. Pouce turned to John Doe who was reaching into a cabinet to pull an envelope off a shelf. "What does this boy do? I can't remember what he does."

"Nothing I do will go to work for you, E. Pouce."

"I wouldn't have you work for me. I don't need help."

"What about your eyes? Why did you take your eyes?"

"I think the boy is lazy. I don't think he even wants a job. I think he's a freeloader. Always has been," said E. Pouce.

"I'm going to let Dusty use the cabin," John Doe showed Lavinia the envelope.

"That's a good idea for him," she said. John Doe put the envelope in Dusty's hand, and he grasped it. "That's the keys and the map and some instructions."

"What were you afraid to see? Why did you blind yourself?"

"Don't be shy about it," John Doe said. "Use the place."

"Does the boy really want me to answer?" said E. Pouce
to Lavinia. "Is his question rhetorical?" She laughed, and
patted his shoulder. "Must I face this question for the first
time finally and come up with an answer for the boy. I
know. I took my eyes so I could finally see. How's that?"
Both Lavinia and John Doe laughed. "Maybe that's the
story he has in his head."

"So don't be shy about it," John Doe said again to Dusty.
"There's a lake by the cabin. Good ice skating. And you'll
get a chance to look at the stars, Dusty. I want you to
spend some time looking at the stars like I told you.
There's lots of food, and firewood, and ice skates. Just
look at the stars and remember what I told you about it."

Dusty had his hand on the doorknob. He pushed and the
door opened. "I took the eyes because they were my
eyes," said E. Pouce as Dusty stepped into the hall, and
closed the door behind himself. He stood in the easy
brown light of the hallway and breathed. A door, he
thought, was merciful. One of the doormen in his grey
overcoat and military hat leaned on a wall at the far end of
the hall and watched him over the edge of an old copy of
People magazine.

The young woman who sat across from Dusty on the
Lexington Avenue Subway downtown looked at him as if
she expected something. She rested one hand on her large
suitcase. But for the man asleep at the other end of the car,
and a young Puerto Rican, from a cadre of Guardian Angels protecting the train, they were alone in the car. The
'angel' eyed Dusty with suspicion. When the young woman smiled at him, and Dusty returned the smile, the 'angel'
moved to stand between them. Dusty lowered his eyes to

the envelope he still held in his hand. The buckle on the 'angel's' belt had been filed to an edge. He wore black leather wristlets and steel studs, and a maroon beret at a jaunty angle. He stood with his arms folded, balancing himself effortlessly in the vibrating subway car, staring at a point on the window behind Dusty's head. Dusty turned the envelope over. He should have handed it back to John Doe.

"You guys do good work," Dusty said to the 'angel', and in his mind a residue of John Doe echoed, 'but on the real Earth the People don't need guardian angels.'

The young man narrowed his eyes and lowered them on Dusty, but said nothing, grinned, and stared again at the spot behind his head. The young woman had slid along the seat so she could still see him. She was smiling. Dusty tried to keep from looking at her, but there was something vaguely familiar about her that made him curious. As they pulled into Union Square a whistle blew from the captain of the cadre in another car. The 'angel' lowered an admonishing finger at Dusty, did a military about-face to look at the young woman, a left-turn and march to the door, a right-turn out of the car just before the door closed.

At the first jerk of the train out of Union Square the man who was sleeping stood up and careened towards them. He grabbed a pole to stop himself, and took off his greasy overcoat. He wasn't wearing a shirt, his body as dirty as his face. A lunge forward threw him into a seat next to the young woman with the suitcase. He flexed his muscles, grinned, mumbled incoherently. The woman crossed the car to sit next to Dusty while the man waved his fists in the air. Dusty grabbed the suitcase and the woman's hand

and pulled her off the train at Spring Street, his stop.

"Where are you going?" Dusty asked.

"Nowhere. I don't know. I don't have anywhere in particular."

Dusty looked at her, her uncomplicated smile, and remarked to himself that his day continued its little shocks. "Maybe you'd better come to my place for a little while, till you figure it out," he said, and he carried her suitcase onto the street.

"I knew you were nice," she said. "Because you look like my husband." They walked down Crosby Street towards his place, picking their way around the attractive refuse. "Not look like him because he's blond and tall and slim, but you're just like him, the same aura, that clouded-over happy glow."

"Where is he?"

"I don't know," she said. "Maybe he's dead. "

Anna, his neighbor, was leaning from her window on the second floor, watching the street. "Listen, Dusty," she said. "I took your mail today because your box don't close. It don't lock." Her arm was extended from her door when they got upstairs with his unemployment check and a postcard in her hand. "Big lobster," she said. The card was a picture of a fisherman with a lobster bigger than his boat draped across the gunwales, "A Cape Breton Catch", in yellow letters across the waves. He showed the card to the young woman.

"Where is Cape Breton?"

"It's in Nova Scotia. I've got some land up there." The message on the blank side was, "Bigger than what you see. Try it in winter." The card wasn't signed, but it was written in the shaky hand of an old man, so he could guess which neighbor of his had written it.

"I'd love to go to Nova Scotia." The young woman sat down on his couch. "Isn't that in Canada?" Dusty stared at her. She did look familiar.

"Listen," he said. "First tell me your name. My name is Dusty."

"Stormy," she said. "Or Storm. Now it's Storm."

"Why do I think I've seen you before?"

"That wasn't always my name," she said. "I changed it after all my children died."

"How did they die?"

"I think it's good to change your name after you go through a big change in your life."

"You don't look old enough to have had children."

"Do you like to fight? My husband used to like to fight. He used to come home with his face all beat up. After the children died he got his Master's degree in anthropology. But he liked to walk out in the streets and he wasn't like anyone else; he liked to go to the scary neighborhoods and get into dangerous situations. I told him I thought it was a waste of his education. One day he said he was going to walk into the South Bronx, practice his Spanish. I never saw him again. That's why I think he was killed in a fight."

"Storm what? What's your last name?"

"You didn't answer me, if you like to fight."

"Storm what?"

"There you go. You act as if life is some kind of knock-knock joke. But some men like to fight. It's the way they get their sex, I think. That's why I was asking you. I

think if men had good sex there wouldn't be any wars."
She looked into Dusty's eyes. "I bet you think I'm a
runaway. You can throw me out if you want to. But my
feeling is you're nice."

"I just met you on the subway, Stormy. What am I
supposed to think?"

"It's not what you think, it's what you feel. You can call
me Stormy, but it's Storm now."

"Okay. Storm what?" Dusty put a hand on her shoulder,
and she moved closer to him.

"I can see the potion we gave you is beginning to work,"
she said.

"What potion?"

"Some tea would be great, if you have some good tea.
I'll make it."

Dusty pulled three varieties out of his cupboard, and she
filled the kettle and put it on the stove. Dusty emptied the
contents of the envelope John Doe had given him onto the
table. There was a detailed map, a key to the cabin, and
car keys with the address of a garage on Morton Street.

"There's someone else you remind me of," said Stormy
as she set the tea on the table. "That was my father. But he
was much much older when I knew him. At least this was
the guy my mother said was my father. You look like
you'll be cranky as he was when you get older. A couple of
years before I married my first husband, and went back to
California, I found out where he lived and went to see
him."

"How old are you, Stormy?"

"Not as young as I look, mister. And see, you said that
just like my father would have: 'How old are you, Storm?'

A little more formal because of his generation. Amazing. You know what his name was? It was Shirley. Shirley Beaufort. He lived in Hoboken when I met him, but he spent a lot of his life in Canada too, was some kind of secret agent up there in World War I. That's why I'd like to go to Cape Breton. I never met a man before or since by the name of Shirley." She sipped her tea and picked up the map on the table. "What's this?"

"That's to a cabin in Maine. I met this guy today who owns the cabin."

"Great," she said. "You know my father and I were suppposed to go to Maine together on his motorcycle. He had this old Cleveland motorcycle from 1917, a monster bike, a real kidney-buster. That was before they learned how to put suspensions on them. He kept it going from the time he was a kid, and we were going to head up to Maine on that. But I moved to California, and then he died. He had this little steam engine he loved too, that he built himself, so he could fire it up and ride on it. He'd take it all over the state fairs, and steam-engine pow-wows in Iowa. Show it off. He was great, a cranky old guy, a real pisser; and a real American too, an individualist with ingenuity. It makes me feel good to talk about him, because I feel real connected when I do, to America, the best of it. That's kind of crazy, isn't it; but I mean this country has gotten so weird, and now it's almost the eighties, and the Klan is back, and the Nazis are back."

Dusty sipped his tea. He enjoyed this young woman. She was both serious and trippy. Empty trucks clattered crosstown to the tunnel on Broome Street. The scent of spaghetti sauce settled on them from the family dinner upstairs.

"I guess everybody has to feel connected to something," she mused. "And you know what he had?" she said, with a burst of enthusiasm. "He had this fine little parakeet he called Coolidge, and his cage was never closed except at night when he covered him to sleep. It was the only parakeet I've ever seen that could talk. When I sat with my dad at the table he'd fly down between us and perch on the sugar bowl, and my dad would say, "Well, Coolidge, what of it?" and little Coolidge would ruffle up his feathers and say,"Government bullshit." Then he'd fly to my father's shoulder and say, "Government bullshit," again. That was all the little bird could say, but my father agreed with it every time. It made him real happy." Storm picked up the car keys and cabin keys. "Hey." She dangled them in front of her nose. "Hey, I've got an idea," she said.

"What idea?" Dusty said.

"Why don't we just go up to this cabin?"

"No. I can't do that. I hardly know this guy. I don't have any money to go to a cabin."

"I've got some money for gas," she said.

"And for that matter I don't even know you."

"Well then it's all even. Nobody knows nothing. Government bullshit. Let's go."

"And I don't even know how old you are, or whether you're telling the truth about kids and husbands. You could be sixteen. You could be jailbait."

"Hey, Dusty, when I say you remind me of my dad, and even of my husband, I mean that's good, and I mean it. You're not as much older than I am as you think you are."

Dusty felt something. His little apartment, a neutral place he'd retreated to after splitting from his family, usually cool, grey, and vacant, was full now of this young woman, the dimly lit atmosphere expanding and contracting like a heart. He couldn't think of anything else to say in protest. He picked up her hand off the table. It was light and chilly, and he put his lips to the small knuckles.

Stormy was asleep almost as soon as she hit the bed, and Dusty lay awake looking at her. All the characters he had met that day did a slow swim across his mind: Salvatore, Lavinia the bag lady, the fat librarian, John Doe, E. Pouce, Lavinia Bread again, younger, with her children. But Stormy asleep in his eyes made them pass as shadows without qualities. He watched her turn onto her stomach, and slipped the blanket off her body, and followed the ridges of her spine to the base where there was a rose tattooed, a red rose with blue bees crawling in its petals.

The car was a two-tone pale blue and lemon yellow '56 Chevy Bel-Air in mint condition. Wide whitewalls, stick shift. "That car was made when I was born," Stormy said. "It's like riding to Maine in my cradle." Dusty drove up the parkway through Connecticut into Massachussetts. Stormy told the stories of her life. "I ran away when I was fourteen. My father was a bus driver, drunk all the time when he wasn't working, and my mother was a devout Catholic with a heavy paddle. Right into Haight-Ashbury, then the Mission District, and a short stint as a hooker. What a horror and a bore. That turned me off to sex before I began, though I've got back into it since. Then I went to

Venice and the Gypsy Jokers grabbed me right away, and before I got away from them I had a tattoo. I wasn't even sixteen. And I was hitching out of there at 4:00 A.M. I didn't care. North seemed good. Picked up by three real gentle people in a van. They didn't know what time it was. They were stoned, and I liked them, and they took me to their commune near Ashland, Oregon. I ate a lot of peyote and mushrooms with them, and I joined in all their rain-dances and fertility rites, and I learned yoga, and I had my first baby there right in front of the whole commune, in the middle of a dome that I helped to build. It was powerful, and if I'd been older I might still be there, but six months after little Sassafras was born I left her there. I was too young. I had to move on, and the commune wanted to raise her. We didn't know which one was her father anyway.''

''Is this all true, Stormy?''

''I don't know. Where are we?''

Dusty glanced at the road-map by his side. ''We're almost to Portsmouth. We'll be on the New Hampshire Turnpike soon. Maybe we'll stop there.''

''Well, true or not, Dusty, my stories got us this far.''

''Then you're telling me you're making all this up.''

''I never said that, Dusty.''

''You are a weird one.''

''Not as weird as when I married Edward. I wasn't even nineteen yet. I had no idea who I was yet. I got addicted to having kids with him. That's the only addiction I ever had, and I'm glad I kicked it. But I still dream about Sassafras. I guess I'll go back to see her some time if the commune's still there. I know Oregon's a better place for her to grow up, than to follow me around. You know I almost never think about all my other kids. Maybe it's because she's still alive, but she's this empty place that's always inside me, like a hollow ball I can surround with thoughts, or I can ignore it, but I'll never fill it up.''

''All your other kids are dead?''

''The Lord giveth,'' she said. ''But sometimes he don't supporteth.''

''How did they die?''

''We'll stop for lunch in Portsmouth, Dusty. I need to eat a fish.''

They drove onto the quaint streets of downtown Portsmouth, and stopped at a seafood restaurant on the inlet. ''You know living with Blast wasn't like anything else. We had something. We could grow together.''

''Who's that? Say his name again.''

''He took that name after the kids died. My husband. The one who disappeared. Blast. He changed, and he changed his name. Just like me.''

''I never thought of it as a name before,'' said Dusty, examining a forkful of scrod. ''Blast.''

''Well he kept blowing my mind open. I don't mean violence, even though he liked violence. And I kept his head moving too. I mean you'd have to meet him. I like you, but it's a different thing. I'm a little crazy, you know.''

''Storm and Blast,'' Dusty grinned out the window at a lobster boat going by. ''What a pair. Now Dusty is the aftermath.''

There was a general store at the dirt road turn-off, and they stopped there to buy gas. ''You be on the lookout,'' the proprietor said. "If you're headed up there to one of them cabins."

"That's where we're going," Dusty said.

"Well there was someone out there all last winter. Broke into a lot of the cabins and took what food was left. Some kind of escaped convict or somebody."

"He's not dangerous, is he?"

"He hasn't hurt anybody yet, but you never know if a man gets hungry. Johnny Layton said the guy shot at him once, but I'd shoot at that drunk if he got too close to me. He's a walking threat to life and limb." He pulled the nozzle out of the tank. Stormy came back from the bathroom. "Last year they tried to go after him on those snowmobiles everybody's got, but those damned contraptions make so much noise an elephant could hide from them. Too damned lazy anymore for snowshoes."

"What's this?" Storm asked.

"He says there's a wild man living out there," Dusty said, pointing up the dirt road.

"Great," said Storm.

"He's got a big beard, and he's real greasy. They say he wears a big fur hat that comes to a point. But no one's had a real good look at him yet. Maybe he's real old. Maybe he's young. I've got a lot of respect for him though. Even if he's deranged he's got something up there." He tapped his head. "Just to survive like that. And I hope you know what to do if you meet him."

"What should we do?" Storm asked.

"Let him be. You're not from around here. You don't know how things have changed. Used to be a man could go out there and die by himself if he wants to, and that's what Maine was like. Everyone left everyone else alone. Any more people are jealous of someone can make it on his own out there, not pay taxes. Since that damned Vietnam I think everyone's got mean." They got back in the car and Dusty started the motor. The proprietor looked in the window. "Good luck to you now, and look out for yourselves."

The cabin was twelve slow miles up the dirt road by a small frozen lake. What little snow had fallen had blown off so the surface was slick as a frosted mirror. Storm jumped out of the car. "Taste this air," she said, stretching her body. "It's full of vitamins."

It was a one-room cabin, with a sleeping loft, the mattress next to the stovepipe. The cupboard was full of canned goods and dry cereal and flour. "Lucky that wild man hasn't found this food yet," Dusty said. "That old guy was probably just trying to scare us." Storm found some ice skates in the closet and immediately put them on, and while Dusty set a fire in the stove she glided across the lake and back. She found Dusty at the woodpile, splitting some kindling.

"Come on with me," Storm said, wobbling up to him on her skates.

"I haven't skated since I was sixteen," Dusty protested.

"Just put on some skates and let's go."

Dusty carried in an armload of kindling, found the skates that fit him, and with Storm's help made his way to the ice. On the lake, with Storm supporting him, he started to remember how to do it, and to glide easily. Their noses and mouths burned in the freezing air. A three-quarter moon balanced on the sunlit spruce-tops.

They moved faster and faster around the lake, leaving their frosty breath behind. Their bodies heated up in their wool shirts. Birches crackled in the wind as they rushed under them. Dusty's spirit was honed by the sound of the blades on the ice, and when he slid like a baserunner to a stop near the cabin he was laughing and singing as loud as he could. "You better look out." He stood up and pulled Stormy to him, feeling under her shirt for her breast. "You better not cry," he sang to her.

"Shh. Be quiet."

"You better not shout, I'm telling you why," Dusty spread his arms and lifted his chin as if to throw his voice over the treetops.

"Quiet, Dusty," Stormy put her hand over his mouth.

"Santa Claus is coming to town," he mumbled, and kissed her forehead.

"Did you notice that?" she whispered.

"You have to believe in Santa Claus."

"There was someone watching us," Storm said. Dusty looked around. "I kept feeling his eyes," she said, and he followed her back to the cabin. "They kept following us around the lake." She closed the door.

"Oh, Stormy. You're just spooked by that cranky old guy at the store." Dusty threw some kindling on the fire. "You know he just wanted to scare us."

"Something is going to happen, Dusty." Storm shook her head. Dusty grabbed her by the shoulders. "I don't want to stay here," she said. He pulled her against his chest.

"Relax, Stormy. I'm here. Nothing's going to happen."

She rested her head on his shoulder and breathed. He

could feel the tremors in her small body. "I must seem really stupid," she said. "You shouldn't listen to me. I always get spooked when I go to the country." She threw her arms around his neck. "I'll be alright." He squeezed her and she sighed, and he knew her eyes were open, as he had seen it so many times in the movies, staring into the void at camera right with other-worldly apprehension, as the picture fades. "I think it's my moon in Scorpio," she said. Something popped in the firebox.

In the morning they opened the door to a fragrance of spruce. A change of wind had warmed the air and lifted a light haze off the lake. Some cardinals whistled back in the branches. Pools of wet mottled the surface of the ice with dark reflections of the woods. The sudden warmth filled the air with whatever was volatile. Squirrels dove through the trees. A cloud of gnats lifted prematurely like a grey gas. A pair of mallards landed on the ice in the middle of the lake, then flew away, leaving a grey spot out there. Dusty crawled carefully over the melt to where the birds had been. It was an egg, left out of season like a forethought. He brought it back and placed it in Stormy's hand. "It's still warm," she said.

On the other side of the lake were two small cabins boarded up, and further away in a clearing halfway up the mountain was a larger cabin half surrounded by lush Norwegian Spruce. Some smoke or a low cloud lay like sediment over the roof. Storm grabbed Dusty's arm when he started towards the cabin. "I want to see if someone's up there," Dusty said.

"It's getting cold again," said Storm. "I want to go back. I don't care if anyone is up there." Storm started back to

their cabin, and Dusty looked one last time up the
mountain, then followed. The bats that had been dormant
in the cold under the shingles were chirping and
squeaking, and made the cabin seem fragile and rusty, like
it could flake away into the trees. Then the snow began to
fall, and it was quiet again.

Dusty lay awake most of the night and listened to the
wind, and watched the snow blow by the window. It had
turned much colder. By morning they could be snowed in.
They should have got out while they could. Storm sat up
suddenly, throwing off the featherbed. "You know
what?" She said. "I lost the duck egg. I left it out there."

"That's okay," said Dusty, pushing her back down and
covering her. "We'll get another one." She fell back to
sleep immediately, but he was wide awake. He climbed
down from the loft and shined a flashlight through a
window into the banners of drifting snow. He threw on a
parka and boots and went to the woodpile, already half
covered, and carried an armload back to the cabin, then he
stoked up the fire and sat by the stove till it started to get
light.

More than a foot of snow had fallen by morning, and
drifted halfway up the door. Dusty found some snowshoes
and shuffled to the outhouse. The wind had died and the
forest seemed to rise through the snowflakes that hovered
in their slow descent like tiny white bats. He sat with the
door open and watched the stuff accumulate. The cold
was dreamy, the snow like sleep as he looked through it.
At first he didn't believe he saw the man leaning against a
tree. It looked like a deformed branch or a large burl; but
no, it was a man. It leaned without moving. Some teeth

showed through the beard covered with snow. It carried the antler of a moose, leaned on its shoulder, the butt end tucked under a bandolier of cartridges. His beard was whitened by the snow, so his age was difficult to determine. He watched Dusty for a while, then tipped his fur cap and disappeared back into the woods into the snow.

Dusty returned to the cabin and put on a pot of coffee. He didn't want to tell Storm about seeing the man, but was going to suggest they leave as soon as possible. He sat down in the heat by the stove and waited for the coffee to perc. The next thing he knew Storm was on his lap, wrapped in her featherbed.

"Hey, you fell asleep, stupid." She kissed his ear. "I smelled the coffee and now I'm up. Coffee smells so sexy when you're snowed in, and I'm going to bake a coffee cake." She stood up, poured him a cup of coffee, and opened the door. "This is so far out," she said. She grabbed a handful of snow and dropped it in her cup.

Dusty got up and closed the door. "I think we'd better leave as soon as possible," he said.

She grinned widely. "Now you're being really unimaginative. We can't leave, anyway. The car has vanished."

Dusty went to the window. Steam from his cup fogged the pane, but he could see she was right. Out there, no car. No road. No lake. Snow. And behind the snow, he knew, someone, or something. Stormy pulled some fluffy pillows from the closet and spread them around. He didn't want to say he'd seen the man. "Now we can do something real sexy," she said.

"I think we ought to try to leave."

Stormy leaned back on the cushions. "Come over here and put your mouth on me."

Dusty looked out all the windows. He knew that at some point if they stayed they would have a visitor.

"Don't even look out there," she said. She got up from the pillows and came close to him. Her robe hung open from her shoulders. "We're snowed in. Now we can do all the indoor sports." She flicked open the buttons of his shirt. "What do you have that begins with a 'c' and ends with a 'k'?"

"Storm. I don't know," said Dusty, still looking out the windows.

She kissed his nipples, then started to undo his belt. "It has an 'oc' in the middle." His belt fell into halves, and she pulled the top snap of his jeans. "Whatever it is, I want to kiss it." She lowered to her knees on one of the cushions, and her robe slipped from her shoulders. Dusty could feel that whoever that was out there was looking in a window. That never turned him on. "We haven't ever done it yet, Dusty, and now's the best time. I was waiting for the right time and now we're snowed in."

"If we're going to get going," he said and snapped his jeans, "we'd better get started."

"Oh Dusty. Don't be silly. There is no boogey man." She unsnapped his jeans again.

"I saw him this morning, Storm."

"Now you're like that old guy at the gas station, who likes to scare tourists." She pulled his zipper down.

"Stormy, please stop. Please get dressed."

"No." She pulled his pants down and with two fingers raised his cock into her mouth. He pulled back and flipped it out.

"I don't think I can do this now, Stormy."

"Yes you can." She grabbed it again and held it with her lips so he couldn't pull away. He looked nervously from window to window. She was clamped to him like a suction cup. He put a hand on her forehead and pushed gently. "Ouch. Come on, Stormy."

"Shit," she dropped back and pulled her robe around her body. "Now I hope he does show up." Dusty tried to touch her, but she stood up and pulled away. "You know how old I was the first time I fucked?"

"We should get dressed and leave, Storm."

"I was thirteen and it hurt. It was lousy. And I always wanted something like this to happen. I always wanted to be snowed in, in a cabin and a wood fire and someone I really liked. And we would do everything and make love and be nice to each other because that's the way we would be."

"I'm sorry, Stormy. I just think we should leave."

"You drive me nuts. Something finally happens, and you get paranoid."

"I'm sorry."

"I'm the one who's sorry." She quickly pulled on some clothes. "Anyway we can't get the car out. We'll be snowed in for a week, at least." She looked at him sassily, down her nose. "I guess I have to be patient. I guess a young woman has to have patience when she gets involved with an older man." She pulled on a parka, and grabbed the snowshoes.

"Where are you going?"

"Do I need permission to go to the outhouse?"

"Hey. Be nice."

"Do you want to come with me? It's a two-seater." She

paused. "I guess that's nasty too. You can watch while I masturbate. Oops. Still nasty. Bye-bye." She climbed out onto the snow.

"Be careful," Dusty shouted after her. He watched her legs move past the window. The sun had broken through, and the wind was up again, veiling the air with a shine of snow. Dusty waited a minute then decided to follow, at least to stand in a place where he could see the outhouse. He put on his parka, and went to the door. A gust of snow flew in when he opened it, and there was the man, huge in his sheepskin coat, grinning weirdly, his moose antler in one hand, dangling at his side. Dusty backed slowly into the room towards the axe leaned against the wall. The man was moving his lips. He followed Dusty in. No sound came out of his mouth. Dusty grabbed the axe behind his back and moved to the center of the room. It crossed his mind that he might have to swing the axe, and kill this man, or maim him. He had watched situations like this in the movies, but had never imagined himself in one. The man slowly shuffled towards him, still moving his lips strangely, and grinning as if this confrontation was a joke they shared. The man was younger than he'd imagined, blue eyes, long matted blond hair, an intelligent face under all that beard. *Straw Dogs*, Dusty thought. Dustin Hoffman. When he started to speak he almost laughed.

"Just tell me what you want. Don't step any closer." Dusty moved the axe from behind his back, and held it in front of his face. The man extended his antler and took another step. His lips were still moving as if he wanted to say something, but couldn't. He had almost a gentle face, but kept shoving the antler at Dusty, challenging him. Or maybe it was a friendship gesture, or a ploy. All the possibilities zipped through Dusty's mind. The man extended the antler and touched Dusty's axe. It seemed harmless. What to do? Swing it? Too late. A deft turn of the antler and the axe flew from Dusty's hands. Stupid. The man stepped forward and touched Dusty lightly under the chin. Lightly, but he felt the bone against his jaw.

"Ice cubes," Storm shouted as she swung the door open. "Little pee pellets." Then she screamed. The man wheeled around, and she screamed again. As he took a step towards her Dusty jumped on his back, but the man shook and Dusty dropped off as if the coat was oiled. The man stepped closer to Storm and lowered the antler, still shaping his lips as if into words. She stared at him as if she was looking into another world.

"O my God," Storm said.

"Don't you touch her," Dusty said. He picked up the axe. "I warn you, don't get any closer." He brandished the axe above his head. Could he really do it? He shifted his feet and planted them, but his legs still trembled.

"My God. O my God. My God," Storm kept repeating. The man reached out as if he would touch her face.

"I warn you again. Don't touch her." Dusty knew he couldn't do it. For one thing the man's head was too high for him to hit it effectively, and his clothes were too heavy for the dull axe to penetrate. He could swing at a leg but the heavy leather boots came up high and he would probably miss the narrow band of pants exposed between boot top and coat bottom. Dusty felt stupid and ineffectual.

"I'll split your skull for you if you move any more." His

dry throat made his voice sound very thin, without conviction.

"O no. No, Dusty. My God. My God. God."

The man dropped his antler, and Dusty quickly picked it up and sighed. "Okay. Okay." The man reached into his coat. "Watch out," said Dusty, as the man pulled out a duck egg and handed it to Storm.

A big smile illuminated Storm's face. "It's still warm," she sang out, and jumped forward into the big man's arms. "This is Blast, Dusty. It's my Blast, alive."

Dusty sank back into the chair by the stove as if the last bit of charge had been drained from him. "Blast," he said, and closed his eyes, and an image of the axe splitting the man's skull repeated itself behind his eyelids. It should have been so easy. He shouldn't have been so helpless. A swing of the axe. He felt his own body twitch, and saw in his mind the big man stumble and collapse.

"He said he's sorry he frightened you," Storm said, and Dusty opened his eyes. They had sat down by the table, and were looking into each other's eyes. He couldn't talk, but moved his lips very slowly so she could read them. She held his hand and shook her head to show she was getting it. She translated some for Dusty.

"He went to the South Bronx, like I said, and a gang of teenagers did grab him, and they cut out his tongue, but they didn't castrate him, so he was lucky. He says he couldn't come back to me without a tongue. Poor baby." She leaned forward and tried to kiss him, but he pulled his face away. "He doesn't want to kiss me without a tongue. So now he came up here and is using himself as the subject for his anthropology research. He says he survived last winter on less than fifty dollars. He ate a bear. My Blast ate a bear, some rabbits and bluejays, and a couple of bags of chicken mash. That was his biggest expense. Sometimes he'd find some Shredded Wheat left in these cabins. He's learned a lot, he says, and he thinks it was worth it."

"Did he come here to look for Shredded Wheat?" Dusty crossed the room to sit with them at the table.

"No," Storm translated his lips. "He said for some reason he never broke into this cabin. He came because he knew someone was here and he was a little lonely. Says he feels like he left the planet, poor baby. He didn't even know it was me. And he wanted to return the duck egg."

They drank coffee and talked all day. Blast left at sundown and Dusty and Storm settled on some cushions near the fire. She kept looking at him, then diverting her eyes to withdraw into herself. He knew what she was thinking about, and felt a little strange himself, superfluous, emasculated.

"Blast," she said. "Blast. The way he lives his life is so interesting. He never does anything without watching himself doing it, and then he keeps notes. He acts out certain roles, and writes them up. That's his profession. That's how he'll get his Ph.D. He's still the most interesting guy I know." She sat with her chin on her knees and stared at the stove.

"You know what we can still do, Stormy?"

Storm sighed and looked at him. "We could go up to Cape Breton from here, like you said you wanted to do. And for the time being we're still snowed in here." He reminded her of her earlier fantasty.

Her glance, that had fallen on him for the moment,

seemed to dissolve him and look beyond. ''I don't think I could live with him any more. I mean there's too much ego and macho, though I can't really call it macho, but it's hard for a woman to get herself together around a man like that, unless she's really together in the first place, going in, and can ignore his demands, which I don't think he wants to make in the first place.''

Dusty wanted to stand up and say 'Look, I'm here', or just to slap her once so she felt that he was present. He played roughly with her nipples. An erection pressed and throbbed against the denim like an angry thwart. He felt dull. He undid his belt.

''He seems always to want you to submit totally to his projects, because he never wants to talk about anything else. No 'How will we cook the eggplant?' in Blast's conversation, but that's okay, because that's the way he concentrates.''

Dusty blew gently in her ear, and kissed her neck and shoulders. She shrugged and rotated her head. He sunk his teeth lightly into the muscle at the back of her neck. His passion was calculated, he realized, to mitigate the stupid anger that he felt.

''But any woman he's with has at least to pretend to be totally absorbed in *his* work, and to respond that way, even if it's only as a sounding board.''

He pushed her back onto the pillows and undid her pants and pulled them off. He grazed her belly with his lips and kissed her navel. ''Your skin smells like smoke,'' he said.

''But that's not where he's at underneath. It's not submission that he wants.''

"Hey. Shut up, Stormy. I'm here. I said your skin smells like smoke."

"What? Oh. Yeah. Like smoke. I should take a bath." Dusty pinched her thigh with his lips.

"Ooh. Underneath." She put her hand on his head. "Underneath he really wants to be with a woman who's free in her own head, and has her own work to do. I know that much about Blast."

Dusty parted the lips of her mound with his tongue and flicked it in. "He wants a woman to match his intensity, and share energy with him. He doesn't want to hear your half-assed ideas about what he's doing. He wants to know what you've been working on." Dusty furiously licked into her muff. Storm lifted his head up by his ears and looked at his face that was shining with herself. "He would even want to collaborate with a woman, who was developing in her own way."

She released him, and Dusty rolled her onto her stomach and tried to break into her from behind, but she was dry and tight. She lifted her head and tried to look back at him as she talked. "He'd appreciate a woman of equal accomplishment. So his demands aren't really demands on you." He suddenly slipped in, as if he'd pushed aside some loose bricks. "He prefers accomplishment in a woman," she gasped. Dusty grabbed the handles of her pelvis and tried to move her. "It's really good for a woman like me, Dusty, to find a man who wants her to accomplish something. I mean you have to want to do it for yourself, but I've always been oriented to men, so it really helps."

"Blah blah blah blah," Dusty shouted into the air.

Stormy rolled over and Dusty flipped out of her. "I'm not into it, Dusty, I'm sorry." He looked at her. No openings.

"We're so snowed in, Stormy," he appealed.

"I'm just very distracted," she said, and she hugged him, staring over his shoulder at the table where Blast had last been sipping his coffee.

He wasn't surprised next morning to find the message on her pillow. She was gone to be with Blast in his new life in the wilderness. "Thank you, Dusty," the note said, "for leading me back to Blast. I mean, isn't it weird how things turn out?" He hadn't led her anywhere. Nothing led anywhere. He looked over the snow-covered forest and understood that he had come to nowhere. He spent most of the day trying to free the car, a futile job since he knew there was no way he could get it out through the snow on the road; but he felt some reassurance just in seeing it, a '56 Chevy Bel-Air, pale blue and lemon yellow, in the middle of nowhere. He started it up and sat down inside with the heater on, and looked at the snow till the windows fogged up.

That night, after a dinner of canned peas and spam, he stepped out of the cabin and walked to the center of the frozen lake. The snow was knee deep. He looked at the dim light in the cabin windows, and at the darkness everywhere else. Something was strange about this. Storm and Blast were off there in the darkness, maybe. Never sure when the dream begins. He looked up to the sky full of dizzying stars. John Doe had been correct. His feet felt not quite sure underneath himself. He was nagged by a vague sense of false destination. He was born on this planet, and those were the stars it accompanied. He looked at them till they started to spin, then fell on his back into the snow, the cold tumbling down on his face. He lay there watching the stars spiral out of their points. Then he got up and without looking at them again he rushed into the cabin.

He had a dream that night precisely of the picture he had seen in the book by P. P. Dent. It gave him a feeling of gratitude to see it so enlarged. He realized, first of all, that the girl with the suitcase in that picture was Storm, and that was why she had looked so familiar. E. Pouce was walking out of the dark room onto the balcony towards him. Dusty jumped to a tree near the balcony and climbed down. He took Storm's suitcase and led her past the table where John Doe was ladling sauce over a huge bat steaming on a platter, and that bat had a human face they both recognized. "I don't want to look," Storm said, and they walked further, around the house to a garden. Salvatore, the man who had talked so much to him in the library, was planting a tree there. "This is an Umbrellone," he said. "It grows in southern Italy. It's beautiful. It will be a tall pine tree that spreads out at the top, and from the pine cones you get the pignoli, and you eat them." He pushed aside some of the dirt to show them the grey ash at the roots. "I put my mother's ashes in the roots so it will grow and she'll be happy. This tree will grow and be my mother. Tomorrow."

Dusty woke up early and snowshoed out to the main road. The general store was closed when he got there, a hand-painted sign on the door telling of a sickness in the family. It was written on part of a torn poster that said,

"Don't let us say we told you so," against a blue sky. He was halfway between Cape Breton and New York and could go in either direction. If a spaceship passed, he'd head for Jupiter. A car was coming south. He stuck out his thumb, and it passed. Suddenly everything seemed very logical. Going either way. Logical. Doing what he vaguely knew he was supposed to do. Another car passed him by headed south. Either way. If not logical, then what else? A truck heading north stopped at the gas pumps, and the driver hopped out, and went around to the outhouse. Dusty jumped into the cab. "Figured you needed a ride," the driver said, when he got in, and they headed for the New Brunswick border in the empty truck.

KEEPER

Dusty stayed in his cookshack when a man named Fletcher appeared unexpectedly on the trail near his tepee. He pushed at the fire. He had expected no visitors, preferred to be alone in these hours, and was reluctant to step out to greet him, hoping he might disappear if not acknowledged. These were hours when he enjoyed nothing to happen. He had met Fletcher only once, at his brother's house, and remembered him to be a peculiar person, obsessed with the story he had to tell, about himself. Dusty watched through a chink in the cookshack wall. The man stood quietly by the tepee, looking into the sky as if he expected to leave the ground. The light of early sunset laid a pale cayenne glow on his face that made him seem more than alive, like a shining spirit. The spruce darkened slowly. Blue heron sailed low over the water and settled on the rocks to stand for one last fish before going to roost. Grey bats, asleep all day in the folds of the smokeflaps, were starting to move. They would fly and feed on insects around the poles. The chili bubbled lightly on the stove. Fletcher turned and slowly approached the cookshack. Dusty had a premonition that this really wasn't happening. From under the silence the rumble of a fishing boat returned to the tiny Inverness harbor hidden behind the headland a mile away. White-throated sparrows exchanged blue sentences from the chokecherry to the ash. Dusty was jealous of these summer hours at his place, when his mind could come to rest, no visitors expected, no strollers on the beach, and he would settle down to eat alone inside the long, lush narrative of a northern sunset.

Fletcher had a pack on his back, and held a small covered cage in front of himself like a lantern. Dusty stepped out of the cookshack.

"Hi," said Fletcher, stepping towards him. "I wondered if I was in the right place. I hope you remember me."

"Sure. Peter's friend. The sailor. Why don't you put your stuff down?" Dusty felt how cool his voice came out, but there was no reason to fake a welcome. Fletcher set the cage on the table, and Dusty helped him take off his pack.

"It's a long way down here. You didn't tell me how long that trail was when you invited me."

"Once you know it it doesn't seem long."

"I bet when you invited me you didn't expect me to come."

Fletcher looked so vulnerable that Dusty couldn't take this cue to say something mean. "It's true. I tell a lot of people about this place, but not many manage to get here. Congratulations."

Fletcher swung onto a bench and leaned on the table. "A primo view you've got here, and what a great table." From one side of the table you saw the ocean, and from the other side the hills of Foot Cape.

"Like everything else here I just nailed this table up out of driftwood planks and poles. Whatever was around." Dusty took some pride in the way he had developed his place.

"It's beautiful," said Fletcher. "A basic place." He pulled his little cage towards himself.

"I'll finish cooking the chili," Dusty turned back to the cookshack. Fletcher lifted the cover of cage and peeked under. "Psst."

"Hey," Fletcher shouted, as Dusty threw some wood in the stove. "I hope you don't mind that I came."

"Don't worry," Dusty said. "As long as you appreciate my chili." Fletcher leaned on the table, and Dusty watched him gaze at the sunset, his peculiar intense profile, pointed as an arrow, thrust out as if he were on a trajectory towards the horizon.

At a recent visit to his brother Peter and his brood, the first in many years, Dusty met Fletcher, and casually invited him. He invited a lot of people to his camp in Cape Breton, but never expected them to show up. It was too far from anywhere. People seemed to understand that he wasn't really asking them to come, but they enjoyed the fantasy of a wilderness vacation as he described his place to them: the unspoiled coast, the tepee, the driftwood shacks. Dusty had put this place together as an adventure for his family, and now that the family was dispersed he enjoyed to be there alone whenever he had the time to go.

He had walked into his brother's living room and Fletcher was there. He leaned towards Dusty without introduction and said, "I'm deeply involved with these bats, in case you're wondering who I am. So I'm visiting here because your brother works at the university and I wanted to talk here with Professor Knowland F. Knowland, he's the bat expert." More peculiar, Dusty thought, than his interest in bats, was Fletcher's compulsion to tell about it immediately, even before he said hello. He looked into the strange face, broad from the front, thick stubble of beard, tufts of hair sprouting from the ears, the face a map of many problems, unlike the clear vector of his profile.

"So you guys met each other already," Pete said, entering the room. "You know you both worked on ships. Fletcher here is a seaman. We graduated high school together."

"I just picked up a job once when I was in Europe," Dusty said.

"Well I'm a union member, for better or worse. No big deal. Like any other job, a pain in the ass. It's a living."

"Sounds great to me," said Peter. "Work half a year."

"Yeah, but you lose touch. A seaman loses touch. You're out at sea and your world turns inside out and what do you know. Like I come back from this last trip, and I go to the apartment I rent, I mean you know my room in it, and it's full of these little bats, little blue-eyed bats, all over it. And nobody knew anything about them. That's why I came here, because I read in the library about Professor Knowland F. Knowland, and I been keeping in touch with your brother Peter, so I came." One of Peter's little girls jumped into Fletcher's lap, and he sat back in the chair, quietly stroking her hair.

Peter sat on the edge of his recliner staring at Dusty as if he might be the answer to a question he had been burdened with for a long time. He rolled a scotch-on-the-rocks between his palms. "So you find yourself married," he blurted out, "and then you've got the kids and the mortgage and the wife's analyst to pay for, and here you are." He took a sip. "The whole shot."

"So I came to ask the professor about my bats," Fletcher added. He looked at Peter. "I don't get it. You got some nice kids. What does a seaman get? Six months unemployment. Sea legs. Clap in every port. And now I got some bats." The little girl on his lap made a face.

"Peter always loved to complain," Dusty said. In the midst of the velour upholstery, the neatly matted prints, the indirect lighting, it was hard to take his brother's troubles seriously. "Hey Peter, you've got a steady job, a job for life. How many people have got that?" Three more kids came in and sat down at their father's feet.

"You spend your life picking your nose, and reading books nobody cares about. You spend your life talking to adolescents."

"Don't knock it," said Fletcher.

"When he was a kid we used to call him 'Whine'."

"Merchant seaman seems like a good choice to me now," Peter slugged down his scotch.

"Yeah, and spend your life with morons and assholes and misfits." Fletcher kissed the girl in his lap on top of her head. "If I could do it again, and found the right woman, I'd have a bunch of kids."

"How come you survived it? How did you do it?" Peter asked Dusty.

"What?" Dusty asked, though he knew his brother meant the wife and kids experience. He didn't relish continuing this conversation that was leading them back into old sibling conflict. "Who said I survived it? I just did a day at a time, Peter; until we couldn't do it anymore." That line could have gone on the soaps, Dusty thought.

The kids stiffened visibly when Tasha, Peter's wife,

came in. The youngest boy hid his toy truck behind his father's chair. Dusty remembered Tasha as the ideal of bovine contentment, a mother of kids, blissfully married. Now she almost throbbed with anxiety and resentment. Her smile was like a sneer overlaid with a grin, a studied stretching of the lips calculated to show all men present that she was equal or better. She stared at Peter till he stood up. "That's right," he said. "I get the dinner tonight. Hope everyone likes curry." The kids made faces. "I'll help you make it, daddy," said his eleven-year-old daughter.

"Don't let him get you to do all the work, Nance," said Tasha. "And you guys go out to play. Uncle Dusty isn't used to children."

"They don't bother me," said Dusty.

The kids hesitated, but their mother glared at them till they left, all but the little girl still asleep in Fletcher's lap. Tasha settled into the recliner Peter had vacated and lit the butt of a half-smoked cheroot. "Been about eight years."

"Yeah," said Dusty. "Something eats up years. You had three kids last time, and Terry was the oldest, right? He was in third grade. Must be almost out of high school. The kids look great. We look a little tired, though."

She blinked a few times, waiting for Dusty's comments to pass then waved her cigar around as if to purify the air. She took a few puffs, then pointed the burning end at Fletcher, who sat very still, with the little girl sleeping in his lap.

"I'd take a job as a merchant seawoman. I'd ship out tomorrow if someone came in here and told me I could."

"That ain't likely to happen," Fletcher mumbled perfunctorily. Dusty had the sense they'd been over this territory before and she was just reviewing it for his sake.

"Of course it ain't." She smashed her cheroot in the ashtray for emphasis. "There's no such thing as a merchant seawoman, yet." She waited for Dusty to absorb the weight of this point.

Terry arrived at the front door, mumbled a greeting, and rushed out through the back. "What an asshole he's gotten to be," said Tasha, and she jumped up to follow him, leaving Dusty and Fletcher and the sleeping daughter in the room.

Dusty tasted the chili. Even a little hotter. "Do you like spicy?" he shouted at Fletcher, who was rolling a cigarette.

"Hot's okay, but I don't like sweet." He cupped his cigarette and lit it in the wind.

Dusty lifted a stove-lid and the fire roared up. He dropped in some more wood, and put on the coffee pot. Some violet clouds spread on the horizon, and somewhere an owl. "You hear that owl?" Fletcher said as if to himself. "Owls eat bats."

With the kid still asleep on his lap Fletcher slid forward and leaned towards Dusty. "I'll tell you what happened when I went to see the Professor."

"Sure," said Dusty.

Fletcher settled back in his seat. "You know, I wouldn't have bothered the guy, I mean to have a dumb seaman come to ask a professor about some little bats, but there was this Indian I shipped with last time, Lester Half-hawk. He was an oiler, and I'm an engineer, so we were together a lot, and he kept telling me these Indian stories, and I didn't know if they were real stories or what, but they passed the time and telling them kept Lester off the juice. I didn't try to remember them or anything, except this one story came back to me after I got home, about a tribe that lived on Manhattan Island before the twenty-four bucks, and they disappeared, or they all were killed, but this story believed they would all come back when the time was right, when the buildings got too high, he said, and they would come back in the form of tiny bats, and each of those tiny bats would enter the body of one of the people living in Manhattan, and grab his soul, and fly away with it. You can believe I remembered that story when I got home and found my walls covered with little bats. I mean that was more than a coincidence. So that's why I came to see the Professor."

"Did you tell the Professor that legend?"

"No way I could tell him anything. He was a flipped-out professor, like a Groucho Marx professor. ''There are no blue-eyed bats,' was what he said, and he shoved my cage aside. I said, 'Wait just a second, Professor.' He was one of them small professors, wiry, nervous, a little white goatee that jumped around as he talked. And his eyes never stopped to focus on anything. They bounced all over the room as if he was afraid of being caught in one place at the same time. So I felt like I was wasting his time, but I said, 'Now wait a second, Professor. What about these little bats right here in this cage? These little bats have blue eyes.' I moved the cage in front of his face again, and lifted the cloth right off. His eyebeams hit my cage, and richocheted off like a bat in flight. 'There are no blue-eyed bats. The African epaulette bat has a dull grey cast to its eyes,

Epomorphus, but I've seen it only in photographs.'

"So I told him, 'Hey, Professor, I don't want to waste your time and hold up your experiments, but don't be a jerk. These blue-eyed bats here are right in front of your eyes. Take a look once. You'll give me some satisfaction for coming all the way out here, and you'll make out alright yourself. You'll see a bat you never seen before.' I mean I don't know what these professors get their jollies from. But this little squirt wouldn't look at them. He stood up, got his pipe and a pouch of tobacco, and reamed and packed the pipe with a vengeance. 'The study of bats can be worse than frustrating as you have no doubt discovered for yourself.' His eyes flew here and there. Yeah, I said to myself, especially when you got to talk to a bunch of screwballs. 'There's disappointment, danger, even tragedy,' said the Professor, putting a lighter to his pipe.

"'And bats, Professor? Tell me about blue-eyed bats.' I tried to put it to him but the screwball ignored me. I thought it was time to get out of there. I wouldn't get anywhere with him, but he called his secretary and told her he didn't want to be disturbed, and he settled back in his seat and smoked his pipe, and I knew I was in for a long one. 'I want to tell you about a collecting trip I once took into the jungle of Ecuador.'

"So I figured, wait the guy out. Maybe after he relaxes he'll take a look at my bats. I mean there's a lot at stake with my bats. I mean we're talkin' all the souls from the island of Manhattan, and maybe the boroughs of Queens, Bronx, Brooklyn, and the ferry to Staten Island."

"'About ten years ago now,' the Professor began, 'I received in the mail an unusual specimen that a fisherman had snagged in the tropics. This man had been fly-fishing along the banks of the Alogongo and the bait was grabbed in the air by a bat. It looked most like the Carollia Perspicillata, one of a species whose powers of audition I had been studying, but with an unusual ear conformation that was either an aberration of this individual, or the indication of a whole new subspecies. I decided to organize a collecting trip to the headwaters of the Alogongo where I was assured by my correspondent a large population of bats inhabited caves in the hills of the surrounding watershed. It took me several years to arrange my affairs and get a sabbatical. I had experiments to finish. I had to dispose of a dying marriage et cetera et cetera . . .' ''

Fletcher swung off his seat and approached Dusty in the cookshack. ''This place you got down here, this is a magical place. I feel lucky to come here.''

''Peter has never visited me down here. I know the kids would love it,'' said Dusty.

''Your brother's got that chick he's married to. He's got his own problems. All those professors he's got to talk to. I don't envy your brother.''

''Taste this.'' Dusty held out a spoonful of chili. Fletcher pulled his head back. ''Phew. That's hot. That's good chili.''

''Twenty minutes, I figure, and we can eat it. Meanwhile why don't you stow your stuff over there.'' He pointed at a driftwood tower built by one of his sons. ''It'll keep the rain off.''

Dusty watched him grab his stuff and go to the tower. There was something different about Fletcher, less substantial than the man who had told him the story, like he had aged, or evaporated. Maybe it was the bats' influence. The story Fletcher told remained in Dusty's mind like the shadow of an intricate thing.

''...Professor talked and my little bats started flying around in the cage, like doing amazing tricks. I didn't want to be impolite but my little bats were knocking themselves out, and I wanted him to notice them. I said, 'Look, Professor. Bats. Bats right here.' No way he would look. He sucked on his pipe and blew big clouds of smoke in his own eyes. I needed him to know about my little bats and the situation of souls in New York City, but he kept talking. '. . . Narrow-gauge railroad to the interior, after which there was no way to go but on foot. Our packers, taciturn little Chingayo Indians, carried my collection cases and equipment. I had for a companion a young archaeologist from Illinois, a brilliant young Jewish woman of some twenty-six years, Susannah Gorchow her name, alas. She laughed like a man. I don't know if you're Jewish, but I find certain intelligent blue-eyed Jewish women irresistible. Her eyes were violet. She was working with the archaeology of bat imagery. It appeared in the weaving and on the pottery of contemporary Indians, and she had records of some studies done by an astroarchaeologist showing that in their perception of the night sky, which in the Southern Hemisphere is full of starless dark patches, they take at least one of the configurations of darkness to be a huge bat, which in their mythology, as far as it is understood, is the resting place for the spirits of men while they sleep, and the first station for those spirits after they die. She hoped to find some

subjects to tell her more. A fascinating companion in a
tepid rain forest full of parrots and snakes. She spoke to
me in French. 'Voulez-vous dejeuner á ce belle poste ci?
Ce n'est pas le Howard Johnson. Ha ha ha.' She carried a
can of paté in her pocket, and we ate it there, our final
taste of civilization. Then we climbed and slipped and
splashed up and down one of the most miserable trails I
have ever followed. At sundown we came on a wretched
little shack. It was inhabited by a couple of miserable,
rheumy, pink-eyed Norwegians who sat there on some
straw mats when we entered with machetes in their laps
and told us they had no food for us, and we weren't welcome to sleep inside with them. It rained on us all night.
In the morning we paid dearly for some leaky dugout
canoes and started up the river towards a village they
claimed was there, settled by some Japanese. We were
hungry and wet and cold. What a river. Masses of floating
rubbish narrowly missed our tiny boats. Mats of water
hyacinth sheltered schools of piranha, and crocodiles slid
off the banks to cross our bows. The rains had roused
hundreds of tiny frogs to activity and their tinkling chorus
like windchimes came from all sides as the boys continued to pole us up the river . . .' "

The little girl stirred on Fletcher's lap. From the kitchen
came the sounds of Peter cooking, and his older daughter
giggling while she worked with him. "I gotta admit I was
pissed when I understood that Professor had kept me
there to listen to his story, but didn't have time to even
look at my little bats. He chewed on his damn pipe. He
looked everywhere else, and the smoke swirled up into
the ventilators, and he kept talking, '...miserable, the

same forlorn appearance as the black vultures we passed sitting dejectedly over a dead calf by the riverside, their heads drawn down between their drooping shoulders. Occasionally we halted by the riverside to rest, or to lunch on a cluster of small bananas fortune had sent us. Susannah moved close to me. In the bow a native draped incongruously in a woolen shawl chewed coca leaves and...'''

The story wound on like a river, and Dusty watched his little niece asleep in Fletcher's lap, his mind flying off to his own recollections about the ship he had worked on, a Norwegian tramp that stopped at Taranto to unload its anthracite and load some steel pipe to be delivered through the Bosporus to Odessa. He hung around the old city with a Philippine friend of his, Bataan. It is an ancient slum on an island between the two newer sections of the city. The streets were so narrow they could stand in the center and touch the walls on either side. Kids followed them everywhere, begging money. And the sailors off a few Russian freighters, unaccustomed to liberty in the West, moved through the crowds of Italians like schools of fish.

They ate in a seafood restaurant near the fishmarket, huge bowls of a rich grotesquerie of mussels and clams and ugly bottom-fish. Bataan returned from the bathroom a little paranoid, and before the soup came he left Dusty there without a word. He waited for him to come back, stared into the sluggish face of the sea-robin cooling on his soup, and sipped a little around the edge. Bataan had a keen sense of trouble and Dusty knew he should have got out of there. Two men grabbed his arms, and he stared into the grin of a commandante of the carabinieri.

       " ' . . . At length to reach the village of Xigadiga (pronounced sheegadigga), an Indian word for the sound of a canoe riding through the reeds, suddenly coming aground on a spit of mud. In this season the village was a lake of mud, thatched huts built above it on platforms supported by poles. The people proved congenial and gave us food and shelter, a good thing because we learned that it would be four days before the mail-boat arrived to carry us the rest of the way up the river. The people were very gentle. They giggled a lot and made great sport of the unpleasant task of picking the leeches off our legs. From the vantage of our accommodations, a little hut on stilts above the central square, Susannah and I could watch the natives luxuriate in the warm mud. They stripped off their loincloths, young and old alike, and dived into it from the ladders of their huts, rolling over, blowing bubbles like African hippos. It looked like such pleasurable sport we couldn't resist the temptation that in a civilized context would seem so contrary to the rules of hygiene. We stripped, the first time I had ever seen Susannah in the buff, and she had a quite nice conformation of limbs, her breasts small with nipples standing up like little snouts.' The Professor paused to relight his pipe. My bats were bored stiff. Was this a two-pipe story, I wanted to ask. A three-pipe story? 'These natives were fascinated. They had never seen white bodies in the buff before, and they loved the spectacle as we dove into the mud. They played fanfares on their crude flutes and beat on log drums. The mud, we discovered, provided relief from the itching of our numerous insect bites. No scratching an itch in that climate, because flies swarmed on the slightest abrasion to lay eggs in the wound, causing some painful swelling. The mud was relaxing to body and mind, and even the insect bites were a kind of blessing, because we discovered that to relieve the general itching it was quite efficacious to rub our bodies together lightly in such a way as not to break the skin, and we found quite naturally that that contact led to further intimacy and finally to the blossoming of a love that had been implicit all along in our delight in each other's company. There has never been a more tender nor a muddier honeymoon. The natives were more than happy to let us...'''

The Commandante in the room where Dusty was detained kept a pipe in his mouth, but said it was too expensive to light it. "Next time you come to Taranto bring me a gift of tobacco. American tobacco is best, but very expensive in Italy." Dusty sat in the sparsely furnished room for several days with this commandante. He left only when Dusty slept, on a straw mat on the floor. Though the officer wouldn't talk about it, Dusty's guess was that they would keep him till his ship sailed. They didn't want an American on the crew headed for a Russian port. The Commandante practiced his English. "Gioia del Colle, you know it? Twenty kilometers from Taranto. Secret missile base. When Americans first come there the town gave a big celebration, lights all over the street, a festa for twenty-two days. Every two hours the mayor makes a speech to welcome the Americans. The American colonel made a speech too, a very big man." The silos of the missiles of this top-secret base rose among the olive trees, some of the oldest in Italy. "So the Colonel was very happy, because the people of the town were happy to have the work, and the soldiers were happy for the big party. But when he got his electric bill he wasn't so happy. Four hundred and fifty-thousand lire. The mayor of Gioia was 'furbo', how do you say it? Clever. Shrewd. He attached the electricity from the whole town to the Colonel's meter. Why not? Rich American. The Colonel had to pay. The American government would not pay.'' A bedraggled corporal brought in two bowls of pasta. The Commandante was laughing. ''To pay. Money.'' He took a mouthful of the pasta, chewed it, spit it back into the bowl. ''Porca putana,'' he exclaimed, and shoved the bowl back at the corporal. ''Ci porta la pasta fatta corretamente alla dente, o non ce ne porta. Capito.'' ''Si, Commandante, mi dispiace, ma insomma . . .'' The corporal took the bowls away. ''Mannagia la miseria,'' said the Commandante. ''Choongum. Pasta like choongum.''

'' '. . . Several hours' ride over mountain trails. If I had known beforehand how treacherous those trails were I would have tried to convince Susannah not to follow. Our gear in pack-saddles on the mules, and ourselves on what we were told were sure-footed horses that knew the trail. Our mounts took the bits in their mouths, and though we tried to rein them to the inside they preferred to ride the outer edge of the trail, their bodies and ours hung out under the rushing clouds. We had a sense at first that we were invulnerable, immortal, didn't need to touch the ground because we were mounted not on ordinary nags, but had between our knees the airborne progeny of Pegasus. Would it were true. O how I've wept for a horse that could fly. I heard one stumble behind me. It happened so quickly. It was Susannah's horse. I turned and saw her body flying off into the canyon some two thousand feet below. The same body that over the weeks past I had come to love as if it were my own, falling, falling. How ironic that the woman to whom I was prepared to dedicate my life from then on perished for want of those extremities, those infernal wings, so abundant on those creatures to whom my life had been devoted up to that point.' The professor started to cry. What was I supposed to do? What was he gonna do next? I mean was I supposed to put my arms around him like he was a woman? I mean I never even went to college. I covered up my little cage of bats. He talked again. 'They convinced me it was no use to go after her. The bottom of the canyon was more than a week away from where we were. I had no choice but to sadly push on. At length we arrived at the abandoned camp of some prospectors adjacent to the caves we had set out to explore. Oh, Susannah...'''

"Look, my ship is due to pull out at five A.M. tomorrow. What am I doing here? Just helping you with your English?''

"They had a key club on this base. You ever have a key club?''

"Commandante, will I get out of here in time to sail with my ship?''

"I would never say that all Italian wives are faithful, quite the opposite, but to make adultery into such a game, so public. Italians are never that organized about love.''

Dusty stood up. "Commandante, I demand that you at least let me contact...''

"Ah, ah, ah . . ." The Commandante pressed a buzzer under the lip of the table he was leaning on, and the two carabinieri stationed outside the door entered and stood at attention. "There were seventy couples, and every Friday night they met in the enlisted man's club - a few officers with them too - and they all threw their keys into the middle of the floor, and then each man picked up a key, and by luck whatever key he got that was the woman, the wife, he spent the weekend with. An Italian doesn't understand this. An Italian likes to seduce a woman, a little romantico. But when the Colonel found out he was very angry about this, and he made all the men to stay on the base, and the women were left alone at home."

Dusty had noticed that the two guards seemed almost to be sleeping. He slowly moved closer to them, figuring to sprint through the door at a certain moment, but before he made his move they grabbed him and pulled his arms behind his back. "Okay," he said. "So you're sincere."

"That was when our ragazzi started to invade the bedrooms of the American women. They called it 'la guerra di mezzanotte', the midnight war. Italian boys are so romantic, and the American women love them a lot, good fucking dark boys..."

Fletcher moved the little girl to the floor by his feet, and she lay there with her blue eyes open sucking her thumb, staring at Dusty. "He showed me a picture," Fletcher said. "He carried a walletful of pictures of bats like my mother's got a folder of her grandchildren, or high school girls carry pictures of boys. This one was ugly, with a little flap of skin on its nose, and a mouth like a bulldog, and ears beaten in. He kept talking to me. 'The chamber could

be entered only by lying flat and pushing forward with the
toes. A feeling of profound depression came over me, that
the walls might at any moment collapse and hold me there
forever. After some more hours of careful descent we
came to a small antechamber that could have made the
most virtuous man feel he had been assigned to one of the
empty wards of hell. The floor was a seething mass of
enormous cockroaches, a deafening rustle as they
struggled about rubbing against one another. It was
hideously hot. Big centipedes moved back and forth across
our legs. One room was hotter than the last, and there
were no signs of bats yet, but I was determined to go on
through the stench and heat just because I had come this
far. We soon descended a broad, well-like shaft to a cooler
region of this vast network of caves. Here the only passage
was by a long shelving ledge that afforded us a slippery
foothold. Our pale lamps made the shadows leap around
us like demons. Stones kicked loose after several seconds
made a faint splash where like "Alph, the sacred river,"
ran an underground stream said to harbor blind fishes. At
length the ledge widened and we found ourselves in a
large chamber at the bottom of a vaulted dome. I shined
my light around. "Alogongo," I shouted, and the word
bombinated through the chambers of the cave. But not a
bat. There were no bats at all. I was hoping for any little
one, even if it wasn't a Carollia, which usually roost in
trees anyway; just some small specimen I could collect to
redeem somewhat the tragic consequences of my fateful
trip, but not one creature there to begin to replace the loss
of my Susannah. I shouted her name, Susannah Gorchow,
and it rebounded off the surface of the domed chamber,

and I shouted it again and again so it would reverberate forever within the hollow cliffs of Alogongo.'''

"The missiles," said the Commandante, "were set up at Gioia under a joint Italian-American command." So what did it mean to him, Dusty thought? He lost a job. He wouldn't get to Odessa. They fed him well, and he'd had worse company than this commandante. "The Americans controlled the nuclear warheads, and the Italians controlled the missiles themselves. The consoles were set up in trailers outside the missile silos. How is my English?"

"Fuck your English, wop."

"Very kind of you, Mister Dusty. Gioia is 'happiness', you know that? Gioia del Colle, happiness of the hills. So in each trailer an American lieutenant and an Italian tenente sat facing each other. Twelve hours they sat, and each had a key, the American for the warhead, the Italian for the missile. It was supposed to fire only by both keys. One day there was a big inspection by the NATO generals, a disaster, of the whole missile installation, and all the generals crowded into one of the trailers where the two lieutenants were sitting. They were such lonely lieutenants because the Italian spoke no English and the American no Italian. They took the key from the Italian lieutenant, to show how it worked, lifted the cover, and tried to insert it. No fit. Not even into the keyhole. Nothing. The Generals were disturbed. They turned to the American and asked for his key..."

A loud bell clanged in the hall outside and the Commandante stopped talking. He looked at his watch, stood up, and saluted Dusty. "We are free to leave, Mr.

Dusty. You can go now."

"But what about the key? Did the American key...?"

The Commandante put his pipe in his pocket and left without answering. The room was suddenly empty, pale yellow. Dusty could imagine how that story ended, what happened with that key, but what use was imagination, like fish gills pumping in the belly of the boat. He had come, in a way, to depend on the Commandante, and now felt deserted by him. He opened the door slowly and looked into the hallway. No one but a cleaning woman in the building. It had got to be Sunday without his knowing, and his ship had sailed on Friday. The woman was mopping the floors of the massive fascist building. She said, "ngiorno," and he walked into the street.

'"There were no bats. Not a bat, I tell you. Not a miserable creature in the cave.' This professor started foaming at the mouth and shaking his fists in the air. I didn't know what was going to happen next. 'All that distance. All that expense. My reputation, and I lost my Susannah. And this terrible sickness. For what? Ten thousand miles at enormous sacrifice, and not a bat. Not even one bat. That's all I can say. No bats.' I felt sorry for him. He was swaying around like a drunk man, his fists waving in the air. He brought a fist down on top of my cage and smashed it, but the little bats flew to safety under my collar. This professor was berserk. He jumped onto the desk, and I stepped back because I didn't want him to jump on me. He swung his arm around like a windmill and heaved his pipe through the window. 'Out, out,' he shouted, and before I could grab him he hollered out one last, 'no bats at all,' and crashed through the window himself.

"I ran into the secretary's office where she was talking on the phone and I said, 'Hey, your professor just jumped through the window.' She held her hand up, as if there was something more important she was saying on the phone. 'The guy jumped through the fucking window,' I said again when she put the phone down. 'We know. We know,' she said, like a nurse in a loony bin. 'This happens when he talks to a visitor. I've already talked to maintenance and they're coming over to fix the window.'

"I ran around the building. It was just a three-foot drop from his first floor window, and he wasn't even hurt, just lying there more or less relaxed now, smiling, crumbling some autumn leaves in his hand, as if this was just what he needed. 'Why do you want to get involved in this ugly business?' he asked. 'You're young. You still have time. You're not even a zoologist. Why this interest in bats?'

"'It's not the bats that I'm interested in, Professor. Not the bats themselves.'

"'What then?' He jumped up spryly and tossed the leaf crumbs into the air.

"'I need to find out about their ability to capture the souls of men,' I said.

"'Oh, that,' he said, and for the first time that afternoon this professor looked me right in the eye. He was crying again. This was so weird. He said, 'In Queensland I ate the bats regularly. Flying foxes. They tasted good, like hare.' He was sobbing. 'I made them into hassenpfeffer.' Then the Professor got up and walked away. Enough of that, I figured. I didn't follow him any more.''

Dusty stepped out of the cookshack. The wind was coming down off the hills and tasted like evergreens. He could hear Fletcher arranging his gear in the tower. "Another few minutes and we can eat," he shouted. The edge of the mountains glowed faintly with the moon that was going to rise full that night.

After his story about the Professor, Fletcher fell silent, and the little girl stood up and crossed the room to Dusty. "You sleep in my room," she said.

"Okay little niece," said Dusty, touching her hair.

"You know what else I have in my room?"

"No."

"Guess."

"You've got me in your room."

"No, silly. I mean all the time. Every little minute."

"Okay. I give up. What have you got?"

"I've got a whole place full of munchmellow people. A whole place." She spread her arms to show how big a whole place was.

Peter came in from the kitchen with his arm around his older daughter and announced dinner. He was a good cook. The curry was delicious, but Tasha made a point of eating a hamburger. "I used to enjoy all that foreign food," she said. "All that exotic, but not any more."

"Tasha belongs to AA," Peter said. "It's not what you think. This one is American America. It's a new organization here."

"I didn't tell the Professor," Fletcher said, still intensely focussed on Dusty. "But I'd eaten the bats before too. I fried them up and they were delicious. Little tiny things, that shriveled up to the size of a currant, but they came out crisp and delicate, little bursts of taste. I just took handfuls of them off the wall and tossed them in the pan."

"If we want an American culture," Tasha said, "we've got to work on what's American. You feed the soil if you want to grow roots. So I eat many hamburgers. It's not bad, it's good. American cars. American jobs. American America."

"That's some of the jargon," said Peter. "Can you believe it? Tasha put away her hippie and found a redneck in her closet."

"Rednecks are closer to hippies than they are to college professors." A resigned scowl crossed Peter's mouth, as he turned the curry with a spoon. Tasha went on, "The rednecks will be the survivors, and the salvation of America. Just watch."

"Watch what? The holocaust? The salvation of what?"

"Look, I don't mean they're going to save some New York art made with a piece of string, or some literature you can't read."

"C'mon, Tasha. You know it's just chic for you to like rednecks at this moment. You don't even know a redneck."

"You never listen to me."

"I don't listen to the Ku Klux Klan, either."

"Why not?"

"I roasted them like hibachi on little sewing needles. They were good that way," Fletcher said. "And I used them once for stuffing in a chicken."

"I still eat chicken, Colonel Sanders."

"And you were a goddam good cook, too," Peter said.

"That's the only time you ever listen to me is when I tell you how I used to cook something."

"Well I don't think that shit you eat now is good for you,

and you used to agree with me, all that chemical beef.''

''Go take a chic leak,'' Tasha turned to the kids. ''Who does the dishes tonight?''

''I'm sorry you had to come all this way to listen to this,'' Peter said to Dusty. The kids seemed to ignore the argument. They worked out the dishes without dispute. ''We decided best to let the kids hear us argue,'' Peter said. ''Gives them a sense of reality. You know there's still a lot of love between Tasha and me. We still have to work some things out.'' Peter put his arm around his wife and kissed her.

Tasha smiled. ''Thanks for the dinner.''

''Don't rub it in. You didn't eat any of my dinner.''

''I always wonder what these bats eat,'' Fletcher said.

''I didn't have to cook it either,'' she kissed him again.

''We promised,'' said Peter, his arm around Tasha. ''To end every argument with a kiss.''

Dusty took the whole pot of chili to the table. It was a big crusty, cast-iron dutch oven that kept bubbling after he took it off the fire. Fletcher was back at the table, facing the mountains this time.

''When does the moon come up?'' he asked.

''Don't know,'' said Dusty. ''Any minute now.'' He ladled some chili into the bowls. ''Since my kids have stopped coming here with me I tend to make the chili real extreme. A little 'picante' jolts the consciousness, especially when you're alone.'' It was changing, Dusty thought. The story had been Swiss Family Robinson when the kids were included in the fantasy, and now for him it was a retreat, lonely and calm. Fletcher didn't taste the chili. He stared behind Dusty towards the brightened edge of the mountains.

"Have you been to see Peter since I met you there?"

"No, not there."

"I wondered how they were doing. How the kids were doing. I didn't think they'd get divorced but…"

"I've been in my room," Fletcher said.

"With the bats." Dusty looked at the covered cage still sitting on the table. It made him a little anxious that Fletcher hadn't yet tasted the chili, a vestige of raising his kids.

"I wanted to figure out what they ate," said Fletcher. "I mean, how they survived, and if each of them really did hold onto the soul of some New Yorker. Wouldn't you want to know?" Fletcher caught Dusty with his eye that seemed already full of moonlight. "If you were in possession of bats like these?" He lifted the cloth from the cage.

Dusty was caught by this question with his mouth full of hot chili. "Of course. Yeah. Of course I would." His eyes were tearing.

"Yes, yes, yes," said Fletcher. "Yes I did. And one night my roommate was having a party, and I wanted to stay in my room, because a lot of the little things were giving birth. They had chosen the wall separating my room from the rest of the apartment as their maternity wall. It was fine. It made me feel good. Each teeny baby was born sucking on a nipple smaller than a flyspeck. There was a hum coming off the wall like real contentment, that I heard even under the speakers blasting in the living room. I wanted to hold one of the little mothers in my hand, wanted to feel it give birth. That was when I reached in with a finger to take one off, and I felt something really weird. My finger," he held up his forefinger, "actually sank into the wall beyond the little bats. I thought there was maybe more than one layer of them, so I pushed real gently and my hand went in up to the wrist, and I still didn't feel any wall, but around my hand there was this prickling of energy. Then the whole forearm went in—NO WALL. I pulled the arm out and looked at it. Not a mark, but it tingled like crazy, like all the molecules were popping. It was raining out, so just to prove it to myself I went over to the wall that separated my room from the street and stuck my arm through up to the shoulder. I could feel the difference in the temperature outside, and when I pulled back my hand was wet. My hand was really wet."

"It was wet, huh? Your hand was wet?" Fletcher still hadn't touched his chili.

"Yeah. Yeah, from the rain outside. I mean it wasn't a wall there, only this solid front of bats to separate me from everything. And I don't know how they were still structural. I put my hand back in and waved it back and forth, like moving it through water packed solid with minnows."

"Why don't you eat some chili?" Dusty said. He looked at the cage Fletcher had brought. It was one of those frail cages of sticks the Chinese use for crickets. He couldn't see any bats in it.

"So then I decided to go into the party and tell them about it. Now that wasn't easy for me to do because Lydia was there, and she was an old girlfriend of mine who came to the party because she wanted to see me, and I really didn't want to see anyone like that, not until I figured all this stuff out. But I did want someone else to see what I saw, because I was feeling really crazy at that moment as you can well imagine, and I wanted someone to tell me it was happening. Lydia was already knocking on my door anyway. 'Hey, Fletcher, come on out here, babes, this is a party.'

'''Listen,' I said. 'First you come in here. I need to show you something.' I was in my space, I mean IN IT, and that was where I had to stay.

'''If it's those bats you talk about I don't want to see it.'

'''How do you know? You never seen my bats.'

'''Bats make me feel weird, even talking about them.' She opened the door a little more. 'You come to the party.'

'''Watch,' I said. 'I can put my arm through the wall.' I did it for her. I put my arm in right to the shoulder.

''She acted as if she didn't see it. 'Come. Come to the party.' She pulled me by the other arm through the doorway into the living room. Everyone was dancing close to a slow number. Lydia was one of these ample red-headed women and she pulled me up against her body so I disappeared in her soft tits. 'I got a lot of hair,' she said. 'The bats'll get in it.'

'''That's a silly superstition, Lydia.' I leaned back to look at her face. She was a good woman, but you wouldn't call her smart. 'Those bats...I mean I can walk right through that wall.'

'''Look, I don't like to talk about them, even. They make me feel weird, Fletcher. They come in the night. They suck your blood.'

'''Forget it. I'm going back to my room. Look, you keep

your eye on that wall, and in a few minutes I'll be coming through it, not through the door, through the wall, and when you see that happening you tell everyone to watch. Okay?'

"She hesitated a little, and looked at me with some sad eyes because she wasn't getting what she wanted, but then she said okay even though it made her feel a little stupid. I went back to my room. To get it across at all I knew I'd have to give a powerful demonstration. It crossed my mind that if these bats held everybody's soul in New York, maybe nobody else was capable of seeing them, like trying to look into your own eye without a mirror; but it was gross for me to presume that I was the only one aboard with a soul. And I even thought that maybe there were no bats, maybe there was nothing for anyone to see, maybe just my imagination was bothered like that, and I was crazy, or the world had cracked apart and I was caught in the cusp and I'd lost sight of everything else retreating around the bend, if you see what I mean. I said to myself, now this is really crazy, Fletcher, to believe that these bats had replaced wallboard and brick and stud and joist, and that they would yield their space so you could move through a wall, I mean, just for you, to separate the bonds of energy or whatever it is that makes a wall a wall."

"I don't see any bats in this cage, Fletcher," said Dusty. He held the cage close to his face. Fletcher's eyes were fixed on the hill at Dusty's back. "You should eat a little chili, anyway," Dusty said.

"I'm gonna try to tell you what it was like, Dusty; but you've gotta remember that you can't really describe what it feels like to walk through a wall. You've gotta experience it yourself. I figured you had to do it naked, because it wasn't right to put some clothing through a wall, so I stripped and relaxed. There was a light humming in the air that put me right at ease. I slowly moved up against the wall. It was iridescent blue from all the little eyes focused on me now. It was like coming flat against the surface of the sky, not a cloud visible in any direction. I didn't have to take a step. I didn't even have to think about it, because it was pulling on me, sucking all the gravity out of my weight, and I was about to take off. As soon as I moved to finger a few of the creatures aside I felt the release, zero gravity, and I was launched, and this mellow-like temperature began to fill me like water coming into a sponge. There was no resistance. None. Entering the bats was like being held aloft by the meekest wind. I've tried to think of what it was like when my body was entirely within the wall, but it's hard. Maybe it's something like taking a bath, if you can imagine each of your molecules being scrubbed separately by a tiny bat. Does that help?"

"Yeah. Each molecule. That's good," said Dusty.

"And then there's this smell, a scent, that I never got anywhere else, that you smell it in your whole body, and in your mind, not in your nose, too subtle for that, distinct and sweet, and that, I assure you, is the odor of time emanating from the forms of things, all things opening once like flowers, petals falling in the wind of the endless events, the transcription of events. Doesn't it sound crazy? I mean, you know, I'm not even sure I'm saying it. Like you penetrate the wall, but the bats penetrate you, and there's room for everything, nothing lost, nothing added. And Dusty, I tell you, my understanding of what my emotions were changed in that moment; I mean I can't even call them *my* emotions any more. I feel like it's me now, and the emotions, and we share a space, like live in the same apartment. I disregard them, just visualize each little piece of emotion carried away by a tiny blue-eyed bat flying through time-scented bazaars of energy. Don't get me wrong, Dusty. This isn't an idea I have, but I know it, I see it, and there it goes... No way to explain this, but I want you to promise me, Dusty, that one of these times you yourself will penetrate a wall, and then you will immediately need no explanation. Do you promise me that? " Fletcher looked for once directly into Dusty's eyes. Fletcher's eyes were bright blue and moving in their depths.

"Okay. I'll do that. But only if you eat some of your chili right now." How paternal that sounds, Dusty thought. "And I honestly can't see any bats in this cage, Fletcher."

"So I did come through the wall, and no one was looking. Not even Lydia. She was way on the other side of the room. Then my roommate looked at me and said. 'Hey get a look at Fletcher. He's streaking.'

"I was just standing there. Sabrina, a tall, skinny woman, wearing a sheer crepe dress, came over to dance with me. 'I love naked men,' she said, jabbing her bones against me. And my roommate, his name is Sonny, said, 'Now we've got a real party going,' and he started to strip, and pretty soon the whole party was naked. Then I knew it was no use, I mean they'd never figure it out. I went back to my room and packed some gear, and then descended slowly through the outer wall and into the rain, and I headed up here to see you because I wanted to get far away, and I remembered you invited me. In a way, you know, I didn't want to leave, because those little bats helped me to understand what little I know about the nature of stuff. Anyway now I'm here.''

''And you're welcome for a while. I'm glad you're here,'' Dusty said. ''But you should eat some chili.'' Fletcher's arms rested in a broken circle around the bowl, but he showed no interest in the contents. ''And to tell you the truth, Fletcher,'' Dusty said, lifting the cage, and shaking it slightly. ''I don't see any bats in this cage.''

Fletcher gently picked the cage from Dusty's hand, as if he were picking a bubble off the surface of a dream. He held it in front of his face. ''Then don't look at them,'' he said.

''I want to see them,'' Dusty said.

Fletcher stared through the cage. Dusty looked at his full bowl. Not a bite taken. He would have mentioned it once more, just once, but the words stopped in his mouth when he looked at Fletcher again. The whites of Fletcher's eyes had disappeared. He was staring out through two wide blue spheres. His shoulders raised up around his face so they almost covered his ears. A smile opened on his face, so strange that he seemed to be attentive to the echo of a sound Dusty couldn't hear in this world. Then as a curtain closes on the last actor present who will never deliver the conclusive line, Fletcher opened his wings wide behind himself and holding the cage high he rose on the slowly undulating membranes unfurled from his side. ''Fletcher,'' Dusty said softly, as if he were remembering his name. He didn't even have time to doubt what happened, or question it. He saw it. Fletcher rose in a leisurely spiral, his blue eyes drilling down on Dusty; and his black shape rose against the constellations already dimmed by moonlight, and it hid the stars of Bootes, the Corona, and the Big Bear with its wings.

Dusty breathed at the table, slowly in and out. He looked out at the last dark shades of sunset and could see on the water that the moon had finally risen behind him. He watched some fear rise in himself and then fly away. Had this happened at all? He picked up Fletcher's bowl. If only he had eaten a bit of it. Had he been sleepwalking by himself through a dream? If there had only been one other person there who might have seen it, maybe Nick who had built the tower in which Fletcher stowed his gear. Dusty turned to look at the tower. The moon was right behind it. It seemed higher than the hills. Fletcher's gear would still be inside it, all he had to do was open the door. He remembered his son's mild obsession with it as he built the tower, started at ten, finished when he was sixteen, hauling driftwood boards and 4 x 4's from the beach, fitting them precisely as he could. And he put a bed in it, that wasn't long enough for him by the time he was sixteen, so he had to open one side and cover an extension for his feet to sleep. Now the tower looked like it had always been there. Dusty emptied Fletcher's bowl of chili into the pot, and walked to the tower. Its west wall was still warm from the sun. The moon filled his campsite with silver light. The tower was full of everything, he knew it, full of gear and nostalgia. He looked up at it extended to the stars as if ready to be launched. No, he thought, don't open the tower. Don't look in. It's the same door at this time when you get to madness or to sentiment. When something rises questions go unanswered. Some day maybe his brother would come and use whatever was in there, maybe not. This was a structure full of everything, or full of nothing. He removed his hand from the wall, turned his back on it, and took seventeen steps away from the tower, twenty-six steps away from the moon.

BOUNCE

"These weigh some tons," said Dusty, as he and Vinny and ten other of the neighbors got under each of the green spruce beams and grunted together to hoist them slowly on to the studs.

"Now you're going to have a real house," Dusty said, stepping back to look at it when they had raised the last beam.

"Yeah," said Vinny Falconieri, a mile-long grin on his face. "Vinny the Ginny's little cabin grows up." Vinny jumped onto the rough floor of his new structure, and framed in the beams and studs he held up his arms like a winner. Dusty started to applaud, and all the men and women, the kids, the dogs howling, they all applauded, and Vinny banged his foot on the floor, and the applause followed him into a beat, and Vinny started to dance, just threw his head back and whirled, and Dusty jumped onto the floor to dance with Vinny, and someone pulled out a guitar, and someone else a fiddle, and Sally Lens jumped up and shook her tambourine, and all the young folks and the old ones, and all the families were dancing in their coveralls and their jeans, in their long beards, their 'Sunday' skirts hooping out, and the circle of spruce around the clearing swayed under the evening Cape Breton sky, and the gulls, rising way up and flying inland cried warnings of a big storm on its way.

After the feast, when most of the people were gone, a

few sat around the little cabin in the light of kerosene lamps: Lennie Axelrod and his wife, Roz, were still there, and Sally Lens, the dancer, with her boyfriend, Roger, and Sybil McPhalls and her little daughter, Laurel, and Marie, the young Micmac woman who lived with Vinny was cleaning up at the sink.

"So this be it," Vinny said. "This be the place where I sit it out. Cape Breton Island." Dusty was grinning, an incredible joy bubbling in his heart. The glass of red wine trembled in his hand. Roger picked up a guitar and played a few chords. "You want to know why I chose this place?" Vinny went on. "I'll tell you. Because everything right began here. Because this is where all the stories begin."

"What's that mean?" Dusty asked.

Vinny pointed at the map of Cape Breton Island on his wall. "Look at it. Have you ever thought about why it looks the way it does? It's a peculiar piece of real estate, right? How do you think it got to look this way?"

"I know. I know," said little Laurel who was listening with mouth and eyes wide open.

"What is it, darling? What do you know?" Vinny picked Laurel up and turned slowly, holding her in the air.

"One day, a very very long time ago," she said, "God was running too fast, and so he tripped, and he fell down, and his hand landed on Cape Breton Island."

"Of course. That's right. That's what happened." The child beamed, and put her finger in her mouth and looked at everyone in the room. Vinny put her down and she ran back to her mother and hugged her. He went to the map. "You see Lake Ainslie, that's where the thumb hit, and the fingers are St. Anne's Bay, and St. Andrews Channel, and East Bay, and the meat of the hand is Big Bras D'Or lake."

"You think that's really what happened?" Lenny asked, a little removed by the wine.

"Oh, Lenny," said his wife. "You're so ingenuous. You don't know a story from reality."

"But that is what happened," said Vinny.

"Vincent, I mean you don't really believe that something happened that way. You were speaking figuratively."

"I'm ready to go back to the States," Lenny was an aging expatriate from the Vietnam war resistance. "I don't care about any of this."

"I speak the truth. Vinny Falconieri does not tell anything he does not know is true. Just check out this scenario for a few minutes." Vinny sat on the edge of his chair and leaned forward. "It's ten or twenty thousand years ago, and you're on the Pacific Coast, and suddenly you see a bright star jump onto the horizon in the west, and it's coming your way, moving at incredible speed."

"Oh shit, shit," said Sybil, holding up a bag of her home-grown grass. "I hope someone here has some papers. I thought there were some papers in here."

"You try to watch it, but it's so bright, brighter than the sun coming at you, and you cover your eyes, and it shines red right through your hands, and if you don't get dead from the hurricane winds and thunder, or the heat, or the shock waves of super-heated air exploding as this huge chunk of rock passes, trailing a tail of plasma and vaporized rock hundreds of miles long, you can watch it streak eastwards."

"That's all I care about doing. I want to go back to America," said Lenny. "I want to get Rolfed."

"Lenny, you know you can get Rolfed in Toronto," said Roz. "He's so ridiculous sometimes. He always wants to get Rolfed."

Dusty moved to sit next to Sybil on the bench, and took the glowing joint from her hand, and pulled the smoke deep into his lungs. He didn't enjoy marijuana much any more, but the beam-raising, and Vinny's story, rated a few tokes. He laid an arm around Sybil's shoulder, and she moved closer to him. She was a powerful woman. He admired her independence, how she lived poor, raising her child alone. She was intimidating, but exciting. Laurel climbed onto Dusty's lap, and pressed her head into his chest. "Your heart goes bump bump bump," she said. "Because it loves you," Dusty whispered in her ear.

Sally Lens stood up and began to move to Vinny's story. "I need to dance," she said. "I love to move to stories." Her loose yellow skirt swung out over her pale blue leotard as she whirled, fanning light breezes against their faces.

"This is not a story," said Vinny. "This is the truth." He pulled on the joint and passed it to Lenny. Roz snatched it from Lenny's hand.

"That stuff makes him impotent," she said.

"Okay. So you survive, and you get up and look to the east, and there's this swath of destruction as far as you can see, where the huge meteor has passed, burning forests, exploding mountaintops, and it's travelling thousands of miles an hour heading for the east coast, and underneath it, modestly moving at five hundred miles an hour, carrying Cape Breton along with it on the easternmost tip of this continent, is our whole earth, poor little planet. And if that meteor was going a little faster, or if the earth were a little slower, it would have missed Cape Breton, but everything was right on target, and in a split second one hundred and sixty cubic miles of Cape Breton were blasted to powder."

Roger had fallen asleep and right on cue the guitar he was holding crashed to the floor. Sally picked it up and danced with it as if it were the body of a friend.

"So guess what happened," Vinny teased little Laurel.

"What?" Laurel asked sleepily from Dusty's lap. Then she sat up straight. "I know. All the lobsters in the ocean cooked and made a lobster party." She settled back, her lips wetting Dusty's t-shirt.

"That's right, honey." Vinny kissed her on the forehead, then turned and danced with Sally as he went on talking. "And there was even more, and I'm not making this up. I learned a lot of this from an expert, this guy named David Dow, who's an engineer and a geologist and studies missile impact. He's real convincing. Just you think of Krakatoa, when it blew up in the nineteenth century with incredible violence, and removed only about a cubic mile of material. Tens of thousands of people were drowned in the tidal waves that lasted for days, and the dust from Krakatoa stayed in the air for years after it got blasted into the stratosphere. Well you know this Cape Breton meteor was one hundred and sixty times worse. Tidal waves inundated all the coasts of the world. A mushroom cloud like thousands of H-bombs exploding at once. Violent storms everywhere, like nothing else we

know, and the sea water boiling for months, sending fog
everywhere."

"O wow," said Roger, opening his eyes.

"I was waiting for someone to say that," said Vinny.

"This is great," said Roz. "I feel like I'm in a book by
James Michener."

"I never read a book by him," Lenny said.

"Everyone's read a book by Michener," Roz said.
"Hawaii, the one about Spain. It's real stupid. Real
middlebrow stuff. I started Hawaii, but I never finished
it."

"Here comes Ms. Bennington again," said Lenny.

"Of course this affected the whole planet," Vinny went
on, "and it was during the early history of modern man, so
all these legends of floods, and how the earth shuddered
and groaned and the sky got dark for months, and the
story that Lucifer fell from the sky as a fallen star, stories
from all over the planet, South America, Polynesia, Africa,
Asia, were all spun out of this one catastrophic event here,
right here on Cape Breton Island."

"Bennington has nothing to do with it. You don't even
know anything about Bennington, Lenny."

"I know Bernard Malamud taught there. John Gardner
taught there. Anne Waldman went to school there."

"So I'm hunkering down right here," Vinny went on,
oblivious, "and this is where I'll stay while this planet
goes through all its catastrophes, and survive or not, to
hell with it, Vinny's sitting tight at the origin of all the
stories of the world." Marie, who hardly ever spoke, rose
from leaning against the counter where she had sat down
after finishing the dishes, and stepped slowly towards

Vinny, singing, "Tu tu tu tu tu tu tu," like a bird of easy heart, and they embraced, her dark black hair flashing gold down her back in the kerosene light, and they stood in the center of the room, swaying in the rich silence that penetrated from the dark clearing around the house.

"Well," said Roz, first break the silence. "I guess we'd better leave before the storm hits." She threw Lenny's cap onto his lap.

Lenny sighed and stood up. "What a place," Lenny said. "Cape Breton." He put on the cap. "Wrent-a-Wreck" was embroidered on the insignia across the front. "I don't care about any of this," he said. "I just want to go back to the States. I want to learn Tai Chi."

"He wants to get Rolfed. He wants to learn Tai Chi. You're slow enough already, Lenny. You don't have to study Tai Chi. Seven years you've been building our house."

"I just want to study Tai Chi," he said.

"Good night," said Roz. "Thanks." She pulled Lenny out the door. Sally and Roger left soon after.

Dusty stood up with Laurel sleeping in his arms. "I am going to dance now," he said, and moved around the floor with the little girl in his arms. He was full of feelings. "I'll dance forever with Vinny, and with the whole world right here in this place, and all the stories will spin out, and the stories will spin out forever."

Sybil took Laurel from Dusty's arms as he turned, and whispered in his ear, "Dusty Wier, you're hot."

"What?" Her warm breath startled him, sent a chill down his back.

"You've got it. You're hot." She put Laurel down on the

couch, and covered her with a light blanket. "I guess I'm here for the night. I hate to move her when she's asleep like this."

"Sure. You can stay here. No problem," Vinny said. "There's a couple of sleeping bags in that chest. You can sleep with Dusty?"

"With me? Here?" Dusty shook his head. "Okay. Good idea."

Sybil grabbed Dusty's buckle, and tugged on his belt. "See what I mean? You're hot." Dusty grinned at her. "We'll sleep outside, Mr. Grin," Sybil said. "Under the new beams."

"It'll rain on you," Marie sang.

"That's good," said Sybil.

They dragged a thin foam mat and some sleeping bags out onto the rough floor under the beams, and they lay staring up at the clouds lit yellow and green with distant lightning.

"What do you think?" Sybil whispered. "Will we get wet here?"

"We'll get everything here," Dusty replied.

She took his hand from his chest and placed it between her thighs, and bit his shoulder through his shirt. "Dusty, you're a very sexy man, but you always wear awful tasting shirts."

"That's what I want to do," Dusty said, still moved by something innocent that had risen in himself.

"What?" Sybil asked.

"Everything, Sybil. Just do everything."

"Well, there's nothing to stop you here," said Sybil, as the frame of the unfinished house filled with thunder.

"This could be the beginning of the new world, Sybil."

"Dusty, how are we ever going to get along? You're this incurable romantic and I'm...I'm..."

"You're a horny woman."

"Yeah. I love it." She pulled at his zipper, gave up, and slipped her hand under his belt.

Dusty rolled over to kiss her. "Well," he said, "at least we've got compatible afflictions." A warm mist came down like a bouquet of lips, enveloped their embrace.

* * *

Dusty pulled his pack out of his little pickup and filled it with groceries. He looked across the bay to the horizon. When it was clear as this he could make out Prince Edward Island crumbling the horizon-line to the south. Only an eye intimate with the view could see the island at all, and then it had to be still enough so the edge of land wasn't mistaken for shifting swells. And it had to be morning, the sun low in the east to illuminate the dunes and small houses he imagined were there, to distinguish the edge he saw against the sky, that gave him the sensation of both *this* and *that* in the world, which he preferred to the uneasy monotone he'd been suffering for the last few days, as a persistent haze erased the horizon and made him invent the island, and the distances, and the separation of sea and sky.

Dusty parked his truck at the head of his trail, just off the dirt road that penetrated Broad Cove Banks, from Kennedy's Canteen, past MacLean's campground now closed, past Foot Cape and Cape Mabou roads, for nine

miles or so to Sight Point, where a trail begins that leads
you by Mackinnon's Brook all the way to Mabou. The
road is narrow and rough, and winds through forests of
spruce and fir, and opens suddenly around a bend onto a
cliff that dives to the sea, a coastline that cracks the
shadows of the mind: to precipitous meadows lavender
with vetch or stippled with cornflowers and daisies or ripe
with strawberries in July, and his thoughts hoist over the
horizon to settle on other coasts never seen, and their
spectacles of mammals and shells.

From the summer camps at the end of the road kids set
out for picnics at Mackinnon's Brook, carrying their
peanut butter and jelly, their despised sardines, their
six-packs of Pepsi. They descend the creek-bed to the
small, bowl-shaped cove big seas carved from the cliff. An
empty eagle's nest, woven from big branches, rests in the
overhanging cliff. They stretch out on the flat stones above
the tide and peel their oranges. The kids are happy to rest
after the hike, and some of them sleep.

Their counselor, Terry Metz, a high school senior from
Worcester, Mass., self-conscious about his weight, but
good-natured, a sense of humor about it too, climbs to the
pasture above the little cove with Dooley Shaykin, from
New York City, a junior counselor with big breasts and a
thick waist, and a face bothered by acne. Terry has been
coming to the camp for several years and knows a lot
about the wild stuff that grows, especially if it's something
to eat. He is thrilled to get off alone with her finally,
promises to show her where the cranberries grow, and
some wild strawberries that ripen late close to the sea, but
taste better than anything because of the salt wind. "But

we don't want a lot of little kids following us, because they just run around and make a lot of noise and ruin everything." She agrees, so they sneak off together through the high grass and wild rose brambles leaving the young ones to sleep while the tide comes in. Terry is more interested, of course, in Dooley's breasts than he is in wild cranberries. They are big and they are firm and he wants to touch them, and has been maneuvering schedules since he got to camp so he would have a chance to be alone with her breasts. Dooley loves Terry's eyes, very pretty blue, that drop whenever he talks to her to stare at her breasts, as if he has a weight in his chin that pulls his eyes down to what her mother always said were her jewels. She wore only a light cotton t-shirt, her Save-The-Seals one, that showed her nipples off in the wind. Terry was cute, how he'd jerk his head back up and look at her face and grin as if embarrassed. Sometimes it embarrassed her to display them, but it did keep her from being totally ignored by boys, because she was, otherwise, she felt, just plain and fat.

"I've never been too good at any sports anyway," she said. "My mom was this great water-skier, you know she was from Florida. She liked to show off her bod in a bathing suit, but would never admit it. But I think it's dumb. I like to swim okay, but I don't get fanatic about it."

"Yeah, I used to be on a baseball team, but I hated it," Terry said. "It's such a boring game to play. You stand there in the outfield and you stand there and fall asleep. And I wasn't very good at it anyway. The only hit I ever got in the league was a bunt, and I didn't even hit that with the bat. I hit it with my eye.''

Dooley looked at his eye, which dropped immediately to look at her breasts. They came to a soft patch of clover in the meadow, and as if they had been simultaneously struck down they both fell and lay on their backs, and forgot their mission to hunt for cranberries. They watched a procession of clouds shaped like scimitars, their cutting edges luminous against the deep blue. Terry caught a spot of red out of the corner of his eye, some strawberries near his face. He picked a few, big ones for wild berries, as fat and long as the top joint of his pinky. He put them on Dooley's slightly parted lips. She let them lie there for a moment, then sucked them into her mouth.

''You're exactly right,'' she said.

''What?''

''Just one little berry and my whole mouth is full of taste.''

Reginald got to the camp on one of two scholarships that came to The Settlement where he lived with other problem kids. He took the one to Canada, and Plooky got the one up in Maine, because he didn't want to be too far away from his sister who was often strung out on drugs. Reginald and Plooky were the only two kids at The Settlement together enough to be out in the world, if you could call being with some rich kids in this north wilderness 'the world'. If Plooky had come here with him he would probably relate better to everyone; but that's the way it was, sometimes you've got to be alone. He liked some of the kids here okay, but couldn't emphathize with their complaints home asking for money, their extravagant back-packs, their top-of-the-line hiking books.

He went everywhere they did on his Converse All-Stars.
These kids liked to steal to impress him, just to be weird.
He didn't mind stealing himself, if he really needed
something, but never to show off. Halfway back from
town, in the back of the van, they'd all empty their
pockets in the middle of the floor to show what they'd got.
It was all like doing something illegal to them, like
disobeying their parents, not like survival. They were a lot
richer than the shopkeepers they took the junk from, who
were easy marks because they weren't used to shoplifters.
They liked to give all the stuff to Reginald, because he was
their one charity case. He didn't want all those flashlights,
pocket-knives, pens, even a box of regular Tampax, but
he'd take it just to return it to the shelves of the poor
shopkeepers next time he was in town, and he had to be a
lot slicker than they'd been when they were ripping it off,
because people in town always stared at him to figure out
if he was black or Micmac. He'd heard of Robin Hood,
and he was just the opposite.

He walked away from the other kids, up the stream bed
towards the mountains. Wild irises bloomed in the marshy
places along the banks. He loved all this nature. For him it
compared favorably with the streets. The banks of
Mackinnon's Brook got steeper towards the mountains,
rose about sixty feet on either side. Reginald climbed the
one on his left. Tiny mushrooms growing out of the moss
smelled like garlic. He picked one and looked at it close—
tan, translucent, fluted like a little umbrella. It made him
happy. He came up on a level place full of fallen trees and
brush. He saw a little clearing on the opposite bank,
where people had camped, a circle of stone around a fire

pit, some logs arranged as benches. Smoke seemed still to be rising from the center of the stone circle. Strange smoke. He rubbed his eyes and looked again. There was a form to the smoke, like it was becoming substantial. He looked up to the top of the trees and the sky beyond, blue, crossed by two intersecting con-trails. He turned back. The smoke was someone, the shape of a young boy that moved away from the firepit like a jellyfish in the sun. It was like a 3-D reflection in a cloudy mirror, like a hologram he'd seen once in a museum. He felt his arm and pinched his belly to make sure he was actually there. This was like living in one of the ghost stories his Grandma Venable used to tell him when he was little.

"What time do you make it to be, boy?" asked the apparition.

Reginald looked around to see if there was someone else. No one else, of course. "You talking to me, spook? Whatever you are." Some weird things had happened to him, but this was the most weird yet. One thing he remembered his grandma said was that you've got to be tough with a ghost, or else it can get the best of you. "Because if you talking to me, you watch who you be calling 'boy', spook."

"Time's all I'd like to know," the apparition asked again.

"Okay. I guess it's close to noon by now. I don't got no watch."

"I mean, I'd like to know which year. I don't know what year this is yet."

"Which year this is? This is 1983, chump. Been that since January first, since New Year's Eve. And now it's summer, in case you're wondering."

The ghost stood there quietly, as if it was thinking about things. "Wait a second," Reginald said. "I'll come over there. Don't you go nowhere." Reginald dropped down into the stream bed. He wanted to see this up close, if he was really seeing it. He climbed up the other side, didn't expect it to be there. He was making this up and he knew it; in fact, he hoped it was there and he hoped it was gone at the same time. But there it was, standing in the campsite, even more substantial. He knew them duppies liked to spook around some houses, but he'd never heard of one spooking in the woods before.

"I just don't know," the ghost said, when Reginald got close to him. "I never been out in 1983 before. I'm always here, don't you know, but I don't always come out in every year. What did you say was your name?"

Reginald opened his mouth but no sound came out. Up this close to the ghost he was suddenly freaked. This was too weird. The ghost's body was of a young boy, but he had an old voice, old and full of echoes. The eyes were very blue, and there was long black hair, and he wore some rags of old-fashioned clothes, all of this perfectly transparent.

"My name is Duncan. Don't be afraid of me. What could your name be?"

"Reginald," he finally said, and a great relief. "I come from New York City."

"I thought that perhaps you were a Micmac Indian. I never been with a Micmac Indian."

"I got some Indians back there in me when they was fuckin' with some slaves, so there might be some Indian in me. Everyone was fuckin' everyone back then, just like now, except they had babies, because they didn't have the pill, the diaphragm, none of that shit."

"So I am Duncan Mackinnon, and this is my place, and this is where I am forever."

"That's a long time, Duncan. That's forever." Reginald felt something sad about Duncan, the way he had said that. This was a deep ghost, a friendly ghost. "In the projects we had a kid named Dunkin'," he said to cheer up the ghost. "He was fourteen years old and six foot nine. We called him Donuts." Duncan didn't smile, missed the point. Reginald stepped around him to look at a bright orange mushroom growing near some birches. He loved the way the mushrooms grew. He picked this, a pretty one, the cap covered with white scales, like barnacles. He turned to show it to Duncan, but the ghost was gone. "Duncan," he said. "Duncan." He kicked the ashes around in the fire-pit, a long time since there'd been a fire there. "Where are you? Where'd you go, Duncan?" It was stranger than being afraid of him, to suddenly miss him now. He walked a little way up the overgrown old road that went to Mabou, calling Duncan's name. Nothing. He stopped. This was stupid. There was nothing. He'd probably been making it up for himself anyway. He turned around and headed back for the ocean, holding the mushroom in front of himself.

"Don't you go eatin' that toadstool," said a voice, Duncan's.

Reginald looked around. Nothing to be seen. "Shit," he thought. "I'm making all this up too. I'm going crazy."

"Just don't you eat that."

"Duncan?"

"I eat one of them toadstools myself, and that's how I get dead. That's how I do myself in at that time." The voice seemed to come at him down a long tube.

"Duncan, where are you hiding? I can't see you nowheres."

"You know once I saw you lift up that toadstool I slipped me back about six seconds, because I don't appreciate such toadstools."

"So where are you now, Duncan?"

"I'm close, but I'm not available."

"So you a real dead man, Duncan?" Reginald couldn't figure if he was making this up, or if this was a real opportunity. There were a lot of questions he could ask someone dead. "Are you really a real spook talking to me here in the woods; I mean, really?" Questions like what does a dead person eat? Does a dead person need shoes? Does he find his mama if he never ever met her?

"Aye, you know I am dead at this time, but I don't comprehend all of it myself; because at the time I was alive I am still alive, and those are hard times, so I don't like to come out then, though I'm with my family then, but when I come out at a time like this I have been dead for many many years."

"This shit just don't make no sense to me, Duncan. When you die you be dead. That's dead. Someone pops you in the head with a police thirty-eight. That's it." Reginald climbed the bank to the meadow full of daisies and buttercups. "Isn't that it?"

"I'd like you to lay that mushroom down," said Duncan. "Pick some flowers instead."

"Okay. Alright." Reginald tossed the mushroom over his shoulder and picked a handful of daisies, and some curved sprays of purple vetch.

"I once could pick these flowers too," said Duncan's voice, sadly. "But I cannot pick them no more, at least not at this time when I'm here because my hands will pass right through them, and that's a disadvantage, to have no substantial hands. But I love the flowers here, and I love them back then too, because everywhere else was trees, and here there is always natural meadows, with strawberries I could eat that one summer when I was here. That's what I want to tell you, Reginald, how we got here, we Mackinnons, how we crossed from Scotland on a boat, and they put us down right here."

"Sure," Reginald said. He brushed the flowers across his face. "Tell me the story." He'd have to postpone his questions about the dead.

"It is perplexing to understand it these days, especially on a fine summer day like this, the hardships the settlers of this Broad Cove once had to endure."

Reginald continued his walk slowly down the meadow, with Duncan's voice following him like a trail of dust.

"See, most of us was brought here by boat from Scotland, because after the Highland chiefs lost the battle of Culloden the poor Scots fell on hard times, and we was starving, and this Cape Breton needed settlers, because even though the British had won the battle of Louisbourg here, the French was reproducing themselves so fast they was threatening to repopulate this island with French. So we was Catholics too, you see, and valued the large family, so they packed us up with promises, and they

shipped us here. 'Cha till mi tuille. We shall return no
more,' my father said, and after that he spoke no more
Gaelic to us. His name was Malcolm Mackinnon, and he
was a proud Highland husbandman and farmer, with a
warm Highland heart. First they took us to Pictou, where
we got us some supplies, not much because we was all so
poor, and they gave us some livestock - a cow and six
chickens for each family, and they showed us on a map
where our land would be, and then they took us on
another sailing boat, a small one, and brought us up here,
to this very coast. I climbed onto my father's back and
watched with him as Chief Surveyor Black, and Captain
Lord, both Britishers, pointed out on the map and
indicated on the shore the landmarks of what would be
my father's homestead. They showed us this very cove, at
the mouth of this brook, and my mother kept saying, "So
bonnie. Such bonnie meadows. Praise the Lord." But how
little she understood yet of the bitterness those bonnie
meadows would soon be in her life.

"It is a beautiful day, that day. Clear as a melody. Not
much waves, either, and lucky for us. They dropped my
father's little boat into the water, and put all of us in it, my
sisters crying all the time, and our allotment of supplies,
about a month of biscuits, some dry meat, the chickens, a
sack of flour, and my father tied our little cow to the back
of the boat, and they dropped her in the water, and she
swam all the way to shore as my father rowed. We came
up on this beach, and here we were. This was quiet as a
breath. My father put us down on the beach, and here we
were. I couldn't even stand up. I rolled around on the
sand, I was so happy, and I rolled over and over. The little

cow shook itself off, and my father untied it, and it ran up the bank to this meadow. I looked out to sea and the boat that had brought us was almost out of sight around the headland and we were alone to survive or not, according to our ambition and our luck.

"My father says, 'You follow that cow, Duncan. Do not let her out of your sight, because if we lose her, or her calf, it will mean hard times for us in the New World.'

" 'Aye, Father. I will,' said I, and I followed the cow up to somewhere near this very spot. Now a man can be displaced, but a cow is always at home, just so it has some grass to eat. I followed it to the fresh clover, that it must have smelled just as soon as it touched the beach, and I was pleased to sit there alone with it while it ate the clover on that warm May afternoon, my stomach still awash from the weeks at sea."

Reginald walked slowly across the meadow where it began to level off before the bluff that fell to the beach. "Right here. Right at this spot. This is where it happens," says the voice following him. He looks around. A place like anywhere else in the meadow.

"My father is a small, wiry man, powerful and brave. Always patient, too much patience, some say, to allow him to succeed at a homestead like this one. And I follow his orders and sit here all day in this spot, and watch the cow eat the clover, and it was such a balmy day at that. And watching that cow eat, and then stop to chew her cud, 'Sleepy,' I say, because that's the name I give her, chewing her cud, her eyes closed, 'This be the best day.' My father was working all day to put up a little shelter for my mother, who was pregnant, and my three sisters. She loses the baby, in fact, that winter, and the family lives through the year in a dark, dugout shelter, built up with sod, with our little boat on top of it for a roof, and anyone who has done that one winter will never get over it. And that's what they put up with, these Mackinnons, these MacIsaacs, these McLellans, and MacDougalls that settle on this island of Cape Breton.''

The voice grew silent, and Reginald could hear other kids screaming by the beach. ''I'm going nuts,'' he said to himself. ''Listening to a voice that I can't even see the mouth. Not even a ghost to look at. But I can't be making this up. There's a cow in this. I never heard nothing about a cow before.'' That was why he kept on listening. A cow. ''Hey, Duncan. Where are you? Are you still here?''

''It just made me stop to think,'' said the voice.

''Listen, Duncan, give me a chance to see you again. I want to see what a little spook looks like again. I won't do nothing with no mushrooms.''

''And I've been thinking about all the courageous people, those ones who did the brave things here, and were never heard of again. You know my father was one of them brave men.''

''Just give me another look at you, Duncan. Just so I can be sure of something. No mushrooms. I promise.''

''So as the sun was setting my father comes up to this spot, and he looks at the cow, who seems alright to me, just maybe a little full from having eaten so good, and my father says, 'O Duncan, now what did you do? O noooo.' You see I'd let the cow eat too much clover too fast, and I didn't know about this. I'd never learned before about the bloat.''

"Duncan, you just a jive spook. You won't let me see you again, put my mind at rest. You a jive monkey-ghost."

"So then my father rips up a handful of clover and holds it in my face. 'You should never, lad. You should never...' He throws the clover down and strokes the swollen belly of that little cow. 'Now don't you let her eat no more,' he admonishes me. "Aye, father, I will not," say I, and I know that cow will eat no more that day. He rushes across the brook to where that mountain ash still grows, and cuts a length of it, and peels the bark, and hollows it into a tube, and puts a sharp point on one end of it. The little Sleepy cow complains funny and low, getting real uncomfortable, and it tries to move but it can't. I feel real sorry for it, and sorry that my own ignorance has caused it such misery, though I can't be blamed. Father comes back with that sharp wooden tube and a big stone in his other hand, that I think for the moment he is going to use to bash my head."

"My grandma used to use her big cane across the back. Whap. Whap. Whap," Reginald said.

" 'What will you do with that stone, Father, and with that stick?' I ask him, but he is in no mood to answer my question. He walks up to that little cow that is lying on its side just looking so sad just trying to breathe. My father rubs its ears for some moments and speaks to it real nice, then he takes that sharp tube and holds the point down behind the ribs, where the poor creature is swollen even more than with her calf, and he drives the tube in with a sharp blow from the stone that makes my heart jump. Gas rushes out of the stomach with a loud whistle, and a sour smell fills my nose, and my father sends me back to be with my mother and the girls, and he stays up all night with the creature, and it lives alright, but loses its calf, and never freshens, and my mother has to slaughter it that fall, after I die, and my father is gone, just to feed herself and the girls. You know my father never returns.''

''Stop a second, bro. You know this is too nice a day to listen to all this sad story.''

''Funny, isn't it?'' says the voice of Duncan Mackinnon.

''What's funny, Duncan? What's funny?''

''I suppose you could call it a sad story when you hear it as I tell you from a beginning to an end of it, but for me it's just the way things are in the moments as they happen. Everything's just in proper balance. Everything is as it is.''

''Shit it is. You died and you were young. I don't want to die.''

''I'd be dead at this time under any condition, Reginald.''

''Don't talk about it.''

''Well I'm going to finish telling you this story, and you can listen to it if you want to, or else you can go back over there.''

Reginald looked down the stream bed where he could see the other kids messing around, making noise. He'd rather listen. ''I'm listening. Tell the story.''

''See, my father, he leaves that winter on foot across Cape Breton Island to Sydney, to register his land and get another cow if he can, one that might freshen in the spring. And before he leaves my father says to me, 'Duncan, my son, while I am gone you are the man here, and you must watch over this place like a man.' 'Father, I will,' says I. 'And you must take care of your mother and your sisters, and see to their comforts to the best of your abilities, because you are the man.' And I say, 'Father, I will,' and certainly I would have done so to the best of my youthful ability, had I not eaten that mushroom and died soon after he left. See, Malcolm Mackinnon does not come back ever, not that spring, nor the next winter, nor the next spring. Some say he takes off for Halifax with a wild Micmac woman he meets in Whycocomaugh, and they end up in North Carolina, and others say he falls through the ice and drowns when he tries to walk a short cut to Sydney across Great Bras D'or, and that's what I think is the true story, because my father is not one who will abandon his family so easily just for some personal satisfaction. So I eat the mushroom soon after he leaves and there I die in the midst of the most startling dreams. My mother keeps my body frozen in the snow until the ground is soft enough to lay it under, and they live that winter on meager supplies, a stroke of luck when my mother kills a baby seal on the ice for some meat, but the girls' bones go soft by early spring and they never really recover their form even when food becomes plentiful. And when the ground softens up the girls work real hard to dig my grave, and they have no proper coffin, so they wrap my body in spruce branches and put it away, and my mother aborts the new baby, and she plants a garden, and they catch many salmon as they run up the brook, and they smoke the meat of it to store for winter, and they dry the wild berries that's plentiful and luscious that year, and find wild onions, and eat the trout all summer, and if my father were there they'd all be happy, but alas he never comes, and they face another winter in the dugout under the boat, of loneliness and cold, and comes the next April they leave the land here and set off up the coast to look for other people, and they get as far as Margaree Harbor where there is a small community, a few houses, and only one of my poor bent sisters ever marries, and the other two remain as spinsters in Margaree, and that's where they stay for the rest of the days of their lives.''

The voice stopped, as if it would say no more. ''Duncan,'' Reginald whispered. ''Where'd you go?'' He looked around. ''Don't leave me yet.''

''It's that depression over there in the clover,'' Duncan said, his voice dimmer, further away. ''That's where the dugout was, with the boat for a roof, where my poor people spent two of their miserable winters.''

''Please, Duncan, don't go away from me yet. I got some questions I need to ask you.''

''I cannot stay here no more, Reginald.''

''Just a few questions. I never talked to nobody who was dead before.''

''Alright,'' said the fading voice. ''I'll answer three questions and then I'm gone, but ask them quickly.''

''Okay. Okay. First of all...'' Reginald knew he had a million questions, but didn't know how to say them.

''Let's see. First of all, if you be dead, how come you talk to me? Who gives you the permission? ''

Terry Metz heard this question, as if a bird had dropped it on his head, but he didn't want to remove his mouth from Dooley's breast to see who was there. That wouldn't be smooth, and Dooley was breathing just nice, just very deep and excited. She was a lot hotter than he had expected her to be, because once his hand just grazed her breast she grabbed it and pressed it down, and then she took the back of his head and pressed his face into it. She could let herself feel it, and how it felt good, and still stay in control before it went too far. She was old-fashioned that way. She knew how far she wanted to go. Some of her friends didn't know that, and already had diaphragms they would forget to put in. She preferred her own way. She wasn't ready for everything yet. Neither was Terry. He had never done it, and had never even got this far before, not this fast, and he wasn't sure of what to do if he'd have to go further. She pressed his face so hard against her breast he had to twist to free his nose to breathe.

"Okay, Duncan. Now tell me this. When you dead do you get to be with all your old friends again? Do I get to talk to old Ptomaine Harry again?"

Terry recognized Reginald's voice. Dooley was breathing like she was asleep. When Terry lifted his head from her breast to see where Reginald was she sighed so loud he had to cover her mouth. There he was, not ten feet away from them, shaking his head as if he was listening to someone. Dooley sat up, blinking her eyes dreamily. Terry pulled her t-shirt down over her breasts. "What?" she asked, not focusing yet. She touched her breasts that were still tingling. "It's Reginald," Terry said. "He's right here. Shh."

"Okay," said Reginald. "When you dead, do it ever hurt? Do it ever pinch, like this?" Terry saw Reginald pinch his own forearm, then stand there, nodding, as if he was listening to someone talk.

Dooley leaned her head on Terry's shoulder. "I want a

kiss,'' she said.

"Shh.'' Terry whispered. "Reginald is right here.''

"So what,'' said Dooley. "So are we. And this is the free world.'' She wriggled around to kiss Terry on the lips. Terry let her kiss him but couldn't get into it while Reginald was right there.

"Yeah. Right on. I get it. That's right. But just one more question, Duncan. I just thought of the question I wanted to ask. Look, Duncan, when I be dead; I mean, do someone who be dead always come back just like you? Just don't go yet. Just answer that one first. Will I be hopping around from time to time like you do? Shit. Don't go. Oh, well, damn. Motherfucker's gone. Goodby Duncan. Thanks a lot.'' Reginald turned and looked down and saw that he was standing practically on top of Terry and Dooley. "Damn,'' he said. "Could you hear that stuff, about Duncan talking about what it's like when you're dead.''

"Why are you up here by yourself, Reginald. You know you're supposed to have a buddy with you all the time.''

"Who's Duncan?'' Dooley asked.

"Duncan Mackinnon. They owned this whole place here, and he told me a sad story of their family, except he explained it wasn't really sad, and he was telling me about what it's like to be dead.''

"You should be down there with the other kids, Reginald.''

"He said that the first house they lived in, it was really like a little dugout with a boat on top, was right here where you guys are. All his sisters, his mama...''

"Sure, Reginald,'' said Terry. He stood up and looked

towards the sea. Several kids were running towards them through the meadow, calling their names. Suddenly it seemed urgent. "Terry. Quick. Come here. Terry." Terry and Dooley started running towards the kids. Reginald got there first, and they grabbed his hand and then Terry's and Dooley's and pulled them back towards the cove where they had left the kids, playing safely. The tide was almost in, pounding the little beach with big waves. The kids pointed out past the waves where some of the others were hanging on to driftwood they had pushed out to play on while the waves were light. They were still out there, hanging on, trapped in the undertow.

*   *   *

Dusty leaned his pack against the little truck and started to fill it. He laid some light groceries in first, in the big compartment, and removed the kerosene lamp from its box so it would fit. He stuffed his newspaper, rolled up, into the chimney to give it support. The six-pack of Keith's fit in the bottom compartment with the potatoes, onions and two cans of milk. The lamp oil went in one of the pockets, the staples and plastic in another, and his mail and the Cape Breton magazine in a third. The pack was heavy, and it crossed his mind that he'd better be careful, because for days at a time there was no one but himself who walked this trail. When his kids spent summers with him there was constant traffic on it, but now they were working in New York and Chicago and he was alone there, and a serious injury on the trail could leave him there for days, weeks. He'd stopped using his chain saw for that reason, and cut all his stove wood with a bow saw now. The chain saw was a curious toy. There was always a slight temptation, working with it, to see what it looks like going through your own leg. It wouldn't be bad, he thought, to die in Cape Breton, at his own place, looking out to sea, but he wasn't going to volunteer. He slipped his arms through the pack-straps and stepped forward. This was heavy, alright. It swayed and turned him around to face the red barn that belonged to Sarah MacDonald. Rory, their youngest son, once played his bagpipes in front of the house on warm days like this, but no more since he went to Alberta to make his money working in the oil-sands. Dusty could still hear those pipes in the colors of the barn, and the light wind bending the grasses, and he heard them still sometimes below when the sea was calm and the sound of the pipes would reach down to him over the spruce and raspberry thickets like a quartet of angels. Sentiment clung to the Cape Breton landscape like that. This was a place that held the residue of everything from the heart, everyone still remaining on the trail that he and his family cleared, cutting away fallen snags and brush, his wife and two of the boys working up from below, himself and Nick working down from above, till they met just below Halfway Hill, and the trail was clear. And the cookshack held it, built as was everything else, out of driftwood planks and found materials, the old wood stove bought for twenty bucks, and carried in by small boat from Dunvegan, hauled up the bank with the help of friends, and settled on some railroad ties near the clearing where they would later put the tepee. Dusty stood on the stove top and, while his wife held them, drove in the poles

that formed the frame of the shack, and they hammered
driftwood planks of all sizes and shapes onto those poles,
putting up the windward wall first, so they could squeeze
together and get some protection near the warm stove
when the wind blew. Each board they put up had its own
character and obscure history, each one carried up the
beach on one of their shoulders, or floated home on their
little boat after a long scavenging run up the shore, some
boards so hard and seasoned they bent several nails before
they allowed themselves to be penetrated and fastened.
And the rhubarb they planted, and the comfrey and
day-lilies still held the spirit of Olivia, who hadn't been
there for many years, and all the places that he stopped,
under the tepee poles, for instance, where the driftwood
furniture they'd built still lay, all the voices of all the
gatherings of friends, all the presences of lovers since his
marriage broke up, all the feelings of long evenings
around the tepee fire, playing cards or Scrabble with the
boys, seemed to haunt the place, bringing dead issues
back to life, spooking his solitude. All his memories rose
with the warmth every time he lit a fire in the stove. And
there was Bonnie's laughter in the fronds of raspberries,
and Jane bathing by the stream, and Linne in the hum of
each mosquito. And Avrum, Nick and Rafael coming
down the trail and coming down the trail. All of it stayed
put, all the murmurs of all the hearts, and who would
believe the planet could sustain it all, all the loves and
betrayals, all the openings of laughter, the tragedies on a
bench, settling back each year like an ancient dew onto
this landscape that renewed itself each spring as if nothing
would ever change, as if around the corner big difference

and big indifference weren't in collaboration.

Sally Lens, who lived further up towards Sight Point, passed in her old station wagon and honked at Dusty. He waved, then turned to start down the trail. It followed the old fence line of the field where Sarah MacDonald's husband, Daniel, had run sheep when he was alive. "I can't eat the damned lamb. It makes me sick," his wife always said. "I don't eat the lobster," she'd say, when her Daniel had his lobster license, making a face that showed her revulsion for it. He kept a garden, but she didn't like vegetables. It was difficult to find out what she ate, nourished probably by love, and the rum they drank together.

He walked past a stand of birches into a wild cherry woods, that made him think always of Olivia, because one of the last compatible things he did with her was to pick the cherries here. There was one tree she called the grandmother of all the pincherries, and they stayed by it all afternoon, pulled down branches laden with tiny ones like little rubies lit from within when the dappled afternoon light slanted through the branches. They cooked them into jelly that trapped this color of light, that tasted winy and sweet and bitter and intoxicating as summer evenings in the middle of winter. Below these woods near the trail was the birch stump, almost decayed now, where he had sat talking with Vinny Falconieri, and Vinny had first put the idea of giants in his mind.

"Dusty," he said. "Sometimes when you sit down there alone in the morning, and you look out at the water, do you ever see anything? I mean, do you ever sense anything under the water?"

"Under the water? What do you mean?"

"Like something big. Something strange? Something sleeping there?"

"What are you talking about?"

"I saw something out there."

"Most peculiar thing I ever saw was one morning at sunrise when I was up doing Tai Chi..."

"Tai Chi is like magic."

"I don't know about that. It's exercise. It's a way to move. It's just a form."

"It gives you a special aura, Dusty. Like I knew you before you did it, and now you're different."

"Okay, anyway, Vinny, I was doing my form, and every time I turned so I was facing the sea there was this big thing seemed to be swimming towards shore."

"That's what I was telling you. This big thing."

"Okay, yeah, so I finished the form, and I walked to the edge to get a better look at this, and it came into shore. That was like a miracle morning. The sunlight was just skimming the tops of the waves, and out of them, onto the beach, this gorgeous deer rose up, this buck with a huge rack. He stepped onto the sand and shook himself off, and there he was, tawny as a lion, sniffling the wind, turning his head right and left."

"That wasn't a deer," Vinny said.

"It was a deer. I saw it. I don't know where it came from. They say they can swim all the way from Prince Edward Island."

"That was no deer, Dusty. It was one of them."

"Them?"

"Dusty, you've never been here in the autumn, or the

winter. That's when you get the sense of them."

"What is 'them'?"

"I come down here a lot in the fall, just to get away from the house for a while. You know what I love about Marie a lot is that she understands you need to be alone. And she needs to be alone too."

"So what do you mean about 'them'?"

"Well, I'd sit here and watch the ocean when it was calm, you know, and it was real soothing, at first, until I saw this something."

"What something?"

"It was like this knee, like a huge knee bending up out of the water, then settling back. It was right north from where you look out from the bank near your cookshack. Then this arm came up, a huge arm out of the water."

"Did you see a flying saucer, Vinny?"

"Hey..."

"You were drunk."

"I was sober, Dusty. Vinny don't come down here and drink by himself. I was in my straight mind."

"It was just blackfish. You saw a school of blackfish and it bent your mind a little. You spend a lot of time alone."

"I know the little whales, Dusty. I know the blackfish. This was not whales. This was something else."

"Okay," said Dusty. "Okay. What do you say it was?"

"Look, you don't stay here in the winter, so you don't get into the people the way I do, but over the winter, when the nights get long, they start to tell me things, and that's when I learn something about this place."

"When the day gets short people must make up stories just to get through the nights."

''I don't know if you ever noticed, but the fishermen don't ever drop their traps in that area where I tell you I saw what I saw. Daniel MacDonald told me they always lose their traps when they put them in that general area. I told him I thought there was something big under the water there and you know he didn't deny it.''

''You've been here too many winters, Vinny.''

''And I'll be here for the rest of the winters. I'm the Cape Breton wop. Why don't you ask me what did Dan MacDonald say? Because you know I'll tell you anyway. He didn't say anything, Dusty; but he told me to follow him, and he took me on a walk.''

''A walk? In the winter?''

''It was spring. The winter was pretty dry, and it warmed up one day, so he just said, 'Follow me,' and I sure as hell followed him, even though I'd told Maria I'd be home at one o'clock for lunch. A nice thing about living with a Native Canadian person is that there is no time. One o'clock is a state of mind that happens whenever you get there. So is lunch. Lunch is like a wavelength, not a specific period of time, and that goes for everything. I'll explain it to you some day. Anyway, Daniel took me up the mountain there, up Cape Mabou, through some woods I'd never been in before, and I thought I'd walked all over this island. I mean, I don't stop. This is like a virgin forest, with these old, old spruce, their roots arching up out of the ground, in a blanket of moss. Those old trees always amaze me, how little green at the top it takes to keep them alive, like some old people who take just a little food in the evening. And mushrooms, Dusty, you'd love the mushrooms in these woods. I don't know anything about them, but I know you do. There was one that smelled like almond extract."

"That's the fetid Russula."

"And all kinds of red ones, and little ones. Anyway we passed through the woods and pushed into some bayberry and wild rose brambles over our heads. Then into a stand of young spruce, and I never realized how high the mountain went up. So then we came to a spot where he stopped finally, like any other spot up there, where there was a ledge of rock. The ground was real moist there, some little frogs jumping already where we put our feet. Daniel squatted down right there. 'We're real close to it now,' he said. 'It's not the prettiest spot on this mountain, but it's my spot, and it's real private, and when you live in a family with fourteen other kids you've got to find your private spot. I needed a place to be alone, so I found this place. I'd come here every day, and they would look for me, and they'd never find me here. This is the first time I've ever shown this secret place to anyone. And I've only come here once or twice myself since I was a boy.'

"Dan started to pull out some rocks from under the ledge. 'I put these stones down in here some thirty-five years ago, and haven't removed them since.' He uncovered a little cave opening and shoved his head in. 'See I plugged this up,' he said when he pulled his head out, 'when I got too big to crawl in there any more, but why don't you look.' I put my head in the hole, and it was dark at first, but slowly my eyes got used to this faint misty green light in there, and I could see it was a huge chamber in the mountain. 'You been inside that cave?' I asked Daniel MacDonald.

"'I been in there,' Daniel said. 'When I was real small I went in there, and I'd drop down to the ledge below there and disappear, but when I got a little bigger I was afraid I wouldn't be able to get out again.' Daniel lifted a handful of water from the spring, and tasted it.

"'It still has a slight taste of the whiskey. You should taste it.'

"'Whiskey?' I said.

"'You taste it.'

"I pulled some up to my mouth, and it tasted like good, pure water to me. 'I don't taste any whiskey,' I said. I didn't. If I'd tasted whiskey I would have told him.

"He tasted it again. 'I guess you had to know it then to have a sense of it now,' Daniel told me, and he licked his finger. 'But there's still a trace in it. It used to be, when I was a boy, that in the spring, in the first few days when the water ran, it ran as the clearest, smoothest whiskey, delicious. I knew that as a boy, and I kept it a secret, and at an early age I was drunk all the time up here on the mountain, and none of my family knew what it was. They couldn't understand my lethargy, how I hated to get out of bed in the morning, and how I stayed away all of the day.'

"'Did you ever see where the stuff came from?'

"'I wish you could just go there, Vinny, and hear it for yourself. If you could just be inside there, then you'd know something of the magic of these hills from Foot Cape to Mabou.'

"'There's probably another entrance to that cave. The light in there has to come from somewhere.'

"'If you could just hear them at work in there. Their voices are so deep.'

'''Hear who?'

'''The men of the distillery.'

'''The men?'

'''Aye. They were men.'

'''Did you ever see them?'

'''No. No, I was afraid to leave the ledge you stand on as soon as you get inside, for fear I'd never get out again. But I heard them here. My father used to tell about what lived under the hills in the old country, but he knew very little about what was inhabiting beneath this place.'

'''So you think there are men working under this mountain?'

'''I know it. I heard their voices. This is where they have their distillery. I've tasted their whiskey.'

'''They are big men?'

'''They are...' Daniel threw an arc with his hand that flew higher than the tops of the old trees, '. . . huge. And I know they are strong. And like all the big ones on the earth they move with special grace. And they are tender giants. And they love the summer.'

''I tell you, Dusty, that all sent a real shiver up this Ginny's spine, because I'm sure I've seen one of those giants sleeping under the water down at your place. Out of the Golden Age. 'I would sure like to go look for those men,' I told him.

'''I rambled all over this hill, after I became too big to go in there anymore, just to find another entrance if I could, but I never found one. I'm not saying there is none, mind you. Every man might find his own, though I imagine it would be a might easier for a young boy. But you can look for it yourself if you want to, if you have the time to do it.

My advice to you, though, is that you do not mention this cave to anyone. Do not tell a soul.'

"We started down the hill as the sun was going down, and some little clouds were rushing up at us from the horizon. You know those evenings here. Dan said no more about the men of the distillery. We stopped and picked some of the last blackberries and ate them."

"Blackberries?" said Dusty. "You said it was the spring."

"Did I?" Vinny grinned. "Well, the story started in the spring and is ending in the fall. About the blackberries Daniel said, 'I'd bring some of them down for Sarah, but I know she won't eat the berries.' And he never said anything more about it, Dusty. And to the day he died he never mentioned the men of the distillery again."

*   *   *

Dusty lifted his pack and continued out of the woods, through the upper raspberries to Halfway Hill and down the trail by Drunken Lady's Gulch, through Raspberry City, and Borneo, to his own place, where he put the pack down by the table near the cookshack. He looked south towards Sight Point. The budworm had stripped the needles off the spruce in the last few years, and had erased that restful cast of blue that once lay on the hillsides, and after everyone rushed to cut the pulp before the dying trees were worthless, the treeless slopes covered quickly with pale green raspberry. No one could do a thing to stop this minor natural disaster. It was part of a long rhythm Dusty had power only to observe, as he observed changes in his own life: elements of it drifting away like flotsam, an occasional fire in the dead spruce left on the mountainsides.

He put away his groceries and went to George's cabin to read and write in his journal. He had been down here for over a month alone and preferred to spend his time in this little shack that looked north up the beach as far as Cheticamp Island, beyond Sea-wolf Island. George Schneeman built that cabin out of spruce logs Dusty had split lengthwise with a chain saw. That had been a summer full of people, George and Kati and their three boys, Dusty and two of his, and anyone else who occasionally came down the trail. A big party that year, pot full of clam chowder, chili, baked spuds, fresh bread, Moosehead and Keiths chilled in the stream. Everyone there, all Dusty's friends. The cabin had a special feeling only George could give it, a domestic cheeriness made from his love for being at home, making his art - paintings and frescoes and drawings - in the midst of his family.

Dusty sat in this cabin with his journal open to a blank page, and his collection of Rimbaud open to "Le Bateau Ivre" and he watched the fishing boats slip out of the little inlet at Inverness Harbor, and head for the cod a mile off shore, or for the snow-crab in the deeper waters. His notebook page looked like a design for a garden patch with its paths of syllables through the crossed-out words. This was going to be a novel 'mitt...blow this...—-bing...drona's apart...'' He grabbed his binoculars that sat on a shelf near his hand to look at the people he spotted walking up the beach. People rarely walked on this beach, some kids and their dog sometimes, or an older man taking his constitutional, but that was just a few times in a summer. This was a couple coming over the rocks, she in a scant beige bikini, he in a pair of jeans and a t-shirt, his blue sweater thrown over his shoulder. She stepped out ahead of him, jumping from rock to rock, more daring in bare feet than he was in sneakers. She paused to wait for him. Her small torso nested on firm legs, a strong butt, tiny breasts. She hugged him, rubbing boldly against him. He looked around as if he could sense someone spying on them. The woman led him to a patch of sand beach and embraced him again. She stepped away and dropped her bathing suit and moved slowly into the water with her arms out for balance. She turned to watch as he reluctantly took off his clothes, looking furtively up and down the beach. She shifted her legs impatiently, the water so calm she just wrinkled the surface with her knees. Dusty had never seen such a thing happen here in all his time of gazing at the beach. He'd followed gulls with his binoculars and cormorants and the great blue heron, and he'd watched terns dive, and colloquies of ravens light on the tops of dying spruce, but never a bonus like this that could make him feel so lonely, so wicked with his eyes. He was finally naked, and he stepped into the water, folding his arms around his chest against the cold. She threw her arms around his neck and circled his hips with her legs and they both fell into the water. Their laughter, made melancholy by distance, reached him as a slight shock wave. He lowered his glasses. "I don't want to look at this," he told himself. He caught them again, heading back to shore. She stopped and kissed him, moving her body into his, then she settled down out of

sight behind a rock, and he stood above looking down at
her a moment before he too disappeared out of sight on
top of her. Dusty was grateful for that. He wanted to see it,
but he sure didn't want to be looking at it. He panned his
binoculars out over the calm water. The air was slightly
hazy, and still. A mile or so out two fishing boats moved
around each other as if wafted on the air. The low beat of
their idling engines echoed at him off the hills. This was
one of the harmonious moments in the atmosphere of this
place that pulls everything together, land and sea and sky,
and all the creatures and objects enmeshed there in the
flux of form and matter and energy. This was one of the
moments that sets the spirit loose to flow into everything
opening to receive it. One moment of harmony and
disintegration. And that was why he saw it just then. He
panned slowly back to shore and saw this disturbance in
the water. Something large lifted from below and settled
back; just a brief moment of seeing this, like a Loch Ness
vision transplanted to this new world Inverness, that
happened so quickly he saw it and doubted it in the same
moment. Yet the image remained, the way it rose and
reimmersed itself like a huge serpent, but not a serpent,
rather an enormous leg, the foot rising highest out of the
water, shin and knee emerging, then sinking back. He
kept the glasses trained on the water still rippling where
the thing had happened. Once the water calmed and the
sand settled he could sense the huge form submerged
there to which the leg was attached. He had the distinct,
unsettling sense of something there. He looked back at the
beach. The couple had risen, still embraced, their bodies
covered with a crust of sand. They stood like another

stone tipped up and carved by the tide.

Dusty put the binoculars back in their case, closed the journal and the Rimbaud, and capped his pen. He put on some sneakers and crossed the raspberry patch in front of his outhouse, through the tepee poles to the cookshack and table. He grabbed his bottle of tequila and sat down. Someone stepped out from behind Nick's tower and approached him from behind.

"Nick really built that tower, didn't he?"

Dusty turned to see Lenny, his hands in the pockets of his surplus fatigues. "Lenny! I didn't even hear you come down. How long have you been here?"

"A little while. I thought maybe you were looking for mushrooms or something. Roz wanted to know if you wanted to come up for dinner."

"I've got some chili here," Dusty said. He poured a cup of tequila for Lenny.

"You've always got some chili here. I like your chili. Roz is cooking the vegetable stew as usual." Lenny swallowed half his tequila in one gulp. "I hate the fuckin' health-food nuts."

"Lenny, while you were sitting here, did you see anything under the water?"

"Sesame salt. Fuck it. Brewer's yeast. I didn't look under the water. What do you mean, see anything?"

"I think I saw this big leg lift up out of the water."

"Well that's good," said Lenny. "A big leg is good." He filled his cup again with tequila. "I always forget how beautiful it is down here. I stay up there working on that damned cabin all the time and I forget there's an ocean here. I brought my grandmother down here after you left last summer. She thought it was beautiful. You know she's real spry at seventy-six. She couldn't believe how nice it was. So I finished insulating the loft, and the closer I get to finishing that cabin, the more I want to leave this place." He lifted the cup of golden tequila in front of the sun that was slowly setting. "Yeah, so you saw a leg. I bet it was big, wasn't it?"

"What can we do?" Dusty asked.

"I told you what I want to do. I want to leave and go back to New York, or Boston. I want to go back to mother concrete."

"Why don't we take my boat and try to row out and see it?"

"See what? You're joking. Drink some more tequila, Dusty. Roz has dinner almost ready. Goddam vegetable stew." He tipped down more tequila. "You know, if I didn't have to love that woman I'd eat more meat."

"I'm not joking." Dusty filled the cups again. Good tequila was the smoothest burn in the world, slipping down the throat.

"When my grandmother came down here she saw something out there too. She's a crazy woman. I love her."

"What did she see?"

"She saw a German U-boat. She always likes to tell me the story of the U-boat captain she was in love with in World War II. She looks into the ocean and she always sees a U-boat."

"I think I saw that movie too," Dusty said.

"She lived in Gloucester during the Second World War, in a little house on the beach outside of town. That's where my dad was born just before the Depression. My grandfather was a fisherman then, before she started selling insurance after the war. But one night she says there was a knock on her door. I don't know if any of this is true, but she loves to tell this story. It keeps her young. Her face gets really pretty when she tells it.''

The golden tequila poured through the sunset into their cups, gilding the edges of the story.

'''Your grandfather was out fishing all night,' she says, 'and your father and Aunt Minnie and Aunt Clara were all in bed asleep, and I was listening to the radio, ''The Inner Sanctum,'' with the squeaky door. You probably never heard of it, but they had good radio programs in those days. Scared me to death, but I liked to be scared. You weren't even a twinkle in your father's eye at that time. So I dozed off by the radio, and then there was this knock on the door, and it really scared me because I'd been listening to this horror show anyway. At that time there was a blackout. There were no streetlights allowed because of the war, and if you needed a light on in your house you had to keep some black shades drawn. Even cars, you weren't supposed to drive them after sundown, but if there was an emergency then the top halves of all the headlights were painted black, just so the German bombers wouldn't see anything if they flew over the town. So whatever was outside usually was really in the dark, and I was afraid to open the door, especially when my Herman was gone. I'd forgot how bright it could be just with the moon, and there it was three-quarters and glowing just over the shoulder of a handsome Captain of a German U-boat. He spoke to me like a gentleman, in perfect English. The tide was exceptionally low, and he was stranded on a sandbar just below the house. I could see it sitting there like a fat cigar. I invited him in, with two of the sailors accompanying him. I guess it was unpatriotic, but I've always liked people better than nations.' My grandma said that. Sometimes the Captain had sailors with him, sometimes not. Sometimes the story was that the Captain sat down at the piano and played her the most lovely Brahms. Sometimes she said he talked to her for hours about literature and philosophy until the tide was up, because he respected her intelligence and sensitivity as a spark lying dormant, and he blew that spark into a flame, and she fell in love with him, and when he left he kissed her hand. That was the Captain of her U-boat.''

''Did he ever come back to see her?''

''Sometimes she says he did, and sometimes she says it was only once, but that she loves him forever. You know she never told that story at all till after my grandfather died. And when she came down here with me to look out at your ocean and we were sitting at this table she suddenly stood up and pointed out to sea and said, 'There it is. There's my Johannes.''

Dusty lifted the empty tequila bottle and looked at Lenny through it. ''That's the way it is, Lenny. Everybody's got his ghosts and his stories.'' He put the bottle down. ''God bless it full, goddam it's empty. At a certain point that's all that's left, the stories. And that's how you keep going.''

''You're getting sentimental, Dusty. You must be drunk as me.''

''I'm not drunk,'' Dusty stood up. ''It could have been

the leg she saw, for an instant, like I did." He walked to the edge of the bank. "Hey, Lenny," he shouted back to the table. "Let's just take the boat and go out there and see what it is."

Lenny grabbed the empty bottle and followed Dusty to the edge. "You mean the boat?" He waved the empty bottle at the green and crimson western sky, then tipped the last drop onto his tongue.

"Yeah. We'll take it out, then we'll see about things once and for all." Dusty laid a hand on Lenny's shoulder. "I like to be conclusive."

"Of course. Why not. Good." Lenny held the bottle over his tongue. "Shit." He tossed it into the brush. "Some of us must be drunk."

"I feel very intelligent," Dusty said. "I can see anything right now." He started down the bank, then turned back to Lenny. "Hey, glad to have you aboard, Lenny. Glad you're with me."

"Where you going?"

"To the boat."

"I don't see a boat." Lenny stepped off the bank to follow Dusty. "Where do you see a boat?"

The water was flat, not the slightest swell, as Dusty rowed them out. Lenny sat in the bow, dipping his hand in the water and singing, "You can get anything you want, at Alice's Restaurant." Dusty rowed a few strokes, looked, and rowed again. "I don't want a pickle," Lenny sang. It was the hallucinatory time of evening, just enough light left to give the visible world a slight credibility. They came to an expanse of water that seemed even calmer than the rest, as if they were gliding on a piece of glass, a window to the bottom. Something was glowing, Dusty thought he saw it, under the boat, like the moon on a slanted surface of rock, but the moon hadn't risen yet.

"Do you see that glowing?" Dusty whispered to Lenny.

Lenny trailed his hand in the water. "...a friend of mine..." he hummed. He had just a smattering of lyrics.

"It's real subtle," Dusty said. "It's in front of you right there now, Lenny. That small light." Lenny looked into the water. Dusty kept the boat moving along the edge of glowing that he seemed to see better with his peripheral vision. A heavy scent of spruce lay on the water, and the stars began to pump out small light overhead, and over Lenny's thin singing voice a deep note of the evening flowed basso and contralto from the still bright open mouth of the horizon.

He rowed quietly along the line of the leg of their silver giant. Lenny hummed monotonously, his eyes closed. "Hey, Lenny," said Dusty. "You think we're drunk? You think we're too drunk?"

"Of course it is," said Lenny. "It's drunk as shit out here." Lenny waved his head from side to side, humming through his loud breath, as the boat slowly flew skywards in their deep mutual dream. Dusty turned to look back at the shadow of the shore. "Jesus," he mumbled. They were far out. He had never thought they could get so far by merely rowing. "Look," said Lenny, and Dusty turned back. He crawled to the bow and they both looked into the deep at whatever they saw glowing down there.

"That looks like it could be a face," said Dusty.

"I should never drink tequila."

"What do you think that is, Lenny?"

Lenny looked as if he was about to cry. "Roz says I hallucinate with too much tequila. I think that's a tequila vision."

The face in the deep seemed modeled out of silver mined on the moon. It turned slowly from side to side, as if having its own dream.

"We both see it, don't we," Dusty asked. "You see that, Lenny, don't you?"

"Let's get out of here," Lenny looked around. "Don't you have a motor on this boat?" He leaned too far over the bow and dropped into the water, hardly making a splash. He didn't even try to swim, but sank directly as if he was being reeled down.

"Lenny," Dusty shouted. "O my God." He dove in and followed him down. It was cold below, and Dusty couldn't see anything but a mild glow, and thought he felt a sound so deep it was almost below audibility. Just by luck he bumped into Lenny's sunken body, grabbed his hair, and tugged him slowly to the surface. Lenny was still breathing, but his eyes were closed. Dusty didn't dare let go, for fear he'd sink again, so he pulled him to where the boat had drifted almost out of sight, and grabbed the gunwale, and banged Lenny's smiling head against the side of the boat. His eyes opened. "Fuck," he said. "I'm in the water."

"Get back in the boat."

"I'm in the fucking water, Dusty. How did I get in the water?"

"Get in the boat, asshole." Dusty held the boat steady while Lenny climbed in, then he climbed in himself.

"I had a dream," said Lenny. "It was all tequila."

The moon was up now, full moon, and Dusty looked back at where the apparition had pulled them down, a glow of moonlight opaque on the surface. "Do you realize what we saw?" Dusty started to row. "Do you realize what that was?"

"Just another tequila moonrise," Lenny sang. "I am freezing."

A wind had come up, chopping the water, and Dusty rowed back to shore, riding the rising tide that made it easy to row. He saw a flashlight beam swinging among the tepee poles and trees in his camp, and a voice calling, almost drowned out by the sound of increasing surf. The boat hit the beach and pitched Lenny onto the sand. He rolled over and stood up singing, "Set sail in the ship John D.," and they pulled the boat in and climbed the bank to find Roz sitting at the table.

"I expected you guys for dinner two hours ago." She played her flashlight first on Dusty's face, then on Lenny. "O my God," she said, and pulled Lenny to her, and touched him all over. "You're all wet, Lenny."

"We used to have a subscription to WET, but you never let us renew it."

"You get hypothermia," she said, "and I made the banana muffins and I picked all the green beans. Dusty, you got some big towels? Lenny's really susceptible."

"We saw this thing and he fell out of the boat. I had to jump in to pull him back. Tell Roz what we saw, Lenny."

"What the tequila sees, and what I see..." Lenny shrugged.

"Get the towels. Please. Quick." She stripped off Lenny's clothes, and lifted her sweater and shirt to her

armpits and pulled him against her large breasts to keep
him warm. "Please. Quick. Dusty, I know what I'm doing.
Lenny could really get sick. All we need now is
pneumonia."

Dusty took her flashlight and went to his cabin and
changed his clothes, and brought back a change of clothes
for Lenny.

"Took you long enough," said Roz. "Now I'm freezing
too." She wrapped Lenny in a towel, and started to pull off
his pants. Dusty went to the cookshack and lit some
kindling in the stove. He shifted the pot of chili onto the
heat, and walked to the edge to look at the ocean. A bright
half-moon layed an hallucinatory shimmer on the waves.
He heard Roz cooing over Lenny and kissing him. In his
mind he could still see the huge head turning under the
water. August twelve it was, the sun in Leo. And where
was the moon? He walked back to the table. Lenny had
seen it too, but he would never remember. He would deny
it and forget. He liked to avoid extremes. That was why he
had chosen to go to Canada, rather than to join war
protests at home. He didn't expatriate out of political
conviction, but because he saw it as the quickest way, in
the face of the Vietnam war, to return his life to normal.
So Lenny would easily attribute this experience to an
interlude of drunken hallucinations, its details fading like
the details of a dream. He would deny it in the morning,
insist it was nothing but the tequila. Dusty couldn't deny
any of it. He'd seen the thing twice. It was his forever.

Dusty set down the pot of chili and a loaf of bread he'd
baked the day before. He lit a lantern in the cookshack
and brought it to the middle of the table. "Nice it's a warm

night," he said.

"Too bad I didn't bring the banana muffins. They would have gone good," Roz said.

"And that moon is nice," Dusty said. "Look at all the bats. They like the warm nights."

"I thought they were swallows. I hate bats," Roz said.

"You don't even know bats," Lenny said. "Why do you hate bats?"

"I don't know. Just something about them."

"She's got phobias," Lenny told Dusty. "Before she came to Canada she didn't have any phobias."

"Canada doesn't have anything to do with it," Roz said. "The chili is delicious, Dusty. And so is the bread."

"It's got meat in it," Lenny said.

"So what. I eat meat. Occasionally."

"You never give us any meat."

"We can't afford meat. We've got to eat the garden."

"Dusty, you know why I want to leave Canada?"

"Meat?"

"We all know it, Lenny. You want to get Rolfed." Roz kidded him.

"Shut up, Roz."

"You want to learn Tai Chi, in New York," Roz insisted.

"I'm not a Canadian. That's why. I'll never be a Canadian."

"Nobody's a Canadian, Lenny," Dusty said. Everybody came here from somewhere else, except the Micmacs, the Eskimos, the Kwakiutls, the Crow. And even they came from somewhere."

"See what I really identify with is the American search for identity. I feel like I've got no real roots."

"Roots are a fantasy."

"That's what I mean. I float around. I'm nuts like all the Americans."

"Nobody will disagree there," Roz said, fondly.

"I love it. That's what I mean. I love the American way, the way we don't know who we are yet. And for a long time we looked for it in England, or in Europe, and we brought whatever we could back to this continent: symphony orchestras, museums, operas, and that was the east coast. But we still haven't got anything from ourselves. The blacks made something American with music, but the story of African roots just confuses things. An American black in Africa is weird. None of us really knows how to live on this continent. And that's why the automobile, and all the superhighways. Every American suspects that maybe he doesn't belong where he is, so he wants to get somewhere else as fast as possible. Maybe the South is different. But there it's economics and privilege. If you can make money and feel enfranchised there maybe you can play some gone with the wind games. Otherwise you leave. Only illegal aliens have got it straight in the U.S. now. They know they don't belong."

"Relax, Lenny. You're just building a theory," said Dusty.

"It happens every time," Roz said. "You get him wet, give him a little chili, some meat in it, and he becomes a philosopher."

"This is why," Lenny said. "America is the most dangerous country on earth. I mean you get the sense they don't live on the earth, that they think they have someplace else to escape to when they use those crazy bombs, when they fuck up the whole ecosystem, as if they can make the place inhabitable and still inhabit it. All the leaders are disenfranchised people. I mean, Ronald Reagan exists on film. He's some sick devolution of affability and charm. It's an image. And Alexander Haig has risen out of the underworld of snakes. These people are destroying their own world, and they don't even understand about it.''

''So you want to go back to America for that?'' Roz shrugged.

''Okay, Dusty, when you look at an Indian; I mean, a Native American, in the face, what do you think? I mean the history of what we've done, what a lot of people still do, when they look at one, is to categorize him as an animal, so they can kill him, and that was the eighteenth and nineteenth century, and that sick war in the Philippines where they invented the forty-five, and the same license we took with human beings in Vietnam; or else you look at the face of some Navaho or Micmac and say to yourself, wait a minute, who is this, and who am I, and what are we both doing here, and through the sixties and seventies some of us were asking that, and we went to Asia some of us not to kill but to find some tools, to meditate with Hindus and Buddhists, do the martial arts with the Daoists, dance with the Sufis, and here we ran around on this continent from one Macdonalds' arches to another Burger King, and what did we find out? That we still haven't figured out how to live on this planet without destroying ourselves.''

''What's the point of getting all excited, Lenny?'' Roz felt his forehead. ''Now you're too hot.''

Dusty stared at the southeast horizon, where Sagittarius leaned up from the hill. "Whatever happens, this is a balmy night. And as far as I can figure it out, Lenny, that's what's important, that's what life is about, some good days, some balmy nights."

"So I'm hot, Roz. So what? What do you know about it? The only thoughts you ever have is about your garden. I'm talking about what I care about. I'm an American. We've been in exile here for almost fourteen years."

"And we still live in one room."

"Only Americans can face the situation, Dusty. I'm talking about the situation of the whole planet. And do something about it. Europeans won't do it. They're worn out and tired and cynical and greedy, or like the Germans they get crazy and fanatical. The United States is the only place where there's still enough idealism to save the situation, and that's the good side of the USA, what I want to get back to, because we have the ability to embrace in the American soul the best of every culture, and to guide our continent back to viability and comfort through some hints given us by some sacred people, the Native Americans, who lived here well and harmoniously with the earth before we came."

I feel like I should come forward and be saved," Roz said.

"Hey, the Indian nations themselves weren't too nice to each other. There was some heavy bloodshed."

"The Canadians aren't the same. The Queen comes here, or the Prince of Wales, and they all line up and sing "Hail To The Queen," as if they can actually identify their enormous continent of polar bears and black flies and

moose and caribou with that little island of stiff upper lips
and questionable automobiles. When the Duke and
Duchess of Argyle came here you know what all these
people did? They put on their kilts and started to speak
Gaelic. It was like the Battle of Culloden, and the hardships of their own people at that time had never happened, were totally forgotten."

"It's great they have some traditions to hold on to."

"Don't kid yourself. This ain't the new world, Dusty.
That's why I want to go back to the USA. We have the last
chance there to work at keeping the whole thing
together."

"Lenny," Roz said. "You can't walk around with all the
troubles of the world on your shoulders."

Lenny carved at the edge of the table with a bread knife.
"That's why I like you, Dusty. I can talk to you. You know
this has to be a new planet. And it has to be everyone. And
it has to start in the USA. And that's why I want to go
back."

That's all Lenny said. They listened to the moonlight. A
light breeze stirred the tops of the spruces. At another
distance an owl loaded the silence.

"Well, I guess Lenny is dry now," Roz said. "So we'll be
going."

She stood up, switched on her flashlight, and led Lenny
up the trail. He left without saying another word, without
looking back.

* * *

There came Reginald, running up the beach towards the party. It looked like everyone was going to show up, even Dusty's sons, with Olivia, their mother. And the Clarks who were building a dome in Upper Margaree, with all their friends Dusty didn't know sitting in a circle, passing a joint; and Nina from Scotsville by Lake Ainslie, who looked even more unkempt-Hollywood-image now that she'd given up her acting career to live in Cape Breton with Willy, an ex-con carpenter and logger she'd met through the mail. There was a whole platoon of expatriate fishermen from Meat Cove messing with a bonfire on the beach, their women running around naked, a line of men with a jug of wine sitting on the edge of the bluff, watching them. There was Fletcher, to Dusty's total surprise, standing alone in the middle of the field, wrapped in a heavy trenchcoat, rotating slowly, always in some private ritual. He hadn't anticipated a party this big.

"Are we gonna play ball, or not?" Lenny shouted, tossing a softball back and forth with Roz.

"Anybody bring some charcoal starter?" Vernon stepped out of his house holding a bag of charcoal. He was throwing the party. He and his wife had finished this house two years earlier. They'd taught themselves to build it as they went along, learning carpentry and plumbing and wiring; and they had little Daria, and raised her for a couple of years together in the midst of their construction. Now the wife was somewhere else, he said, in Chicago or somewhere, fucking men with her boots on, he laughed, bitter and philosophical and stupid about her. He had moved to San Francisco with the little daughter and was getting rich buying old houses and renovating them, and he returned to Cape Breton for only a few weeks a year to get together with all the people he knew for this one big party.

"I want to show you something," Dusty turned to the touch of a hand on his shoulder. It was Fletcher.

"I never expected to see you again."

"Come on," Lenny shouted. "Let's play before it's time to eat."

"Everyone's having a good time, Lenny. They're at the beach. They're getting stoned. Leave them alone." Roz threw the ball wild and Kevin McPhee's big dog caught it and ran away in a wide circle.

"It wasn't my idea to play softball. Vern asked me to organize it and that's what I'm doing." He took off after the dog.

The sky was like navy blue velvet behind Fletcher. Though high noon surrounded everyone else, Dusty saw stars in the sky around Fletcher's head. Fletcher was grinning, his sly, pointed smile.

"Why don't you take off your coat?" Dusty said. "It's hot."

Fletcher backed a few steps away from Dusty as he undid the belt around his waist.

Near the house Willy was showing off his new pistol to some teenagers, slapping it out of the holster at his hip." I would have done it. I would have taken on Cole Younger and Jesse James and Billy the Kid. That's how a man got to know how good he was. Slap leather, Pancho." He turned on one of the kids, practicing his quick draw.

"Macho asshole," said Rosalie, the goat lady from Toronto, to Sybil McPhalls.

"I don't mind macho," said Sybil. "I just don't like guns."

With his hand on each lapel Fletcher spread his trenchcoat wide. From behind his back the white head of a bald eagle appeared, turned one way and then another, then looked upwards and flew loose, hitting the bridge of Dusty's nose with the tip of its wing as it started on a wide spiral into the sky.

"Fletcher?" Dusty said, expecting himself to ask some questions, but no words came to ask about what he needed to know.

Now a great blue heron stretched its neck out, and found Dusty with its bright yellow eye, then followed the eagle, beating its wings heavily to rise, and it sailed out towards the island. Now a raven slowly came from the wings of the coat making complicated noises as if to argue with the wind.

"So many birds," Dusty said. "How many birds are there?"

More birds than people," Fletcher said. "More bats than birds."

"Put your gun away now," said Nina, stopping Willy's hand on the holster.

"We're gonna start the softball game now," Lenny announced again.

"The game is about to start," Nina told Willy.

"I'll tell you something," said Bill Gillis, who'd come from Baddeck. "In Cape Breton a man don't show off a gun like that. That's just not done here."

Willy tilted a bottle of Moosehead into his mouth. "Okay. So I'll play center field. See this arm. It's like a rifle.''

''Brute,'' Nina whispered in his ear.

A pale grey dove squeezed out from under Fletcher's beige flannel shirt, onto his outstretched arm, and cooed to all the angles of the air, then fluttered up and flew under the bank onto the beach where Vinny and Marie were tossing a frisbee and guarding the kids who played at the edge of the waves.

''A dove on the beach,'' said Marie, ''is a sign.''

''A sign of what?'' asked Vinny. He tossed the frisbee so it caught an updraft and lofted high above her head. Kevin McPhee's big dog watched it rise.

''I don't know,'' she said. ''A sign is a sign. My people are Micmac people.''

''Hey, Vinny, come on. You're captain of the other team,'' Lenny shouted from the bank. ''If we want a game we've got to start.''

''Why me?'' Vinny shouted back. ''I don't even enjoy baseball.''

''This is the first annual Cape Breton Olympic softball game, and they want you to be captain, so you have to come up.''

A slight fussing in Fletcher's sleeves and a pair of white-throated sparrows appeared, one in each hand. They tumbled to the ground and pecked in the grass around Dusty's feet.

''C'mon Dusty,'' said Vinny. ''You're on my team.''

''Fletcher,'' Dusty said, wanting to say something about the birds, but could say only, ''Birds...'' He turned and started for the house.

''First come look here,'' Fletcher stopped him. He

spread his coat again and stepped closer to Dusty as if he would envelop him in the wings. Dusty saw, like an iridescent lining in the coat, the whole colony of minute, blue-eyed bats. "This is New York City," Fletcher said, "and most of the surrounding suburbs."

"I never know, when I'm around you, what to believe," Dusty said. He looked closely at the lining again. "Do you think they are going to like it in Cape Breton?"

"Not to worry," said Fletcher. "Everyone is here. They fly at night."

The sparrows flew up to sit on Dusty's shoulders like epaulettes.

There came Reginald, running up the beach towards the party. He paused to pick up something shining in the sand. This was a barette, 'Sylvia,' the name on it, partly rubbed off. He knew who Sylvia was. He threw the barrette back into the waves and kept on running.

"The kids look great," said Olivia, when Dusty stopped next to her by the house.

"You're playing left field, Dusty," Lenny said, holding up a roster he'd scribbled on a brown paper bag.

"I can play left field," Roz said. "Why can't a woman play left field?"

"All the women are out in left field," Vinny said.

"Very funny, pig," said Roz.

"You play second base, Roz, and that's it. Or else you go back to the kitchen."

"They do look terrific," Dusty said to Olivia, and he touched her shoulder. "And they're not kids any more. They're men." It was the first time he'd touched her in many years.

"Hey, Dusty. Look who's here." Vernon shouted at him from in front of a station wagon with some girls getting out of it, his nieces. There was his brother, Peter. Dusty ran up and embraced him. "What's going on? What a day to get here. How did you find out about this?"

"I thought we'd surprise you. We always threatened to visit you up here."

"Dad," the youngest girl, she was sixteen now, impatiently tapped on her father's shoulder.

"Wait a second, Susan. I'm talking to your uncle. You should say hello to him, at least."

"Hello Uncle Dusty," she said, shyly. "But Dad, he said we could take out his boat and ride to that island, Dad." She looked ready to bust with excitement.

"How did you guys find me here?" Dusty asked.

"We just saw someone in town who I thought would know you, and sure enough he knew where your place was, but he told me you'd probably be here, and he gave me these directions."

"Everyone shows up for the First Annual Cape Breton Stoned Olympics," Vernon said.

"I never thought I'd ever see you guys up here." Dusty hugged Susan, who grinned uncomfortably. "Where's Tasha?"

"The way of all wives these days," Peter said. "She went out to Oregon to live with her girlfriend on a macrobiotic commune. Her girlfriend has cancer."

"Dad, can't we go? I want to go out to that island. It looks so neat."

"Do you want to go to the island?" Peter asked the other girl, older, quieter. "Sure," she said.

"I guess we're going out to the island," Peter said. "We'll see you later."

"Be a little careful," Dusty said. "It's rougher than it looks."

Sybil McPhalls' little girl, Laurel, ran out of the circle of children and clamped onto Dusty's leg, and rode it as Dusty walked back towards the house where the game was about to begin. "You've got a birdy on your shoulder," she said. The sparrows alternated, one pecking near his feet, the other resting on his shoulder. He picked her up so she could reach out and touch the little bird. "Ooooh," she cried, clapping her fists together, as the bird pecked lightly at her hand. She jumped down and ran to her mother who had stepped out of the house with a bowl of tabouleh salad.

"Sybil, you're pitcher for us," said Vinny, followed back from the beach by Marie and a tail of little kids.

"I don't know how to pitch," said Sybil. "I never did it."

"Not to worry. Even Valenzuela had to start somewhere."

Willy lifted a little girl and shouted, "Hey, little girl," as he tossed her in the air.

"No. Stop. Mommy," cried the terrified girl.

"See my new gun," Willy said, pulling it out after he lowered the girl to the ground.

"Your boyfriend is crazy, Nina," said Sybil. "What is this with his gun? He's perverted."

"You're right," said Nina.

There came Reginald, running towards them up the beach. He stopped to pick up a tennis shoe tossing in the breakers. He recognized this tennis shoe, threw it back into the waves, kept on running.

"Are we playing ball or not?" Lenny shouted again to penetrate the wall of drunkenness and friendship.

"Afternoon, softball fans," announced the announcer. "I'm broadcasting from the gulf shore of beautiful Cape Breton Island, and we have a beautiful day here for a ball game. The sun is shining. A light breeze blowing into left field just stirs the flags at the tops of the flagpoles around the stadium."

"What should we use for second base?" asked one of the McPherson brothers. Lenny had four McPhersons on his team: first base, left field, shortstop and third.

"Just use one of them stones," said another brother.

"How do you like to slide into a stone?"

"So we don't slide in this game."

"The teams are about ready to take the field," the announcer announced, "and on this fine day we are about to start the First Annual Cape Breton Stoned Olympics softball extravaganza."

"No wine on the playing field," Roz said, following William McPherson to third base and pulling the jug of wine from his hand.

"Why not?" asked Bill.

"Because you don't catch the ball with a jug of wine in your hand."

"I catch it better," said Bill, grabbing the wine back. "And this is a party anyway. I'll just put it down here by the base and anyone can have a taste on the way in to score."

"If you play a game," said Roz, "you play it to win.

That's the way you have fun."

"Come on, Roz," said Lenny. "Let it go. You're not George Steinbrenner. I never heard you like this."

"When you play baseball you've got a team, and a team does not drink wine on the baseball field," Roz insisted.

"Just shut up, Roz, and play second base."

"I can play third base too," Roz said.

"McPherson's playing third."

"The teams are getting set," the announcer announces.

"I can pitch."

"Sally is pitching. We need you on second."

"Come on," said Vinny. "Start the game, before it gets dark."

Dusty looked into right field at Fletcher pounding his baseball mitt. Dusty wouldn't have taken Fletcher for a type to play ball. And beyond him were the waves, like a trim of fur around the island sitting like a hat on a table. It was getting a little rough. Dusty could barely make out the little boat, with his brother and family riding in it. Everything here was mellow. Someone was singing to all the kids, and they were quiet, and around the house the people not playing ball were drinking wine, and smoking grass, and playing cat's cradle. Sybil McPhalls was batting lead-off for Vinny's team. Out there the boat was out of sight. Perhaps it had reached Sea-Wolf Island. There were many disturbing stories about that island, peaceful as it looked out there, about the disappearance of lighthouse keepers. Sinister stories. Rough crossings. Sally Lens warmed up, pitching to John Doe, who had volunteered to catch for both teams. So even John Doe showed up, with everyone else, even Elizabeth Zinberg-Pouce and her new mate, Franco, from Switzerland, kicking a soccer ball around in center field to the distraction of outfielder Bunky MacDonald, a fiddler of great local reputation. E. Pouce not there, however. Vinny's team out in order top of the first, and Dusty trots out into left field and E. Pouce comes to mind.

"So three up three down top of the first," says the announcer. "And here we are on a beautiful day for the First Annual Cape Breton Stoned Olympics Softball Game, not a pie in the sky, not a fence on the horizon. Now Sybil McPhalls sets up on the mound for Vinny's team, and looks at Micmac MacWaters leading off for Lenny's . . .

There came Reginald, running up the beach towards the party. He paused for something purple carried by the tide onto a rock. This was a bathing suit. He picked it up, a small one worn by a child, by little Delilah Jacobi from the camp. She was a smart-ass kid. He liked her. He threw the suit back in the water and kept on running.

"All I have to do is to stop thinking about him, and E. Pouce will disappear," thought Dusty in left field.

Though E. Pouce was busy he always made time for his mother, especially when she was in the hospital. The project he was on now satisfied him more than any of his previous; in fact, it was a kind of culmination. It was inspired by a book by Kurt Vonnegut. This was the first time a book of fiction, a fantasy, had ever directly affected his business in the world. On the book's inspiration, he had devised a system that linked into all the information and communication networks of the civilized world, and even much of the uncivilized, in such a way that from a central location known only to Pouce he could monitor any exchange, and he had managed to feed back his own pattern of control into the whole grid, a web of coordination he could impose, connecting secretly what had been remote and independent systems; so that now he could virtually throw a switch and all systems would short out, communication stop, and then the commerce of the whole world, the chains of command - military, economic, social, all the governments, all the remote personal interactions would terminate, and at that point Pouce could impose his own punishing overview on the whole previous mess, and observe gleefully what he thought of as the ultimate redemption, the canonization, of Grandpa Pouce. And then he could leave. He was the great spider of the software systems. How much more satisfying to implement it, than to fantasize about it, Mr. Vonnegut, thought E. Pouce. He preferred the risks of real life to the harmless fantasies of a silly book. This was his private acid rain, his nuclear accidents, his toxic wastes. Grandpa Pouce at his good and meanest could never have predicted such a simple effect, such a singular end to all the troublesome life. It was elegant. A might slower developing than E. Pouce would have liked, but at the right time the result would be so refined, so sophisticated and pleasing, that patience wasn't difficult, to wait for the final devolution of the ultimate retrograde. Meanwhile he took time to visit his mother in the hospital, and afterwards, in the late afternoon, they had scheduled a meeting, the bastards who ran his shipping companies.

Visiting hours had almost passed. The lounge near the information desk was crowded with relatives and kids, noisy as a playground. Behind the glass-enclosed pharmacy counter two men fought silently, one bleeding, the other slashing the air slowly with a scalpel. Pouce tapped with his cane towards the elevator. In a hospital everyone ignored this apparently blind man, his featureless face. He enjoyed looking blind, though his people had developed, before he removed his own eyes, the technology of micro-sensors connected to his optic nerve that allowed him to see even better without them. He liked it better without the original equipment (his had been greenish) because it prevented that stupid feeling that anyone was looking through them into his head to figure out what he was thinking. He didn't think. He moved. He was Pouce, the juggernaut. The elevator door opened and he tapped his way in. Two Thai nurses wheeled in a wheezing patient, the i.v. tubing swinging like vines against E. Pouce's face. They chattered softly in Thai, and watched with furtive interest as a black attendant stepped onto the elevator with a radio at his ear. The doors closed and the elevator crawled upwards, and the attendant turned his volume up, put his radio down, and began to dance. The patient moaned and raised his head and his tongue crawled out of his mouth like an eel, and stayed there when he lowered his head back to the pillow. The attendant wiped his thumb against his tunic, held the patient's nose with the mouth open, then tamped the tongue back in with his thumb. The nurses giggled softly. E. Pouce kicked the radio over with his toe, then crushed it with the heel of his boot.

"What for you do that, motherfucker?"

"I'll create the same effect on your physiognomy," said E. Pouce, as the elevator stopped on the fifth floor, his floor.

"That was my Sanyo. You a blind motherfucker. Where I get another Sanyo?" He watched E. Pouce step off the elevator. "I don't mess with no blind man," he told the nurses.

E. reached back in and snagged the tubes of the patient's i.v. and held it as the door closed on it. The tubes jerked as the elevator went up and stuck in the door.

E. smoothed his collar and fixed his lapels. Mother Pouce didn't tolerate flaws in his appearance. Particularly when she was in the hospital she liked his appearance to be correct. Hospitals were like one of her most persistent hobbies, one of the centers of her social life. She lived for the attention of her doctors. Their hands on her body made her feel creative, she said. For her the hospital was like an artists' colony, her Martha's Vineyard, where she most enjoyed to express her wildest impulses. Her doctors, whom she retained on a generous private salary, would check her in on her slightest caprice, the hint of a liver attack, a flutter of the heart, a trumped-up ulcer. She took a different name each time she went in, so E. couldn't ask for her at the desk, but had to look for her in each room. The paging system called persistently for Dr. Ronald Padgett, one of her doctors. He looked into one room where a patient lay under an old-fashioned oxygen tent. He was wired into a vital functions monitoring system, signals dancing gaily across the screen, as if happy the subject was alive. E. Pouce waited at that door to ask the attendant about his mother: five foot one, over seventy, white hair, lean, high-pitched voice. The attendant crawled around by the head of the bed, messing with some wires, singing, "Let My People Go" in a shrill voice. She stood up and turned to the patient, a bare wire in each hand, that she slowly brought together till a spark sizzled between them. When she saw E. Pouce at the door she started giggling: an old woman, about five foot one, grey hair, lean.

"Such a good son, comes to see his mother in the hospital. Nice boy."

"What are you doing, Mother? You should be back in your room. You should be in your bed."

The man in the oxygen tent was heavily sedated, clutching a beeping page box. The hospital intercom called for Dr. Padgett again. Urgent. Immediately to surgery.

"The doctor said I could go home today. Besides, this is my room, son. And I've got my Dr. Padgett right here." She handed E. the loose wires. "Be careful with them. I'll just be a minute here. Don't let them touch each other." She snapped the oxygen tent open and climbed inside with the doctor. E. always admired how spry she remained, hardly slowing down even into her seventies. She yanked the i.v. needles out of the doctor's arm and neck, and poised herself above him like a picador.

"This is my doctor," she said. "I bought him." She sank one of the needles into his protruding tongue, and another into his eye. "Okay. That's good," she said, coming out of the tent. "You know, son, one thing I never told you before? I'm not really your mother."

"Mother, you tell me that every time I see you. Aren't they calling Dr. Padgett to surgery?"

"He's my doctor. I'm taking care of him here. They won't get him to surgery this time. Do I look like your mother?"

"You certainly do act like my mother."

"Oh." She hit her forehead with the back of her hand. "I almost forgot what I was doing. You know, as you get older you forget." She turned off the monitor and took the bare wires from E. and crawled back into the oxygen tent. She placed the wires carefully in her teeth and undid the doctor's pants. "It's not what you think, son. I'm not averse to that kind of thing, but never in intensive care." She smeared some conducting cream onto his genitals, and taped the wires there close together, then crawled back out of the tent. "I just want to see what happens. I think you get your scientific curiosity from me."

"You are the only mother I have ever known, Mother."

"Well don't blame that on me. If you had any gumption you would find yourself another one."

In his stupor the doctor waved his head back and forth. His tongue, with the i.v. still in it, stuck from his mouth like a swollen foot.

"O, I fear things don't look so good for the doctor, son. O my heavenly spigots. Poor Doctor Padgett. He showed so much promise as a brain surgeon. His hands could do the finest filigree." She reached up and touched E.'s face. "I'm so glad you came, and just in time to take me home from the hospital. You know I was just having some fun with you. I am your mother, and I'm so proud of you. You're an excellent Pouce, and a tonic for me. You make me feel so good no matter how sick I am. It's just that, and you should know this, I never slept with your father. Oh we played a little stinky pinky but we never really did it. So you know what that means?"

"I'm a virgin birth."

"Hah. You were an immaculate conception. What fun. Now there's just one thing I have left to do here. I hope you don't believe me." She placed her hand on the switch of the monitor. "Ready?"

"Mother," he said, his tone somewhere between exasperation and pride. "You're toying with life and death."

"Isn't that the way we do it?" She hit the switch and there was an explosive crackle as a spark flew across the doctor's genitals and his body stiffened into an arc, and the tent filled with white smoke, and the bed blew in an instant into a conflagration.

"All I have to do to get rid of E. Pouce," said Dusty, out loud, "is to stop thinking about him. Stop telling his story."

"That's what you think," said E. Pouce.

The oxygen tent melted down onto the body.

"I'm going home today, son, so please get my clothes out of the closet. My overcoat is there, and a wool dress, and my blue scarf." E. went in through the smoke and came back with the clothes.

"I'm so glad you finally got rid of that wife."

"I guess she came to see you." The room was filling with smoke. They left and closed the door and his mother dressed in the corridor.

"She was such an embarrassment. She dressed like I don't know what. Like a farmer's wife."

They were still calling for her doctor over the page. Mother Pouce opened the door and smoke poured out around her. She cupped her hands and shouted at Dr. Padgett through the smoke, "Remember, Doctor. Never

put your wishbone where your backbone ought to be."
The nurses spotted the smoke and ran towards the room.
E. Pouce took his mother by the elbow and led her away.

"The best thing about going to the hospital," she said, as
they stepped into the elevator, "is how much better you
feel when you leave." They paused as they stepped
outside the building and before hailing a cab listened to
the alarms inside the hospital. "The birds in the trees,"
said Mother Pouce, "don't sing any sweeter."

"Lenny's team down in order once again top of the
second," says the announcer. "Vinny's team at bat. The
first hitter is second baseman Pablo Bernstein of
Dungarry, followed by Vincent Falconieri and Dusty
Wier."

"That's exactly what I did," Elizabeth Zinberg-Pouce
tells Dusty, who lifts a bat, the first in many years, and
wraps his hands around the grip. "I just put Pouce out of
my mind, and I'm much happier for it."

"And you look so much younger, Elizabeth. You look
just great," Dusty says, swinging the bat over his head to
loosen up. He can feel it. He feels a base hit in his hands.
"And your new man looks like a nice guy. He's good
looking."

"Yeah," she says. "I like him too. I'd just rather he was
a real Italian. He's romantic enough, but he's Swiss, and
he's a little dull; I mean, not stupid, but everything has to
be accounted for. I can't explain it. I think I love him. He
treats me good."

Franco still kicks the soccer ball around center field, and
keeps an eye on her and Dusty. "It's wonderful for you,"
Dusty says, and kisses her on the cheek. Franco picks up

the soccer ball, puts it under his arm, and starts towards them. "Your man looks like he gets jealous."

"Yeah. Isn't it ridiculous. I love it."

"You're up, Dusty," shouts Vinny, from first base.

There comes Reginald, running up the beach towards the party. He stops short and looks at a small, swollen body the waves have washed against some broken lobster traps. He bends down to look at the face, and he recognizes it. He straightens up and keeps on running.

"Falconieri on first," says the voice of the announcer, "on a line-drive single over second, and now Dusty Wier steps into the batter's box. He bunted last time at bat."

"Hey, Dusty," Sally Lens shouted from the mound, and she blows him a kiss.

"Pitch the ball," says Dusty. "Don't be a female. This is baseball."

"Lens looks over her shoulder checking the runner at first, then she looks at John Doe, doing a good job of catching for both teams, and she shakes off the first signal, checks the runner again. Falconieri has good speed. Here's the pitch. O does Wier take a big cut at the ball. The sparrow flies up from his shoulder, settles on the ground. The other sparrow flies to the other shoulder. Strike one. Dusty took a healthy cut at the slow ball. He steps back out of the batter's box."

"It's been a long time since I've swung a bat," Dusty says to John Doe.

"You can't swing a bat," says John Doe. "Nobody does it. Nobody ever swings a 'B' either."

"C'mon Dad, you can hit one," shout his boys, from the bench.

"You can't swing any of the alphabet," John Doe advises Dusty, "except maybe sometimes for 'Y', which is sometimes a vowel, and sometimes a consonant. That's why it's so hard to swing 'b.a.t'."

Dusty looks at Fletcher, playing right field. Baseball, he realizes, is the great American pastime. It brings together so many diverse types of people. And this game is a great game. Almost everyone is stoned. And Dusty's heart is full of love for all the players and all the fans observing.

"Wier steps back in, looks at the pitcher. A personal duel has developed between them. McPherson plays him in from the bag at third. Always a threat of a bunt when Wier is at bat. His power is to right, where Fletcher plays him deep. Here's the pitch. Into the dirt. Runner holds at first."

"So much food," says Olivia, placing a casserole on the picnic table. "Who's going to eat all this?"

"Don't worry," says Marie. "Vinny will eat most of it."

"Sybil made these brownies," says Rosalie the goat lady. "Probably full of hashish."

"Sybil is so sixties," says Arno Myring, a writer from Toronto, who doesn't play baseball, but enjoys sitting by the picnic table and fixing a toy truck, as a gaggle of little ones crowds around him to listen to his stories.

"I bet you little guys never heard of Shaughnessy O'Diddley Dewdrop."

"Who's that?" asks a little boy.

"That's Shaughnessy. Say it."

The kids repeat the name.

"O'Diddley..."

"O'Diddley."

"Dewdrop."

"Dewdrop," the kids shout.

"Shaughnessy O'Diddley Dewdrop. He's a kid, just like you kids. He lives in the projects in a big city. He has a friend called Fudge Bitters who lives in the basement, and Fudge Bitters hates chocolate."

"Nobody hates chocolate," says one kid.

"And this is the story about how Fudge Bitters gets all the chocolate in the world and hides it away from all the children in the world. And this is how Shaughnessy O'Diddley Dewdrop helps all the children find it again."

"And eat it again," says Laurel McPhalls.

"Yes. To eat it again."

"O I know all about him," says little Laurel.

"Wier digs in in the batter's box. Here's the pitch from Sally Lens. Slow slow pitch. Sparrow jumps from Dusty's shoulder, lands on ball. Wier swings and lofts this one high into right field. It's a solid shot, but Fletcher is playing him just right and it looks like an easy out. He drifts under the ball, sparrow still riding it. Should have no trouble with this one. Under the ball now, a dove, beating its wings. How about that? A dove underneath lofts the ball higher. There's nothing written in the rule books about this one."

"What do you think the world would be like without chocolate?"

"Yucky," say several kids in unison.

"Falconieri comes around to score. Wier holds between second and third, turns to watch the ball still rising. A blue heron comes up under it and carries it still higher on the point of its beak."

"My grandfather told us it was the birds who carried the embers from the campfire into the sky, to build the sky. That was how they put the stars in heaven," Marie tells the women around the table.

"Fletcher still circling under the ball. Circling under the ball, and the ball still rises on the beak of the heron. I never thought I'd ever say anything like that to you baseball fans. Fletcher, the right fielder, spreads his coat. It's like wings, folks, and he rises, glides up after the ball and rises. This is not to be believed. If I wasn't here myself I would not believe it. I am here, in fact, and this thing is incredible. This is Mary Poppins of the outfield. Better than Mary Poppins. This is Superman in a trench coat. What a shot by Dusty Wier, and what a leap, what a play by the right fielder, Fletcher."

"A world without chocolate is like a dream of the meanies," says Arno Myring to the kids, "and Fudge Bitters is a meanie, even though he's Shaughnessy O'Diddley Dewdrop's friend."

"My friend Sooky is a meany. She likes to pinch."

"Well, all the children of the world were unhappy because of Fudge Bitters, that meany, who hid all the chocolate. And a world full of unhappy children is an unhappy world."

"She bites too. And in some places they kill little children."

"Baseball fans, that ball is still rising. What day is this in the history of the ball game? But there's no doubt about it. This day will be remembered. And holy cow, from higher up, what's that? An eagle. Fletcher any more just a little flake in the sunset over right field. This eagle swoops, snatches the ball from the heron's beak, and lifts. What a blast by Dusty Wier.''

Both teams put down their gloves and bats and walk towards the beach where the eagle rises over the water with the sphere in its claws.

"I told you," Vinny whispers to Dusty, "that Cape Breton...this place... that something is happening here.''

"What'll happen to our game?" Roz asks. "All we have is one ball. I didn't even get a chance at bat.''

"It's easy," says Lenny. "We get to eat instead.''

"Soup's on," Olivia calls out, ringing a brass cowbell. The picnic table is packed in front of her.

"Food," the kids shout, and they jump up to attack the table.

"Wait a little minute," says Laurel McPhalls. "We need to know about that chocolate first. What about the unhappy children?''

"No chocolate till after dinner," says Arno Myring.

"What happened to all of it? What did Shaughnessy O'Diddley Dewdrop do with that blushing blue giraffe?''

"Even Shaughnessy O'Diddley Dewdrop says no chocolate till after you eat your dinner.''

There comes Reginald, running up the beach towards the party. He keeps on running by three small bodies from his camp washed onto the pebbles in a heap. He keeps on running.

Dusty feels the wind, sees a heavy chop on the water, and thinks about his brother and his nieces on the island now. No provisions. Dangerous at best to try to return with the water this rough. Fletcher flown almost out of view. Eagle still lifting the ball.

"What is this?" the announcer announces. "What will be the outcome of this game?"

"At least we've got lots of good stuff to eat and lots of wine," say some McPhersons.

"It grows," says the announcer. "The ball is growing. The eagle carries it. It's like the eagle carries the new moon into heaven."

"The eagle is carrying the new moon into heaven," Lenny says. "That's what this is."

"Don't be ridiculous," says Roz.

Willy pulls his gun, and with one arm around his girl empties its chamber into the sky.

"The moon into heaven," says the announcer. "And now look. Look at it. Holy cow. How about that. Out of the water. I can't believe it..."

Total silence. Everyone watches the water. Vinny gets under Dusty's legs and lifts him on his shoulders. Dusty raises his arms and belts out a high note.

"Sometimes I feel like we live in a movie by Fellini," says Roz.

"There is no movie by Fellini," says John Doe. Lavinia, his wife, has him covered up to his navel in sand.

"O," the announcer continues. "O. Look at the water. And the ball. Eagle has released the ball and it drops slowly, comes down like the moon coming. And out of the water, baseball fans, ladies and gentlemen, out of the water rises an enormous, a huge baseball mitt, the huge glove on the huge hand out of the water, waiting to catch the setting of the new moon. It's a Roberto Clemente model, an old Roberto Clemente mitt, bigger than life, as was the great outfielder bigger than life himself. Roberto

Clemente, one of the tragic stories of modern baseball, and this glove, bigger than all of Three Rivers Stadium where he played his last years. And where has the eagle flown now? And where is the poor right fielder? The huge mitt is under the huge ball. And don't go away yet, folks. The game is not over yet.''

The participants stand on the shore and silently watch, their fans beside them. There comes Reginald running up the beach towards the party. Everyone on the shore watches sea and sky and food gets cold. And there comes Reginald running towards them up the beach. Everyone ponders, everyone wonders, everyone asks himself about the idea of a softball that has become the moon and the biggest baseball mitt to ever try to field a fly ball. And what is the credibility, Dusty wonders, of such an announcer? And what do they believe is actually happening on this afternoon of September 24 19—?